Marin Thomas grew up in the Midwest, then attended college at the U of A in Tucson, Arizona, where she earned a BA in radio-TV and played basketball for the Lady Wildcats. Following graduation she married her college sweetheart in the historic Little Chapel of the West in Las Vegas, Nevada. Recent empty nesters Marin and her husband now live in Texas, where cattle is king, cowboys are plentiful and pickups rule the road. Visit her on the web at marinthomas.com.

Books by Marin Thomas

Harlequin American Romance

The Cash Brothers

The Cowboy Next Door
Twins Under the Christmas Tree
Her Secret Cowboy
The Cowboy's Destiny
True Blue Cowboy
A Cowboy of Her Own

Rodeo Rebels

Rodeo Daddy
The Bull Rider's Secret
A Rodeo Man's Promise
Arizona Cowboy
A Cowboy's Duty
No Ordinary Cowboy

Visit the Author Profile page at Harlequin.com for more titles.

Marin Thomas

NO ORDINARY COWBOY & A RODEO MAN'S PROMISE

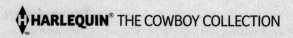

HARLEQUIN® THE COWBOY COLLECTION

ISBN-13: 978-0-373-60164-6

No Ordinary Cowboy & A Rodeo Man's Promise

Copyright © 2015 by Harlequin Books S.A.

The publisher acknowledges the copyright holder
of the individual works as follows:

No Ordinary Cowboy
Copyright © 2013 by Brenda Smith-Beagley

A Rodeo Man's Promise
Copyright © 2011 by Brenda Smith-Beagley

Printed in U.S.A.

www.Harlequin.com

CONTENTS

NO ORDINARY COWBOY

To Kimberly Nichols,
who submitted the highest "name the dog" bid
through *New York Times* bestselling author
Brenda Novak's 2012 Online Auction
for Diabetes Research. Thank you, Kimberly,
for helping out this worthwhile cause!

Madeleine, aka "Maddie," was a joy to write
in this book, and I hope I did justice to her
real-life namesake. The dog in *No Ordinary Cowboy*
possesses your Maddie's best characteristics—
she's wickedly smart, has a great memory,
can be stubborn on occasion and is
devoted to those who love her.
I wish you and your Maddie much happiness!

CHAPTER ONE

"LADIES AND GENTLEMEN, it's time for the chuck wagon races here at the Yuma Good Ol' Days Rodeo!"

Lucy Durango ignored the announcer—her attention remained glued to Shannon Douglas, a former high-school classmate who'd climbed onto the back of Sidewinder. Shannon wrapped the bull rope around her left hand while several cowboys perched on the rails, ready to lift her to safety if the bull reared.

The pungent scent of manure, livestock and sweaty cowboy saturated the warm April air as Lucy inched closer to the chute. *I must be nuts.* Time would tell if the idea she'd come up with for her Pony Express fundraiser was brilliant or just plain idiotic.

"Before we kick off our next event, we've got a special treat for you." The announcer gestured toward the bull chutes. "Shannon Douglas, a resident of Stagecoach, Arizona, is here this fine Saturday afternoon to prove cowgirls can ride bulls as well as cowboys!"

Half the fans cheered—the other half booed. Lucy had been to enough rodeos in her lifetime to understand some men would always object to women competing in roughstock events. The cowboys who surrounded Shannon's chute supported her, their words of encouragement ringing loud and clear.

One of the men helping Shannon was C. J. Rodriguez, an up-and-coming rodeo star. The *Stagecoach Gazette* had run a feature story about Shannon and C.J. touring the country together to promote women's bull riding. Lucy thought Shannon and C.J. made an interesting couple—the tomboy and the rodeo Romeo.

"Shannon is sponsored by Wrangler—" the announcer said "—and recently returned from rodeos in New Jersey and New York."

Sidewinder balked, and C.J. reached over the rails, grabbing Shannon's arm to keep her from sliding beneath the bull.

The blood drained from Lucy's face. Was she out of her mind? Probably.

No, definitely.

"Ladies and gentlemen, Shannon Douglas will be riding Sidewinder, a bull from the Pat McLean Ranch in Solvang, California. Sidewinder's a four-year-old veteran who twists like a snake when he bucks."

The chute door released, and Sidewinder exploded into the arena, the force of the move throwing Shannon forward, her face narrowly missing the bull's sawed-off horns. Sidewinder had been aptly named—his midsection bent into a tight coil, then unwound in a violent burst of energy as he kicked out with his back legs. Shannon defied the odds and clung to the bull. When the buzzer sounded, the bullfighters sprang into action, distracting the animal. Shannon launched herself into the air, hit the ground hard then bounced to her feet and sprinted for the rails. Once Sidewinder lost his rider, he settled down and trotted off to the bull pen.

Applause echoed through the stands of the outdoor

arena. "Let's see what the judges think of Shannon's performance." All eyes were glued to the electronic scoreboard in front of the judges' table. "Eighty-four!" The announcer chuckled. "Not too bad for a girl."

After nodding her thanks to the cowboys who congratulated her, Shannon removed her protective gear and Lucy crept closer, waiting for the hoopla to die down. Once the fans dispersed, she stepped forward. "Congratulations, Shannon."

"Hey, Lucy. I haven't seen you at a rodeo since…" Shannon's smile disappeared. "Sorry, I didn't mean—"

"It's okay." Until today, Lucy hadn't been to a rodeo since her brother, Michael, had died. "Do you have a minute?"

"Sure." Shannon stuffed her gear into a canvas bag then nodded for Lucy to follow her.

"I want to talk to you about a fundraising idea for the Pony Express."

Shannon nodded. "How's your taxi service for inebriated cowboys doing these days?"

Lucy tried not to be offended by Shannon's description of the Pony Express as a free taxi service for drunken cowboys, because it was so much more than that. Seven days a week the van service offered cowboys who'd celebrated a little too much a ride home from the local bars. Keeping an impaired cowboy from running his truck off the road wouldn't bring her brother back, but it would honor his memory.

"Hector—" a retired ranch hand, divorced four times, father of seven, grandfather of twelve, born-again Christian and a recovering alcoholic was the driver for the Pony Express "—is keeping busy."

"I have to make an appearance at the Wrangler booth," Shannon said. "Let's talk there."

Once they reached the sponsor's tent, Shannon spent several minutes chatting with rodeo fans and signing programs. Lucy had almost given up hope of speaking to the lady bull rider when a Wrangler employee insisted she take a break.

Lucy and Shannon walked behind the tent where Wrangler had placed folding chairs and a large cooler filled with drinks. Shannon fished a Gatorade from the melted ice. "Help yourself."

"No, thanks." Now that Lucy had Shannon's undivided attention, she got right to the point. "I need to raise money for the Pony Express."

"I thought I read somewhere that you'd gotten a federal grant for the business?"

When Lucy had started the taxi service two years ago, the local newspaper had run a feature story on her new venture. "Earlier this year I learned that my grant is being cut in half because of budget shortfalls." If she wanted to keep the Pony Express going, she needed to hold an annual charity event to make up the gap in funding.

"Won't your father give you the money?"

Everyone across southern Arizona knew the Durangos were filthy rich—that didn't bother Lucy. What irked her was airing the family's dirty laundry, but she'd risk becoming the subject of gossip to keep the Pony Express in business.

"My father feels I should have put my college degree to better use than catering to drunken cowboys." The taxi service had been Lucy's attempt to honor her brother's memory, and in doing so, help her grow closer to her father. Her good intentions had backfired when her dad cut off access to Lucy's trust fund, which would have provided the cash she needed to keep the business afloat for the remainder of the year.

"You want me to ask if Wrangler will make a donation to the Pony Express?"

"I have something different in mind." Lucy crossed her fingers and forged ahead. "I need you to sway the powers that be at Wrangler to allow me to ride in three of your local rodeos."

"Ride?"

"Bust bulls."

Shannon's mouth sagged.

The reaction wasn't unexpected. Lucy had considered several ways to raise money, but in the end had decided to ride bulls because that's what her brother had been famous for. And, selfishly, she'd hoped her father would be pleased with her for shining the limelight on Michael, if only briefly.

"I'm going to ask people to pledge a dollar amount for every second I stay on the bull," Lucy said.

"You want me to convince Wrangler to allow you to compete against me?"

"Do we have to challenge each other? I mean—" Lucy snorted "—it's not like I would beat you."

Shannon shook her head. "You'll get hurt."

"You take a chance every time you ride a bull."

"Yes, but I'm an athlete."

Okay, so Lucy had never played a high-school sport. Not everybody was coordinated, but that didn't mean she couldn't hang on to a rope for a few seconds.

"Not only do I put in endless hours on a bucking machine," Shannon said, "but I lift weights and do exercises to develop my balance and equilibrium. Even after all that, I feel like a weakling when I'm riding a bull. It would take months for you to get into shape."

"I run on the treadmill four times a week." That had to count for something.

"I don't have time to teach—"

"I'm not asking you to teach me how to bust bulls." Lucy hadn't thought that far ahead. "I just need you to ask Wrangler to let me ride." She wasn't above begging. "Please, Shannon. I have to keep the Pony Express from going under." If the business went bankrupt, she'd never make amends for the role she'd played in her brother's death, which had caused all those who'd loved Michael much pain and anguish.

"I'll see what I can do, but no promises," Shannon said. "Wrangler might appreciate the fact that you're raising money for a good cause."

"And they might be willing to mention the Pony Express when they promote your events." Lucy smiled sweetly. "I was hoping the rodeo committees would allow fans to place pledges before I ride." Lucy handed Shannon a Pony Express business card with her contact information. "I'll wait to hear from you, and good luck with the rest of your rodeos this month."

"You're welcome to hang out for a couple of hours." Shannon's offer stopped Lucy's hasty exit. "I'm heading over to the Horseshoe Bar later to listen to the band, Cowboy Rebels."

"Thanks, but it's going to be a busy night for the Pony Express." Busy night aside, Lucy couldn't get out of the arena fast enough. She'd done an admirable job, ignoring the memories of watching her brother rodeo, but right now the smells and sounds of bucking stock and cowboy roughhousing suffocated her. If her plan succeeded, she'd have to find a way to block out the memories each time she rode.

Head down, she strode through the cowboy ready area toward the exit. When she turned a corner, she plowed into a solid wall of muscle. Off balance, she stumbled backward and a strong hand steadied her.

"Lucy?"

Tony? Her heart slammed against her rib cage. It had been two years since she'd stood this close to Tony Bravo, and his masculine scent—a hint of soap, cologne and pure male musk—brought back memories of the clandestine hours she'd spent in his arms in the months prior to her brother's death.

She licked her lips nervously, and his brown eyes narrowed.

"You okay?" He gave her shoulders a little shake.

"I'm fine." The heat from his touch sent tiny shivers racing down Lucy's spine as she lost herself in Tony's gaze. The man had the sexiest eyes—dark chocolate irises that blended seamlessly with black pupils beneath long lashes. She could easily fall into the bottomless depths and never find her way out. "Sorry. I wasn't paying attention to where I was walking."

He released her and removed his hat then ran his hand over his short black hair. "You here alone?" he asked.

The guarded question didn't surprise her. Not after her father had directed the sheriff to bar Tony from the church during her brother's funeral.

"Yes, I'm by myself." She sucked in a deep breath,

immediately regretting the action when another whiff of Tony's tantalizing scent went straight to her head. "Are you competing today?"

"Yeah." The corner of his mouth lifted, and a tiny ache gripped Lucy's heart. It hadn't been that long ago that she'd woken in the wee morning hours to find Tony watching her with the same hint of a smile curving his lips. Michael's death had torn them apart, and when Lucy had needed Tony the most, he'd disappeared. After the shock of her brother's passing had worn off, she acknowledged that things had worked out for the best between them. If Tony learned what she'd done—rather, didn't do—the night Michael had died, he wouldn't want to be with her anyway.

"How's the Pony Express business?" he asked.

"Fine." The moment felt surreal as they chatted about mundane things, when it felt like only yesterday that they'd been madly in love and crazy for each other. "How's the border patrol business?" Tony was one of the good guys—an agent for the Yuma Border Patrol Station.

"Good." His gaze drifted down her body, stalling on her breasts before descending to her toes and reversing direction. Was Tony recalling the times she'd waited for him in his motel room when he and Michael traveled the circuit?

"How's your mother?" Lucy asked. Maria Bravo worked as a waitress at the Fiesta Travel Stop between Yuma and Stagecoach.

"Fine."

Okay. Everything and everyone was *fine*. There was nothing left to say, but Lucy couldn't summon the strength to move her feet toward the exit. "Is your mother still volunteering with Meals on Wheels?"

Tony nodded.

"I'm glad she's keeping busy," Lucy said. Tony's father, a U.S. Immigration and Customs agent, had been killed in the line of duty when Tony was a baby. Antonio Bravo had gotten caught in the crossfire of a botched drug deal near the border. Rather than return to her hometown of Nogales, Mexico, Maria, a Mexican immigrant at the time of her husband's death, had become a U.S. citizen and had raised Tony in Arizona.

Conversation stood at a standstill.

"I'd better go," Tony said. "I'm first out of the chute this afternoon."

"Good luck with your ride."

"I drew Swagger. Should be interesting to see who struts their stuff better—Swagger or me." He settled his hat on his head and touched a finger to the brim then disappeared among the milling cowboys.

Lucy made it to the exit then did an about-face and returned to the stands, finding a seat on the bleachers near the chutes. Memories pinched her heart, but she couldn't make herself leave—not after running into Tony. She'd believed she'd put their short affair behind her, but seeing him today had unsettled her and awakened a need for answers—answers she feared would open Pandora's Box.

"Ladies and gentlemen, now that the chuck wagon competition has ended, we're ready for the final event of the day. And don't forget the barbecue and music jamboree following the rodeo."

A group of young women wearing pink leather shorts and fringed halter tops strutted in front of the crowd waving signs that advertised the local restaurants competing in the barbecue cook-off.

"Folks, Tony Bravo is up first in the men's bull-riding event. Bravo hails from Stagecoach, Arizona."

The stands erupted in applause and boot stomping, and there were sexy whistles from a group of buckle bunnies near the chutes. What woman wouldn't find Tony's tanned skin, jet-black hair and muscular physique sexy?

"Turn your attention to chute seven. Bravo's coming out on Swagger, a five-year-old Charbray from the Swanson Ranch near Alpine. Only one cowboy has ridden Swagger this year. Let's see if Bravo tames this wild bull."

Hands clasped tightly in her lap, Lucy watched Tony prepare for his ride. He adjusted his protective face mask and zipped his Kevlar vest. Not long ago he and her brother had chosen not to wear the gear. They'd believed themselves invincible—Michael's death had proved one of them wrong.

The chute door opened and the reddish-brown bull jumped into the arena. Tony struggled to maintain his balance, his right arm flailing in the air, snapping back and forth as if connected to his body by a rubber band. Swagger kicked sideways and Tony slid off balance but managed to right himself before the next buck. Lucy counted the seconds in her head. Four…five…six— *Shoot!*

Tony catapulted over the bull's head and she flinched when he landed on his right shoulder and bounced across the dirt. The bullfighter waved his arms, attempting to distract Swagger, but the bull wasn't finished *swaggering.* As Tony struggled to his feet, the animal charged. Tony dove to his right, barely avoiding a collision. Lucy expelled the breath she'd been holding in a loud gasp when Swagger trotted out of the arena.

"There you have it, ladies and gentlemen. Tony Bravo

gave his best effort but Swagger keeps his bragging rights. Better luck next time, cowboy."

Lucy headed for the parking lot. Now that she'd asked Shannon to find rodeos for her to ride in, she'd better show the cowgirl that she meant business. First on her agenda—find a mechanical bull to practice on.

Lucy's father had purchased her brother a high-tech bucking machine that he and Tony had trained on in the barn at the Durango Ranch. On a few occasions during high school, Lucy had hidden in the hayloft and spied on the boys. Sweat had stung her eyes and hay dust had filled her lungs, but the discomfort had been worth it when Tony removed his shirt and she'd gotten an eyeful of his rippling muscles.

After Michael died, her father had instructed Pete, the ranch foreman, to get rid of the bucking machine. One day while Lucy was in Yuma running errands, she'd driven past Tony's pickup on Main Street and noticed the equipment in the truck bed. She wondered if Tony still had the machine. If he did—could she convince him to allow her to use it?

A WEEK LATER, Lucy still hadn't heard from Shannon, but she'd moved forward with her fundraising plans, hoping Wrangler would eventually agree to promote her cause. She'd spent the morning in her small office in the barn, working on her company website. She'd added a PayPal form and a pledge counter so visitors would see how close she was to reaching her goal of $20,000. Once she knew for certain that she'd be competing in the rodeos, she'd upload the new pages.

Nothing left to do but wait until Shannon contacted

her; Lucy decided to head into Stagecoach for a root beer at Vern's Drive-In. She wished one of her girlfriends from college lived nearby, but after graduation they'd taken various jobs across the country, and Lucy had returned to Stagecoach. Before her brother had passed away, she'd dreamed of working in Chicago and renting an apartment near Michigan Avenue. She'd wanted to experience living somewhere other than the hot, dry desert.

The drive-in was deserted when Lucy arrived, but once the sun set the place would be hopping with teenagers. She left her truck running and walked up to the order window. Vern's daughter, Sherry, had taken over the business years ago when her father retired to Palm Springs.

"Howdy, Lucy. What can I get for you?"

"A large root beer, please."

"You want a frosty mug or a to-go cup?"

"To-go."

"Comin' right up." Sherry disappeared for a moment before returning with the drink.

Lucy handed over two dollars then tossed her change into the tip jar. "Thanks, Sherry."

"Sure thing. See you next time."

Back inside her truck, Lucy angled the air vents toward her face and guzzled her drink. Once she'd quenched her thirst, she backed out of the parking spot and turned onto the highway. The drive between the ranch and Stagecoach was nothing less than boring—rocky brown landscape dotted with green cactus. Mesmerized by the wavy heat lines radiating off the pavement, Lucy slammed on the brakes when an animal shot across the road in front of the truck.

"Maddie!" *Blast that dog.* The purebred boxer charged

across the desert. Lucy pulled off the road and turned on the truck's flashers. She rummaged through the glove compartment until she found the whistle, then got out of the truck and blew hard.

The brown speck in the distance skidded to a stop. A stare-down ensued.

"Come back, Maddie. It's too dang hot to chase you."

The seven-year-old boxer had been a shadow of her old self since Michael died. No one had witnessed the accident, but everyone assumed Maddie had been riding in the bed and was thrown clear when Michael's truck flipped and landed in the ditch. Not long after, Maddie had found her way back to the ranch and barked nonstop until she'd woken the family.

Lucy blew the whistle again. Maddie trotted forward then stopped and sat. *What kind of game are you playing, girl?*

Michael had come across the dog walking along a deserted highway on the outskirts of Flagstaff, and the pair had been inseparable until his death. Maddie had begun running away a month after Michael was cremated. At one point, Lucy and her mother had searched for days. Finally, when they'd driven past the site of the crash, they'd discovered the dog waiting in the hot sun for her master to return.

After that incident, her mother had insisted Maddie be put down, but Lucy had refused to allow her parents to euthanize Michael's dog. Instead, she'd suggested they build an outdoor kennel and keep Maddie penned in. The darn dog must have dug her way to freedom.

A horn blast startled Maddie, and she took off like a jackrabbit, disappearing behind a thicket of scrub brush.

Lucy shielded her eyes from the sun as a black truck drew closer and parked behind her vehicle. Tony Bravo.

LUCY HAD BEEN back from college for two years, and he'd managed to avoid any direct contact with her until she'd plowed into him at the Yuma rodeo. Now here they were, running into each other twice in one week.

"Car trouble?" Tony strode toward Lucy, grateful his mirrored sunglasses hid his eyes from view as he looked her over. Seeing Lucy up close in her tight jeans, sassy boots and formfitting T-shirt reminded him of the nights he'd stripped her clothes off in a motel room and they'd both been caught off guard by the explosive passion between them. Their series of one-night stands, strung together over the course of five months, had ended abruptly. After letting Michael down in the worst possible way, Tony hadn't deserved to be happy, and because he hadn't had the guts to tell Lucy the truth about the night her brother had died, he'd walked away from her without a word of explanation.

"Maddie ran off," she said.

He scanned the horizon, realizing he hadn't seen the dog since Michael's funeral, when she'd sat beneath the tree across the street from the church. The memory of that afternoon flashed through Tony's mind, but he slammed the door shut before the images came into focus.

"Will she come back?" he asked.

"Eventually." Lucy didn't sound confident.

Tony returned to his truck and grabbed the gallon of water he stored for emergencies and an empty fast-food salad bowl from yesterday's lunch. He filled the bowl with water then placed it on the ground near Lucy's feet. "If she comes back, she'll have water to drink."

"Thanks." Lucy walked several yards away and blew the whistle. "It's been over six months since her last break for freedom."

Tony wasn't surprised Maddie had run to the place Michael had crashed his truck. Dogs were intuitive animals, and Maddie's internal clock had alerted her to the importance of tomorrow's date—the second anniversary of Michael's death. The sun had faded the white wooden cross Lucy had placed in the rocky ground after the accident. Michael's name was barely discernible. Tony's chest tightened when he recalled his last conversation—rather argument—with his best friend. Tony wanted a do-over of that night so damned bad. "Maddie's how old?"

"Seven."

Tony studied Lucy's face. Her cheekbones were sharper than he remembered, making her blue eyes appear larger beneath the light brown lashes. She'd pulled her curly blond hair into a ponytail, and the little makeup she wore revealed a flawless complexion. He squeezed his hands into fists to keep from dragging a finger down her cheek to test the softness of her skin.

"Interesting uniform hat." Lucy pointed to his head.

Grinning, he tugged the brim of his Stetson. "I'm a cowboy first, then a border patrol agent."

Lucy laughed, the gesture showing off the tiny dimples in her cheeks. "Guess I'll head home. Hopefully Maddie will turn up tonight."

"I'll spread the word to my coworkers to be on the lookout for her when they're driving in the area."

"Thanks, Tony."

He watched Lucy get into her truck and drive off. Once the vehicle disappeared from sight he turned and spotted Maddie trotting through the desert in his direction. The sly dog had waited for Lucy to leave. Maddie stopped at the water bowl and drank it dry.

"Long time no see, girl."

The dog lifted her head, water dribbling from her jowls.

Tony dropped to one knee and Maddie bounded closer, putting her paws on his legs and licking his face. "Guess I'll have to take you home." He grabbed the plastic bowl and opened the truck door. The dog jumped inside and sat in the passenger seat. After Tony started the truck, Maddie sniffed the air vents, then relaxed, her tongue hanging out the side of her mouth as she panted.

Tony steeled himself against the ache in his heart when he scratched the boxer behind the ears. Maddie pressed her head into his hand and he rubbed harder. "I've missed you, girl. We had some good times with Michael, didn't we?" The dog had traveled everywhere with Michael, and Tony had been in awe of their powerful bond.

"I miss him, Maddie. More than you know."

The dog lay down on the seat and rested her head on Tony's thigh. His throat tightened at the affectionate gesture. He shifted the truck into Drive and sped down the road. Tony had planned to speak with Cal Durango about a human-trafficking ring in the area, but had hoped to have more evidence before he asked the ranch owner for access to his property. Thanks to Maddie, Tony would be confronting Lucy's father sooner rather than later.

CHAPTER TWO

"You KNOW HE hates me, don't you?" Maddie's alert brown eyes shone with sympathy. Tony strangled the steering wheel as he drove along the highway on the outskirts of Stagecoach. He wasn't looking forward to facing Cal Durango. The man blamed him for his son's death and he had a right to.

Not a day passed that Tony didn't regret leaving the bar after Michael had assured him he'd find a ride home if he drank too much. If Tony could travel back in time, he'd have stayed until Michael had finished celebrating, or he'd have coaxed him out of the bar before he'd had one too many beers.

He turned down the road leading to the Durango ranch house and passed beneath a stone archway with the iron letters *DR* at the top. A mile later, he parked in front of the sprawling hacienda with the covered front porch that ran the entire length of the home. The house sat in the shadows of a rocky incline that blocked the wind and provided shade from the afternoon sun. The yard had been landscaped with palm trees and colorful vegetation reminiscent of a California resort, not the Sonoran Desert.

Tony stepped down from his truck. "Get the hell off my ranch, Bravo." Cal Durango sat on the front porch, smoking one of his expensive Cuban cigars.

"Be happy to hit the road as soon as I unload this cargo." Tony snapped his fingers. "Come on, Maddie."

The stubborn boxer wouldn't budge.

Tony reached for her collar, but Maddie scrambled into the backseat.

"Damn dog's a nuisance. Should have put her down long ago." Durango acted tough as nails, but Tony knew the death of his son had cut him off at the knees and he was a broken man on the inside.

"Got a leash?" Tony asked.

"Here's one." Lucy stepped out the front door. Had she been eavesdropping? She skipped down the steps and clipped a tether to Maddie's collar. "Naughty girl." Lucy tugged the dog from the truck. "She must have come back after I left."

"Left where?" Lucy's father stood on the top step and glanced suspiciously between Tony and his daughter.

"Maddie misses you, Tony," Lucy said, ignoring her father's question.

"Enough about the damned dog. Get off my ranch, Bravo."

"I'd like a word with you first." Tony moved closer to the porch.

"A word about what?"

"We believe—" Tony had yet to convince his boss of his hunch "—that underage girls are being kidnapped and brought over the border then sold into the sex trade in the Midwest."

"How awful," Lucy said.

Durango chomped on his cigar. "And this concerns me how?"

"We suspect members of a Mexican cartel are crossing

into the United States between the San Luis and Luke-ville ports of entry then making their way north through Stagecoach." Tony paused for a moment to allow the information to sink in. "We have reason to believe the men are using your ranch as a shortcut through the area."

"You got any proof of that?" Durango puffed on his cigar.

"Witness reports spotting young females walking on your property along highway 41."

"Reliable witnesses, or illegals you didn't catch at the border?" Durango asked.

"Reliable witnesses. I'd like to take a look around your place."

"Have your boss call me. I'll consider giving him access, but not you."

"Dad!" Miffed at her father's rude behavior, Lucy spoke to Tony. "Thank you for bringing Maddie home."

Tony flashed a half smile and her pulse fluttered with yearning, just as it had each morning he'd kissed her goodbye after each of their motel rendezvous. They'd kept their affair a secret because Tony's mother had been old-fashioned and expected her son to marry a Hispanic girl. Of course, Lucy's father wouldn't have approved of Tony, because he hadn't come from a wealthy, prestigious family. They'd also worried that their parents' objections to their relationship would distract Michael from his quest for a national title.

Each time she and Tony had seen each other, they'd fallen more and more in love, and the strain of keeping their affair a secret had worn them down. Finally they'd decided to tell their parents during Lucy's spring break in April, after Tony and Michael returned from the rodeo in Prescott. But Michael had died that night, and Tony had refused to see Lucy or take her calls. He'd broken her heart when she'd needed him most.

Shoving the memories aside, Lucy blamed her sudden queasiness on the fact that tomorrow was the anniversary of her brother's death, and although she'd tried to avoid thinking about it, the pain was a constant presence in her heart. If she knew what was good for her, she'd also keep her feelings for Tony locked away and focus on her fundraiser.

After the taillights of Tony's truck disappeared, she said, "Dad, don't make it difficult for the border patrol to do their job."

Her father stared unseeingly into space.

"If illegals are cutting across the ranch, what's going to stop them from coming up to the house and robbing us, or worse?" Lucy said.

"Bravo's making a big deal out of nothing, because he's looking out for himself."

"I don't understand."

"He requested a transfer to the border patrol office in San Diego."

"How do you—" *Never mind.* Her father had eyes and ears all over the state.

"He needs credit for cracking a big case in order to get his transfer."

"You don't believe Tony deserves the promotion, do you?"

Her father retreated inside the house, the smack of the screen door answering Lucy's question.

When would he stop blaming Tony for Michael's death?

When you tell him the truth.

Lucy's eyes burned with tears. She'd hoped the Pony Express would make up for her grave blunder the night Michael had died, but maybe she was fooling herself—there were some things in life one couldn't make amends for.

"Back to the kennel for you, girl." Lucy put Maddie in the outdoor cage and secured the lock. On the way to the office in the barn, she silently cursed. She'd forgotten to ask Tony if he still had her brother's bucking machine. Now that she thought about it, she'd wait to ask him until she heard back from Shannon about the rodeos. No sense stirring up trouble until she knew for sure that she'd be riding a real-life bull.

"Hey, Mom, it's me," Tony called out as he entered his mother's trailer.

"In the kitchen!"

He found her sliding a cake pan into the oven.

"You're late." She closed the oven door.

"Sorry." Tony hugged her. "I should have called." But he'd been too agitated, his mind a jumble of tangled thoughts after running into Lucy along the highway then dealing with a stubborn dog and a mulish Cal Durango.

"Problems at work?"

In his line of duty there were always problems. "No." He watched his mother dish out the chicken pot pie she'd made for their once-a-week supper together. "I ran into Lucy Durango today."

"Oh?"

"Maddie took off and Lucy was out searching for her."

"Did you find the dog?" His mother set their plates on the table and sat down.

"Yeah." He omitted the part where Maddie had waited for Lucy to leave before approaching Tony. His mother would insist the dog missed Tony and that he should visit Maddie once in a while—as if Lucy's father would allow him near the dog, never mind his daughter.

"Mr. Bonner lost his cat last week—flattened by a semitruck."

"Nice visual before we eat," Tony said.

"Sorry. No more animal talk at the table."

Tony would be lying if he didn't admit that he missed Maddie and all the dog represented—a friendship with Michael that had begun with an I-dare-you game on a school playground and had evolved into a brotherly bond. Tony had lost a part of himself when his best friend died, and Maddie brought to the surface all the pain buried inside him.

"How did you do at the rodeo last weekend?" His mother's brown eyes twinkled as they roamed over Tony. "You're not sporting a cast or bandages."

"I got thrown." Tony was twenty-seven, but some days he felt like an old man. He used to be a decent bull rider before he'd begun working for the border patrol. Now he was lucky if he lasted eight seconds on the back of a bull in one out of ten rodeos. He should retire his spurs, but he was reluctant to give up those few hours a month when he could keep his memory of Michael alive.

"Any news on the transfer?" his mother asked.

"Not yet." Six months ago, after two years of pre-tending he'd moved on from Michael's death and his affair with Lucy, he'd finally admitted that he wouldn't be able to put the past behind him until he left Stagecoach.

"The cost of living is much higher in California."

His mother was not in favor of her only child leaving town. Tony would miss his mom, but San Diego wasn't so far away that he couldn't make a monthly trip to Stagecoach. "You could relocate to America's Finest City with me."

"I'm comfortable at my job, honey. I don't want to start at the bottom of the waitress ladder."

"I bet Juan would move with you." His mother and the grill cook at the truck stop had been dating for several years but his mother wasn't interested in tying the knot—her heart still belonged to Tony's father.

"You haven't said how Lucy's doing." His mother quirked an eyebrow.

"She's fine."

"Just fine?"

Actually, Lucy was more than fine. After two years of catching only glimpses of her from a distance, seeing her up close at the rodeo had stolen his breath. Her smile had reminded him that he'd lost more than his best friend because of a stupid lapse in judgment. He'd also lost the girl who'd captured his heart. Tony shoveled a forkful of food into his mouth, chewed and swallowed. "Lucy was at the rodeo last weekend."

"Really?"

He had been more than a little surprised he'd bumped into her in the cowboy ready area. After Michael died, the Durangos quit attending rodeos, while Tony continued to ride, wanting to hold on to the one thing that had been a huge part of his friend's life.

"I noticed the Pony Express van parked in front of Gilley's Tap House the other night."

Never in a million years had Tony believed Lucy would start up her own business in Stagecoach. No one talked about it—at least not out loud—but it didn't take a genius to understand that the free taxi service was Lucy's way of honoring her brother's memory. The van served as a solemn reminder of how Tony had failed his best friend.

"You're awfully quiet," his mother said. "What's wrong?"

"I've got a lot on my mind."

"Still no leads on the Mexican gang smuggling girls across the border?"

"No." But he was positive that if border patrol agents staked out the Durango Ranch, they'd catch the bastards transporting their human cargo through the desert.

"I hope you get a break in the case soon." His mother pointed to Tony's plate. "Do you have room for seconds?"

"No, thanks." He carried his plate to the sink. "I'll tighten the bathroom faucet before I leave."

"You're not staying?"

Unless he received an emergency call from work, Tony watched TV with his mother for an hour or two after supper. Approaching the anniversary of his best friend's death, he wouldn't be good company, so he fibbed. "I've got paperwork to catch up on."

"I made the cake for you."

"Juan will appreciate your chocolate cake."

"He's on a diet." Juan was a big man who made no apologies for his big appetite.

While his mother cleared the table and washed the dishes, Tony went outside and unlocked the storage shed.

His father's tool kit sat on the ground inside the door. A half hour later, Tony had fixed the bathroom faucet, oiled a squeaky doorjamb and loosened the sticky window at the front of the trailer. Then he kissed his mother good-bye and headed to Yuma.

He'd only driven a few miles when he found himself parked in front of the Saguaro Cactus Lounge, staring at the blinking Budweiser sign in the window. Some days, life called for a beer.

Today was one of them.

"Don't worry, Hector. You stay home tonight and feel better. I'll be out soon to pick up the van." Lucy disconnected the call.

Poor Hector. One of his granddaughters was taking a culinary class in Yuma and had cooked a chicken sausage seafood gumbo for the family. Hector had barely made it back home before being hit with food poisoning.

Lucy left her office in the barn and returned to the house for her purse. Dinner would be on the run tonight.

"Where are you off to?" her mother called out.

Lucy put the brakes on outside the sun room where her mother sat reading. "Hector's not feeling well. I'll be handling the calls for the Pony Express tonight."

The lines bracketing her mother's mouth deepened, but she refrained from voicing her disapproval. "Call when you get to Hector's."

Lucy swallowed a sharp retort and left the house. A twenty-four-year-old shouldn't have to report in to her mother, but Michael's death had changed the family dynamic in more ways than size. Sonja Durango wanted to know every move her daughter made. Full of guilt,

Lucy had been happy to keep her mother informed of her whereabouts, believing it would only be a matter of time before she got over her fear of something happening to Lucy. But months turned into a year, and now two, and still her mother hadn't eased up on monitoring Lucy's activities.

The drive to Hector's took twenty minutes. He lived in the foreman's cabin on the Ace of Spades Ranch, west of Stagecoach. Bill Gunderson no longer ran cattle on his land now that he and his wife spent half the year on the East Coast with their son's family. In exchange for watching over the property, Hector lived there rent-free.

When she pulled up to the cabin, Hector's mongrel dog emerged from his underground den beneath the porch. "Hey, Blue. It's Lucy." Holding out her hand, she approached the chained dog cautiously. Blue sniffed then wagged his tail. "You remember me, don't you?"

The tail wagged harder. Hector had found the stray dog limping on the property. Blue had been suffering from mange and the vet had confirmed he was going blind. Losing his sight made Blue more aggressive and fearful of strangers, so Hector no longer took the dog with him when he left the ranch. Blue spent most of his days under the porch in the cool dirt cavern Hector had dug for him.

"Where's Clementine?" Lucy glanced across the porch and spotted the gray cat lounging on the chair by the door. "Hey, Clementine." The cat's tail twitched once. Clementine barely tolerated Blue until the nights grew cold, then she slept with him beneath the porch.

"How about some fresh water, kids?" Lucy refilled the large water bowl from the spigot connected to the side of the cabin, set it on the bottom porch step then texted her mother that she'd arrived at Hector's.

"Hector, it's Lucy," she called out as she let herself inside the cabin.

"Keys are by the door." The muffled voice came from the hall bathroom.

"Hope you feel better soon." She placed a set of keys to her truck on the table then left the cabin. After giving Blue one more pat on the head, she drove off in the Pony Express passenger van. She'd almost made it to the highway when her cell phone rang.

"Pony Express, Lucy Durango speaking."

"Lucy, it's Bob out at the Saguaro Cactus Lounge."

"It's only eight o'clock and you have a pickup for me?"

"Not yet but I figure he'll need a lift by ten."

"You're prebooking a ride?"

"Yep."

"Is he a regular?"

"Nope."

If the cowboy wasn't a regular, it usually meant the guy was drinking off a heartache. "Who is he?"

"Tony Bravo."

Tony? At least he wasn't on duty. "Did he say why he's drinking?"

Bob chuckled. "Border patrol agents don't need a reason to drink."

"I'll be there in a few minutes."

She disconnected the call then turned onto the highway. Tony had never been a big drinker. Even when he and Michael celebrated their twenty-first birthdays, the guys hadn't gone on a bender because they'd had to rodeo the following day.

There were only a handful of vehicles parked in the lot when she arrived at the bar. As soon as she entered the tavern, Bob nodded to the stool where Tony sat hunched over a beer glass. He was drinking tap beer—the cheap stuff.

Lucy passed a pair of cowboys throwing darts and four more playing cards before she slid onto the stool next to Tony. She tapped a fingernail against the bar, keeping time with the George Strait song playing on the jukebox. Tony ignored her. After a minute, she broke the silence. "I'm sorry you didn't make it to eight last weekend."

Keeping his gaze on his beer, he said, "Thought you'd left the rodeo before my ride."

"I stayed." She'd missed watching Tony and her brother tangle with bulls. "Tough draw."

"Hardly." He guzzled the amber liquid in the glass.

"Just so you know, I'm here on official business," she said.

"This is my second—" he counted the glasses on the bar "—third beer."

"Bob reserved a seat for you in the van."

"I can handle my liquor."

Chilled by the air conditioner mounted on the wall next to Tony, she asked, "You want to go somewhere and talk?"

His dark gaze unnerved Lucy. Did he assume she wanted to talk about the past—more specifically their past?

Tony fished his wallet from his pocket, left a ten-dollar bill on the bar then nodded to the door. "Lead the way."

As soon as they stepped outside, Lucy said, "I haven't had supper. Let's head up the road to Vern's."

"Leave the van here." He threw her his truck keys.

Lucy hopped behind the wheel of the black Dodge and adjusted the seat and mirrors then drove toward town. The drive-in was crowded with teenagers but she found a parking spot. When she lowered the windows, the smell of greasy hamburgers and fries filled the cab and her stomach growled.

"That wasn't very ladylike." Tony grinned.

"Sorry."

A young girl with an order pad stopped at the truck. "Welcome to Vern's. What can I get you?"

"Two cheeseburger baskets with root beers."

"Be ready in a few minutes." The waitress dropped off the order at the service window, then chatted with her friends sitting at the patio tables.

"I thought Hector drove the Pony Express van," Tony said.

"He does, but he's sick tonight."

"You should hire a second driver. It's not safe for a woman—"

"Don't think you're saying anything I haven't heard a million times over from my parents. I know it's risky, but I don't do it often." Before Tony badgered her more, she said, "Tell me about this human-trafficking ring you're trying to bust."

"For the past year we've been tracking a well-known drug cartel with routes through Arizona. After the first of the year, they switched their cargo from drugs to teenage girls."

"Why?"

"Prostitution is a lucrative business, and from a cost perspective, the gang spends less money transporting

humans across the border than growing and process-
ing weed."

"And you're sure the gang is cutting through our ranch?"

"Yep."

"That doesn't make me feel very safe."

"You shouldn't feel safe. There's no telling what these
guys will do if they feel threatened or cornered." Tony
cleared his throat. "I want to set up a sting operation on
your property. Put a couple of lookouts in the desert so
we can mark their trail and get close enough to identify
individual members of the gang."

"Here you go." The young girl arrived with their food
and Tony got out his wallet.

"My treat," Lucy said. She handed the girl a twenty.
"Keep the change."

"Thanks for the burger." He devoured it in five bites.

"You must be hungry," she said.

"I don't know why. I had dinner at my mom's tonight."

Lucy hadn't seen Maria Bravo in a long time. "I
should visit her at the truck stop when I'm out that way."

"She'd like that."

"What did you think of Shannon Douglas last week?"

"She's impressive." Tony dug into his French fries.
"Have you seen her compete before?"

"Last weekend was the first time."

"I competed in the Canyon City Rodeo last summer,
and after watching Shannon and her lady friends, I couldn't
figure out if the women were stupid or really brave."

"Shannon's got a lot of talent."

"I won't argue with that. She's been a tomboy all her
life, but the others—" He shook his head. "They looked
like you."

"What's that supposed to mean?"

"They're the kind of girls who enter beauty pageants not rodeos."

"I'll take that as a compliment." Lucy's pulse raced when Tony's gaze momentarily dropped to her breasts.

"You're as beautiful as I remember."

Feeling short of breath, she said, "You're a chauvinist, Tony Bravo. Just because a girl is pretty doesn't mean she can't be tough, too."

"Hey, I'm all for women's rights. I work with female border patrol agents and they handle the job as well as, if not better than the male agents. But bull riding is best left to men."

If Shannon called with good news soon, Tony's opinion would be put to the test, because Lucy intended to ask for his help in preparing for the rodeos. There was no sense bringing up the subject now and giving him an opportunity to talk her out of it.

"I was surprised you stayed in Stagecoach after you graduated," Tony said, changing the subject.

"Really? Why?"

"Memories." Tony balled up his burger wrapper. "I've been trying to get out of this place for a long time."

Lucy wanted to ask if Tony was on the run from the memories of their brief affair or Michael's death. She, on the other hand, preferred to smother herself in the memories. "My father said you put in for a job transfer to San Diego."

"I'm ready for a new challenge."

That was a bald-faced lie. Tony had told her plenty of times how much he loved Arizona, and that when he stopped rodeoing he intended to become a border patrol agent so he could stay put. Lucy's heart ached that her mistake was forcing him to leave the home he loved. If she confessed that she was the reason Michael had driven home drunk from the bar, would Tony change his mind about leaving?

The truth won't bring Michael back.

The thought made Lucy feel even guiltier.

"If we're successful in shutting down this human-trafficking ring, I'm positive I'll get my transfer."

"I doubt your mother is happy about you transferring."

"At least I'm not moving across the country." He waved a hand. "Forget about my job. I want to know why you're driving wasted cowboys home. Don't you want to do something worthwhile with your business degree?"

She was doing something worthwhile—saving lives. But how many lives would she have to save to make up for Michael's? "For now, I'm content running my nonprofit business." Until she found the courage to come clean with her parents about the circumstances surrounding Michael's death, Lucy didn't have a whole lot of options.

"Have you ever been threatened by a passenger?"

Although she'd never admit it, there had been one passenger last year who'd made her keep her pepper spray close at hand. After that night she'd informed the bar managers where she was taking the cowboys. If she suddenly disappeared from the face of the earth, the sheriff could ask a few questions and figure out her route. "Most cowboys are decent, God-fearing men who treat women with respect, whether they're drunk or not."

"That may be true, but a girl like you—" Tony leaned closer and his masculine scent went straight to Lucy's head "—would test any cowboy's morals and values."

CHAPTER THREE

WAS HE NUTS?

Tony had no business kissing Lucy, but he did anyway. Emboldened by her soft moan, he thrust his tongue inside her mouth, her sweet taste reminding him of the nights they'd shared on the rodeo circuit. His body shook with need, memories fueling his desire.

On the verge of losing control, he ended the kiss—or tried to. Lucy's mouth followed his when he pulled away, their ragged breathing filling the truck cab. *Damn.* The joke was on him. He'd kissed Lucy because he'd been trying to make a point about her safety, but the sizzling chemistry between them proved that two years of trying to put this woman behind him had been in vain. He'd better keep his guard up, or she'd make him forget his reasons for leaving Stagecoach.

Lucy pressed her fingertips to her lips and mumbled, "What did you do that for?"

"Do you want me to apologize?"

"Do you want to apologize?"

"Not really," Tony said.

A woman like Lucy came along once in a man's lifetime, and he'd blown his shot with her. Who was he kidding? Even if they had gone through with their plan to tell their parents about their relationship, Cal Durango would have made Tony's life miserable until he'd broken up with Lucy. No way would the wealthy, prominent businessman have allowed Tony anywhere near his daughter.

"Tony."

"What?"

"I'm still mad at you."

"For what?"

"For ignoring me after Michael died."

Tony tensed. He didn't want to discuss this.

"Why didn't you return my calls after his funeral?" she asked.

"I wasn't in the right frame of mind."

"Okay. I'll buy that, but we were all grieving, Tony, and I really needed you."

"I'm sorry." The walls were closing in on him. "I couldn't be with anyone."

"I thought what we'd shared meant something to you."

The wounded look on Lucy's face squeezed his heart, but he remained silent. There wasn't anything he could say in his defense.

"I felt so alone," she said.

Not as alone as he had felt after he'd been banned from Michael's funeral service. He'd gotten the message loud and clear—now that Michael was gone, Cal Durango had no use for Tony. In truth, he might have found the nerve to stand up to Durango and insist he was good enough for Lucy, but he didn't have the right to after he'd ditched Michael in the bar. That decision had sealed Tony's fate and convinced him that the best thing to do was to keep his distance from Lucy.

Unable to stop himself, Tony tucked a strand of blond hair behind Lucy's ear. Maybe fate had brought them to-

gether again so he could apologize for Michael's death—
not that he expected an apology to absolve him of his
sins. "I'm sorry, Lucy. Sorry Michael died." *Sorry things
ended the way they did between us.*

"Michael's death still doesn't feel real to me."

Memories hurled Tony back in time. Lucy had phoned
at 4:00 a.m. with the devastating news that her brother's
vehicle had run off the road and he'd been pronounced
dead at the scene. Lucy had told him not to bother driving out to the crash, because medics had already taken
Michael's body to the hospital.

Tony hadn't known what to do. His mother had been
working the night shift at the truck stop and he was alone
in the trailer. He'd paced the floor, wishing Lucy or Mrs.
Durango would insist he mourn with them at the ranch.
Not until his mother walked through the door several
hours later had Tony broken down. When the day of the
funeral arrived, he'd driven to the church, desperate for
a final glimpse of his best friend, but Cal Durango had
denied him even that.

The pressure building in Tony's chest crushed his
lungs. Forcing the words past his lips, he said, "It was
my fault Michael died."

Lucy sucked in a quiet breath. "It was not your fault,
Tony."

"I shouldn't have left your brother at the bar."

"Why did you?" Lucy squeezed his hand.

The truth wasn't flattering. He'd been angry that Michael's leap to the top of the standings meant Tony had
to sacrifice being with Lucy in order to travel the circuit
with Michael as he made a run for the National Finals
Rodeo title. *Don't blame Michael.* Tony could have quit

rodeo but he hadn't been able to walk away from the deep bond he'd shared with his best friend since childhood.

Tony spit out a lie. "I was tired and I didn't feel like drinking that night." He pulled his hand from Lucy's—he didn't deserve sympathy or compassion.

Lucy closed her eyes and leaned her head against the back of the seat. Tony regretted that the conversation upset her. "If I'd known that Michael intended to drink until he was wasted, I would have stuck it out at the bar with him." His apology failed to make Tony feel better, which reinforced his belief that he didn't deserve to be happy after what he'd done or, in this case, hadn't done to prevent Michael's death.

A shrill ring startled them. Lucy answered her cell phone. "Pony Express, Lucy speaking." She tapped the truck horn and the waitress removed the food tray. Lucy put the truck into Reverse and backed out of the spot. "Not a problem. I'll be there in thirty minutes or less." She disconnected the call.

"Where to now?"

"Willie's."

Willie's Wet Whistle had been a favorite haunt of Michael's.

"The Cowboy Rebels are playing to a packed house and Carter—" Lucy looked both ways before pulling onto the road and heading back to the Saguaro Cactus Lounge "—said a couple of guys have reached their limit and he wants them gone before they pick a fight."

"Carter should call the cops if his customers are giving him trouble."

"He'd rather I haul the cowboys away than risk the sheriff's deputy closing him down for the night."

Tony hated the thought of Lucy alone on the road with drunken men.

She's not your girl. You have no say in what she does.

Lucy turned into the lounge and parked next to the Pony Express van. Before they got out of his truck, he said, "Mind if I ride along with you tonight?" What the heck else did he have to do but go home and worry about Lucy's safety?

"Okay." Lucy smiled. "I doubt the passengers will give me any trouble with a border patrol agent riding shotgun."

"YOU MISSED THE TURNOFF," Tony said.

Shoot. Lucy had been thinking about Tony's confession that he was to blame for Michael's death. "Sorry." She slowed the van, checked her mirrors and made a U-turn. She hadn't believed she could feel any guiltier than she already did, but Tony's admission twisted the screws tighter.

Tell him it isn't his fault. Tell him it's your fault.

Too late. The lot at Willie's was jammed, so Lucy parked in front of the entrance—an oversize royal-blue door that sported a silhouette of a cowboy. The dance hall reminded Lucy of an airplane hangar—a windowless aluminum building with a rusty tin roof. Giant swamp coolers circulated damp air while the metal doors at both ends of the building had been rolled up, allowing the music to spill into the desert.

"Wait here," Lucy said.

"Are you kidding? I want to see you in action." Tony followed her into the bar.

Lucy winced at the loud music as she wove through

the maze of sweaty bodies and worked her way up to the bar, where the owner poured drinks. Carter spotted her and nodded. The former Phoenix Cardinal linebacker had retired in Yuma and opened Willie's five years ago. When Lucy reached him, he motioned to the guys sitting at a nearby table.

"Bobby Ray and Billy John," Carter shouted above the noise. "Good luck." He handed Lucy a set of keys.

Tony intercepted the pass and snatched the key ring.

"You hire a new driver?" Carter glanced between Lucy and Tony.

"Carter Hawkins... Tony Bravo," Lucy said. They shook hands.

"I remember you," Carter said. "You rode bulls with Lucy's brother."

"And you had a pretty good career with the Cardinals," Tony said.

"I did." Carter grinned. "Still ride bulls?"

"Every now and then. Tonight I'm riding along with Lucy."

"Good." Carter pointed to her customers. "Billy John is harmless but Bobby Ray's a hothead." One of the waitresses called Carter's name and the owner walked off.

"I'll handle these guys," Tony said.

Tony's take-charge attitude didn't offend Lucy. He wouldn't be a good border patrol agent if he wasn't self-assured and confident. "Let's go," Tony said to the men.

The cowboys stared with stony expressions. Time to pour on the charm. "Evenin', gentlemen." Lucy smiled sweetly. "You've bought yourselves a ticket on the Pony Express." The line sounded corny but most of her customers chuckled.

Casting evil glares at Carter, the men rose to their feet and stumbled toward the exit. Once they stepped outside, Lucy asked, "Where are you fellas from?"

"Yuma," Bobby Ray said.

She unlocked the side door on the van. "You looking for a ride into town then?"

"Unless you're offerin' a different kind of ride tonight?" Bobby Ray leered at Lucy, and Billy John snickered.

Tony stepped forward, but Lucy blocked his path. She'd use Tony as backup only if necessary. "Sorry, but you won't find that kind of ride in this van."

"Aw, c'mon, sugar."

When Bobby Ray made a move toward Lucy, she grabbed his forearm and spun, tossing him over her shoulder and onto the ground. Before the cowboy knew what had happened, Lucy had planted her boot heel against his windpipe. "Rule number one. Don't mess with the driver. Got that, Bobby Ray?"

Tony whistled low between his teeth. "Nice job."

Secretly pleased she'd impressed Tony, Lucy said, "If you gentlemen mind your manners, I'll give you a lift into Yuma. If not, you sit in the parking lot until the sheriff arrives. What'll it be?"

Bobby Ray grimaced. "Yuma."

"Shut up and behave, Bobby." Billy John helped his friend off the ground. "Sue Ann will have my head if I don't come home tonight."

"Either of you carrying a weapon?" Lucy asked.

"No, ma'am." Both men raised their arms in the air.

"Lift your jeans up over your boots." Satisfied neither cowboy carried a knife or a gun, Lucy said, "Get in."

Tony closed the van door then hopped into the front passenger seat.

"Who are you?" Billy John asked Tony after Lucy started the engine.

"Tony Bravo. Border patrol agent."

"Someone give me an address." Lucy input the information into the GPS as Billy John recited it.

"How often do you end up at the wrong house?" Tony asked.

"Never. But Hector's landed in a few strange places."

"That was pretty impressive," Tony said. "Where'd you learn to flip a guy onto his back?"

"I took a self-defense class in college." She left out that she'd dated her instructor, Keith, for nine months.

"I'm glad you know how to defend yourself, but you should have a partner if you're going to drive the van."

"Quit harassing me. You're worse than my parents." Lucy had thought long and hard before making the decision to start up the Pony Express. She'd weighed the pros and cons, but in the end the only thing that had mattered was saving lives.

Halfway to Yuma, Bobby Ray crawled into the third seat and fell asleep. His quiet snores served as background music to Billy John's conversation with Tony about border security.

Lucy followed the GPS map and ended up at the Desert Sands Apartments. "Which way?" she asked, turning into the entrance.

"Third building on the right." Billy John unbuckled his belt when the van stopped. "How much do we owe you?"

"Nothing. The Pony Express is free, but if you're feeling generous you can leave a tip to help pay for gas." Lucy held out a mason jar and Billy John dropped a five-dollar bill in it then roused Bobby Ray.

Tony steadied the man as he stumbled from the van.

"Stay home the rest of the night, okay?" Lucy said.

"Yes, ma'am." Billy John lugged his friend up the sidewalk to the apartment.

Lucy waited until the men went inside before pulling away. Tony remained quiet, but she sensed he had something to say. "You might as well spit it out."

"I underestimated you."

"How so?"

"You're a rich, spoiled girl."

"Yes, I am." Or she had been until her father cut off her inheritance.

"I never imagined you caring about what happens to lowlifes."

"Just because a cowboy drinks a little too much doesn't mean he's scum. Most of the guys who catch a lift home from the Pony Express are hardworking ranch hands or down-on-their-luck rodeo cowboys."

Lucy tuned the radio to a country station and returned to the Saguaro Cactus Lounge. Tony remained quiet during the drive and she found his silence comforting, not nerve-racking. As soon as she pulled into the parking lot of the bar her phone rang. Shannon Douglas. "Sorry, I have to take this call."

"No problem. Thanks for the ride-along, and watch yourself tonight." Tony hopped out and shut the door before she had a chance to hand him his truck keys. He'd probably forgotten she had them from earlier in the evening.

"Hi, Shannon, what's up?" Lucy's blood pumped faster through her veins as she listened to the good news.

"Great. Thanks so much. I'll arrive at the rodeo a couple of hours before my ride." Lucy grabbed the pen and notepad she kept in the van and scribbled down information about the Ajo rodeo in the middle of May. "I promise I won't embarrass you."

When Shannon lectured her on the importance of being in top physical shape, Lucy said, "Don't worry. I'll be fine. I've found someone to help me train for the rodeo." She crossed her fingers, hoping she hadn't told a lie.

After disconnecting the call, she let out a whoop of joy. Shannon had persuaded Wrangler to allow Lucy to ride in three summer rodeos to raise money for the Pony Express. The two rodeos following Ajo were yet to be determined. Lucy left the van and waited for Tony to come out of the bar.

"Looking for these?" She jingled the keychain when he stepped outside. "I have a huge favor to ask, but I'm positive you'll say no." She handed over the keys.

"Then why ask?"

"I have no one else to turn to."

"What do you need help with?"

"Teach me to ride bulls."

His mouth sagged.

"Please, Tony. I've organized a fundraiser—"

"No."

"Is that a *no* or a *maybe no?*"

"No means no, Lucy."

"I realize this came out of left field, but—"

"You have no business on the back of a bull." Good

God, Tony thought. The woman was small-boned, five-feet-six or -seven inches tall at the most, and probably weighed less than one-ten, sopping wet.

"This is important, Tony."

He'd worked for the border patrol long enough to tell the difference between people who were serious and sane and those who were serious and insane. Lucy was dead serious—whether she was sane or insane was anyone's guess. "Why do you need to ride a bull?"

"I'm raising—" A rowdy group of cowboys leaving the bar interrupted her.

Tony took her by the arm and helped her into the front seat of his truck. He started the engine then flipped the air-conditioning on high, hoping the blast of cold air would mask the scent of Lucy's honeysuckle perfume.

"Hear me out," she said.

Did he have a choice?

"When I came up with the idea for the Pony Express I expected my father to object, but he didn't."

"Why not?" Tony sure in hell would have.

"My mother told him to back off, because she was worried I wouldn't remain in Stagecoach."

"You had plans to go somewhere else?"

"Right before I graduated, I received a job offer from a marketing firm in Phoenix, but because my mother was having a difficult time coping with Michael's death I declined the job and moved back home." Lucy waved a hand in the air. "Anyway, my father expected the Pony Express to fail, so he stayed out of my way as I got the business off the ground."

"What does all this have to do with bull riding?"

"The federal grant I receive to run the Pony Express

was reduced by half. When my father found out, he cut off access to my trust fund, which I'd been dipping into to keep the business afloat."

Tony thought he might have done the same thing if it had been his daughter.

"If I don't find a way to raise $20,000 this summer, the Pony Express will go bankrupt before the end of the year."

"Besides gas and maintenance on the van, what other expenses do you have?" he asked.

She counted off on her fingers. "Hector's salary and his—"

"Hector isn't a volunteer driver?" Shoot, his mother didn't get paid to deliver food to her Meals on Wheels clients.

"I pay Hector a small salary and his benefits."

"What kind of benefits?"

"Health insurance." A second finger popped up. "I also pay liability insurance in case I'm sued."

Liability insurance was smart. Even though the Durango Gold Mine had stopped production years ago, drunken cowboys might sue, hoping to get their hands on part of the Durango fortune. "Okay, I can see where your business needs cash flow to survive, but how will riding bulls pay the bills?"

"Shannon Douglas talked Wrangler into agreeing to let me ride bulls as a fundraising event for the Pony Express. The first rodeo is in Ajo the second weekend in May."

"Wrangler's paying you to ride?"

"No. I've set up a website where people can pledge

a specific dollar amount for each second I remain on the bull."

"What happens if you get injured after the first rodeo and can't ride?"

"That's where you come in," she said.

"Me?"

"Teach me how to ride without getting hurt."

"If there was a way to do that, there'd be more bull riders in rodeo." He wanted no part of her foolish scheme. "Sorry, no can do."

"You're the only person I trust," she said.

"No." Her father would have his head if he taught Lucy rodeo skills.

"Okay, then you must know someone on the circuit who'd be willing to show me the ropes."

Was she kidding? Once the guy got a good look at Lucy's pretty face and sexy body he'd try to do a lot more than just show her the ropes.

"If you won't help, I'll find a cowboy who will." Lucy reached for the door handle.

He snagged her arm. "You're dead set on riding bulls to raise money for the Pony Express?"

"I'll do anything to keep the business running."

A sixth sense warned Tony that helping Lucy was not in his best interest, but he didn't trust anyone else to show her how to protect herself from serious injury.

Her blue-eyed gaze implored him. "If the Pony Express goes under then Michael will have died in vain."

Nothing anyone said or did would validate Michael's death, but Tony refrained from saying so.

"Every drunken cowboy I prevent from getting behind the wheel is a life that Michael's death saved."

Maybe Cal Durango wouldn't object to Tony helping his daughter if he kept Lucy from killing or injuring herself. "Okay, I'm in, but I want something in return."

"What?" she asked.

"Access to the Durango Gold Mine."

"Dad said he'd speak with your supervisor about allowing the border patrol access to that area of the ranch."

"I want to go out there before anyone else." Tony wanted to be the one to find evidence that the property was being used to transport young girls through the desert.

"What if I can't get my father to cooperate?"

"Then no bull-riding lessons." He prayed she wouldn't call his bluff.

"When do I get my first lesson?"

"Six o'clock tomorrow night at my mother's."

"You won't cancel out on me?" she asked.

"You hold up your end of the bargain, and I'll hold up mine."

Lucy flashed her sassy dimples at Tony and got out of the truck. How the hell was he going to help Lucy and keep his hands to himself when each breathing, living part of him wanted to have his way with her?

CHAPTER FOUR

SUNDAY MORNING DAWNED bright and early—too early. Lucy had dropped off the last Pony Express passenger at 3:00 a.m. With only five hours of sleep under her belt, she dragged herself from bed and stumbled into the shower. The lukewarm water revived her, and thoughts of her first bull-riding lesson with Tony washed away the remaining vestiges of sleep.

She dressed quickly and pulled her damp hair into a ponytail before leaving her room and following the scent of freshly brewed coffee through the house. Today marked the two-year anniversary of her brother's death. Bracing herself, she entered the kitchen, where her mother flipped pancakes at the stove and her father read the newspaper at the table.

"Good morning, Lucy." Her mother smiled.

"Morning." Lucy fetched the orange-juice pitcher from the fridge, poured herself a glass and sat at the table across from her father. "Good morning, Dad."

An unintelligible grunt echoed from behind the paper.

"Thanks," Lucy said when her mother placed a plate of bacon and a stack of pancakes on the table. Sunday was the one day of the week her mother cooked—the housekeeper had the day off.

"Is scrambled okay?" her mother asked.

"No."

"Sure." Lucy spoke at the same time as her father.

"You'll eat whatever I put on the table, Cal."

Yeah, Mom. Lucy hid a smile behind a fake cough. Her father was the stereotypical spoiled, wealthy man who loved being coddled, but Lucy's mother drew the line at bending over backward to please her husband.

"Is Hector feeling better?" She whisked eggs in a bowl then poured them into a frying pan.

Taking her cue from her parents, Lucy pretended this was just another ordinary day. "I hope so." She yawned. "I'll call him after breakfast." Her father ignored the conversation, continuing to read the paper while his food grew cold.

"What are your plans today?" her mother asked, setting the scrambled eggs on the table and taking a seat.

"I need to drop off the van at Hector's and pick up my truck." Lucy shoveled a forkful of eggs into her mouth and contemplated how to broach the subject of granting Tony access to the ranch. She tapped a finger against the newspaper. Her father folded one corner down and stared.

"Heard any news on the human-trafficking ring?" Lucy asked.

"I spoke with Jim Fencel." Mr. Fencel was a member of the Arizona State Legislature. "He said the border patrol gets leads all the time that are dead ends."

"What if this one isn't a dead end and Mexican gang members are transporting kidnapped girls across the ranch, Cal?" Lucy's mother joined the conversation.

"Border patrol helicopters fly over the ranch once a week and use heat-sensing cameras to track any movement on the ground. If there was activity on our property they would have notified me by now."

The Durango Ranch encompassed 126 square miles and the area near the mine was dotted with thick scrub, offering ample cover for trespassers. A helicopter could fly overhead and not spot a thing. "It's your civic duty to allow the border patrol access to the ranch," Lucy's mother said.

"My civic—"

"Cal," she interrupted. "They're helpless little girls." She buttered a slice of toast. "And we can't have our name associated with that kind of illegal activity." Of course her mother would be concerned with protecting the Durango name.

"Dad, if cartel members believe our ranch is a safe haven and inaccessible by the border patrol, then it's only a matter of time before they grow bolder and rob the house or steal our vehicles."

"You're being melodramatic, daughter."

"When was the last time you drove to the mine?" Lucy asked.

"I don't remember."

"Eat." Her mother pointed her fork at the remaining food on Lucy's plate.

Ignoring the command, Lucy pleaded her case. "Mom and I won't feel safe when you travel unless we know no one is hiding on the property."

"I haven't denied the border patrol access to the ranch. They're taking their sweet time investigating."

"Maybe they're busy investigating another case. Tony could stop out there and have a look around."

"I don't want Bravo anywhere near the ranch." Her

father's stubborn scowl provoked Lucy to speak without thinking.

"Do you hate Tony so much that you'd risk the ranch being vandalized or one of us getting abducted just to keep him from doing his job?"

Her father's fist slammed down on the table, rattling the dishes. "Bravo's the reason Michael's not sitting at this table with us!"

Her mother's fork clanged against her plate.

So much for ignoring the significance of the day. "It's not Tony's fault, Dad." *It's my fault.* Lucy's conscience demanded she confess, but fear of jeopardizing the progress she'd made in her relationship with her father kept the truth bottled up inside her.

"Tony should have never left the bar if he knew Michael was drinking heavily."

"You always put Michael on a pedestal, Dad, believing he could do no wrong." Unlike her. "He was twenty-five. An adult. Michael was responsible for his own actions."

Each night since her brother's death Lucy went to bed and repeated in her head—*Michael was responsible for his own actions.* And each night she waited for the words to ring true in her heart.

Two years later she was still waiting.

"Bravo was Michael's best friend," her father said.

"In the beginning you forbade Michael to be friends with Tony," Lucy's mother reminded him.

"And for good reason. Look how things ended."

Lucy changed tactics. "If you despise Tony that much, why not give him access to the ranch to prove you're right about the cartel and he's wrong?" Her father's pain and bitterness over Michael's death was so deeply entrenched that she didn't see any other way to get him to agree to her request unless he believed it would put Tony in his place.

"You're right." Her father's grim expression lightened. "Bravo needs to be taught a lesson in humility."

Lucy choked on her orange juice. If anyone needed that lesson, it was the man sitting across the table from her. "So you'll allow Tony to search the property?"

"Not alone. You go with him to make sure he doesn't steal anything while he's out there."

Although the mine had closed, not all of the gold had been extracted from the Venus Vein—discovered in a network of underground tunnels. A cave-in near the vein had killed a miner, and after further testing, her father determined that it wasn't worth risking more lives for the small amount of gold left in the shaft. He had officially shut down production in March 2001.

He pointed his finger at Lucy. "You take Bravo to the mine. Make sure he doesn't go anywhere else on the property."

"Sure." Sweet relief rushed through Lucy. Now, nothing would stop her from preparing for the Ajo rodeo. Whether Tony approved of her fundraising idea or not, he'd be forced to teach her basic bull-riding skills if he wanted access to the ranch.

Everything was falling into place, leaving her with only one worry—how best to tell her parents about her newest fundraising idea. She'd have to inform them soon, because she intended to post flyers in Stagecoach and Yuma. Sooner or later, word would get back to them and pandemonium would erupt. She rinsed her dirty dishes and loaded them into the dishwasher. "I'll be in my office for a couple of hours before I take the van back to Hector."

"Your father and I are having dinner with the Friedans tonight," her mother said. Robert Friedan was the branch manager of the First Trust Bank in Yuma—the bank her father kept part of his fortune in. "We won't be home until late."

"Have a nice time." Lucy kissed her mother's cheek. "Thanks for breakfast."

The next few hours flew by as she made phone calls and sent out emails asking for help with the fundraiser. Her college friend Christine had offered to spearhead an Alpha Delta Pi pledge drive for the Pony Express. With Lucy's sorority connections, she was able to convince Arizona State University and the University of Arizona to work their sorority-girl magic and collect donations from their sister chapters across the country. After discussing a PR campaign with Christine, Lucy designed a flyer and pledge card before finally leaving her office.

When she walked past Maddie's cage, the boxer twitched her tail but didn't move from her spot in the shade. Certain the dog knew the significance of today's date, Lucy didn't have the heart to leave her alone. "Wanna go for a ride, Maddie?"

Maddie sprang to her feet, her tail wagging faster than a windshield-wiper blade. Lucy snapped on her leash, and as soon as she opened the passenger-side door of the van, the dog jumped inside. Once Lucy got the air-conditioning running, she texted her mother that she was taking Maddie on errands with her, then headed for the main road with her canine partner.

"HEY, BRAVO." Steve Hernandez paused in front of Tony's desk. "Don't you have Sundays off?"

·"I've got paperwork to catch up on." Tony had stopped at the office because he'd been tempted to hole up in his apartment all day and drink until the alcohol obliterated Michael's death from his memory.

"A group of us are going to Buffalo Wild Wings after work."

"I'll take a rain check." He shouldn't be looking forward to giving Lucy her first bull-riding lesson, but spending time with her on the anniversary of Michael's death felt strangely right.

"Hot date?" Steve grinned.

Lucy was definitely *h-o-t*. After the first time they'd made love, he hadn't been able to keep his hands off her, wanting to savor the connection they'd shared. "No hot date," he lied.

"You're not still moping over your breakup with Evita, are you?"

Almost a year had passed since he'd ended his relationship with Evita, and to be honest, he only thought of her in passing. Tony shook his head. "I promised my mother I'd stop by and visit her tonight." It wasn't anyone's business but Tony's if he was meeting Lucy there.

"If you change your mind, we'll be at the restaurant."

As soon as Steve left, Tony's boss poked his head out his office door. "Bravo, get in here."

Deputy Chief Patrol Agent Cesar Romero's abrupt demeanor didn't faze Tony. The former Marine never minced words and rarely socialized with the men under his command. The boss man was all work and no play.

"Shut the door," Romero said when Tony entered the office.

Tony did as ordered, then stood by the closed door

until his boss nodded for him to sit in the chair across from the desk. "Did you finish the paperwork on the drug bust last week?"

"I emailed it to Rosalinda." The office assistant was the go-to person for everything in the department. Nothing landed on the boss's desk until it passed through Rosalinda's hands.

"The human-trafficking ring is on the back burner until we finish investigating the four dead bodies found in the Hilo Basin."

Tony had feared his boss wouldn't take his hunch seriously. If Tony expected Romero's help in securing a transfer to San Diego, he needed to make his boss look good. Finding evidence of trespassers on the Durango Ranch would earn him brownie points.

Romero shuffled through a stack of papers. "Anything new come up in your chat rooms?"

Each of the border patrol agents was assigned to an internet chat room where illegals talked about border crossings and drug trafficking. "Nothing out of the ordinary."

"Word came in a few minutes ago that a group of illegals were caught with explosives near Smuggler's Gulch." The gulch was a large rocky canyon that followed a dried-up riverbed along the California border.

"The men were members of the Sinaloa Cartel," Romero said. Months ago his boss had predicted the famous cartel was on the verge of expanding their Texas operation to New Mexico and Arizona. Now there was proof the gang had infiltrated the Grand Canyon State.

"Then it's possible the Sinaloa are behind the human-trafficking ring," Tony said.

"Get me proof, Bravo, and I'll back you one hundred percent."

"Yes, sir." Even if Lucy didn't come through for him, Tony would find a way onto the Durango Ranch.

"That's all. Get out of here."

Tony left the office. He had an hour to kill before Lucy showed up at his mother's and he planned to use the time to shower and change into a pair of shorts. He kept extra clothes at the trailer because he often crashed in the guest bedroom after pulling all-nighters on the job. Sunset Trails Mobile Home Park was closer to the border patrol station than his single-bedroom apartment on the north side of town.

When Tony arrived at his mother's, Maria was sitting on the covered porch sipping lemonade. "This is a nice surprise," she said as he climbed the steps. Today her hug was extra long—she remembered the importance of the date. He returned the hug, conveying without words how much her love meant to him. "Lucy's coming over—" he glanced at his watch "—in a half hour."

His mother sucked in a quiet breath. "But today's the anniversary of Michael's—"

"It's okay, Mom."

"Shouldn't Lucy be with Cal and Sonja?"

"She wouldn't come over if they had family plans."

"I'll throw together a tuna casserole." Tony's favorite comfort food. He followed his mother inside. "I haven't seen Lucy in forever," she said.

After all this time, she still had no idea he and Lucy had been involved in a relationship when Michael died.

"Lucy wants me to give her pointers on bull riding."

Tony walked down the narrow hallway of the double-wide, his mother hot on his heels.

"Lucy has no business on the back of a bull," she said.

He entered the guest bedroom and grabbed a change of clothes. "She's riding in the Ajo rodeo next month."

Maria's eyes rounded. "Cal and Sonja didn't object?"

"Her parents don't know." Advertising the event would take care of that minor detail soon enough.

"Why in the world is Lucy rodeoing?"

"She's trying to raise money for the Pony Express," he said before shutting the bathroom door. Standing under the low-flow showerhead was like getting caught in a summer sprinkle rather than a dousing rainstorm. Mindful of the area's water restrictions, he soaped up quickly and rinsed off. He spent most of his workday outside, requiring at least two showers per day in a state where water was a priceless commodity.

After drying off, he slapped his cheeks and neck with aftershave and shrugged into clean clothes, refusing to examine why he was sprucing up when he'd get sweaty all over again hauling out the mechanical bull from the shed.

He'd stowed the machine after Michael's death and promised himself that he'd never use it again. He should have given it away, but he'd kept it as a reminder of all the good times they'd had together. While his mother worked in the kitchen, Tony hauled boxes of Christmas decorations out of the shed. He'd just finished clearing a path to the bull, which sat on transport dollies, when a truck pulled up in front of the trailer.

Maddie sat in the passenger seat, her long tongue hanging from the side of her mouth. As soon as Lucy opened the door, the dog charged Tony, and he braced himself for impact when she leaped through the air. Dropping to his knees, he wrestled with her.

Lucy laughed, drawing Tony's gaze to her dimples, and his heart missed a beat. If one smile from Lucy was all it took to disrupt his life rhythm, then he was a heart attack waiting to happen.

"You should have seen Maddie when I asked if she wanted to visit you." Lucy looked every inch the cowgirl in tight jeans, cowboy hat and boots. And her expensive-looking Western shirt hugged her breasts and showed off her trim waist.

Forcing his gaze from her figure, he pushed Maddie off him and fetched a bowl from the shelf inside the shed. Michael had left the water dish at the trailer for the times he stopped by with Maddie. The pink plastic dish with a princess crown painted on the side had amused Tony, and he'd accused Michael of treating the dog better than he did his girlfriends.

"Look at that, Maddie, a designer bowl." Lucy laughed.

The dog followed Tony to the water spigot on the side of the trailer. As soon as he filled the bowl, she lapped up the contents then lay down in the shade on the porch.

"Michael complained about Maddie being a female dog." Lucy stared at the boxer with sad eyes. "But I think my brother liked having his best girl by his side all the time."

"Has Maddie been behaving?" Tony asked.

"Only because she's been locked in her cage."

No wonder the dog was depressed. After Michael had rescued her, she'd gone everywhere with him. Maddie was used to being with people and other animals, not spending every hour of the day alone. Tony shook his head to dislodge the image of the boxer in her cage and motioned to the shed. "I need your help with the bucking machine."

Lucy glanced at the trailer door. "I was hoping to say hello to your mother before we started."

"She's making supper for us. You'll have a chance to chat with her later."

"Great." Lucy poked her head inside the shed. "I'm glad you kept my brother's bucking machine."

"How did you know I had it?"

"I saw it in the back of your truck one afternoon in Yuma." She shrugged. "How do you propose we pull this giant monstrosity out of here?"

"It's resting on a pair of steerable dollies. It should roll right out." He slipped past Lucy, the sultry scent of her perfume drifting up his nostrils.

"What do you need me to do?" she asked.

Stand there and let me sniff you. "Press this button." He pointed to a red tab. "When I say so, pull on your end and I'll push on mine."

"Sounds easy enough."

Tony got into position. "Okay, hit the button."

Lucy obeyed.

"Nice and slow so you don't run over your foot." He hadn't expected Lucy to help much but the machine lurched forward and Tony acknowledged she was stronger than he'd given her credit for. Once they'd cleared the shed, they rolled the bull behind the trailer. Tony had poured a concrete slab six years ago when he'd bought his mother an outdoor cooking grill, but the grill had ended up at Juan's house when the two of them begun dating.

As he positioned the machine, Lucy said, "I know you don't approve of me rodeoing, but isn't landing on cement cruel and unusual punishment?" The dimples in her cheeks twitched.

Man, she was cute. "You won't fall off."

"You sure of that?"

He grinned and set the dollies aside. "Trash day is Wednesday. Someone's bound to throw out an old mattress."

"I'm not landing on some flea-infested, urine-stained padding."

"Don't worry, princess, we'll cover it with sheets." All this talk about mattresses had Tony fantasizing about enticing Lucy into his bed.

"You're in for a big surprise, Tony Bravo." Lucy made a mulish face.

"Oh, yeah?" He laughed.

"I don't intend to fall off."

He could damn well guarantee she wouldn't tumble from the machine, because he'd be standing by her side, ready to catch her if she slid. Lucy made a move to mount the bull. Tony's hand shot out and caught her boot heel, holding her leg suspended in the air. "Your first lesson comes with a price, remember?"

Lucy didn't attempt to yank her leg free and Tony struggled to keep his gaze averted from the fancy stitching across the back pockets of her designer jeans. "I have good news for you. Dad said I can take you out to the gold mine."

"What happens if I find evidence of trespassers?" Damn, he was impressed with Lucy's balance—she wasn't even teetering.

"We'll cross that bridge when we come to it."

Fair enough. Lucy had matured into a self-confident young woman capable of holding her own with him, and Tony found that sexy as all get-out. He released her leg then grabbed her by the waist and hoisted her onto the machine. When she wobbled, Tony placed his hand beneath her armpit to steady her. His palm accidentally brushed the side of her breast and a quiet gasp escaped her.

He was playing with fire. If he didn't keep things between him and Lucy purely business he was likely to get hurt—in more ways than one.

CHAPTER FIVE

TONY PLUGGED THE bucking machine into the outlet at the rear of the trailer. "Hold on while I run the machine through each gear. If it jams, I don't want you to get whiplash."

"What? And take all the fun out of this?" Lucy said, refusing to grab the pommel.

Tony positioned the machine at the lowest level and the motor squeaked for a few seconds then settled into a gentle twisting motion. "Relax your hips," he said. "You look like someone shoved a pole up your—"

"Okay, okay, I get it." She attempted a loosey-goosey posture, but it was all she could do to force herself to concentrate when Tony stared at her breasts.

"Guess what you're doing wrong," he said.

"Isn't it your job to tell me what I'm doing wrong?"

"You're holding the rope with your right hand."

"Oops, I forgot." She switched the rope to her left hand. After years of watching Tony and her brother compete, she'd known bull riders held the rope with their left hands, but Tony's presence flustered her. Maybe it hadn't been a good idea to ask for his help. He was a bigger threat to her than a renegade bull.

"Like this." He grasped her hand and her skin tingled when the calluses on his palm scraped her knuckles. She shivered as an image of that rough hand caressing her bare thigh flashed before her eyes. Tony had been an amazing lover, and he'd taught her things about her body that she hadn't known she could do.

He adjusted her fingers on the rope so her grip felt more secure. "Lean your shoulders forward, not your hips," he said.

She did as instructed.

"That's too much." He stepped behind her and tweaked her shoulders. "Perfect." Five seconds later he shook his head in disgust. "Your hips are moving again."

"No, they're not."

"Yes, they are." His fingers clamped down on her hips, pressing into the bone. Tiny electrical pulses shot through Lucy's stomach and straight down to her...*never mind*.

"Try to move now," he said.

Darn it, he'd been right. With her hips set in place and her spine relaxed she was able to keep her shoulders in place. Her body moved in sync with the machine and she remained balanced. Her emotions, however, were not as easy to steady.

"I knew this wouldn't be difficult once I learned the proper technique." She sounded winded—probably because Tony's hands were still guiding her hips.

"Honey, if this sport was easy, every boy would grow up to be a rodeo cowboy."

"I'm being positive. All I need to do is sit on a bull for a few seconds."

He pressed down on her thigh with his hand. "Clamp your legs against the machine. Riding a bull for a short time is nothing. Dismounting without breaking your neck or getting stomped on is a bit trickier."

"Being trampled isn't in my game plan." Lucy's voice sounded sure, but her insides quaked—although not from fear, but arousal. With each undulating twist of the machine Tony's fingers inched closer to her crotch. If she thrust her hips a fraction forward he'd touch...

"You better not get too cocky, Lucy." He released her leg and she sucked in a lungful of air. "Your father will have my head and my job if a bull so much as swishes his tail in your face."

"Hey, you kids." Tony's mother called from the porch. "Supper's ready."

Tony shut off the motor and helped Lucy climb down from the machine. "Before this goes any further—" his eyes bored into her "—when will you take me out to the mine?"

Lucy had forgotten Tony wasn't giving her bull-riding lessons out of the goodness of his heart. "When do you want to go?"

"As soon as possible."

"How about tomorrow?"

"I've got meetings in the morning, but I can make it out to the ranch by one-thirty." He skirted the cactus flower bed and climbed the porch steps.

Lucy followed. "Stay here, Maddie."

"She can come inside while we eat." Tony clicked his tongue and the dog bolted past him into the trailer. After Tony shut the door behind Lucy, he scratched Maddie's ears. "This is your home away from home, isn't it, girl?" Maddie's tail wagged. The dog hadn't been this happy in a long time—obviously she missed Tony as much as she did Michael.

Tony's mother stepped from the kitchen and smiled.

"Lucy, you're a sight for sore eyes." She spoke perfect English with no accent, which always amazed Lucy. Michael had mentioned that when Tony's mother decided to become a U.S. citizen she was determined to master the English language.

"It's good to see you, Mrs. Bravo." Lucy hugged the older woman.

"Call me Maria, please." She waved them into the kitchen where she'd set the table. "I hope you like tuna casserole."

"I love tuna casserole." The Durango housekeeper rarely made comfort food. Instead she served mostly steamed veggies and grilled meats. "What can I help with?"

"You can fetch the bread from the oven." Maria dished the casserole onto plates.

Both Lucy and Tony washed their hands at the kitchen sink, then Lucy retrieved the loaf of French bread and Tony grabbed bottles of water from the fridge.

Benign chitchat filled the dinner hour before Maria pushed her plate away. "Young lady," she said, "your parents must be beside themselves. You couldn't find a less risky way to raise money for the Pony Express?"

Tony left Lucy to fend off his mother's questions while he cleared the table.

"I want to honor Michael's memory, and riding bulls seemed like a good fundraiser idea."

Maria patted Lucy's hand. "You could get harmed."

"Tony's going to make sure I don't."

"It's bad enough that I worry about my son when he gets on the back of a bull. Now I have to worry about you." Maria shook her head. "I'll see if my manager at the truck stop will let me put an empty pickle jar next to the register to collect change for the Pony Express."

"Thank you, Maria. Do you think he'd also agree to hand out pledge cards and hang flyers in the windows?"

"I don't see why not." Maria frowned. "I can't imagine your father approves of Tony giving you bull-riding lessons." Maria Bravo was well aware that Lucy's father blamed her son for Michael's death.

"My father won't make trouble for Tony." And the only way she could guarantee that was to keep him from finding out that Tony was coaching her.

"I still don't like the idea of—"

"Don't worry, Mom." Tony offered his mother a reassuring smile, but Lucy caught the flash of uncertainty in his eyes before he looked away.

Was Tony concerned her father might make trouble for him? As much as Lucy loved her dad, she never underestimated the power his wealth wielded. She'd witnessed firsthand how his pocketbook influenced politics in the state. If not for her mother's philanthropic work and large financial donations to the performing arts programs at both state universities, her father would have more enemies than friends.

A cell phone rang and Maria excused herself from the table, taking the call in her bedroom.

"It's probably Juan from the truck stop," Tony said.

"How long have they been a couple?"

"A few years."

"Any plans to marry?"

Tony shook his head. "Mom doesn't want to marry again. It was tough on her when my father was killed."

And tough on Tony growing up without a father.

"Charlotte went home sick a few minutes ago," Maria said as she hurried into the kitchen. "I'm heading over to the truck stop to fill in for a couple of hours until Linda arrives for the graveyard shift." She grabbed her waitressing apron from a hook on the kitchen wall. "There are chocolate-chip cookies for dessert. Help yourselves." At the door she said, "And you watch yourself on that goofy machine, Lucy."

"I will. Thank you for inviting me to dinner, Maria."

"Anytime, dear."

As soon as the door closed, Tony said, "Ready?"

"For what?"

"Your next bull-riding lesson."

The thought of Tony touching her body again excited Lucy, but she worried that the more time they spent with each other, the more difficult it would be to say "see ya" after the rodeo fundraisers ended. "I better get going."

"If I'm in charge of keeping you alive, I call the shots." He leaned across the table and lowered his voice. "You'll practice until your sweet little fanny is too sore to sit on."

Lucy's face warmed.

"Come hell or high water, Lucy Durango—" Tony walked to the door "—I'm gonna make sure nothing happens to that pretty neck of yours, because if you get injured, it's my head your father will serve up on a silver platter."

Even though Tony was well aware of the risks of helping Lucy, he appeared determined to stay the course. "I've changed my mind," she said, following him onto the porch.

Tony descended the steps and fetched a can of lubricating spray from the shed then ducked beneath the bucking machine and oiled the motor. When he finished, he said, "Changed your mind about what?"

"Asking you to help me." She motioned to the mechanical bull.

He returned the spray to the shed then strolled toward Lucy, hips swaggering. He stopped in front of her—less than an inch of space between them. His scent swirled around her head. "Who *will* help you?"

"Shannon Douglas can give me pointers."

His dark gaze zeroed in on her mouth and Lucy's pulse raced. She couldn't think with Tony standing so close, but when she attempted to retreat, nothing happened—it was as if the heels of her boots had been staked into the ground.

"Shannon doesn't have time to help you." His mouth curved in a sexy half smile. "Besides, I'm the only one who isn't afraid of your father."

That was the God's honest truth.

"Whether or not Cal approves of me doesn't matter. I'll be transferring to San Diego soon."

A sick feeling grew inside her. Lucy wouldn't put it past her dad to prevent Tony's transfer from happening.

"Never mind. This wasn't a good idea from the get-go." Not just because of her father's guaranteed objection, but because the chemistry was still there between her and Tony and it would take little effort on his part to make her fall in love with him all over again. She walked away.

"Hey, we had a deal." Tony marched after her. "My help in exchange for—"

"Don't worry. I'll take you out to the gold mine." As much as she hated to see Tony move away from Stagecoach, Lucy wanted him to be happy. She hopped into her truck. "Meet me at the west entrance of the ranch to-morrow at one-thirty." She shut the door in his face and drove off, forgetting all about Maddie.

AS TONY WATCHED the taillights of Lucy's truck leave the mobile home park and turn onto the highway, he exhaled a sigh of relief. The woman was too much of a temptation. Keeping his attraction to her under control was more difficult than chasing criminals through a moonless desert without the use of night-vision goggles. But as much as he believed it was best for him to stay away from Lucy, he didn't trust anyone else to give her pointers on bull riding. And he for sure didn't like the idea of Lucy cozying up to another rodeo cowboy for help.

Jealousy aside, picking up where they'd left off two years ago would only end in disaster. They were different people—both changed by Michael's death. Yes, the fire still burned hot between them, but he didn't deserve a second chance with Lucy. He'd made his bed—now he had to lie in it. He'd give her a few days to search for a new bull-riding mentor, but he was confident she'd crawl back to him. Then it would be up to him to make sure they kept their relationship purely professional.

Easier said than done.

He threw the tarp over the bucking machine, closed the shed door then went to lock up the trailer for the night. When his boot hit the first porch step, he froze. "Maddie."

The dog's ears perked. "How'd you get left behind?" He sat down and Maddie rested her head on his leg.

Come to think of it, he couldn't recall seeing the boxer when Lucy had driven off. "Sneaky girl. You hid on purpose, didn't you?" What was he supposed to do with the dog?

Call Lucy. He reached into his pocket for his phone, but the dog's big brown eyes stopped him. "You can't stay at my apartment," he said. "No pets allowed."

Maddie licked Tony's hand.

"We had some wild times, didn't we, girl?" Tony's mind flashed back to the afternoon he and Michael had taken Maddie hiking. The dog had spotted a rattlesnake coiled on a rock and barked a warning when Michael stepped within striking distance.

Tony's phone jingled with a text message. "I think I know who this is."

Is Maddie with you?

He texted back. Yep.

On my way.

Tony texted, She can stay here tonight.

Sure?

Yep.

K.

You're not driving and texting are you?

:-) No.

I'll bring Maddie when we meet at the ranch.

K.

Tony returned the phone to his pocket. It beeped again.

Night.

The single word sounded intimate and Tony put the phone away before he texted, Sweet dreams. "You hungry, Maddie?"

The boxer went to the door.

"Guess so." He let her into the trailer. "Hope you like tuna casserole." Maddie followed Tony into the kitchen and waited patiently for a handout. He set a plate of food on the floor along with a fresh bowl of water, and the dog devoured the meal.

"Now what?" he asked when her sad eyes latched onto him. "Because of you, I'm stuck sleeping here tonight." Tony walked down the hall to the guest bedroom. Maddie followed him and hopped onto Tony's bed, resting her head on his pillow.

Ignoring the dog, Tony took his uniform to the laundry room and stuck it in the washer so he'd have clean clothes for work tomorrow. Returning to the bedroom, he rummaged through the dresser, throwing clothes on the bed as he searched for his favorite Diamondbacks T-shirt.

He changed into the shirt then gaped at the dog. Maddie had nosed through the pile of clothes and dragged one of the shirts onto the pillow, then nestled her face in it.

Damn it, Maddie. Tony's throat closed as he struggled against the urge to flee, but there was nowhere to run from the memories. The crumpled T-shirt had belonged to Michael. Tony sucked in a ragged breath then stretched out across the bed.

"He shouldn't have died, Maddie." Tony counted to ten—twice—but the damned tears leaked from his eyes. He rested his head next to the dog's on the pillow. "Why Michael, Maddie?" He'd thought he'd cried every last tear for his friend in the days that had followed his death, but Maddie reminded him that he couldn't outrun guilt.

Why hadn't he coerced Michael's backside off that bar stool?

Michael wasn't drunk when I left.

I figured he'd call his father if he needed a ride.

That's what Tony had told himself, but he'd known Michael wouldn't reach out to his father. Cal Durango had worshipped the ground his son walked on. Michael had confided in Tony that his father had ridden broncs in high school but a back injury had ended his career before he'd graduated.

Cal Durango had lived vicariously through his son—taking credit for Michael's rodeo wins as if he'd been the one riding the bulls. He'd also given Michael unlimited funds to pay for motel rooms, food and entertainment on the road.

Tony had worked part-time jobs in order to cover his entry fees. The only reason Durango tolerated Tony was because he'd looked out for Michael. Michael's name drew a lot of attention from rodeo groupies—bimbos hoping to become wife and heir to the Durango fortune. Tony had made sure Michael remained focused on busting bulls and not buckle bunnies.

The night he'd left Michael at the bar had been a first for Tony. Unfortunately, it had also been a last.

Closing his eyes, Tony drifted off to sleep. Thirty minutes later, the alarm on the washing machine woke him. He switched his clothes to the dryer then noticed Maddie sitting at the front door.

"You read my mind, friend." Tony clipped the leash to Maddie's collar, grabbed his keys and went out to his truck to retrieve his night-vision binoculars and his loaded Beretta 96D Brigadier pistol from the glove compartment. Maddie was a large dog, but a hungry coyote or a pack of javelinas could take her down in a minute. Wild animals aside, the biggest threat to Tony was stumbling upon drug runners. Gear in hand, he locked the truck and walked into the desert—twenty-five acres that belonged to the trailer-park developer. There had been plans to divide the land into more trailer pads but the economic recession had stalled further construction, and for now residents used the area to walk their dogs and ride ATVs.

Tony followed a well-worn path through the scrub brush. Saguaros dotted the landscape, several of them full of bullet holes from delinquents practicing a game called cactus plugging. When Maddie stopped to sniff, Tony raised the binoculars and scanned the desert. Fifty yards ahead he spotted a coyote trotting in the opposite direction, and farther away a jackrabbit. If the rabbit was smart he'd hide before his scent reached the coyote. A sudden movement in the scrub caught Tony's attention.

"Sit, Maddie." The dog obeyed and Tony trained the binoculars on a large mesquite bush. Someone stepped out from behind the vegetation and ran north. Five more bodies emerged from the hiding place. If Maddie weren't with him, Tony would have given chase, but he didn't want to risk the dog getting shot if the suspects had guns. Instead, he followed the group with the binoculars as they made their way across the desert landscape. When they disappeared over a ridge, Tony called dispatch on his cell phone and made his way back to the trailer. He locked Maddie inside then went out to wait for his fellow border patrol agents at the entrance to the trailer park. Ricky Sanez and Danny Barker arrived a half hour later.

"How many?" Sanez asked as soon as he hopped out of the truck.

"Six. They're running northeast. They disappeared over that rocky incline out there. I couldn't tell if they were carrying weapons."

Barker made sure his pistol was loaded, then lowered the tailgate of the truck and pulled down a metal ramp. Once they'd unloaded the ATVs, both men put on helmets and night-vision goggles.

Tony made a move to go with Barker, but the man held up his hand. "You're off duty, Bravo."

"No one knows this area better than me." Hell, this piece of desert had been Tony's backyard for years. He knew every rabbit hole and snake den for a mile in each direction. Besides, if he went back to the trailer he'd think about Michael and Lucy.

"Let him come," Sanez said.

Tony hopped onto the back of Barker's ATV. If they were lucky, they'd find the group and apprehend them without incident.

CHAPTER SIX

TONY WAS LATE.

Lucy sat on the front bumper of her pickup and stared down the highway, waiting for a glimpse of the black Dodge. An early morning thunderstorm had rolled through the area, leaving behind cooler temperatures in the mid-eighties. Triggered by rainfall, the pungent smell of creosote bushes permeated the air and breathed life into the desert.

She adjusted her high-powered binoculars and scanned the area. Aside from an occasional piece of garbage that had blown through the barbed-wire fencing, there were no signs of animals or trespassers. Gold Dust Ridge, where the mine was located, might be a different story.

Although Lucy hadn't visited the ridge in a couple of years, Pete, the ranch foreman, had driven out there six months ago and reported nothing amiss. A lot could change in six months.

A horn honked and Lucy swung the binoculars toward the highway. Tony's truck sped toward her, Maddie sitting in the passenger seat. The pair looked right together, but Lucy's heart ached for her brother—he should be the one driving with Maddie. She zoomed in on Tony's face. His eyes were hidden behind his mirrored sunglasses, but she imagined a smoldering heat sparking from the dark brown orbs.

Last night she'd gotten little sleep—her dreams were filled with visions of Tony making love to her. Before dawn she'd awoken aroused and short of breath, as if Tony had sneaked into her bed and made love to her while she'd slept. She wished they could just pick up where they'd left off, but details of the night Michael had died stood between them, and that was all the reason Lucy needed to keep her head on straight around the border patrol agent.

Come clean, and tell him the truth. The truth made Lucy nauseous. Even if her father forgave her, she doubted Tony would. Tony's truck turned onto the property. After he drove through the entrance, she swung the gate closed and fed the security chain through the bars, then retrieved the cooler of water bottles she'd brought along. When she hopped into Tony's truck, Maddie greeted her with a sloppy kiss. "Hey, girl."

Maddie wagged her tail.

"Did she eat breakfast?" Lucy asked.

"I picked up a bag of dog food on the way to the station this morning."

"You took her into work with you?"

"Yep."

"I hope she wasn't any trouble."

"Maddie was on her best behavior."

Lucy snapped on her seat belt, and Tony hit the gas.

"Does your father know we're going out to the mine?" he asked.

"I didn't have a chance to tell him. He flew to California on business this morning before I got out of bed."

The bumpy dirt road made driving a challenge, so Lucy kept quiet. Tony's head swiveled from side to side taking in their surroundings. He stopped the truck twice to get out and study the ground. After a few miles, Gold Dust Ridge came into view. "Wait here," he said. He grabbed his binoculars and left the truck.

As soon as he shut the door, Maddie whined.

"Big baby." Lucy rubbed the dog's neck. "He'll be back, don't worry."

Tony surveyed the area, then bent over and picked up an object from the ground.

"What did you find?" Lucy asked when he returned to the truck.

He handed her a Mexican peso, then drove on.

Hopefully an illegal immigrant crossing the property had dropped the peso and not a member of a Mexican cartel. When Tony got closer to the ridge, she said, "Go left. It's a shortcut to the entrance."

"If left is the fastest way, trespassers will take the opposite route to throw off anyone following them."

"Okay." Tracking illegals was Tony's area of expertise, not hers. Lucy counted only a handful of saguaro cacti in the area and was saddened that the landscape had been desecrated decades ago when gold was discovered. Years of environmental abuse had left Gold Dust Ridge scarred and ugly.

As soon as the truck drove past the ridge, Tony slammed on the brakes and Lucy grabbed Maddie's collar to prevent her from flying into the windshield. Tony put the truck in Park and got out to investigate a small pile of debris littering the ground. Curious, Lucy joined him and Maddie whined in protest at being left behind.

Tony sifted through the trash—gallon-size water jugs, food wrappers, torn clothing and threadbare shoes. He lifted a jacket by his fingertip. "Look at this."

"It belonged to a young girl." The smaller size and pink color were dead giveaways. All the items appeared to be girls' clothing, including a dirty athletic shoe with sparkly purple laces.

"They're driving the girls in here." Tony pointed to the faint tire tracks left in the sand after the early morning shower.

"The lock on the gate wasn't tampered with," Lucy said.

"They're not using the west entrance." He pointed southeast. "They're driving from that direction."

"There's no gate along that side of the ranch."

"I'm guessing they take down a section of fence then put it back up after they've gone through."

She and Tony returned to the truck and he drove by the debris, careful not to run over any of the discarded items. When they arrived at the mine, Tony let Maddie out of the truck and the dog went off in search of lizards. Lucy and Tony discovered more trash and a smashed cell phone.

"I'd say you have enough evidence to support your claim that the girls are being transported through our ranch," Lucy said.

"Your father will want more than garbage before he admits there's any illegal activity on his property."

Not if Lucy had anything to say about it. If young girls were being kidnapped in Mexico and marched across the ranch right under her family's nose, she'd do everything in her power to convince her father to cooperate with the border patrol in order to stop this heinous crime.

The mine entrance remained boarded up and showed no signs of vandalism. "Is there another way in?" Tony asked.

"If there is, I don't know about it." Lucy followed Tony, stepping carefully over the rocks scattered across the ground. The last thing she needed was a sprained ankle before her first bull ride.

Tony stopped to examine a deep crevice between a pair of large boulders.

"What is it?" she asked.

"Possibly a way in." He switched on the flashlight then got down on his belly and slithered through the gap, affording Lucy a bird's-eye view of his muscled buttocks. After he disappeared from sight, he shouted, "Wait there."

Fat chance. Lucy glanced over her shoulder. "Maddie, stay." The dog wagged her tail but remained focused on the brown-spotted gecko she'd cornered.

Dropping to her knees, Lucy wiggled through the rock opening.

"Figures you wouldn't listen to me." Tony had removed his sunglasses and scowled at her from across the dim chamber.

"And miss out on all the fun?" Lucy remained on her knees. "God, it stinks in here." She pinched her nose and breathed through her mouth. "What's that?" She pointed at the object in Tony's hand.

"Cable tie."

"Police use that when they arrest protesters." Lucy shuddered at the idea of young girls being handcuffed and left in the dark.

"Look at that." Tony pointed to the wall above Lucy's head.

"What does it say?" She couldn't make heads or tails out of the graffiti-like marks scratched into the rock.

"Gang symbols." Tony approached the cavern wall and rubbed his finger over the stone. "That's the Spanish word for *kidnap*."

"Do you think one of the girls did that?" she asked.

"Maybe. Let's get out of here." He motioned for Lucy to exit the cave first.

Lucy wiggled her way back outside where she discovered Maddie waiting, a lizard tail hanging out of her mouth. "Bad girl."

"Maddie's an excellent lizard hunter."

"She doesn't eat them, does she?"

"No." He pointed to the dog's mouth. "The tail's still twitching."

"Maddie, drop it." Lucy stomped her foot on the ground, but the dog stared defiantly.

Holding his hand out, Tony approached Maddie. She relaxed her jaw and the lizard plopped onto Tony's palm. He placed the slime-covered reptile on a rock then pointed his finger and warned, "No, Maddie."

The dog whined but didn't move from her spot.

"You're the only one she obeys." Lucy smiled at the boxer's pathetic face. "You two belong together."

"I'm moving, remember?"

Lucy didn't need a reminder that Tony wanted to leave Stagecoach. "Maddie could go with you."

"Don't even think about it, Lucy." Tony pitched a bottle of water to her, then poured half of another bottle into a bowl for the dog. Maddie lapped up the water before returning to her spot in front of the rock so she could keep watch over the sunning lizard.

"Now what?" she asked.

"I talk to the chief and discuss setting up a surveillance team to monitor activity at the mine." Tony guzzled the remainder of the water. "Did you find someone to help you with your bull riding?"

"Not yet." Lucy had planned to call Shannon later today for recommendations on instructors.

"You're welcome to stop by my mom's and use the bucking machine whenever you want."

Practicing on a mechanical bull wasn't the way she envisioned preparing for the rodeo in Ajo. "What I need is a real bull to test my skills."

"You're talking crazy."

"You don't think I'll go through with the rodeo, do you?"

"I know you'll try, but I'm betting your father stops you."

Why was she surprised that Tony didn't believe she'd stand up to her father? Shoot, she didn't even have enough faith in herself to reveal the truth about what happened the night her brother had died.

Tony whistled for Maddie to get in the truck, but the dog no longer stood sentry by the lizard. Instead, she paced in front of the boarded-up mine entrance, sniffing the ground. "What's the matter, girl?" he asked.

The boxer wagged her tail and whined.

"What do you think she smells?" Lucy asked.

"Not sure. Could be an animal." Tony gripped one of the boards at the bottom and ripped it off. He got down on his hands and knees and directed the flashlight inside the cavern. "Shit."

"What?"

Tony spoke rapid-fire Spanish and Lucy gasped. "Is someone in there?"

"A girl." He got to his feet.

"How did she get in there if the entrance is boarded up?"

"These nails should be old and rusted," he said, peering closely at the planks.

"They look new to me." Lucy ran her finger across a shiny nail head.

"Someone's removing the boards then putting them back in place."

"What did the girl say?"

"She's thirsty and hungry."

"Is she coming out?"

"I hope so." Tony tore off more boards until there was enough room for a person to crawl out, then he spoke to the girl.

Nothing happened. "She's probably scared to death," Lucy said.

Tony spoke in Spanish again, and finally a pair of small bare feet appeared in the opening. Her abductors must have taken her shoes so she wouldn't try to escape.

Once the girl had wiggled out of the cave Lucy said, "Untie her hands, Tony." The bedraggled female child was short and thin—Lucy guessed not more than twelve.

Tony snapped the plastic bands, freeing her hands, then fired off questions. The girl whispered one-word answers—mostly *si*'s. The poor child looked tired and weak.

Lucy helped her into the backseat of the truck and handed her a water bottle. Maddie jumped in beside the urchin and Lucy smiled when the girl hugged the dog. She offered the child more water, then secured the seat belt across her lap.

"What's her story?" Lucy asked when Tony headed back to the entrance.

"She got left behind when the others were taken away."

"How?"

"Fell asleep in one of the tunnels and didn't wake up when the men came for them."

"Amazing that her abductors didn't try to find her."

"My guess is that something scared them and they left in a hurry."

Lucy glanced over her shoulder. The girl was filthy. "How long has she been in the mine?"

"A couple of days."

"I can't believe this has been going on right under our noses." Lucy's father would be livid when he heard a child had been abandoned at the mine, although she doubted he'd give Tony credit for being right about the human-trafficking ring. "How soon do you think you'll organize a surveillance team?"

"Depends on how much information the girl gives us."

"Did she tell you her name?"

"No. Once she believes we mean her no harm, she'll tell us more about herself."

By the time they arrived at the entrance to the highway, their passenger had fallen asleep.

"Tony?" Lucy whispered.

"What?"

"Keep Maddie with you for a couple of days. She

makes the little girl feel safe." And darned if the dog hadn't sensed the child needed her.

"I suppose she'd enjoy Maddie's company while she's in custody."

The big bad border patrol agent was a softy. Lucy hopped out of the truck, retrieved the cooler from the back and set it on the passenger seat. "In case she wakes up thirsty."

"Thanks."

"Let me know how things work out for her."

"I will."

Lucy shut the door. After Tony drove off she closed the gate and secured the chain. As she walked to her truck, she rehearsed how to break the news to her father that, whether he liked it or not, Tony Bravo was going to be crowned a local hero after today's find.

Tony escorted the young girl through a back door at the station. Heads turned as they walked down the hallway with Maddie.

"Where did you find this munchkin?" Officer Luger said when Tony stopped at the front desk.

"Is the chief in?" Tony wasn't giving any details to the biggest blabbermouth in the building.

"Yeah, Romero's in." Luger nodded at the girl. "She a runaway?"

Ignoring the question, Tony guided his charge through the office. When they reached the chief's door, he knocked.

"Come in."

Tony ushered girl and dog inside, then shut the door. Romero's eyes widened. Tony motioned for the child to sit. "Lie down, Maddie." The dog settled next to the girl's feet.

"What's going on?" his boss asked.

"I went out to the Durango mine this afternoon."

Romero sat straighter in the chair. "I told you to wait until I had a chance to speak with Durango himself."

"Lucy offered to take me out there." He skipped the deal he'd made with her.

"Why is this girl with you?"

"She was hiding inside the mine."

"Were there others?"

"She said there were nine others close to her age."

"How old is she?"

"Twelve."

A low whistle escaped Romero.

"She won't tell me her name," Tony said.

The chief spoke in Spanish to the girl but she ignored him and petted Maddie. "What else did she tell you?"

"That she was kidnapped on the way home from school and the bad guys threatened her family if she refused to go with them."

"Damn thugs. Does she know the name of her captors?"

"No. But she said the men carried big guns." Tony turned in his seat. "According to her, they all walked across the border then got into a van concealed by bushes."

"What color was the van?"

"Black."

"Do you think these guys could be the men you spotted running through the desert outside your mother's trailer park the other night?"

"I doubt it," Tony said. "It's too bad they got away, but they split up and it was impossible to track them."

Romero reached inside the desk drawer and removed his sack lunch. He held it out to the girl. *"¿Tienes hambre?"*

She dug through the bag and pulled out a sticky bun to share with Maddie.

"When did you get a dog?" Romero asked.

"That's Maddie. She belonged to Michael Durango. I'm taking care of her for a few days."

"What else have you learned?"

"Not much. The girl slept most of the way here."

"I'll call in Dobbs to process her." Carmen Dobbs was one of four female field agents in the Yuma district. "She'll get a name out of her and a description of the men who kidnapped her."

"How soon can we set up a surveillance team out at the mine?" Finding the girl today was a lucky break, and Tony didn't want the trail to grow cold.

"I'll make a few phone calls while you wait for Dobbs."

"Thanks, chief." Tony nudged the girl's arm and she and Maddie followed him from the room. The kid needed a shower and clean clothes but he'd leave that up to Dobbs. He stopped at the women's restroom and pointed to the door. The girl shook her head—if she'd been without water for a while it would be hours before she'd have to go.

He collected a handful of water bottles from the refrigerator in the officer's lounge then ushered her into an interview room. He told her to stay with Maddie and wait for the nice lady to help her get cleaned up. He returned a few minutes later with a water bowl for Maddie, then locked the door, not wanting the girl to walk out of the station and try to make her way back to Mexico with Maddie in tow.

CHAPTER SEVEN

LUCY PARKED THE truck in the driveway then skipped up the porch steps, eager to find out if her father had returned from California. As soon as she stepped inside the house, his voice bellowed from the office down the hallway.

"Is that you, Lucinda?"

Her father sounded as if he was in a bad mood. Bracing herself, she paused in the office doorway. "How was your trip?"

"Never mind my trip." He glared over the top of his reading glasses and shook one of the fundraiser flyers she'd had printed. "What's the meaning of this?"

"Where did you get that?"

"On the way home from the airport I stopped at the Chevron station in town and noticed this in the convenience-store window." He flung the paper aside. "Is this some kind of joke?"

"No."

He vacated his throne—Lucy and her brother's name for the huge leather chair covered in a brown-and-white cowhide—and stood in front of the floor-to-ceiling window overlooking the Bryan Mountains.

Lucy engaged in a glare-down with her father's reflection in the glass. "Since you cut off my trust fund and the federal grant for the Pony Express was reduced by half, I needed to find a way to make up the loss."

"And riding a bull will bring in enough money to save your redneck taxi service?"

Ignoring the insult, she said, "People still remember what a great bull rider Michael was. It makes sense that I'd honor his memory by using rodeo events to help fund the Pony Express."

"You're trying my patience, daughter."

What else was new? According to her father she'd been doing that since early childhood.

"First, you graduated college with a business degree then turned down a job with the Rushmore Foundation." He pointed his finger at her. "I went out on a limb asking Jacob Nervier to hire you. Second, you came up with the ridiculous idea to drive inebriated, no-good—"

"You were on board with my business plan a year ago."

"Because I didn't believe you had a chance in hell of pulling it off."

Her father never wasted an opportunity to remind Lucy that she was just his *daughter*. At times, she wondered if anything she did would ever be good enough. Cal Durango had pinned all his hopes and dreams on his son. It was too late for Lucy to right the wrongs of the past, but couldn't her father see that her fundraising idea would bring back the excitement of rodeo for him? Only this time he'd experience it with *her*.

"You have to stop this nonsense." The crevices bracketing his mouth deepened and he appeared older than his fifty-nine years. "Your brother is gone. As much as I'd give anything to bring Michael back, I can't, and neither can the Pony Express."

The hairs on the back of Lucy's neck stood on end. "I'm not the only one having trouble letting Michael go."

Her father's head jerked as if she'd slapped him.

"You blame Tony for Michael's death, so you're trying to do everything in your power to ruin his life."

"Watch yourself, young lady. You don't know what you're talking about."

"You wouldn't allow Tony access to the gold mine until I—"

"Because Bravo didn't have a shred of evidence that the ranch was being used to transport young girls through the desert." He flung his glasses onto the desk. "I don't know why we're arguing about this. I gave you my permission to take him to Gold Dust Ridge."

"And I'm glad you did."

"Oh?"

"I just came back from there," she said.

"And?"

"We found a young girl hiding in the mine."

"Is she all right?"

That her father cared surprised Lucy. "Yes. Tony took her to the Yuma Border Patrol Station. His hunch was right."

"Damn it, I can't have young girls being abducted and held captive on Durango land."

This was one situation where her father's clout and influence wouldn't work. "Tony's speaking to his boss about putting together a surveillance team and monitoring activity at the mine."

"When?"

"I don't know. You'll have to speak with Tony's boss."

"Don't think I won't," he said. "I want this gang of thugs captured before the ranch is linked to the kidnappings."

"I'm sure the border patrol will keep you posted on their investigation." Lucy made it halfway to the door before her father stopped her.

"Stay right where you are, young lady." He closed the gap between them and rattled the rodeo flyer in her face. "This nonsense ends today."

Time to throw down the gauntlet. "If you don't want me riding bulls then release money from my trust fund and I'll cancel my rodeo appearances."

Steam spewed from her father's ears. "No."

So be it.

"Lucy, are you home?" Drat. Her mother had returned from her hair appointment at the Bee Luv Lee Hair Salon.

"In Dad's office."

"What's the meaning of this?" Her mother held up a flyer. Lucy had left flyers and pledge cards with all the businesses in town and Helen, the owner of the beauty shop, must have shown it to her mother.

"Can I count on a pledge from you, Mom?"

Sonja Durango nudged her husband. "Do something, Cal. I will not have a daughter of mine riding bulls."

"Lucy is being stubborn." Her father's eyebrows drew together. "Wonder who she inherited that trait from?"

"I forbid you to ride a bull, Lucy," her mother said. "Good grief, you'll be the laughing stock of southern Arizona."

Lucy sympathized with her concern that others would gossip about the family. After Michael's death their mother had been the target of rumors among members of her philanthropic group who'd suggested that if Sonja had spent less time championing her causes and more time being a mother her son might have known not to drink and drive.

Insinuating that her mother had failed to teach her son an important life lesson was the furthest thing from the truth, but because Lucy hadn't come forward about what had really happened the night Michael died, Sonja hadn't been able to defend herself against the accusations.

"My back is against the wall, Mom. I need to make enough money to keep the Pony Express van on the road for the rest for the year."

"For God's sake, Cal, write her a check."

"It's a waste of money."

"I don't care about the money. I won't stand by and allow another child of mine to get killed." Her mother rummaged through her purse.

"Don't you dare give Lucy money," her father said.

"Don't tell me what to do, Cal." Her mother made out a check and handed it to Lucy, staring defiantly at her husband.

Her parents' relationship had been under a tremendous amount of stress since Michael's death, and Lucy refused to add to it by taking her mother's money. "Thank you for wanting to help, Mom, but I have to do this on my own." She set the ten-thousand-dollar draft on the desk.

When tears welled in her mother's eyes, Lucy hugged her. "I'll be fine. I'm going to wear protective gear and a face mask and I'm not riding the same bulls as the men do. The bulls I ride will be a lot less threatening." Hating that she'd upset her mother, Lucy inched toward the door. "Don't forget to tell Mom what Tony and I discovered at the mine today."

"What did you find out there?" her mother asked.

"A little girl," Lucy answered.

"Is that true, Cal?"

"I'm afraid so. Bravo seems to think the girl's tied to the human-smuggling case he's investigating."

"Is she okay?"

"Physically she seems okay," Lucy said. "Tony's got her at the station and they're trying to track down her parents."

"Thank God she wasn't harmed." Sonja sank into the chair in front of the desk. "What will people think of us when they learn young girls are being transported across our property and sold into prostitution?"

Lucy left the room, her parents' voices fading as she walked out the front door. Feeling edgy, she decided to take her frustrations out on the mechanical bull at Maria Bravo's trailer.

"THIS IS A nice surprise," Maria said when she got out of her car.

"Hi, Maria." Lucy hopped off the bucking machine and pulled the plug. "I hope you don't mind that I came out here to practice."

"Of course not. I brought home half an apple pie from work. Will you have a piece with me?" She entered the trailer, leaving Lucy little choice but to accept her invitation.

"Have you spoken with Tony today?" Lucy closed the door behind her.

"No." Maria hung up her waitressing apron. "Did something happen to him?"

"Tony's fine." At least he was when she'd last seen him.

"What's going on?" The older woman washed her hands at the kitchen sink and served the pie.

"Tony and I discovered a young girl hiding in the mine." Before Maria asked, Lucy added, "The girl's fine."

"Was she abducted from Mexico?" Maria asked.

"Tony believes so."

Maria placed the dessert plates on the table. "I hope they track down the men responsible before another girl is harmed." She motioned for Lucy to sit down. "I imagine your parents were upset to learn about the illegal activity on their property?"

Lucy didn't want to discuss her parents. Since she'd arrived at the trailer park she'd been ambushed by memories of the few months she and Tony had been a couple before their abrupt breakup. "It's going to be difficult when Tony leaves." Face flushing, Lucy quickly amended her statement. "For you."

"Yes, it will be."

"Would you consider relocating to San Diego to be closer to him?"

"I can't afford to live in California, and my friends are here." Maria spread her arms wide. "This might not be much, but it's home."

Taking a fortifying breath Lucy asked the question that had nagged her since she'd learned Tony planned to transfer to the border patrol office in San Diego. "Is there more to Tony's leaving than a job promotion?" She really wanted to know if there was a woman waiting for him in San Diego.

"I'm guessing there are too many bad memories here for Tony," Maria said.

No one could outrun memories. Lucy had learned that lesson after Michael had died. Not a day went by that his image didn't pop into her mind or she didn't hear his voice in her head.

"He can't forgive himself for leaving Michael at the bar that night." Maria sniffed.

"It wasn't Tony's fault—" Lucy swallowed the lump in her throat. "Michael drank too much."

Maria flashed a sad smile. "He understands that, but Michael was like a brother to him and Tony feels he should have protected him."

The apple pie Lucy had eaten congealed in her stomach, making her nauseous. Michael had phoned from the bar that fateful night and asked her to pick him up, but Lucy had refused, insisting he call their father for a ride. The impact of her actions went beyond her brother's death and she worried that nothing she did would ever make amends for the pain and sorrow others continued to struggle with.

"I better get going." Ignoring Maria's startled look, Lucy carried her plate to the sink then walked out the door and drove away as if the devil himself chased her.

Concentrating on the road, Lucy blocked out thoughts of Michael and the past. When she neared the site of her brother's accident her foot hit the brake and she pulled onto the shoulder. She gripped the wheel until her knuckles ached, fearing that if she let go, she'd get out of the truck.

Forces beyond her control beat her down. She grabbed her cell phone and started walking. One step at a time, she marched through the desert, keeping her attention on the horizon. She walked. And walked.

Then walked some more.

The late-afternoon sun scorched the top of her head and singed the skin on her arms as the dry dusty air strangled her. She kept walking. Sweat ran down her face, dripped between her breasts and dampened her armpits. Suddenly an invisible energy grasped her arm and jerked her to a stop.

"Michael?" she whispered in a choked voice. She'd visited this area several times after the accident, hoping her brother's spirit would tell her that he forgave her. Where was his voice now when she needed to hear it most?

The ringing of her cell phone jarred her out of her trance. "Hello?"

"What the hell are you doing out there?"

Tony? Lucy turned and spotted his truck parked behind hers on the road. From this distance the vehicles looked like toy cars. She must have walked at least a mile into the desert.

"I'm taking a walk."

"It's 104 degrees."

Not in the mood to spar with him, Lucy disconnected the call and hiked back to the road. By the time she made it to the truck, her T-shirt was soaked through and her hair was plastered to her head.

Tony handed her a water bottle.

"Thanks." She guzzled the cool liquid.

"I was on my way to speak with your father when I saw your truck." He shook his head. "Are you nuts?" He motioned to the empty water bottle. "Walking aimlessly in the desert without water?"

"I wasn't going far."

"Are you having a nervous breakdown?"

She laughed.

Tony shoved a hand through his jet-black hair. "All this nonsense—"

"What nonsense?"

"Bull riding. Walks in the desert." He removed his sunglasses and squinted at her. "Ever since you came back from college you've been on a mission to…"

"Go on. Say it."

"To bring Michael back from the dead."

First her father, now Tony accused her of not being able to let go of Michael.

"You've got to move on, Lucy."

"Like you?"

"Like me what?"

"You can't stand the thought of living here anymore because Michael's gone, so you're running away to San Diego."

Tony couldn't defend himself against Lucy's charge, because she was right. He was on the run, but he didn't care about the demons chasing him. He cared about leaving Lucy behind, still struggling with her brother's death.

"I come out here to talk to Michael." She glanced over her shoulder. "My parents still haven't spread his ashes and this is the only place I can go where I feel a connection to him."

He hated seeing Lucy suffer but how the hell could he stop her pain short of bringing Michael back to life? "Was he out there today?"

"Yes." The soft sigh that drifted from Lucy's throat drew Tony closer. He cupped her face and brought her mouth to his, pausing to allow her a chance to pull away. Her eyelids fluttered closed and her lips parted.

"You frustrate the hell out of me, Lucy." His breath

mingled with hers a second before he kissed her. Forget slow and easy—too much emotion and history stood between them. He swept his tongue inside her mouth and drank in her sweetness. Tony had kissed plenty of women in his lifetime but Lucy was like no other… Her taste…her scent…reached deep inside him and tugged at his heart.

She clutched his uniform sleeve and flattened her breasts against his chest. No sense trying to hide that he didn't want her. He nudged her closer until her hips bumped his erection. She smelled like warm woman, a hint of perfume and the tang of sweat—earthy and sensual. If he hadn't been on duty he would have hauled her into his truck, driven into the desert, stripped their clothes off and made love to her regardless of the consequences.

When his fingers touched the curve of Lucy's breast, common sense intervened and he stepped back. Was he insane—kissing her on the side of the road where anyone could drive by and see them? "I'm sorry. I was out of line."

She pressed her fingers against her lips.

"I'll follow you back to the ranch." He climbed into his truck and waited for Lucy to get into hers.

Once she pulled onto the highway, he kept several car lengths between their vehicles. His thoughts switched to Nina, the little girl they'd found at the mine. Tony's coworker, Carmen Dobbs, had gotten the girl to talk. Nina claimed her cousin had also been abducted, as well as other girls from their school. Tony's number-one priority was to find those girls and reunite them with their families.

TONY TRAILED LUCY up the porch steps and into the house. He hadn't set foot inside the Durangos' home since before Michael had died. Not much had changed from the last time he'd stood in the foyer. The family portraits still hung on the walls. The same heirloom umbrella stand sat in the corner next to the antique grandfather clock. Then Tony's gaze landed on a framed photo that hadn't been there before—Michael and Chicken on a Chain, the bull he'd ridden in Prescott that had vaulted him to the top of the standings.

"Dad?"

Cal Durango stepped from his office. His neutral expression turned into a glower when he spotted Tony. "What are you doing in my house?"

"Tony's here on official business," Lucy said.

"What happened to you?" Durango motioned to Lucy's disheveled appearance.

"I've been practicing my bull-riding skills," she lied.

The scowl on Durango's face deepened and Tony waited for the older man to explode. Instead, he nodded to the paperwork in Tony's hand. "I assume your boss sent you here with a warrant to search my property."

Michael's father was a man used to calling the shots and he didn't like not having a say. Tony placed the forms on the foyer table. "It's a court order allowing border patrol agents access to your property for surveillance purposes."

Cal walked closer. "Lucy said you found a girl hiding in the mine today. What's her story?"

"Her name's Nina. She was abducted while walking home from school in Nogales, Mexico."

"Were there other girls?"

"Yes." Tony refrained from giving any more details, because he didn't want Durango using his power or political connections to interfere with the investigation. "I can't share any information about the case other than we'd like you and anyone working for you to steer clear of the area near the mine for a while."

"Your boss had better keep his men out of that mine."

Only Cal Durango would worry about people stealing his gold dust. "We won't be going into the mine."

"Tell your boss I want to be kept in the loop."

"Yes, sir." Tony would be more than happy to leave Romero the chore of briefing Durango on the investigation. He left the house, his gaze bouncing off Lucy as he walked out the door.

"Tony, wait." Lucy stayed on the porch. "Where's Maddie?"

"I left her at the station with Nina."

"When you get tired of her, I'll pick her up from your apartment."

"Maddie's not staying with me. They don't allow pets."

"Then where—"

"My mother's."

"Your mom doesn't mind?"

"She likes the company."

Lucy fidgeted and Tony worried she wanted to discuss the kiss he'd much rather forget.

"I spoke with Shannon earlier today and asked where I could find a real bull to practice on. She told me to contact P. T. Lewis, who runs Five Star Rodeos."

"I've ridden a few of the bulls that ended up at P.T.'s ranch."

"So..."

Tony knew where Lucy was going with the conversation and he wanted no part of it.

"I called P.T. and spoke with his foreman, Clint McGraw. He said I could ride Curly, the same bull Shannon used to practice on."

Tony was aware of Cal Durango watching him and Lucy through the front window. "You're not going to change your mind about this rodeo fundraising gimmick, are you?"

"No. I just wanted you to know that I've got everything figured out," she said.

"You figure out yet how you're going to keep from getting killed?"

"I'll be fine."

Fine, my ass. Tony hopped into his truck and shut the door before he said something he couldn't take back. As he sped away, Lucy's image in the rearview mirror grew smaller. She wasn't going to give in and find a different way to raise money for her business, so Tony was left with no choice but to intervene and help her. Her safety rested squarely on his shoulders whether he wanted the responsibility or not.

When he got home tonight he'd give Five Star Rodeos a call and find out when Lucy intended to practice on Curly. She wasn't getting within ten feet of a bull unless he was there with her.

CHAPTER EIGHT

LATE FRIDAY AFTERNOON, Lucy slowed the truck as she turned onto Star Road, which led to the Five Star Ranch. The end of April had arrived and that meant Lucy had only two weeks to get ready for the first rodeo in Ajo. She drove along the dirt track, noting the group of horses standing in the shade of a mesquite tree—the once-fierce bucking broncs now idling away their days in leisure.

The road led to a low-lying ridge, then zigzagged up an incline. Lucy stopped the truck at the top of the ridge and took in the view. Miles and miles of desert stretched toward the horizon. At the base of the ridge sat a barn and several corrals near a hacienda-style home. As she drove closer to the house, she admired the giant saguaros guarding the walkway to the front door and the mesquite trees dotting the land between the barn and corrals.

She parked next to a pickup and got out.

"Howdy."

The greeting came from behind her. A tall cowboy and a teenage cowgirl dressed in jeans, a Western shirt and a cowboy hat walked toward her.

"Lucy Durango." She held out her hand.

"Clint McGraw. This is my daughter, Lauren."

"Nice to meet you, Lauren." Lucy shook the girl's hand.

"P.T. left early this morning to pick up a horse."

"If this isn't a good time…"

"We rigged up a bucking chute in the corral." He nodded to his daughter. "My daughter knows the drill."

"I've ridden a bull before." Lauren grinned.

"Do you still ride?" Lucy asked.

"No. It's an exciting sport, but one rodeo was enough for me."

And Lucy had not one but three bull rides to survive.

"Curly's snoozing in the barn. I'll fetch him and put him in the corral."

After Clint walked off, Lucy spoke to Lauren. "Where do you go to school?"

"California. I live with my mom during the school year there and spend the summers here with my dad. I'll be a freshman at Sacramento State this fall."

"Congratulations. What do you plan to study?"

"I haven't decided." Lauren nodded at the ranch house. "P.T. wants me to major in business so I can help him run his rodeo production company, but it's so dang hot here all the time."

"Arizona does have its advantages, though."

"What's that?"

"Cowboys." Lucy laughed.

"I don't think cowboys can handle me." Lauren removed her hat and a long, neon blue ponytail fell down her back. "I'm not your typical cowgirl."

"I would have given my father a stroke if I'd done that to my hair when I was younger."

"My dad's pretty cool. He lets me be me."

Envy stabbed Lucy. If only her father would show that kind of support. "So, you've ridden bulls before."

"Yep. When Shannon Douglas competed in Five Star

Rodeos last summer, one of her friends broke her wrist and I took her place."

"Were you scared?"

"Heck, yeah. But if I had the chance to do it again, I would. It's such a rush. Kind of like the feeling you get on a roller coaster."

Lucy had ridden several amusement park rides in her lifetime but she doubted even a roller coaster compared to the thrill of a rodeo bull.

"Why do you want to learn how to ride a bull?" Lauren asked.

"I'm doing a fundraiser and asking people to pledge money for each second I stay on."

"What are you raising money for?"

"I own a business called the Pony Express."

Lauren snapped her fingers. "I've seen the van driving through town."

"It's a free taxi service for cowboys who've had too much to drink at the bars and need a ride home."

"Cool." Lauren shielded her eyes from the sun and stared over Lucy's shoulder. "We've got company."

Lucy's pulse gave a little leap of joy when she recognized Tony's truck. He parked the black Dodge next to Lucy's truck and Lauren let out a wolf whistle when he stepped into view. "Wow. He's no ordinary cowboy."

"No, he's not." Lucy smiled. "He works for the border patrol."

"He can patrol my borders any day."

Not if Lucy had anything to say about it.

"Ladies," Tony said, stopping in front of the women. He removed his sunglasses and held out his hand to Lauren. "Tony Bravo."

"Tony Bravo…that's like a superhero name."

The sound of Tony's chuckle warmed Lucy's blood.

"I'm Lauren McGraw. My dad's getting a bull ready for Lucy to ride." Lauren glanced between Lucy and Tony. "I'll see if he needs help."

After Lauren walked away, Lucy asked, "What are you doing here?"

"I came to help you."

"I don't need your help." The protest rang hollow in her ears. She was more than relieved that Tony had shown up today.

"Lucy, I'm damned if I do and damned if I don't. I might not be able to stop this ludicrous mission of yours, but I can try to keep you from coming out on the short end of a bull ride."

Before they got caught up in rodeo, Lucy asked, "What's happening with Nina?" The little girl had been on her mind all week.

Tony put his mirrored glasses back on and Lucy wished he hadn't. His eyes were so expressive and she hated not knowing what he was really thinking. "Nina's fine. She's given us information that's helping with our surveillance plans."

"Have you contacted her parents?"

"Yes, but we have to be careful how we communicate with them so we don't tip off the cartel."

"You're certain this is the work of a Mexican cartel?"

"We know who's behind the kidnappings. All that's left to do is catch them in the act."

"Who's taking care of Nina until you reunite her with her parents?"

"She's staying with an agent's grandmother."

"Is Maddie with them or at your mom's?"

"The dog's at the grandmother's house. I hope you don't mind. Nina got upset when she thought she had to leave Maddie behind."

"I'm sure Maddie's having a lot more fun hanging out with Nina than she would sitting in a kennel all day."

"I have to brief the agent on the case tonight. You're welcome to come with me and visit Maddie."

"Are you sure it's okay if I know Nina's whereabouts?"

"I trust you not to tell anyone."

That Tony had faith in her pleased Lucy. "I'd love to go."

"You ready?" He nodded to Lauren and Clint, who were loading Curly into the chute. "Looks like Lauren brought out some gear."

She and Tony walked over to the corral. "I ordered a Kevlar vest and a protective face mask but they won't be delivered until next week," Lucy said.

"What about a riding glove?" Tony asked.

"Shoot. I forgot about a glove." When they reached the corral, Lucy spoke to Lauren. "Do you happen to have a riding glove I can borrow?"

"Sure." Lauren handed her a glove from the back pocket of her jeans and helped Lucy put on the vest and headgear. "If the glove's not tight enough, there's a smaller one in the barn that belongs to my stepmom."

"This one's perfect," Lucy said after flexing her fingers. "The vest feels really tight. Is that normal?"

"You'll be holding your breath most of the time so you don't need to worry about breathing." Lauren winked.

"Truthfully, you don't need any gear with Curly," Clint said. "Once he throws you, he stops bucking and walks away." Clint fished a metal wire beneath the bull and caught the end of the bull rope then pulled it up over the other side of the animal. "You'd never guess that this bull won several titles in his heyday." He nodded to Tony. "Clint McGraw."

"Tony Bravo. I've ridden in a few Five Star Rodeos through the years."

"P.T.'s semiretired now but he still puts his stamp on the rodeos," Clint said.

"What's Curly's bucking style?" Tony asked.

"Straightforward. He doesn't spin much. If he's not aggressive enough, I've got a few bulls that haven't been retired as long."

"Curly will do fine for my first time," Lucy said.

"Need me to stay?" Clint spoke to Tony.

"We'll be fine."

"Lauren can load Curly into the chute." Clint patted his daughter on the back then returned to the barn.

"Curly likes me." Lauren scratched the animal behind the ears and Lucy worried that she was about to ride a big cuddly teddy bear rather than a rodeo bull.

"Hop on and I'll go over a few things with you," Tony said.

Lucy settled onto Curly's back, her inner thigh muscles straining as her legs stretched over the bull's girth. Heat from the animal's hide warmed her legs and fanny, triggering a release of nerves, and the cotton material beneath her armpits grew damp.

"Hold the bull rope in your left hand the way you did on the bucking machine," Tony said.

Fumbling with her grip, Lucy couldn't get a feel for the handle through the leather glove.

"Like this." Tony pushed her fingers deeper beneath the handle then wrapped the end of the rope around her hand, securing it to the back of the bull. The wrap felt tight but still had a little give. "Line up your pinky finger with the center of Curly's back." She did as instructed. "Now scoot forward." Tony pushed her from behind. Lucy wasn't sure if the tingle racing through her body was caused by a spike in adrenaline or Tony's hands on her fanny. Either way, she felt out of breath.

"When you open your hand, the rope should fall away," he said.

Should being the operative word.

"The weight of the bell attached to the rope will help free your hand."

"What next?" she asked, aware of Lauren hanging on Tony's every word.

"Once Curly starts jerking, make note of his rhythm. It'll help you hang on and keep you in better position for the dismount. Use your free arm for balance."

Lucy would need more than one free arm to keep her from flying off Curly.

"Tilt your chin down toward your gloved hand. Every time the bull jumps, you dig in your heels, shift forward at the waist and lunge aggressively over his shoulders. When he kicks, relax your boot heels and come back to a seated position. Let the bull's momentum carry you into the next cycle."

"You want me to treat the bull as if he's my dancing partner," she said.

"That's one way to think of it."

"Should I count the seconds in my head?"

"No. Today, we're practicing your dismount," he said.

"You want me to fall off as soon as Curly clears the chute?"

"Yep."

Lucy and Lauren exchanged puzzled looks then Lauren asked, "Why?"

"The dismount is where you're most likely to get into trouble, whether you stay on the bull for eight seconds or not."

That made sense, although Lucy didn't like the idea of tumbling to the ground without even trying to ride the bull.

"Before you jump, make sure you release the rope. If your hand gets hung up, you'll get dragged."

"He's right, Lucy. You don't want to get caught under a bull."

The image that flashed through Lucy's head chipped away at her courage.

"What happens if I can't get my hand free?"

"Then you fight like hell to keep your balance and stay on while the bullfighters try to help you," Tony said.

Lucy would just have to make sure she didn't end up in that situation.

"When you're ready to dismount, use the bull as a springboard to push yourself off and then hit the ground on all fours."

From what she remembered of watching her brother and Tony ride, rarely had either of them landed on all fours after they'd been thrown. Instead, they'd hit the ground on their heads or shoulders, or done a face-plant in the dirt.

"Before you dismount, look over your left shoulder," Tony said.

She did as instructed.

"Next, swing your right leg over in front of you and release the rope."

Moving her leg took more effort than she'd anticipated because her thighs were spread far apart.

"Once you're in that position, use the momentum of the bull's next kick to launch yourself as far away as possible," he said.

"After that?" she asked.

"Get up and run like hell for the rails."

"Okay, then." Lucy sucked in a deep breath. "I dismount on the bull's left side."

"That's preferable."

"What happens if I'm off balance and fall backward or forward?"

"Prepare yourself for a tough landing then get to your feet and run."

"Don't worry, Lucy," Lauren said. "Landing doesn't hurt as much as you might think."

Well, that was certainly reassuring. Heart pounding, Lucy repeated Tony's instructions in her head. *Look over left shoulder. Release rope. Swing right leg over and release rope. Push off the bull. Land on all fours. Run like hell.*

"Okay. I'm ready." She squeezed the rope tightly, aligning her pinky finger with the middle of Curly's back.

Lauren counted to three then opened the gate.

Even though Lucy believed she was ready—she wasn't. Curly leaped from the chute and the sudden jerk tugged hard on her arm. Tony's instructions were forgotten as her focus switched to the stinging pain spreading through her shoulder.

"Lucy!" Tony's shout startled her. "Lift your leg!"

She jerked her leg over the back of Curly and released her grip on the bull rope, then flung herself toward the ground. She broke the fall with her hands first, then her left hip, before sprawling on her belly.

"Run!" Lauren shouted.

Still dazed, Lucy scrambled to her feet and stumbled a few steps before applying the brakes when Curly stepped into her path.

"You didn't check to see where the bull was," Tony said.

No kidding. Thank God Curly just stood there staring at her as if she were a moron. Lauren jumped into the pen. "C'mon, boy." She loaded the bull into the chute for round two.

Keeping his voice low, Tony approached Lucy. "You okay?"

If she told him that her arm ached like hell, he'd end the training session. "Yeah, sure. Why?"

He pointed to her arm.

Unaware she'd been cradling the limb against her body, she straightened her arm slowly and said, "I'm fine."

"There's no shame admitting you're in over your head."

"Quit trying to talk me out of—" Lucy hadn't realized she'd spoken so loudly until Lauren cleared her throat.

"I think I hear my dad calling me." The teenager made a hasty retreat.

"I admire you for wanting to honor your brother's memory, but not even Michael would have wanted you to put yourself in danger."

She was riding in memory of her brother but also for redemption. Forgiveness. "That was my very first time on a bull and practice makes perfect, right?"

Tony shoved his hand through his short hair. "When your father finds out I'm helping you, he'll have my head and my job."

"You don't have to help me."

He walked away, stopped short then faced Lucy across the pen. "You don't get it, do you?"

"Get what?"

"You backed me into a corner."

"How?"

"I'm screwed. If I help you, then your father will blame me if you get injured, and if I don't help you and you get injured, he'll still blame me."

Lucy conceded that Tony was probably right. "I promise I'll stay healthy and injury-free." And she would, darn it.

"Nothing I say or do will stop you from doing this?" he asked.

"No."

The muscle along his jaw bunched. "Okay, then. Get on and try your dismount again."

Swallowing an unladylike curse, Lucy did as she was told and Curly behaved like a gentleman in the chute. She adjusted her grip, waiting for Tony to give her advice or encouragement. He kept silent. So be it. He'd find out soon enough that Lucy Durango was a lot tougher than people gave her credit for.

After more than an hour in the blazing sun, all Lucy had accomplished was showing Tony what an abject failure she was—she had the bumps and bruises to prove it. Careful to keep her pain hidden, she grabbed a bottle of water from the cooler Lauren had set by the corral before leaving with her father to run errands in Yuma. Clint had instructed Tony to put Curly in the barn after they finished with him.

"Ready to give up?"

"Nope." Tony wanted her to admit she'd had enough and that he'd been right—she was in no shape to rodeo. Fat chance.

Tony watched Lucy struggle to climb the corral rails. Her boot slipped on the bottom rung and her knee banged against the bar. He cringed with her. The woman had way too much courage and spunk for her own good. If he let her, she'd ride until she broke a bone. If she wasn't going to put an end to this torture then he would. "You're done." Tony opened the chute and the bull walked out of the enclosure. How the hell Lucy believed she was going to ride a competitive rodeo bull if she couldn't perform a safe dismount on an old has-been like Curly was beyond Tony.

"I'm not ready to quit today," Lucy protested, limping after Tony as he led the bull into the barn. "This isn't fair."

"Damn straight it's fair. You're too banged up to ride anymore. As it is, it'll take a week for your sprained ankle to heal, not to mention the sore ligaments in your shoulder." And all the other muscle pulls she'd suffered. Tony walked Curly into a large pen at the back of the barn, then latched the gate and faced Lucy. He expected anger, not the tears that glistened in her eyes.

"I'm not a quitter," she whispered.

He wanted to shake some sense into her and at the same time kiss her tears away.

"With or without your help, I'll be back here tomorrow, and the next day, and the day after that to practice dismounting."

"And then what? Just because you learn to fall off a bull the right way doesn't mean there aren't a hundred other ways you could bust your head open." One good jerk by a bull could shove Lucy far enough forward that her face collided with the bull's horn, knocking her out cold.

The scene played out in Tony's mind and his stomach roiled as he envisioned Lucy unconscious and unable to scramble out of the way of the bull's hooves.

"Whether you help me or not, I'm riding in Ajo. Shannon got Wrangler on board and they've agreed to match every pledge I receive for all the rodeos, dollar for dollar. I can't walk away from that kind of money."

"How much have you raised so far?"

Her chin jutted. "The website went up a few days ago and already I've gotten three-thousand dollars in pledges—that's six if you count Wrangler's contribution."

Tony shook his head. Some people were just plain loco.

"Most of the pledges are coming from rodeo cowboys. Shannon's been a huge help in spreading the word at her events."

Lucy had to survive the first rodeo for there to be a second and a third. "You have the money angle all figured out, don't you?" Now it was up to him to figure out how to keep her alive. He left the barn, but slowed down when he noticed Lucy limping on her sore ankle.

"Before we head out to Carmen's to see Nina, we're making a pit stop at a friend's," he said when they reached their trucks.

"Which friend?"

If Lucy was determined to ride fourteen days from now, her body needed all the help it could get healing. "Her name's Evita. She's a massage therapist."

"She better be cheap, because I've only got twenty bucks on me."

"Don't worry," Tony said. "Evita owes me a few favors."

Lucy shut the door in Tony's face, preferring not to think about what Tony had done to earn favors from a woman named Evita.

CHAPTER NINE

EVITA OWES ME a few favors...

A pang of jealousy gripped Lucy as she waited for Tony to get into his truck and leave Five Star Ranch. She had no claim on him. They'd once been lovers, but fate had intervened and they weren't the same people anymore. She yearned for the chance to pick up where they'd left off as a couple, but her actions the night Michael had died made second chances impossible.

Lucy gave the black Dodge a head start so the dust from the tires didn't obscure the road in front of her.

He kissed you at Five Star Ranch.

There was no denying that the chemistry between her and Tony hadn't faded one iota over the past two years. It was as real and forbidden as Romeo and Juliet's. *And just as doomed.*

Admittedly Lucy was curious about Evita. Tony wasn't the kind of man to cheat, and he wouldn't have kissed Lucy if he'd been in a committed relationship.

The sun had dipped low in the sky by the time they parked at a strip mall near downtown Yuma. *Magic Hands* was etched into the dark glass door of one of the units. Lucy had assumed a massage would be a waste of time, but changed her mind when she got out of the truck and took her first step—her thighs and lower back screamed in pain.

Tony grinned.

Bent over like an old woman, she muttered, "Go ahead. Say I told you so."

"Told you so." He chuckled. "I phoned Evita on the way here. She's expecting us." He grasped Lucy's elbow and escorted her to the door. "Evita's got amazing hands. You'll feel good as new in no time."

Needing to block out the image of Evita using her amazing hands on Tony, Lucy focused on her discomfort. Good Lord, she hoped she wouldn't be this sore tomorrow when she got out of bed. The massage parlor was cool and tranquil, and the melodious sounds of Native American flute music and the scent of lavender eased some of her tension.

Tony opened the door to the waiting room. "Evita, it's Tony. We're here."

"C'mon back."

He pointed to an open door at the end of the hall. "Have fun," he said then made himself comfortable in a leather recliner in the relaxation room.

One slow step at a time Lucy hobbled to the end of the corridor. "Hello. I'm Lucy Durango," she said, pausing in the doorway.

"I'm Evita."

Lucy felt as if she'd been punched in the windpipe. Evita was the pretty, dark-eyed-black-haired quintessentially Hispanic girl Maria Bravo had wanted her son to marry.

"Tony said you're a little stiff after your workout today." Evita peeled back the cover on the table.

"If you can help my back, that would be great." Lucy forced a smile.

"You'll be standing tall and straight when I'm finished with you."

"I don't know about tall, but I'll take straight." While Evita set out a selection of lotions and oils on the tray next to the table, Lucy said, "Thank you for staying open late to help me."

"Tony's a great guy. I'd do anything for him."

Lucy wanted to ask the meaning of *anything* but kept quiet.

"Have you ever had a massage before?" Evita asked.

"I've had facials but not massages. I didn't need one until today."

"Take all your clothes off except your underwear, then slide beneath the covers. We'll start with your lower back since that's where most of your discomfort is."

"Sounds good."

Evita closed the door, allowing Lucy privacy to undress. She heard murmurs in the hallway and assumed Tony was regaling Evita with exaggerated stories about Lucy's bull-riding blunders.

When Lucy stretched out on the table her lower back protested, but she gritted her teeth and extended her legs. She'd just pulled the covers over her fanny when a knock sounded and the door opened.

Gathering Lucy's hair, Evita secured the mass with a clip. "I like to chatter while I work, but if you prefer quiet, I won't say a word."

"Talk as much as you'd like." The noise would drown out Lucy's groans.

"First, I'm going to examine your back and shoulders to see which muscles are in distress right now. If I push or poke too hard, just say enough."

"Enough." Lucy camouflaged her grimace with a smile.

"I haven't even started."

"I know, but I ache everywhere."

"You'll feel like a whole new woman in a little while." Evita squirted warm massage oil onto Lucy's skin and the scent of eucalyptus permeated the room. "What were you doing that caused all this distress with your muscles?"

"Tony didn't tell you?"

"No."

"I was learning how to ride a bull."

"What for?"

"I'm holding a fundraiser to help keep my nonprofit company in business."

"You're talking about the Pony Express?"

"Yes. You know about my business?"

"I read the write-up in the Yuma papers a couple of years ago."

"Well, I'm still in business but for how long I don't know."

"What does bull riding have to do with your fundraiser?" Evita pressed her fingertips deep into Lucy's shoulder. "Too hard?"

"Yes, but don't stop." After Lucy caught her breath, she said, "I'm riding in three rodeos this summer, and for every second I stay on the bull, I earn money for the Pony Express."

"Gutsy." A minute of silence passed then Evita said, "I'm sorry about your brother, Lucy."

"Thanks. I miss him a lot. Did you know Michael well?"

"No. Tony and I didn't begin dating until after your brother died, but Tony talked about Michael a lot."

Lucy forgot to exhale, and when Evita pushed against her lower back, the air in her lungs exploded in a loud moan.

Evita's hands froze. "Are you okay?"

"Fine," Lucy wheezed, still grappling with the news that Tony had moved on so quickly after their relationship ended.

"How long did you and Tony date?"

"About seven months. He asked me to marry him last Thanksgiving."

Lucy stiffened and Evita said, "Relax."

Stunned that Tony had been engaged and she hadn't known about it, Lucy said, "If you don't mind me asking, what happened?"

"I don't want to bring up bad memories for you."

"Are you saying your breakup with Tony had to do with my brother's death?"

"Sort of."

Would the nightmare never end? "Tell me, Evita." She needed to know.

"Tony tried to move on after Michael's death, but he couldn't."

"What do you mean?"

"He said he didn't deserve to be happy when his best friend was dead." Evita poured oil across Lucy's shoulders and worked the muscles. "I insisted Tony see a grief counselor and he did a few times, but in the end he confessed that he'd only make me miserable, so he broke off our engagement."

Lucy's eyes welled with tears. The collateral damage

continued to add up. How would she ever make amends for all the pain she'd caused everyone?

"I'm sorry, Evita. I don't know what to say."

"I'm in a good place right now," Evita said. "My business partner, Nathan, and I have been dating for several months and we have a great relationship."

"I hope things work out for you two."

Evita used her magic hands and Lucy drifted off to sleep. Sometime later, she woke up in an empty room. Slowly, she tested her muscles—a few twinges but no sharp pain. Feeling lethargic, she dressed then stepped into the hallway. Evita and Tony were in the relaxation room chatting like old friends—all they'd ever be because of Lucy. She closed the door to the massage room loudly to warn them of her presence.

"You're standing up straight," Tony said as Lucy walked toward him.

"Evita has magic hands just like the sign claims."

"Come back anytime," Evita said. "I'll work you into my schedule."

"What do I owe for the massage?" Lucy opened her billfold and removed a credit card.

Waving her off Evita said, "Nothing."

"I can't accept a free massage."

"The massage was my contribution to your fundraiser."

A lump formed in Lucy's throat. If Evita knew Lucy was the cause of everyone's pain she might change her mind. "Thank you." The darn massage had not only loosened her muscles but also the tight grip she'd had on her emotions. She had to leave before she embarrassed herself. "Meet you outside," she said to Tony.

The sun had set but the temperature remained hot, the day's heat still radiating off the blacktop. She'd just opened her truck door when Tony stepped from the building.

"You feel up to visiting Nina?" he asked.

"Sure."

"What's the matter?" He grasped her arm. "You're awfully quiet."

"I'm quiet because the massage made me tired," she lied.

"Leave your truck here and let me drive. I have to come back this way to my apartment so I can drop you off."

Too emotionally exhausted to put up a fuss, she hopped into Tony's truck and closed her eyes. She had no idea how much time had passed when he nudged her shoulder.

"Lucy."

She blinked in a daze.

"We're at Carmen's grandmother's home."

Lucy got out of the truck, pleasantly surprised that her muscles hadn't seized up, and she felt only a few minor twinges when she walked with Tony to the front door.

The small adobe house sat in the middle of the block. Unlike several neighbors who'd allowed their landscaping to become overgrown and scrubby, Carmen's grandmother had a manicured front yard and a porch decorated with potted plants.

A young woman in uniform answered the door after Tony knocked.

"Hey, Tony, c'mon in."

"This is Lucy Durango," Tony said. "Lucy, this is Carmen."

"Hello." Lucy shook hands with the officer.

"Lucy was worried about Nina and Maddie," he said.

"Those two are inseparable." Carmen shut the door and locked it. "My grandmother wasn't too pleased when she found Maddie sleeping on the bed with Nina this morning, but the dog is so cute, she's won her over." Carmen led the way to the back of the house.

The kitchen was tiny, the walls painted a sunflower yellow. Spanish tile covered the countertops and a bistro table sat in the corner where Nina was eating ice cream and Carmen's grandmother sewed a button on a pair of pink shorts. Maddie sat next to Nina's chair, one paw on the girl's thigh. The dog's gaze traveled back and forth between the bowl of ice cream and Nina's mouth each time the little girl took a bite.

Carmen spoke in Spanish and Lucy caught a few words, surmising that she told her grandmother who Tony and Lucy were.

The older woman spoke to Carmen and Tony translated for Lucy. "She offered us ice cream."

"No, thank you." Lucy smiled at the older woman.

"Let's sit outside on the patio." Carmen grabbed a grill lighter from the counter then cut through an enclosed porch containing a washing machine and an assortment of storage bins. The backyard was surrounded by a cinder-block wall; a picnic table sat on a cement slab near the back door. Carmen lit two tiki torches, which provided enough light to see across the dark yard.

"Have you learned anything new from Nina?" Tony asked.

"She said something this morning that might be useful." Carmen sat across the table from Tony. "Nina mentioned that the men who drove them to the mine looked like cowboys and were dressed all in black."

"Did she see any tattoos?" Tony asked.

"She didn't remember any markings on the men. They wore long-sleeved shirts."

"It's got to be the Sinaloa Cartel. They're known for using clean-cut drivers so they don't raise suspicions among the locals."

While Carmen and Tony talked, Lucy's respect for their profession grew by leaps and bounds. She'd always been aware of the challenges the border patrol faced in southern Arizona but their knowledge of Mexican cartels and the decades-long drug wars more than impressed her.

"When's the chief setting up a surveillance team at the mine?" Carmen glanced between Tony and Lucy.

"We're monitoring chat rooms right now and it looks like the gang might be back this way in a couple of weeks. Will it be a problem if Nina stays here until we can arrange to return her to her parents?"

"My grandmother's happy to have someone to take care of and keep her company." Carmen spoke to Lucy. "Is it okay if the dog stays here until Nina returns to Mexico?"

"That's fine, but I hope Nina knows that Maddie can't go home with her." Lucy couldn't bear the thought of something happening to the dog. She owed it to her brother to keep Maddie safe.

"We'll make sure Maddie remains with us when the authorities take Nina home." Tony stood. "If you see anyone watching your grandmother's house, we'll need to change Nina's location."

They went inside and Tony and Carmen chatted with

Nina in Spanish while Lucy paid attention to Maddie, giving the dog a good scratch behind the ears. "Take care of Nina, Maddie. She needs you."

The boxer's tail swished as if she understood the command. Lucy nodded to the grandmother and waited outside on the front porch while Tony said goodbye. Once the door shut behind him they walked in silence to his truck. Not a word was spoken during the drive back to the strip mall.

"Thanks for your help today," she said when Tony parked next to her vehicle.

He grabbed her hand when she reached for the door. "You won't change your mind about riding bulls?"

"No." The warmth of his callused fingers made it difficult to concentrate.

"There's a junior rodeo in Tuba City next weekend. I know the producer. I'll ask if you can practice on one of the bulls after the rodeo. It'll give you a chance to ride a bull in a real chute, hear the buzzer and work on your dismount."

"Really?" Lucy's heart thumped with excitement.

"Until then, try to practice your dismounts on Curly. Lauren knows what to watch for and can help you."

"I'll call P.T. tomorrow and ask if I can go out there again."

"I'm working a special assignment next week so I won't be around to help you."

"Are you going undercover?"

"Yes."

When he didn't offer any further information, Lucy said, "I think I'll use the hot tub before I go to bed tonight."

The heated look in Tony's eyes curled her toes. "You'll call me about the Tuba City rodeo?" she asked.

"Yep."

"Thanks." Lucy got out of the truck then hopped into hers. Tony tailed her through town before turning off at the second intersection and heading north to his apartment while Lucy continued east back to Stagecoach.

THURSDAY AFTERNOON TONY sat at his desk completing paperwork after a two-day stakeout had failed to turn up any evidence of gun smuggling along the border. Thoughts of Lucy interrupted his concentration. Yesterday he'd phoned her with the news that she could practice on a bull after Saturday's junior rodeo. This morning he'd texted her a reminder to bring Lauren's protective gear if the vest and face mask she'd ordered didn't arrive before Saturday. And right now he struggled against the urge to phone her just so he could hear her voice.

He'd signed on to help Lucy with the rodeos—not that he'd had much choice—but he sure hadn't agreed to all the worry that came with the job. Worry was another word for *care*. He *cared* about Lucy and felt a sense of duty to keep his best friend's sister safe.

Keep telling yourself that and you might just believe it.

Okay, so he still had feelings for Lucy. Strong feelings. Deep feelings. The kind of feelings that yanked on heartstrings. But that didn't mean he had to act on them.

After Michael had died, Tony attempted to move on and forget about Lucy, but that had backfired on him. When he hadn't been able to commit to Evita, he'd finally admitted that he loved Lucy. After avoiding her for two years, he'd expected some of that love to have faded, but the explosive chemistry he felt when he was near her proved him wrong again.

Kissing Lucy reminded him of all he'd lost the night his best friend passed away. During the past couple of weeks he'd caught himself fantasizing about marrying Lucy and he'd imagined them raising a handful of kids. But there could never be a forever-after for them because Lucy deserved to be happy.

And Tony didn't.

The worry, the daydreaming, the text messages—all evidence that the love he'd harbored for Lucy was alive and well and continued to grow. Maybe this was his penance for the role he'd played in Michael's death—having to be around a woman he loved but couldn't have. Didn't deserve.

His cell phone rang, cutting off the therapy session in his head. "Bravo."

"Tony, this is P. T. Lewis over at Five Star Ranch."

"How are you, P.T.?"

"Be a lot better if you'd drive out here and supervise Lucy Durango's practice. I've got a meeting with rodeo officials this afternoon and Clint drove his daughter back to California for a few days. I don't like the idea of Lucy being out here alone in case she gets knocked on her head."

"I'll be there as soon as I can."

Before Tony disconnected the call, P.T. said, "That Durango girl's got gumption. Sure was a shame about her brother."

"I've got another call, P.T." Tony didn't care to talk about Michael. He said goodbye, then hung up and filled out the most important piece of paperwork before hand-ing it to Rosalinda and sneaking out of the office. He had three hours to get to Five Star Ranch, watch Lucy practice then return to the station for a four-thirty meeting with the agents who'd been chosen for surveillance duty at the Durango Ranch.

Forty minutes later he arrived at P.T.'s place. "Need some help?" he asked as he walked up to the makeshift pen where Lucy attempted to coax Curly into the chute.

"What are you doing here?" She shielded her eyes from the sun.

Tony squeezed through the corral rails. "Making sure you don't—"

"Kill myself?"

"Had a couple of free hours before a meeting later this afternoon. Thought I'd drop by and see how practice was going."

"I didn't tell you I was coming out here today."

"P.T. called me."

"He asked you to babysit me."

Babysit was a little harsh. "P.T. said Clint was in California with Lauren and he had to leave the ranch."

"So?"

"He didn't feel good about you being alone out here in case you got 'knocked on your head.' P.T.'s words not mine."

Lucy kicked at the ground with the toe of her boot. "I'm not a naive teenager who needs coddling."

"No one said—"

"You're just like my father." She spat the words out.

"Wait a—"

"You wait a minute, Tony Bravo. I don't need you hovering over me, holding me back."

"Holding you back?" He spread his arms wide. "Does this look like I'm holding you back?"

"You know what I mean. You're sticking your nose where it doesn't belong."

"I haven't stuck my nose into anything." He jabbed his finger at her and she backed up a step. "You're the one stirring up trouble with your stupid fundraiser."

She gasped. "Stupid?"

He stepped forward and Lucy backed up. "You don't have what it takes to sit a bull for eight seconds."

She thrust her chin out. "If Shannon can do it, so can I."

"Shannon's experienced and she's not a spoiled little rich girl."

"I'm not spoiled."

"Yes, you are." He crowded her.

She retreated another step. "No, I'm not."

"You are."

"Am not."

"Are."

The dance continued across the pen.

"You're a bully, Tony Bravo."

Ignoring the charge, he pointed behind Lucy. "Watch out." Curly had left a few presents in the pen.

"Don't tell me—" Lucy's boot came down on a cow patty and her legs flew out from under her. She hit the ground hard, the air bursting from her lungs in a loud "oomph"!

Tony stood over her and smiled at her dazed expression. "You okay?"

"What happened?"

"You stepped in cow poop."

"Eeew!" In her rush to get off the ground, Lucy rolled over and put her hand right in another patty.

Tony chuckled.

Lucy crawled to her feet and flung her hand out, sending cow manure flying from her fingertips. "You think this is funny?"

"Sorry," Tony mumbled.

"You don't sound sorry." Lucy advanced and Tony kept an eye on her manure-covered extremities. When she got too close he backpedaled until he bumped into the rails. "Anyone ever tell you that you're too bossy?" She slapped her poop-covered palm against Tony's shirt then proceeded to wipe her hand clean on his sleeve.

"Damn it, Lucy," he sputtered. "This is my good work shirt!"

"I dare you," she said.

"Dare me, what?"

"Dare you to kiss me." Lucy snagged a handful of his shirt and pulled forward until their mouths were inches apart. Breath mingled. Gazes loaded and locked.

"If you don't kiss me, Bravo, I'm gonna kiss you."

CHAPTER TEN

TONY REMOVED HIS sunglasses, his brown eyes darkening with desire—a warning of the fine line they walked. As his mouth drew nearer, the blood pumped faster through Lucy's veins.

Faint or breathe.

Gasping, she swayed forward. Their chests bumped. Gazes locked. Breath mingled. Then Tony's mouth brushed hers in a soft caress.

A tingle spread through her body, tiny electrical pulses attacking her knees until they trembled. She sagged heavily against Tony and a groan escaped his mouth when she nudged his arousal.

He crushed her mouth beneath his, the kiss firm. Bold. Too brief. "I'm no good for you, Lucy," he said.

"Shh." She pressed her clean fingers against his lips, then a moment later replaced them with her mouth. She lost herself in his scent—sandalwood, dust, sweat. As their tongues dueled, he cupped her breast and massaged the nipple. A fire ignited in her belly, which he put out abruptly when his strong fingers bit into her shoulders and he pushed her away.

"What's the matter?" Her breath came in ragged gasps. "Why did you stop kissing me?"

Ignoring her question he said, "I don't want you practicing by yourself."

Startled by the change of subject, Lucy didn't immediately respond, not that she would have gotten a word in edgewise.

"If you fall and get stomped on, there'd be no one to help you." He put on his sunglasses and paced in front of her. "And practicing is a waste of time if I'm not here to point out what you're doing wrong."

"Any kind of practice is better than no practice."

"Don't you get it, Lucy?" He flung his arms wide. "This isn't about teaching you to ride. It's about keeping you alive."

"Aren't you being a little melodramatic?"

"The best bull riders are the guys who've broken bones, suffered concussions and have had their hand caught in the rigging. Pain and fear is a rodeo cowboy's best teacher. If you don't survive the first bull ride, then you can kiss the Pony Express goodbye."

When he stopped talking long enough to take a breath, she said, "That kiss really knocked you off-kilter, didn't it?"

Ignoring her, Tony removed Curly from the chute then walked him out of the pen.

"Wait!" She dogged his heels. "I'm not through with that bull."

"Yes, you are. Go find a hose and wash off. You stink."

"You're mad because you still want me," Lucy said.

Tony froze midstep for a millisecond then continued into the barn and put Curly in his stall.

"You can deny it all you want, Tony, but it's still there between you and me. The fire. The heat. The wanting."

The quiet click of the stall latch sounded like a bomb exploding in the structure. Tony faced her. Rays of sun streaming through the cracks in the barn's siding highlighted the dancing dust particles around his head.

"Since you appear determined to have this out—" He took off his glasses and slid them into his shirt pocket. "Yes, it's all still there between you and me."

Her heart skipped a beat.

"But it doesn't matter. We can't do this."

His words stung. "Is it because you still have feelings for Evita?"

"How did—"

"She told me you broke off your engagement because you couldn't get over Michael's death and you said you were no good for her." Lucy held his gaze. "Is that true?"

Tony strode halfway through the barn then stopped and faced Lucy. "The truth?"

Lucy braced herself.

"I broke up with Evita because I couldn't stop loving you."

A thrill raced through Lucy but his next words slammed the door on her joy.

"Not that what I feel for you matters," he said. "Too much has happened to go back and pick up where we left off. We're not the same people we were before Michael's death."

"If you're worried about our parents—"

"This has nothing to do with your father or my mother," he said.

Lucy didn't want to accept that. She needed a tangible reason that Tony didn't believe they could be together— how could she fight something she couldn't see? "Your mother likes me. With time she'll come around, and you don't have to worry about my father—"

"Don't be naive, Lucy. Your father would never approve of us being a couple."

"My dad might be wealthy and powerful, but he doesn't run my life. I choose who I want to be with." *And I choose you.*

"When push comes to shove, you won't stand up to your old man."

"If the Pony Express doesn't prove I can hold my own with him then—"

"Don't kid yourself. Your father can shut down the business anytime he wants."

The truth was tough to deny. The reason her father hadn't sabotaged her business already was because he assumed she'd run it into the ground by herself. Tears flooded her eyes as she felt Tony slipping away from her.

"Even if our parents came around to the idea of you and me dating, I can't be with you."

The intense pain in his gaze stole Lucy's breath.

"I admire the hell out of you for wanting to do something to honor your brother's name, but you're meant for better things than the Pony Express."

"I can't leave Stagecoach."

"And I can't stay," he said.

"That's it? What we had two years ago…what we still feel for each other is—"

"Over." The agony in his brown eyes gave way to a steely glint.

Tony still loved her, but for reasons beyond her understanding he wouldn't reach for his own happiness. He might believe he could run from what they'd shared in the past, but one day he'd realize that Michael's death had created a bond between them that not even distance or time had the power to sever.

"Let's go." Tony strode past her out of the barn.

Despair settled deep in Lucy's bones as she stared at Tony's retreating back. Maybe he was right. If they left well enough alone, at least she'd go to sleep at night with the knowledge that Tony still cared about her—that was more than she deserved.

She went into the supply room and cleaned up at the sink. When she left the barn she spotted Tony leaning against the hood of her truck. He wore his sunglasses, his sober face giving no hint of their earlier argument.

"Meet me at the station Saturday morning at eight." He opened the driver's-side door for her. "We'll take my truck to Tuba City."

The firm set of his jaw told Lucy not to bother pleading her case again. Tony had made up his mind—they were finished. She slid behind the wheel and shut the door without a word. As she drove away, tears clogged her throat. What a fool she'd been to believe she and Tony could recapture the love they'd once shared.

When the truck reached the top of the ridge, she pressed the accelerator to the floor and left Tony in the dust.

"LADIES AND GENTS, the Northern Arizona Junior Bull Rider's Association welcomes you to the fourth annual Trio Boys Youth Bull Bash in Tuba City!"

Fans in the small indoor arena whistled and stomped their boots on the bleachers. Junior rodeos didn't draw big crowds, but those who ventured out to watch the teens were enthusiastic and encouraging.

"Competing at the Bar X Arena today are cowboys and cowgirls from as far away as Oregon, Colorado, and Oklahoma."

Tony and Lucy sat in the stands near the bull chutes—close enough for Lucy to view the cowboy's routines.

"He looks a lot older than seventeen." Lucy nodded to a young man climbing on a bull.

The smell of Lucy's perfume interfered with Tony's concentration and he missed half of what she'd said. "Pardon?"

She leaned closer, her shoulder brushing his, and darned if a spark didn't ignite between their bodies. A lot of good his lecture had done a few days ago about there being no future for them. He forced himself to focus on the conversation.

"The kid looks older than seventeen."

Tony checked the program. "He turns eighteen next month. If he wins today, he'll have enough points to make it to the Youth Bull Riders World Finals in Abilene, Texas, in August."

God, he hoped Lucy kept talking rodeo like she'd done during the drive to the arena. He worried that if she brought up the fact that they both still had feelings for each other, his good intentions would fall by the wayside and he'd agree to anything she asked of him.

The past couple of days had been particularly rough. His first thought upon waking in the morning and his last thought before drifting off to sleep at night had been how much he wanted Lucy. How he wished things could be different between them.

"Why does he keep fussing with the rope?" she asked.

Fear. Tony watched the junior cowboy adjust and re-adjust his grip. "He's nervous."

"Folks, Kenny Rainer is about to tangle with Crybaby," the announcer said. "Let me tell you a little story about this particular bull…"

"The bull doesn't look much smaller than the ones you and Michael rode," Lucy said.

"Junior bulls weigh less but they buck and kick just as hard as full-grown ones. This is probably Crybaby's last season as a junior bull before he moves up in the ranks."

"If this kid is good, what's he worried about?"

"Crybaby has never been ridden to eight." Tony pointed to the write-up in the program.

"What bull am I riding after the rodeo?" she asked.

"Whichever one you want." Jim Howl of Howl Rodeo Bulls provided the animals for the event and had told Tony that Lucy could have her pick of roughstock.

"Folks, it looks like Kenny is ready to ride!"

A second after the announcer spoke, the chute door opened and Crybaby exploded into the area. The bull kicked his back legs high before spinning in a tight circle. Kenny tried to hang on, but the force of each spin pushed the teen off balance. He slid down the bull's side, landing near the animal's hooves. Lucy held her breath as Kenny scrambled out of the way. Unlike Curly, who would have trotted off, Crybaby continued to buck and spin until the bullfighters turned him toward the exit.

While the next kid went through his preride routine, Tony gauged Lucy's reaction. Her mouth was set in a firm line and her cheeks lost their glow. It was good that she understood the dangers of the sport and realized women as talented as Shannon Douglas came along once in a blue moon.

"Next up is Jason Bedford from Chiloquin, Oregon. Jason is eighteen years old and he'll be riding Hercules from the Bangor Ranch in Colorado."

A half hour later the bull-riding event ended. Three of the young men managed to make it to eight, and Stephen Cooper from Tulsa, Oklahoma, who'd ridden a bull named Audacity, took first place.

"Have you picked your bull?" Tony asked.

Lucy straightened her shoulders. "Crybaby."

Damn it, he knew she'd go for the biggest one. "No."

"Why not? At least I'll be prepared for the bull I'll draw next weekend."

"Or you'll end up injured and unable to ride."

She opened her mouth then snapped it shut. "When did you become so bossy?"

"I never ignore my gut and it's telling me you're not ready for a bull like Crybaby."

"The one I ride in Ajo will be tougher than Crybaby and I still won't be ready then."

"C'mon." Tony stood. "Let's take a look at Beastmaster."

"He's the smallest bull of the group."

Tony made an attempt to grab the equipment bag, but she jerked it out of reach and kept walking. *Stubborn woman.*

"Beastmaster might be the smallest, but he's the quickest." More important, after he tossed his rider, he trotted away.

Behind the chutes, they stopped at Beastmaster's pen, where the bull rested. He appeared less threatening from the stands but up close he was nearly the size of Curly.

"He'll do," Lucy said.

Now if only Tony's advice that she stick with Beast-master was all she needed to keep her safe. "I have to use the ladies' room." Lucy dropped the gear bag and walked off.

WHEN LUCY ENTERED the women's restroom she headed straight into a stall and puked. Twice. There went her lunch—hotdog and a diet cola.

After flushing the toilet she rinsed her mouth with water then wiped her face with a damp paper towel and leaned against the wall. The reality of her situation had hit her hard when she'd gotten a close look at Beastmaster—even the junior bulls had horns on them.

You've come too far to let fear stop you now.

She'd checked her website before meeting Tony this morning and discovered her fundraising total had reached eight thousand dollars—based on a three-second ride in all three rodeos and Wrangler matching her pledges. In order to collect the money, she had to remain healthy. After witnessing the young men this afternoon, she doubted she'd escape three rodeos without injury—what kind, and how severe, to be determined.

Lord, don't let anything bad happen to me today.

She'd never competed at anything in her life except during sorority rush week in her freshman year of college. She didn't want to be a wimp—not in front of Tony. But would her stubbornness be enough to protect her from injury?

"Lucy?"

Tony's voice echoed through the bathroom opening. No more hiding. When she stepped outside, he looked worried—he should be. The only thing keeping her from tucking tail and calling it quits was Michael. She wouldn't let her brother down.

"What's the matter? Don't you feel well?"

"I'm fine."

"We can walk out of here right now." He lowered his voice. "No questions asked."

It took all of Lucy's strength not to throw herself at him and hang on for dear life. "I can do this."

"Okay, then. Let's go." He grasped her hand and escorted her to the bull chutes. Lucy soaked up his strength, grateful that he hadn't tried to talk her out of riding.

The stands were emptying quickly and the arena was quieting down. "Is the stock contractor here?" She wanted to thank the man for allowing her to ride one of his bulls.

"He's having a beer with friends. His rodeo helpers agreed to load Beastmaster for us. Get your gear on and I'll check in with the guys."

Lucy did as she was told. When she finished securing her vest, she put on the face mask and approached the chute. One cowboy sat on the top rail, in case Lucy needed help, and a second man stood inside the arena, waiting for her signal to open the gate.

"Harley, this is Lucy." Tony nodded to the man straddling the rails.

"Ma'am." Harley tipped his hat.

"And Bob's in charge of the gate."

"Thank you both for your help today," Lucy said.

"Take your time," Tony said.

If she took too long, she'd panic. As it was, her blood ran cold through her veins. She climbed over the top rail and settled onto Beastmaster's back. The bull's muscles bunched beneath her buttocks and Lucy felt beads of sweat dot her brow.

"Ma'am, he breaks to the right when he leaves the chute," Harley said. "Make sure you keep low and inside from the get-go."

Lucy looked at Tony but his face gave nothing away.

Harley held the bull rope out to her and Lucy nodded her thanks. She recalled how Tony had taught her to wrap the rope around her hand and she made sure her pinky finger lined up with the center of Beastmaster's back.

"Tight but not too tight?" Tony asked.

"Got it."

"Shift your hips," he said.

Lucy complied.

"Shoulder."

She repositioned her shoulder.

"Relax your spine."

Not as easy as it sounded, but she tried.

"Remember to dismount on the left side."

"Okay."

"You don't have to stay on until the buzzer," Tony said.

Time crawled to a stop. Beastmaster snorted, the sound echoing like a horn blast inside Lucy's head. *It's now or never.*

She nodded and the chute door opened. The bull vaulted into the arena. Lucy clenched her thighs tightly against the animal's girth, the effort keeping her from shifting.

The first buck sent her butt high into the air, and when she crashed down on the bull's back she swore her tailbone would be swollen for months. The pain quickly diffused to numbness and her thoughts shifted into survival mode. After two bucks the strength in her arms waned and she looked for an opening to dismount. When Beast-master's back hooves hit the ground, Lucy released the rope and launched herself sideways off the bull.

The ground came up fast, knocking the air from her lungs. The buzzer rang through the arena. Tony's voice penetrated her stupor and her body automatically obeyed his instructions. Rolling to her knees, she checked over her shoulder and saw that Beastmaster had run in the opposite direction. Even though the bull was no threat, Tony shouted for her to get to her feet and run for the rails. She had just enough adrenaline left to accomplish the feat.

"Ma'am, you rode Beastmaster for four seconds!" Harley said.

Lucy whipped off the face mask. "Four seconds?"

"Four seconds." Tony grinned.

She'd calculated her eight thousand in donations based on lasting three seconds on a bull. Now, she intended to set her goal higher. She took a step in the direction of her gear bag then gasped and froze.

"What's wrong?" Tony's gaze roamed over her body. "Did you break something?"

Embarrassed, she said, "Yeah, I think I broke my butt." She rubbed her sore tush.

Harley laughed then communicated Lucy's predicament to Bob, who'd returned after putting Beastmaster into his pen.

"C'mon," Tony said. "I've got a donut pillow you can sit on during the drive home."

The men chuckled and Lucy joined in their laughter. She'd survived a real bull ride for four seconds—for now, she'd bask in her success. At least today she'd proven she could manage her fears. There'd be no turning back.

CHAPTER ELEVEN

TONY GLANCED ACROSS the front seat of his truck. Lucy had fallen asleep as soon as they'd left the rodeo grounds. Strands of blond hair had escaped her ponytail and framed her face. She looked vulnerable and soft, and he imagined waking each morning with her snuggled against his side, her quiet breathing echoing in his ear.

In your dreams, buddy.

He shifted his attention to the road. Nothing made sense. There was no rhyme or reason to the universe. People just existed—targets with bull's-eyes on their backs, waiting for the next hit life hurled at them. Was it only yesterday that he and Michael had danced with pretty girls and wrestled bulls? Now his focus was on survival—physical and mental.

Unable to resist touching Lucy, he brushed her hair off her cheek, his finger lingering long enough to rouse her.

"Where are we?" Her voice, rusty with sleep, sounded sexy and intimate.

"Almost to Yuma. I need to speak to your father tonight. I'll follow you out to the ranch."

"Sure." She sat up straight, wincing when she repositioned the donut pillow beneath her.

"Is your bum still sore?"

"Yes." She smiled. "But it's a good pain."

"If I were you, I'd soak in the hot tub tonight and again in the morning, then stretch throughout the day. Don't let your muscles tighten up on you."

Lucy's stomach grumbled. "Sorry. I'm starving."

"We can grab a bite to eat at the truck stop on the way to the ranch."

"Is your mom working tonight?"

He nodded. "You can tell her all about Beastmaster."

After they picked up Lucy's truck at the border patrol station, they headed to the Fiesta Travel Stop. Tony's mother gestured toward the lunch counter when they walked through the door.

"Hey, Mom." Tony hugged his mother.

Maria looked Lucy up and down. "I'm glad to see you're in one piece. How was the rodeo?"

Lucy beamed, and in that instant, Tony felt a sense of pride in her accomplishment today. He admired the courage she'd shown when she'd gone through with the bull ride.

"I lasted four seconds on Beastmaster," Lucy said.

Maria let out a whoop that drew attention from a table of truck drivers. "This calls for a celebration. Ice cream or food?" She glanced between Tony and Lucy.

"Both. I'll have the fried chicken special with a chocolate malt," Lucy said.

"Make mine the same."

"Comin' right up." Maria scribbled on her pad then passed the ticket through the order window before walking off to serve other customers.

They waited for their food in silence. Tony hated the strain between them but figured it would last until he packed his bags and moved to San Diego. Stagecoach would become the place he'd grown up and nothing more.

"Michael…"

Tony held his breath.

"Wow." Lucy rubbed her finger over a burn mark on the Formica countertop. "Sorry, Michael's name just popped out." She exhaled loudly. "Tony. Do you really want to move to California?"

Lucy had guessed his train of thought. "It's not a matter of *wanting* to leave town. I have to."

"Because you blame yourself for Michael's death."

Of course he blamed himself for his best friend's death, but Tony wasn't so naive that he didn't realize he couldn't outrun guilt. The reason he had to leave Stagecoach had a little to do with Michael and a whole lot to do with Lucy. His actions that fateful night cost Michael not only his life but Tony's future with Lucy. Even if Lucy found it in her heart to forgive him for leaving her brother at the bar, Tony didn't deserve to be happy.

"What if it wasn't your fault?" Lucy gripped his arm. "Would you stay in Stagecoach then?"

The truck stop wasn't the best place for confessions, but he had to make Lucy understand that his actions in the past made it impossible for them to be together.

"There's something you need to know about the night Michael died," he said. "After your brother won in Prescott, we were on our way back to Stagecoach when he learned that he'd moved into the top spot in the rankings, and if he continued to ride like he had been, he'd go to the NFR at the end of the season."

"We didn't find out Michael's ranking until a few days

later," Lucy said. "Dad was upset that Michael hadn't told him."

"Your brother called your father, but he got his voice mail and didn't want to leave a message."

Lucy's smile was tinged with sadness. "My dad will appreciate knowing that."

"Michael wanted to stop for drinks at the bar but I didn't want to celebrate with him."

"Why not?"

"Envy." Jealousy was only part of the reason for Tony's bad mood that night. The other part had to do with Lucy, but Tony kept that to himself. "Michael was a great bull rider. I was just a mediocre one." He closed his eyes against the memory of him and Michael arguing.

"I was feeling sorry for myself. I'd been friends with Michael since elementary school and I'd grown up watching how easy life had been for him. By the time we were old enough to rodeo, nothing had changed. Your father gave him money for entry fees while I busted my ass working odd jobs to pay my own way on the road." Tony swallowed hard. "A week before the Prescott rodeo I told Michael I was quitting."

Tony hadn't wanted to lose Lucy. She'd been just about to graduate from college and had job offers from companies out of state as well as in Phoenix. He'd wanted to give her a reason to return to Stagecoach—him. He'd intended to find a respectable job and believed that, with time, he and Lucy could have convinced their parents to accept their relationship.

"What did my brother say when you told him you were quitting?"

"Michael insisted I stay on the circuit, because I was

the only one he trusted to watch his back." Michael had taken advantage of their friendship, placing Tony in a tight spot. In the end, Tony hadn't been able to disappoint him. "I told your brother that I'd stay with him through the finals in Vegas but after that I was done."

Tony had resented having to put his relationship with Lucy on hold, but there had been no other way. If he and Lucy had made their feelings for each other public there would have been a stressful adjustment period for both families, and Tony hadn't wanted that to affect Michael's rodeo performances and ruin his chance of making it to Vegas.

"I was pissed I caved in to your brother and I spouted some things I shouldn't have."

"Like what?"

No point in confessing if he sugarcoated the truth. "I said he was nothing but a spoiled rich kid." Tony was embarrassed to admit he'd been envious of the Durango wealth. "I told Michael to call your father for a ride home if he drank too much and I left the bar." But Michael hadn't listened to Tony. "If I'd stayed, Michael would be alive today."

Lucy's eyes filled with tears and she dabbed at the corners with a paper napkin.

Maria arrived with their meals, her smile faltering at the sight of Lucy's watery eyes. "Everything okay?"

"Yep. I'm fine," Lucy said.

"Holler if you need anything." His mother grabbed the coffeepot from the warmer behind the counter and walked off.

"Leaving Stagecoach won't make you forget Michael," Lucy said.

No, but at least he wouldn't chance running into Lucy and being reminded that his foolishness had cost him a future with her.

"Michael was my dad's favorite." Lucy sniffed. "Did you know that in his younger days my father rodeoed?"

"Michael mentioned it a couple of times."

"Dad's career was short-lived, but he loved rodeo and encouraged Michael to get into the sport."

"What about you?" Tony asked. "Why didn't you barrel race? Your family has the money to buy expensive horses."

Lucy laughed, but there was no humor in the sound. "Dad never paid much attention to me. I was my mother's responsibility."

"Is that why you're riding bulls—because your father loved rodeo?" Lucy might believe she could make her father love her the way he'd loved Michael.

"Maybe a little."

Did Cal Durango even care that his daughter was risking her life for him? "What happens after the rodeos?"

"I don't know. If I can find permanent funding for the Pony Express, I'd like to add additional vans and drivers."

That's not what he'd meant. He wanted to know how Lucy intended to earn her father's love if she stopped riding bulls.

"I thought it would be great if the Pony Express offered rides for school dances, weddings and private parties, but I'd need to find investors willing to sponsor a van or a school to make that happen."

A sense of urgency ate at Tony as he stared at the cooling chicken in front of him. The sooner he and his department apprehended those responsible for the human-smuggling ring, the sooner he got his promotion and the sooner he got the hell out of Dodge and found the peace he desperately needed. Once he left the area, he'd move on with his life and Lucy would move on with hers.

The thought of leaving her behind hit Tony hard. If things had ended differently the night Michael had died, he and Lucy would be married now, and who knows, maybe parents. Or was that only a fantasy? If Michael had lived, Lucy might not have returned to Stagecoach after graduating college and Tony would have married Evita.

He looked at Lucy and felt the pull of her blue eyes. Honest to God, he didn't know how he was going to find the strength to walk away from her when everything inside him loved her.

You'll walk away because *you love Lucy.*

"Let's eat and hit the road," he said.

Forty-five minutes later, they arrived at the ranch. Lucy parked under the carport and Tony kept his truck in the driveway. They met at the porch steps, Lucy leading the way into the house.

"What are you doing here again, Bravo?" Cal Durango stood in the hallway.

"Dad, be nice." Lucy closed the front door and smiled at Tony—not a smart thing to do with Cal staring daggers at them. "Thank you for your help today." She climbed the stairs to the second floor, leaving Tony to square off with her father.

"Speak your mind."

"We're putting a surveillance team out at the mine either Tuesday or Wednesday night next week."

"Well, which one is it?"

Damned if Tony would explain every step in the process of the investigation. "We're waiting for intelligence to confirm the day. Don't allow anyone near the area until you hear from my supervisor."

"I'd better hear from someone by Thursday morning about what was going on out there."

"We'll keep you informed."

"Don't screw this up, Bravo." Durango strolled closer. "I don't want any bad press. Understood?"

"Yes, sir." Tony left the house and jogged to his truck. He doubted he could outrun the demons chasing him, but he was going to give it one hell of a try. Dust spewed from the back tires as he took off like a bat out of hell.

LUCY LIFTED THE binoculars to her eyes and scanned the desert. Two hours until sunset was a long time to wait, but she made sure to arrive at the mine before the border patrol agents.

This past Saturday she'd hovered in the hallway, listening to Tony inform her father of the planned stakeout. She'd made the trek to the mine on her father's ATV yesterday—Tuesday—but the border patrol had been a no-show. Today was her lucky day. From her vantage point along a low-lying slope a hundred yards from the mine she could see agents setting up their lookouts. She hadn't seen Tony in a while and wondered if he'd moved behind the ridge.

"What the hell do you think you're doing?"

Lucy squawked and rolled onto her back. Slapping a hand against her throat, she wheezed, "You scared the crap out of me, Tony."

His eyes were hidden behind his mirrored sunglasses

but the firm set of his mouth didn't bode well for her. "How did you know I was here?" She'd hidden the ATV behind a bush, hiking the rest of the distance to her hiding spot.

"You left a trail wider than the Mississippi." He rubbed his brow. "You can't stay here, Lucy. There's no telling how dangerous things might get if the thugs show up tonight. They'll be armed and you might get hit by a stray bullet if gunfire is exchanged."

The thought of Tony getting shot worried Lucy more than her own safety. "I promise I won't get in the way."

Tony reached down and helped her to her feet. Tightening his grip on her arm, he escorted her to the ATV. "Go home and stay there."

"I'll go crazy if I have to sit at the house and wonder what's happening."

"Then drive out to my mom's and practice on the mechanical bull for Saturday's rodeo."

"I don't want to bother your mother."

"You won't. She's in Tucson with Juan until tomorrow and Maddie's at the trailer by herself. I was planning to drop her off at your house tomorrow."

"Did Nina's parents come get her?"

"Yep." Tony fished his key ring from his pocket and removed his mother's house key. "You can take Maddie back with you after you finish practicing. Leave the key under the welcome mat. It'll be late by the time we're finished here, so I'll crash at my mom's tonight and pick up the key then."

Realizing she wouldn't change Tony's mind about her joining the stakeout, Lucy caved. "Okay." Tony walked her to the ATV and she stowed her binoculars in the small storage compartment.

"I meant what I said, Lucy. Stay away from here."

She hopped on the quad bike. "Be careful." Tony might be the boss out here in the desert, but that didn't mean she couldn't get even with him. She started the engine then glanced over her shoulder before pressing down hard on the accelerator and brake at the same time. Dirt and sand shot into the air and Tony scrambled to move out of the way. Satisfied she'd made her displeasure at having to leave known, she sped off. Let him chew on that tonight while he waited in the dark for the bad guys.

Several hours later Lucy found herself sitting in the dark on Maria Bravo's porch, Maddie sleeping soundly by her side. She and the dog had had a grand time, strolling through the desert and chasing lizards before Maddie ate her bowl of kibble and conked out for the night.

Lucy wished she knew what to do about Maddie. The boxer loved people and shouldn't be kept locked in her kennel all day. Maybe Maddie could join the border patrol team—after all, the dog had saved Nina's life. The Yuma station could use Maddie to calm the children when families were detained for crossing into the country illegally.

Lucy stared at the star-filled heavens, knowing Tony had the same view of the sky. Was it as quiet at the mine as it was here in the trailer park or had all hell broken loose out there? A vehicle entered the park and Lucy checked her watch. Two in the morning. When the truck turned onto Maria's street, her heart thumped heavily. Tony was back. He opened the driver's-side door and Lucy exhaled loudly, unaware she'd been holding her breath.

Maddie bounded down the steps and greeted him. "Hey, girl. What are you still doing here?"

Lucy stood. "I couldn't leave until I knew you were safe."

"False alarm tonight."

"Do you think someone tipped them off?"

"No. Sometimes criminals get spooked and turn back." He stopped at the bottom porch step. "It's awfully late to be driving back to the ranch."

Lucy had texted her mother that she'd be staying at a friend's apartment in Yuma for the night. "I'm not going back." She held her breath.

Tony climbed the steps. He brushed a stray blond curl behind her ear and whispered, "Good."

Her heart skidded to a halt, and when it resumed pounding, Lucy feared the organ would burst through her rib cage. Tony held out his hand and she grasped his fingers. As soon as they entered the trailer, he pressed her against the door. His mouth was hard and eager, and she melted in his arms.

"Don't move." He walked down the hallway, leaving Lucy at the front door. When she heard the shower running in the bathroom, she closed her eyes and envisioned Tony's wet, muscular body standing beneath the spray. Her fantasy ended abruptly when he appeared in the hallway—naked.

Oh, my. Her mouth watered at the sight of his dark skin and sleek muscles. Then he moved, each step bringing her fantasy closer and closer to reality. There was no guessing involved in figuring out that he wanted her. His desire taunted her—dared her to touch him. She wrapped her hand around his erection and kissed his neck. Tony swept her into his arms and carried her to his bedroom, shutting the door on Maddie.

"Are you sure, Lucy?" Tony nibbled her earlobe.

Was she sure she wanted to make love to Tony when he'd already told her there was no second chance for them?

Was she sure she wanted to lie in the arms of a man who believed he'd been the cause of her brother's death?

Was she sure she wanted to be with the man she'd fallen in love with two years ago and had never stopped loving?

"Yes, I'm sure."

Tony tugged off Lucy's clothes, tossing them on the floor as they both tumbled across the mattress. He groped in the nightstand drawer for a condom. "If you want to stop, say so now, Lucy."

She gripped his biceps, her nails biting into his flesh, and hung on for a Wild West ride she was certain she'd never forget.

CHAPTER TWELVE

LUCY WOKE IN STAGES—first, noticing the firm mattress beneath her, then the absence of ocean waves from her sound machine. She opened her eyes and stared at the unfamiliar light fixture on the ceiling. Slowly, the pieces of the puzzle came together. *Tony's bedroom.*

She rolled her head to the side and caressed the indentation in the pillow left by his head. Cold to the touch. How long had he been gone? Raising her arms, she stretched the kinks in her muscles. Their lovemaking had been as fierce and wild as she'd remembered. Tony hadn't left an inch of her body unclaimed and the experience reminded her why she'd lost her heart to him. Once they'd caved in to their desire for each other, they'd held nothing back, and the same had been true last night. When Tony had gazed into her eyes she'd recognized his love for her. It didn't matter that he hadn't said the words—their hearts and souls had beat as one for a brief time.

Gathering a fistful of bedsheet, she buried her nose in the scent of clean male. The euphoria lasted only a moment before the reality of her actions hit home.

Dear God. What have I done?

She hadn't meant for things to go this far between them—at least not before she'd told Tony the truth about the night Michael had died.

You never intended to tell Tony anything.

Tears stung her eyes. Had her subconscious played a trick on her? Had she convinced herself that she'd eventually come clean with Tony when all along she'd known she lacked the courage?

Would the truth change his mind about leaving Stage-coach?

What if the truth makes Tony hate you?

Unable to accept the thought of him resenting her, she slipped from the bed and pulled on her tank top and panties. She opened the bedroom door, took one step then froze. Tony's mother sat at the kitchen table reading the paper.

"'Morning, Lucy." Maria flipped a page in the paper.

"Good morning." Lucy dashed back into the bedroom and threw on the rest of her clothes.

"There's fresh coffee on the counter." Maria's voice drifted down the hall.

"Thanks. I'll be right there." Lucy made Tony's bed—not that his mother didn't already know what had taken place in it. After freshening up in the bathroom, she entered the kitchen and helped herself to a cup of much-needed caffeine.

Maria set the paper aside. "Tony said to tell you that he took Maddie to the station with him this morning."

How early had Maria arrived at the trailer? Lucy checked the wall clock—9:00 a.m. She never slept this late.

As if Lucy sitting at her breakfast table was an everyday occurrence, Maria continued chatting. "They detained a father with three small children overnight. While he's being questioned, Tony figured Maddie would calm the kids."

"I'd thought about asking Tony if there's a chance Maddie could work for the department, but he's transferring…" Lucy's voice trailed off at the worried look in Maria's eyes.

Maria tapped a fingernail against the tabletop. "I don't know how else to say this."

"Say what?"

"Are you crazy, young lady?"

Lucy swallowed hard. "I don't understand," she said, even though she knew perfectly well what Tony's mother referred to.

"You and Tony carrying on." Maria motioned toward the bedroom. "Your father will have Tony fired from his job with the border patrol if he finds out you two are sleeping together."

Lucy opened her mouth to tell Maria that she wanted to be the reason Tony's transfer didn't go through, but she lost her courage.

"You two are playing with fire."

When it came to her feelings for Tony, Lucy wasn't playing, but she doubted Maria wanted to hear that.

"Lucy, your father—"

"It's not really my father interfering with Tony's transfer that you're worried about, is it?"

"I don't know what you mean?"

"You want Tony to marry a Hispanic girl."

Maria left the table and took the dishrag from the sink to scrub at a spot on the counter. "I'm not prejudiced."

"I didn't think you were."

"I—" Maria tossed the rag back into the sink and

faced Lucy. "I admit I'm a little old-fashioned and hoped my son would marry a Hispanic girl." She raised her hand, stalling Lucy's protest. "You're a wonderful young woman, Lucy, and if my son decided you were the one, then I would accept that."

"But...?"

"But you're not a typical Anglo girl."

"If you're referring to my family's wealth, I can't do anything about that."

"Not just your wealth. Your father wants the best for you, as any father would, and my Tony will never be good enough. Your father would make you both miserable. In the end, you'd be pressured to leave Tony just to keep the peace in your family and my son would be devastated."

Lucy regretted dreaming of her and Tony living happily ever after. If being together made their families miserable, what was the point? "You're right. Last night was a mistake. It won't happen again." Lucy retrieved the rest of her things from the bedroom.

Maria waited by the door, tears welling in her eyes. "Be careful at the rodeo this weekend."

Before she broke down and cried, Lucy raced for her truck. She refused to accept that last night with Tony had been a mistake, but after the pain she'd already caused everyone, the last thing she wanted to do was come between Tony and his mother. She loved Tony enough to respect Maria's wishes and not become involved with him. From now on, she'd act as if last night had never happened.

"NERVOUS?"

The question jarred Lucy from her trance. "Shannon. When did you get here?"

"I've been here all morning." The professional bull rider sent a glare toward the bull chutes.

Lucy tracked Shannon's stare—several buckle bunnies had circled C. J. Rodriguez and were flirting with the cowboy. "Does he draw them everywhere he goes?"

"'Fraid so." Shannon returned her attention to Lucy. "Where's Tony? I thought he was helping you prepare for the rodeos."

"He is…was…" Lucy shrugged. "He might have had to work today." She didn't know where Tony was because she hadn't returned any of his phone calls since the night she'd slept with him. She'd spent Thursday and Friday pampering her sore muscles and focusing on stretching exercises as he'd instructed her to do.

"Here's how everything's going down," Shannon said. "Once the other roughstock events are finished, they'll introduce bull riding and you'll be the first one out of the chute. The announcer's going to mention why you're riding today and then he'll ask the fans to help support the Pony Express by filling out a pledge card or putting money into the cowboy boots being passed through the bleachers."

"What boots?"

"A few of the cowboys who knew Michael wanted to help out and one of them suggested passing a boot to collect cash."

"Wow." Lucy's throat tightened. "That's really nice of the guys."

"There's something else you need to know." Shannon looked worried.

"What?"

"They're going to show Michael's ride in Prescott on the JumboTron."

The blood drained from Lucy's face. Her parents had refused a copy of the videotape of her brother's last ride from the rodeo producers.

"You don't have to watch it, Lucy, but the cameras might zoom in on you while the clip is playing."

Lucy noted the stares directed her way and stood a little taller. She was here for Michael and she wasn't going to let him down. "Do you know which bull I'm riding?"

"Migraine."

Lucy hoped the bull hadn't earned the name because he left his riders concussed.

"Migraine's a straight-forward bucker. He doesn't spin much, and more important, he doesn't charge a fallen rider."

"How old is the bull?" Lucy asked.

"Eight. He's at the tail end of his career. Just make sure you jump clear of him when you dismount. Migraine tends to keep bucking after he loses his rider and you don't want to get stomped." Shannon motioned to Lucy's bag. "Can I see your gear?"

"Sure." Lucy waited for Shannon's verdict.

"Nothing but the best. Good."

Lucy wasn't sure if that was a criticism or a compliment.

"I've got to get back to the Wrangler booth. Try to relax. Everything's going to be okay."

As Shannon walked away, Lucy couldn't help but think that after today, nothing would be okay.

WHERE WAS SHE?

Tony stood in the shadows of the cowboy ready area at

the Ajo rodeo and he'd yet to catch a glimpse of Lucy. His gut had been tied in knots the past two days after she'd ignored his text messages and refused to return his calls. The only explanation for Lucy's silence was that she'd regretted making love with him. Well, he felt the same way. He accepted full blame for what had transpired between them, but it was too late to turn back the clock.

All that mattered at the moment was making sure Lucy made it unscathed through her first bull ride. There was a small part of him that had hoped she'd scratch, but instinct said she wouldn't. Once she set her mind to something, she followed through.

He admired the hell out of her gumption and would have been able to handle her decision to ride today a whole lot better if they hadn't made love. But they'd crossed a line, and in doing so, Lucy had reestablished her claim on his heart. The only thing that mattered now was keeping her safe—for Michael and her parents' sakes, but mostly for his.

A flash of pink caught Tony's eye. Lucy wore a fancy shirt with white fringe across the yoke. He studied her, searching for signs of nervousness, but his mind drifted to the bedroom, and instead of smelling the earthy odors of animal, hay and cowboy sweat, the scent of honeysuckle filled his head. Today Lucy wore her long hair in a braid, but he envisioned the strands loose and flowing through his fingers.

Tony shook his head to dislodge the image of Lucy's naked body from his mind. He'd fought his desire for her because he'd believed if he held her in his arms the experience would awaken the sleeping demons inside him. To his surprise and relief, Lucy had managed to make him feel whole and clean inside—not tainted with guilt. The heavy pressure that resided in his chest had disappeared the moment he'd pulled Lucy into his arms. It didn't make sense—not after what he'd done to her and her family.

It would be so easy to hold Lucy close and use her as a shield between him and his conscience. He liked being able to breathe without flinching and didn't want to return to the way things had been—living in the shadow of his guilt and trying to outrun the past. He took a fortifying breath and stepped from his hiding place.

Lucy's eyes widened. "You came."

"Of course I came."

"You didn't have to—"

"Yes, I did. We're in this together." Lucy's smile zapped Tony in the heart. "What bull did you draw?" he asked.

"Migraine."

"Have you had a look at him yet?"

"No."

Ignoring the queasy feeling attacking his intestines, he grasped Lucy's hand and tugged her after him. When they arrived at the bull pen he had to force himself to release her hand. He asked a rodeo worker to point out Migraine. The Chambray bull sported a gleaming red coat and a white splotch on his belly. "He's on the small side."

"Shannon said he doesn't spin or charge."

"Good. You should be able to handle him." Tony knew Lucy had trained well, but it was the hundred-and-one-million things that could go wrong between one second and eight seconds that concerned him. "Don't tie the rope around your hand too tight and don't—"

"Tony." Lucy squeezed his arm. "I'll be fine."

"Ladies and gentlemen, it's time for the final event of the day—men's bull riding!" The announcer's voice rang over the loud speakers.

Tony and Lucy returned to the chutes and he said, "Get your gear." While she put on the Kevlar vest and her riding glove, the rodeo helpers loaded Migraine into the chute and Tony helped fish the bull rope beneath him.

"Folks, today we've got a special event here at the arena. Many of you may remember a young bull rider by the name of Michael Durango who was making a run at an NFR title the year he passed away. Before I say more, turn your eyes to the JumboTron."

"I should have warned you," Lucy whispered.

The ringing in Tony's ears blocked out Lucy's voice. Gaze glued to the giant video screen, he couldn't look away from the footage of Michael's ride.

His friend's image—larger than life—filled the hushed arena. Michael settled onto the back of Chicken on a Chain then fussed with the bull rope. He appeared as real as ever and it took more courage than Tony imagined to watch the video. Then Michael raised his head and stared straight at Tony and grinned. An excruciating pain—sharper than the agony he'd experienced the night Lucy had phoned with news of Michael's death—ripped through Tony's body, leaving him winded.

He felt the warm glide of Lucy's fingers across his hand and automatically squeezed hard. He couldn't tear his gaze from the screen as the gate opened and Chicken on a Chain made Michael work for his eight seconds of glory.

Tony was in awe of how Michael had managed to keep his balance and survive a series of vicious bucks.

In that moment, he acknowledged that his friend's success hadn't just been the result of hard work—the cowboy had been blessed with God-given talent. No matter how often Tony had practiced, he would never have achieved the same level of accomplishment. The NFR had been Michael's destiny and he'd been robbed of it.

Tony's heart pounded as he lived and breathed each second of Michael's ride. When the buzzer sounded, the arena in Prescott went wild. Michael's dismount was nothing less than spectacular as he launched himself through the air. He hit the ground but rolled to his feet in an instant, then looked over his shoulder and found Chicken on a Chain staring him down. Instead of running for the rails as if his Wranglers were on fire, he stood defiantly and dared the bull to charge.

Tony grinned. *You always were a frickin' show off, Durango.*

The bull charged and Michael turned and ran for the rails, barely reaching safety before the animal's horns clipped the bottom of his boots.

"There you have it, folks," the announcer said. "Michael Durango took over the top spot in the standings with that ride." When the noise in the arena leveled off, the announcer continued. "Later that night, Michael passed away in a car accident." A hush fell over the stands. "Today Michael's sister, Lucy Durango, is riding in his memory."

Lucy perched on the top rail and waved to the crowd. The cameras zoomed in, displaying her image on the big screen.

"Michael's rodeo buddies are passing their boots through the stands collecting donations for Lucy's charity—the Pony Express." When the applause died down, the announcer said, "The Pony Express is a free shuttle service for cowboys who've celebrated a bit too much at the local honky-tonks and require the services of a designated driver."

Hoots and hollers echoed through the arena. "Folks, Lucy Durango will attempt to ride Migraine, and for each second this young lady stays on the bull…"

Tony blocked out the announcer's voice and spoke to Lucy. "Remember to relax your spine." If she remained too stiff when the bull left the chute, she wouldn't last through the first buck.

"I will."

There were so many things he needed to warn her about, but all he managed was a nod.

She straddled Migraine then fiddled with her grip on the rope, lining up her pinky finger in the middle of the bull's back. Tony scanned the crowd for Cal and Sonja Durango but saw no sign of the couple—probably best that they weren't present. Viewing Michael's final ride would have opened old wounds.

While the announcer droned on about Wrangler matching Lucy's donations, Tony sidled up to the chute. *Look at me, Lucy.* She must have heard his silent plea, because she turned her head. "You're going to be okay." He didn't want her to try to hold on too long. "Don't be a hero."

"Heroine." She flashed a shaky smile behind the face mask then shifted her focus to the gateman and tipped her head. The chute door opened and Tony scrambled to the top rail to watch the action. Time froze—even the bull appeared to move in slow motion before his eyes.

Migraine's first buck threw Lucy forward and she struggled to stay centered. At the three-second mark, she slid parallel with Migraine's side and he prayed to God she wouldn't end up beneath the bull. His heart stopped beating as he watched her struggle to free her hand from the rope. When it came loose she managed to use the heel of her boot to push off. Her landing wasn't pretty but she'd kept enough distance between her and the bull to avoid a stomping.

Run, Lucy!

She sprang to her feet and dashed for safety while Migraine headed in the opposite direction.

"Woo-wee, folks! Lucy Durango made it three seconds on the back of Migraine! Let's show that courageous girl we appreciate her effort!"

The fans applauded and Lucy waved her hat to the crowd before stepping through the gate into the cowboy ready area.

Tony was there to greet her. "You did great."

"Thanks." Was it his imagination or was her smile strained? Cowboys congratulated Lucy, but the wrinkle across her brow deepened.

"What's the matter?"

"I bruised my wrist."

His gaze dropped to her hands. "Which one?"

"The right."

"Let me help you with your gear and then we'll have a medic check you over." First the helmet, then the vest. The fact Lucy didn't protest Tony helping her confirmed she was in pain. He packed her gear in the bag then escorted her to the first-aid area, where he hovered as a medic examined her wrist.

"A bad sprain," the paramedic said. He used a compression wrap on her wrist and forearm, then handed Lucy an ice pack.

"Hey, Lucy!" Shannon Douglas appeared. "What happened?"

"Sprained wrist. It's nothing."

"Will you be able to ride next weekend?"

"Sure."

"That's good." Shannon patted Lucy's shoulder. "The rodeo committee is counting the donations and they'll send you a check next week. I gave them your address."

"And Wrangler's matching that amount, right?" Lucy asked.

Shannon frowned. "I thought you understood."

"Understood what?" Tony invited himself into the conversation.

"Wrangler will match your donations dollar for dollar, but only if you ride in all three rodeos."

"I assumed it was per rodeo." Lucy swayed and Tony grasped her arm, worried the stress of the bull ride and her injury was making her light-headed.

"I'm sorry I didn't explain it better," Shannon said.

"Don't tell Wrangler about my sprained wrist."

"Mum's the word. Gotta go. My ride's coming up." Shannon left and Tony picked up Lucy's gear bag. He guided her to the exit, stopping first at a concession stand to buy her a soft drink. The sugar and caffeine would keep her alert. Once they reached the parking lot, he asked, "Can you drive?"

"Of course."

"Call me on my cell if you suddenly don't feel well."

"I'll be fine."

"We'll stop to eat on the way," he said.

"I'm not hungry."

He didn't know whether to be hurt, angry or indifferent to the fact that Lucy didn't want to discuss what had happened between them the other night. When they reached her truck, he tossed the gear bag into the backseat. "If you change your mind about grabbing a bite to eat—"

"There's no need to babysit me, Tony. I'm a big girl."

When she opened the truck door, Tony put his hand against the frame. "Wait."

She made eye contact and he cringed at the coolness in her gaze. What happened to the girl who'd been glad he'd shown up at the rodeo today? Miffed, he blurted, "About the other night—"

"It was a mistake."

A mistake? Shit. When Lucy put a guy down, she buried him ten feet under. "Do I owe you an apology?"

"There's nothing to be sorry for. We were both consenting adults. No harm done." She refused to meet his gaze. "Are you going to let me get into my truck?"

Tony removed his hand from the door. "Rest your wrist and don't practice this week."

"You worry too much, Tony."

You don't worry enough, Lucy. "Drive safe." Tony watched the truck turn out of the parking lot and disappear from sight.

As far as days went…this one sure as hell sucked.

CHAPTER THIRTEEN

SUNDAY MORNING LUCY stood in front of the office window in the barn, which offered a view of the gardens behind the house. She couldn't recall the last time she'd seen her mother do yard work when the temperature had already reached eighty-five by ten o'clock.

Watching her mother pull weeds brought back memories of days gone by when Lucy would hold the weed bucket and follow her mother around the yard. They'd chitchat about insects, flowers and lizards, and her mother would warn Lucy to look before she stepped in case there were snakes hiding in the rocks. Feeling nostalgic, Lucy left the barn.

"Hey, Mom." She approached the stone path where her mother knelt on a foam garden pad.

Her mother sat back on her heels and wiped her shirt sleeve across her brow. "I can't believe how big this bush has grown since Michael planted it."

Lucy dropped to her knees and tugged awkwardly with her left hand at the crabgrass growing beneath the Red Bird of Paradise shrub. Her brother had bought the bush as a mother's-day gift five years ago.

"You know what, Mom?"

"What, dear?"

"I think you should spread Michael's ashes beneath

this bush, then when you come out here to garden you can be with him."

Tears welled in her mother's eyes and Lucy held her hand. They sat in silence for several minutes before her mother nodded. "That's a wonderful idea. I'll talk to your father about it."

As they worked side by side, her mother kept glancing at the elastic wrap around Lucy's right wrist. Lucy wanted to reassure her that she wouldn't get injured in the next rodeo, but doubted her mother would believe her.

Her mother saved them both from the uncomfortable subject. "Whatever happened to that young man you dated before your brother died?"

"What young—" How could Lucy have forgotten the tale she'd spun to cover her tracks when she'd left the ASU campus to meet up with Tony on the road? Drat. What was his name?

"I think you said his name was Eric."

Her mother's recollection triggered Lucy's memory. "Eric Smith. I met him at a frat party."

"That's right. Where was he from again?"

"Chicago. We'd only been on a few dates, but he was nice enough."

"Why don't you invite him out to the ranch for a visit? Or maybe we could schedule a shopping trip to Chicago."

Lucy and her mother hadn't chatted about girl things like shopping and boyfriends in a long time and suddenly Lucy wished with all her heart that Eric Smith was real.

"I lost touch with him after I moved back home, Mom."

Her mother stood. "I think that's enough weed pulling." She returned the mat to her garden bench then said, "I made a pitcher of sangria last night. Would you like a glass?"

"It's a little early to drink, isn't it?"

Her mother's eyes twinkled. "It's five o'clock some-where, isn't it?"

Lucy laughed. "Okay, you talked me into it."

Her mother disappeared inside the house and Lucy made herself comfortable on the outdoor sectional.

Her mother returned with the pitcher and two hand-blown glass goblets. She poured the drinks then settled into the chair next to the sectional and put her feet up on the ottoman.

"This is tasty, Mom, thanks."

"I worry about you, Lucinda."

"Me? Why?"

"I never expected you to settle down in Stagecoach."

"Why? You did." Her mother had been born and raised in Southern California and had met Lucy's father when they'd both attended Stanford.

"I didn't have a choice. I loved your father and he was expected to take over the mine after he graduated."

"Any regrets?" Lucy asked.

"What are you referring to—your father or living in Arizona?"

Lucy laughed. "Arizona."

"The desert has grown on me, but there are times I miss the lushness of California."

"Is that why Dad planted so many palm trees in the yard?"

"I think he was worried I'd change my mind and return to California so he brought the Golden State here to me."

"It's a lucky thing for Dad that the ranch sits above an underground spring. There's no way all this vegetation would survive without water."

"After all this time, I still don't understand why you chose to go to college in-state when you had the grades and the opportunity to go anywhere you wanted."

"I wasn't ready to leave home," Lucy said. That was the truth. By her senior year of high school, she'd developed a huge crush on Tony. He hadn't given her the time of day and she'd naively believed that once she went off to college he'd see her as a desirable woman and not his best friend's sister. That never happened the first year of school, and eventually Lucy moved on and dated other boys. But it was no surprise that her two serious relationships in college hadn't worked out in the end—the poor guys had never measured up to Tony.

Her luck had changed when she'd gone to one of her brother's rodeos on a whim. Afterward, she'd celebrated with Michael and Tony at a local honky-tonk. She'd worn a pair of extra-tight jeans that night and a sexy tank top with rhinestones that sparkled and drew the stares of several cowboys. Tony asked her to dance to a slow song, and right there on the floor their attraction to each other exploded in their faces and the rest was history.

"Tell me the truth," her mother said. "And I mean it, Lucy. I want the truth—don't lie to me."

"Okay."

"Are you staying in Stagecoach because of me?"

"No!"

"Then why? Is the Pony Express really what you want to do with the rest of your life?"

"It's a noble cause, Mom."

"I'm not saying it isn't. But you were meant for better things, Lucy."

So was Michael.

"There are other ways you can honor your brother's memory."

Really? "How?"

"Be happy. You'll never find a young man to fall in love with if you stay in Stagecoach. Michael wouldn't want you to remain single all your life." Her mother smiled. "And I'd like to be a grandmother before I leave this earth."

Lucy chuckled.

"What's so funny?"

"I can't picture you as a grandmother."

Her mother smiled. "I know I've been busy with my charities, but after Michael died… I'm ready to slow down and appreciate the little things in life."

"Grandchildren aren't little things. They're loud, smelly and rude."

Her mother's laughter soothed Lucy's bruised soul. "Grandchildren will drive your father crazy and won't that be fun to watch."

"Mom!"

"Seriously, dear, you need to make plans for your life. You know your father will help you find a job if you want to move to Chicago."

"You're trying to get me to give up the Pony Express, aren't you?"

"I'm doing what any mother who loves her daughter would do—I'm trying to help you move on from your brother's death."

Lucy wanted to ask her mother when *she* would move on but held her tongue.

"And, I confess, I'm worried something will happen to you when you drive that van."

"I appreciate your worry but—"

"Lucy. You're the only child I have left. I love you and I don't want to lose you, but more important, I want you to live your life for you and not in your brother's shadow." She waved a hand in the air. "Sometimes when tragedy strikes, a person needs a fresh start. Your father and I are tied to the ranch so we'll never leave the area, but you're young. You can start over in a new place."

"Do you want me to leave?"

Her mother dropped her gaze to the drink in her hand. "I'd love it if you remained in Stagecoach, but only if you can be happy here."

"What if I find a man right here in Stagecoach?"

"That would be wonderful, but I doubt you will." She sat forward in her chair and hugged Lucy. "Just know that you have my support if you feel the need to move on."

"What about you, Mom? Are you ready to move on?"

Her mother's gaze shifted to the Red Bird of Paradise. "I'm getting there, dear."

Lucy squeezed her hand. "I love you, Mom."

"And I love you, too, sweetheart."

Her mother's love wrapped around her like a warm cloak and Lucy savored the feeling, knowing the truth would destroy their bond.

THE CONSTANT CLICKING of the office printer did little to drown out Tony's thoughts as he sat at his desk staring at the case file in front of him. Monday morning was either boring, because nothing had happened over the weekend, or busy, because all hell had broken loose.

The only hell breaking loose this past weekend was Lucy's bull ride in Ajo. Since then, Tony had lost count of the number of times he'd checked his cell phone for messages—not one from Lucy.

He shoved a hand through his short hair. If only they hadn't slept together, his heart wouldn't feel as if it were being ripped to shreds. He wished he could talk to his mother about his feelings for Lucy, but he knew what side of the fence she stood on and she'd only point out all the reasons they shouldn't be together.

Aside from the usual Monday-afternoon meetings, his day remained wide open. He'd already called P. T. Lewis and informed him that Lucy had sprained her wrist in Ajo and shouldn't practice on Curly this week. Shoot, someone needed to give P.T. a heads-up, and it wouldn't be Lucy. The Cibola Rodeo was six days away. If Lucy felt an urge to practice, she could use the bucking machine.

Tony set aside the file he'd been reading and logged on to the internet. He clicked on the Favorites menu, then on the Pony Express website. He stared in astonishment at the flashing dollar amount displayed on the home page—eleven-thousand dollars.

The competitor in Tony wanted Lucy to go the distance to see how much money she could raise, but the guy who was losing his heart to her wished she'd walk away from the final two rodeos and not risk further injury.

Tony wasn't sure how long he'd been glued to the computer screen when he became aware of the giant belt buckle in the shape of a gold nugget on the other side of his desk. Bracing himself, Tony exited Lucy's website then lifted his head and stared into Cal Durango's steely eyes. Intuition insisted Lucy's father hadn't stopped by to chat about the department's surveillance plans at the mine. Noticing his coworkers had stopped talking, Tony stood. "Let's talk in the hallway." He led the way out of the office, closing the door behind Durango. "What brings you into Yuma today?"

"You're the one helping my daughter kill herself, aren't you?" Durango didn't mince words.

"I did my best to talk Lucy out of her fundraising idea, but she's stubborn. She wouldn't listen."

"And because she wouldn't listen, you decided to take her under your wing and teach her everything you know about bull riding, which, if I recall, isn't much."

The insult jarred Tony, but he held his temper in check. "I'm not teaching her how to ride, I'm teaching her how to survive."

Durango's eyes widened, but he recovered quickly and delivered a counter blow. "You won't be happy until you take both my children from me, will you?"

Tony curled his hands into fists and it took every ounce of strength not to throw a punch at Lucy's father.

"You stay away from my daughter or—"

"Or what?"

"Or I'll make sure your transfer to San Diego doesn't happen."

Lucy's father had the power to manipulate other people's lives, and Michael's death was all the motivation the man needed to carry through with his threat.

"I'm not Lucy's keeper." Even as Tony said the words, he expected Durango to hold him responsible for his daughter's actions.

"The choice is yours, Bravo. Stop Lucy from competing this Saturday or you'll find yourself stuck in Arizona forever." Durango marched over to the exit and paused with his hand on the door. "You should know better than anyone that you can't outrun your mistakes. They'll follow you to the grave."

Once the door closed, Tony gulped in a deep breath. Durango had laid the blame for Michael's death at his feet—where it rightfully belonged. He slammed his fist against the wall, wincing when pain shot up his forearm. As soon as he returned to his desk, his boss called out to him.

"Bravo, get in here."

Now what? "Sir?" Tony paused in Romero's doorway.

"What did Durango want?"

"It was a private matter, sir. Nothing to do with our surveillance plans at the mine."

"Sanez decoded a message in a chat room last night," Romero said. "The cartel may be making their move soon."

"How soon?"

"Don't know. I've got everyone monitoring their assigned chat rooms right now." Romero got up from his chair and peered through the miniblinds covering the window. "I'm worried a snitch is tipping off the cartel."

"Someone in one of the chat rooms?"

"Maybe. What do you know about the foreman out at the Durango ranch?"

"Not much, why?"

"Barker was on patrol and spotted the man working on the west side of the property."

"Durango agreed to steer clear of the mine until we were through with the investigation."

"Durango is complying but not his foreman. The cowboy's fixing fence that isn't broken, picking up trash and—"

"Making sure he's visible from the highway." Tony finished his boss's sentence.

"Anyone traveling along that road is likely to see the man or his truck."

Durango was sabotaging the investigation, insuring that Tony couldn't claim credit for his hunch that a Mexican cartel was involved with human trafficking in the area.

Romero stared at Tony. "I'll ask again. What did Durango want with you a few minutes ago?"

Time to come clean. "He warned me to keep away from his daughter."

"You're involved with Lucy Durango?" The boss's eyebrows drew together. "That's a conflict of interest. You shouldn't be on this case."

"I'm not involved with Lucy...romantically." According to Lucy, making love had been no big deal. "I've been giving her tips on bull riding."

"I don't want you going within a hundred yards of Durango's daughter, you got that? If I hear of you contacting her, I'm pulling your transfer request."

"Yes, sir." Damn Durango and his meddling.

"And I'll help you keep your promise, Bravo."

"That won't be—"

"I'm assigning you to the station five watchtower."

Manning that particular watchtower was boring as hell and his boss used the duty as punishment for agents who didn't listen to orders.

"For how long, sir?"

"Until the cartel makes their move, then you can rejoin the team."

"When should I report to duty?"

"Tonight. Hernandez is out there now. I'll radio him that he's got some R & R coming."

"Anything else, sir?"

"Yes. Just so we're clear—" Romero cleared his throat "—I'm putting you in the tower because I don't want you screwing up your career."

Tony understood his boss had his best interests at heart. "Yes, sir."

"You're welcome. Now get the hell out of my office."

Ten minutes later Tony had cleared off his desk and stopped outside the officer's lounge where Maddie was sleeping on the couch. The dog had made herself at home in the department. Tony had been bringing her to work ever since the morning after he and Lucy had made love at his mother's trailer. If Lucy would return his calls, he'd tell her to come get the dog.

Tony grabbed her bowls and the dog-food bag, then snapped his fingers. "Let's go for a ride, girl." The dog leaped off the sofa and trotted after Tony.

If Tony was going to be stuck in a watchtower for days on end, he might as well take Maddie. The dog was a good listener and kept everything Tony said confidential. Maybe the boxer would help him figure out how to make his heart immune to Lucy.

HE'S NOT COMING.

Lucy stood among the cowboys behind the chutes at the Cibola Rodeo and Horse Show an hour and a half north of Yuma along the California border. Even though she'd told Tony that their lovemaking had meant nothing, she had hoped he'd show up at the rodeo to offer his support. She'd done as he'd suggested and had not practiced on Curly this past week. She'd told those who'd inquired about the wrap on her arm that it was a minor sprain, but moving her wrist still stung like heck.

To say she was nervous about executing her dismount was an understatement. She suspected the landing today would be rough and painful.

"Hey, Durango!" Shannon Douglas wore a big grin as she walked toward Lucy. "You've got a regular army of helpers out there in the parking lot asking for boot donations."

Lucy's heart swelled with gratitude. Word about her fundraiser had spread through the circuit and money was pouring into her website from all over the state. She had her brother to thank for people's generosity. Michael had been a favorite among rodeo fans. He'd given autographs and had always taken the time to speak with the kids who worshipped him.

"I'm getting closer to my goal," she said. Lucy hoped to reach the twenty-thousand-dollar mark once Wrangler matched today's earnings.

"Did you take a look at your bull yet?" Shannon asked.

"Yes." She'd drawn Trickster. Maybe it was her imagination, but the black bull appeared larger and more menacing than Migraine.

"Trickster's only four years old. He's new on the circuit and he's sloppy."

"What do you mean, sloppy?"

"He doesn't have much of a rhythm to his kicks or spins. My advice is to stick like glue to his back, but if you lose your balance, take the first opening and dismount. Trickster's not known to turn on his riders but he also doesn't run for the gate right away. When you hit the ground, get to your feet as fast as you can."

"Got it," Lucy said, watching the crowd.

"Tony's not coming today?" Shannon asked.

"I don't think so." Lucy sensed Shannon wanted to ask why. Instead, the cowgirl changed the subject.

"Same drill as last time. You and Trickster will kick off the bull-riding event this afternoon after they play the video of Michael's final ride." Shannon's sympathetic smile made Lucy's eyes sting. She shoved aside the melancholy—she couldn't afford to lose sight of her goal before she straddled two thousand pounds of pissed-off bull.

"I'll be back before you ride." Shannon strolled away.

Lucy owed much of her fundraising success to Shannon—the lady bull rider had gone above and beyond to help raise money for the Pony Express. Left alone to wait, Lucy put on her protective gear and stood in the shadows, keeping her eyes averted from the JumboTron.

Once the announcer said her name, she stepped forward and waved to the crowd while rodeo helpers loaded Trickster into the chute and fished the rope beneath the bull. After the hoopla died down, Lucy closed her eyes and envisioned Tony's face. She wanted to make him proud of her.

After she counted to five, her nerves settled down and she climbed the chute rails and eased onto Trickster. The heat radiating off the bull's back warmed her muscles and her adrenaline kicked into gear. She lined up her pinky finger with the middle of his back then Shannon appeared at her side.

"Tell me when it feels right." Shannon wrapped the

rope around Lucy's hand, sparing Lucy from having to use her injured wrist to pull the rope tight.

"That's good, thanks." Once Shannon moved away, Lucy mentally checked off Tony's list of bull-riding dos and don'ts.

"Remember to locate the bull as soon as you hit the ground." Shannon's voice interrupted Lucy's concentration.

Lucy dipped her head—a rookie mistake. The gateman had been watching for her signal and mistook the movement as *ready to ride*. The gate swung open before Lucy had leaned forward over the bull's shoulder and she almost lost her seat when Trickster cleared the chute. Once inside the arena, she fought with every ounce of strength she possessed to remain on the bull. Her bottom smacked up and down, jarring her spine and forcing the air from her lungs. Then Trickster twisted his back end, launching Lucy into the air.

Unprepared for the dismount, she instinctively stretched out her arms toward the ground instead of tucking her right arm against her body and absorbing the impact with her shoulder. Her hands and arms bore the full weight of her body when she hit the dirt. For an instant, she thought she'd escaped injury, then she spotted the bull's hindquarters spinning toward her and she dove sideways to avoid his hooves.

The sudden movement twisted her right arm and she felt the snap of her wrist. Pain raced along her arm, across her shoulder, straight up her neck and into her skull. Her arm gave out beneath her and her face mask slammed into the dirt.

Get up! Get up!

Tony's voice echoed inside her head, spurring her into action. She rolled to her feet and checked over her shoulder—Trickster continued to buck and spin. Lucy ran for the rails then attempted to climb to safety using only her left hand. Her boot slipped on the metal rung and a rodeo helper sprang into action, grabbing her by the waist and hoisting her to safety.

Lucy gasped for breath.

"That was five seconds." Shannon patted Lucy's back. "Next time you'll make it to eight."

There might not be a next time. Lucy fumbled with the chin strap on her face mask and Shannon frowned. "What's wrong?"

"Nothing. I'm fine." Lucy managed to remove the headgear and awkwardly stuffed it into her bag. She grasped the handles with her left hand. "I'd stay and watch you, Shannon, but I have to get back to the ranch."

"No worries. See you next week in Cowlic."

Gritting her teeth, Lucy headed to the parking lot still wearing her Kevlar vest. When she reached the truck, she rummaged through the center console and found the bottle of ibuprofen she kept there. She swallowed three tablets, using her spit to wash them down. With one hand, she carefully maneuvered the pickup out of her spot and drove south to Yuma, where she planned to stop at the E.R. and have her wrist x-rayed.

An hour and a half later, Lucy's arm and shoulder were numb. Her wrist had swelled up and she was forced to loosen the elastic wrap on her arm. Once she arrived at the hospital a nurse helped her fill out the paperwork then escorted her to a cubical and took her vitals. While Lucy waited to be taken for X-rays she checked her phone messages—nothing from Tony. Would he call tonight to find out how she did?

The orthopedic surgeon diagnosed a clean break and put a hot pink cast on Lucy's arm. He advised her to see her own doctor before sending her on her way with a prescription for pain pills and a warning to steer clear of bulls for at least six weeks.

Fat chance. Lucy had to compete in Cowlic seven days from now. Otherwise Wrangler wouldn't match her donations. Once she completed her final rodeo, she would gladly leave bull riding to the professionals like Shannon Douglas.

After stopping at a drugstore to fill the prescription, Lucy swung into the drive-through of a fast-food restaurant then continued on to Stagecoach. She wanted nothing more than to return home so she could take a big-girl pain pill and fall asleep.

By the time she parked in front of the ranch house it was dark outside. She wasn't looking forward to her mother's reaction when she learned Lucy had broken her wrist. If she was lucky, she'd be able to sneak up to her room and put off the meeting until tomorrow morning. When her boot hit the bottom porch step, the outside light went on, blinding her. Her father's silhouette filled the screen door.

"Hey, Dad."

The door creaked open and he stepped outside. "What happened?" He nodded to the cast on her arm.

"It's not a big deal."

"What's not a big deal?" Her mother joined them, a gin and tonic in her hand. A twinge of empathy shot through Lucy. No doubt her mother had paced the hallway for hours, worried over her.

"It appears our daughter has a broken arm."

Lucy's mother gasped then shoved her drink at her husband and rushed down the steps.

"I'm fine, Mom. It was a clean break. The doctor said the bone will heal in no time." Lucy allowed her mother to usher her into the house.

"What happened?" she asked.

Lucy resisted the temptation to say that she'd fallen in the parking lot. "I landed wrong after I got bucked today."

"This foolishness has to stop, Lucy."

"Not now, Dad." She was in no mood to go toe-to-toe with her father. "Let me get cleaned up then I'll tell you all about the rodeo." She climbed the stairs to the second floor and her bedroom, where she took a pain pill then checked her cell phone again.

Still no text from Tony.

He hadn't wanted her to ride today, but didn't he care how she did? Mentally, emotionally and physically exhausted, she collapsed on the bed. She'd rest for a few minutes then take a shower.

CHAPTER FOURTEEN

LUCY WOKE TO voices in the hallway outside her room. She sat up on the bed and waited for the walls to stop spinning. Her father's voice grew louder and her mother shushed him. Lucy crossed the room and stood behind the door, listening through the crack.

"You can't let her ride in Cowlic, Cal."

"This is all Bravo's fault."

"Then make him stop."

"I thought I had."

Lucy's scalp tingled.

"What do you mean?" her mother asked.

"I paid him a visit at the border patrol station and told him that if he wanted a job transfer to San Diego he'd better keep his distance from Lucy."

Her father had threatened Tony?

"She's going to get herself killed." Her mother's voice quivered. "Stop her, Cal. I can't lose both my children."

Tears welled in Lucy's eyes.

"I'll phone the rodeo producers in Cowlic and make it clear that our daughter is to be banned from riding any animal on four legs."

Lucy had no doubt her father would carry through with his threat. Whether she was ready or not, it was time to come clean with her parents.

Did you think you could avoid the truth forever?

In no shape to go nine rounds with her father, she opened the door and stepped into the hallway.

"You're up," her father said.

"I need to talk to you and Mom." Lucy headed for the stairs.

"Damn straight we're going to talk, young lady."

"For goodness' sake, Cal, settle down." Her mother grabbed Lucy's uninjured arm and descended the steps with her, then walked her into the living room at the front of the house. "Do you want something to drink, dear?"

"Water, please." Her mother hurried from the room, leaving Lucy and her father to square off.

"Was Bravo at the rodeo?"

"No." Now she knew why. "Is it true? You told Tony to stay away from me?"

"I don't know what's gotten into you, Lucy." Her father shoved a hand through his hair. "Ever since your brother passed away you haven't been able to…"

"Go ahead and say it."

"Let him go." He glared, defying her to contradict him.

"Let who go?" Her mother returned with Lucy's water.

"Tony has nothing to do with my rodeo fundraiser. I asked him to teach me how to last a few seconds on a bull. At first he refused, but I blackmailed him."

Her mother gasped. "Lucinda Durango."

"I told Tony that if he'd give me a few pointers on bull riding, I'd convince Dad to give him access to the gold mine for his investigation."

"Then it is his fault!" her father shouted.

"Tony tried to talk me out of it," Lucy said. "But when

he realized I intended to compete with or without his help, he insisted on teaching me how to remain as safe as possible."

"A lot of good his advice did." Her father motioned to her cast.

"Tony wasn't at the rodeo today." Lucy swallowed the lump in her throat. Even though she understood why he hadn't shown up in Cibola, she was disappointed that he'd picked his job over her.

You're the one who told him making love didn't matter. That it wasn't a big deal.

"I don't understand what's going on between you and Bravo, but damn it, Lucy, he's responsible for Michael's—"

"No, he's not."

"If he'd stayed at the bar and given Michael a ride home, your brother would be alive today."

"No, Dad." Lucy shook her head. "I was the one who turned my back on Michael the night he died."

Her parents stared in shock.

The words crowded her throat, but forcing them from her mouth was the toughest thing Lucy had ever done. "After Tony left the bar, Michael called me. He said he'd had too much to drink, and he asked me to come get him."

Her mother pressed her fingertips to her mouth and tears slid down her cheeks.

"I told Michael to call Dad for a ride." Lucy dropped her gaze to the Persian rug.

"Why?" her father choked out.

"I didn't want to help Michael because I was jealous of his relationship with you, Dad." Where was the relief she thought she'd feel at finally confessing her guilt? Swiping angrily at a tear, she said, "You believed Michael walked on water because he was good at rodeo. I—" her voice cracked "—wanted you to see that he wasn't as perfect as you made him out to be."

Her father stared dumbstruck.

Lucy looked beseechingly at her mother. "Dad never had time for me. He was too busy grooming Michael to be a rodeo superstar." She swallowed hard. "Had I known that Michael would risk driving himself home to avoid disappointing Dad, I would have driven out to the bar that night and picked him up." Lucy chanced a look at her father, but he'd turned his back to her.

"I know there's nothing I can do to save Michael now, but I've been trying to make it up to you." Her voice broke on a sob. "I started the Pony Express because I wanted to honor Michael's memory and I'd hoped that you'd be proud of me for doing that." Tears poured down her face. "Please stop blaming Tony, Dad. I'm the reason Michael's dead." Lucy fled the room, her heart shattering into a million pieces when neither parent stopped her.

Back in her room she paced the floor, anxiety and sadness suffocating her. She had to get out of the house. Grabbing her cell phone and truck keys, she returned downstairs and passed by the living room, where her parents remained immobilized by her confession.

Once in her truck, she sped toward the highway. She glanced in her rearview mirror, hoping to spot her father or mother signaling her to return.

The porch remained as dark and empty as Lucy's heart.

LUCY PULLED OFF the road near the west entrance to the Durango ranch and checked the dashboard clock. Midnight. Up until now she'd been successful in ignoring thoughts of Michael and her parents, but she suspected her subconscious had been hard at work the entire time she'd been driving.

She stared at the chain on the gate, anger and despair warring inside her. What lay in the desert beyond that gate—the Durango Gold Mine—was the root of all evil, or so she wanted to believe. Easier to blame a tangible object for the pain in her life, instead of her own actions.

What would her life have been like if there had been no gold mine? No wealth or power connected to the Durango name? She gripped the steering wheel with her un-injured hand until pain shot up her forearm.

Her mother's horrified expression flashed through her mind and tears welled in her eyes. Lucy couldn't possibly understand the depth of her mother's pain. Both her parents must have felt a devastating sense of helplessness at not having been able to prevent their son's death. Even so, Lucy was positive their pain couldn't compare to the agony ripping her insides to shreds. Jealousy over her brother's relationship with their father had been no reason to leave Michael sitting at the bar. Her own stupidity and immaturity had robbed her parents of a son, her of a brother, Tony a best friend and Maddie a loving master.

In the end, Lucy accepted that no matter how awful she felt, how much she regretted her actions, how hard she worked to make amends for her past, there was no way to fix this. Nothing would bring Michael back.

She could ride a million bulls and it would still never be enough to earn her parents' forgiveness or allow her to forgive herself. As she sat in the truck, the reality of her situation hit home. Now that her parents knew the truth they'd want nothing to do with her, and she couldn't blame them. Lucy's throat tightened. Any hope of a relationship with her father had died when he'd turned his back on her in the living room, but maybe her mother wouldn't abandon her. A mother's love was unconditional. With time maybe she would forgive Lucy, but even if she did, every time she looked at Lucy she'd know her daughter had been the one responsible for her son's death.

Driven by an invisible force, Lucy left the truck to unlock the chain and open the gate. A reckless feeling took hold inside her as she returned to her vehicle and drove on. A voice inside her head demanded she stop, but Lucy pressed the accelerator to the floor.

Whatever fate awaited her in the dark desert was well deserved.

TONY SCANNED THE desert with a night-vision camera, Maddie resting on the floor by his boots. Nothing but darkness lurked outside the watchtower. "Looks like the bad guys have taken a break for a while." He set aside the camera. "Where's Lucy, Maddie?" The dog's ears perked.

Tony had waited all afternoon and evening for a text from Lucy, telling him how she'd done at the rodeo, but she hadn't reached out to him. The longer he went without hearing from her, the greater his anxiety grew, but he refused to consider something bad might have happened.

Damn it, he hated being stuck in the middle of this dried-up wasteland. He'd been banished to the post five days ago and the only thing he'd encountered was a herd of javelinas.

He had one more day left before he and Maddie could return home. Tony's boss had radioed him earlier with the news that they'd received a tip from a chat room, suggesting members of the drug cartel planned to smuggle a group of girls across the border on Tuesday or Wednesday night. Tony and the other agents were heading to the Durango Gold Mine on Monday evening in the event the cartel arrived a day early.

His cell vibrated and he glanced at the display screen. "It's Lucy, Maddie. Let's see how she did at the rodeo."

SOS. Gold mine.

Fear swept through Tony before instinct kicked in and he shifted into border patrol mode. "Maddie, come." He descended the watchtower stairs and jogged to his truck, the dog running ahead of him. Once he was on the road driving toward the Durango ranch, he phoned his boss.

"What's wrong?" Romero said as soon as he answered Tony's call.

"I just got a text from Lucy Durango. She's out at the Durango Mine and she's in trouble." A nagging uneasiness had plagued Tony all day but he'd attributed it to his worry that Lucy would get injured at the rodeo.

"What kind of trouble, Bravo?"

"I don't know."

Romero swore. "It's possible our chat-room snitch tried to mislead us and the girls were brought across the border tonight."

"I'm headed there now," Tony said.

"We're right behind you," Romero said. "And Tony, don't do anything stupid."

"Roger." Tony disconnected the call and pressed the gas pedal to the floor. *What the hell were you thinking,*

Lucy? Why the heck had she gone out to the mine at this time of night? He gripped the steering wheel until the bones in his fingers ached. If he thought about what the cartel might do to Lucy if they caught her, he'd go insane.

When he arrived at the west entrance to the ranch, the gate stood wide open. He switched on the parking lights and drove through. A mile from the mine he flipped off the truck lights and parked. Using night-vision binoculars, he scanned the area. Lucy's truck sat parked in front of the mine where several boards had been removed from the entrance. Nina had described the van her kidnappers had used to transport the girls but it was nowhere in sight. Tony could only hope that Lucy's call for help had nothing to do with her stumbling upon the cartel.

"Stay here, Maddie." Tony lowered the windows partway to allow air into the truck. "No barking." He shut the door quietly then headed toward the mine, gun drawn.

Senses on high alert, he cut a trail through the desert. He froze fifty yards out when angry Spanish-speaking voices echoed through the dark. The worst possible scenario—the cartel had captured Lucy.

Heart thumping hard, Tony inched closer and hid behind the rear bumper of Lucy's truck. The men continued to argue and Tony shivered as his sweat-soaked shirt turned icy against his skin. The Sinaloa Cartel was known to torture witnesses and snitches—no way would they allow Lucy to walk free tonight. He removed his iPhone from his pocket and sent a short text, alerting his boss to the situation. As he slipped the phone into his back pocket, two men armed with semiautomatic weapons and dressed from head to toe in black emerged from behind a cluster of rocks.

One of the men lit a cigarette while the other entered the mine. A moment later, Lucy stumbled out. Relief that she appeared unharmed left Tony light-headed and he breathed deeply through his nose, forcing himself to remain focused. Lucy's life depended on him keeping a level head.

He'd made a huge mistake leaving Michael at the bar two years ago. Getting Lucy out of this predicament alive was his chance to make amends to Cal and Sonja Durango. And if that wasn't motivation to do things right, then needing to save Lucy because he loved her was reason enough not to screw up. The thought of losing her terrified him.

While the men argued, Tony watched Lucy. Her hands were tied behind her back and a gag had been placed in her mouth. Thank God she didn't understand Spanish or she'd probably faint if she knew her captors were discussing how to dispose of her.

Forcing his fears aside, he assessed the situation. Two against one—not bad odds. He could fire off two rounds before they sprayed bullets in his direction.

Without warning, the taller of the two men turned toward Lucy's truck and fired at the front tires. Amazed he hadn't been hit by a stray bullet, Tony watched in horror as the man backhanded Lucy across the face. She dropped to her knees.

Tony's blood boiled. *Don't be stubborn, baby. Just do as he says.* Romero and the other agents would arrive at any moment—but that moment could mean the difference between life and death for Lucy. The tall man disappeared behind the rocks while the other man went into the mine and led out eight girls with their hands tied behind their backs.

Evil bastards.

Lucy slowly got to her feet and the girls huddled around her. The sound of an engine rumbled in the air and a black cargo van drove into sight. The tall man got out and told the girls to get in. Lucy remained behind and Tony could only imagine the terror she was experiencing.

It was now or never. Tony had to make a move. The girls were safe inside the van so he inched toward the front of Lucy's truck, stepping over her smashed cell phone.

The tall man's next words chilled Tony to the bone. There was no time to think—only react. He stood, steadied his arm on the roof of the truck and fired twice, hitting both men in the upper shoulder. The tall man sprayed bullets across the windshield of Lucy's truck as he fell to the ground.

"Run, Lucy!"

Tony's shout propelled her into action and she fled into the mine. Tony kept his eyes on the wounded men—the tall one lay motionless but the shorter man crawled toward his weapon a few feet away.

"Toca la pistola y te mueres!" The man froze. The bastard wanted to live to see tomorrow. Too bad, because Tony was in a make-my-day mood.

Tony heard whimpers inside the van and warned the girls to remain where they were. *"No te muevas, niñas."*

The gunman grimaced and spat, *"Eres un hombre muerto caminando."*

Death threats were nothing new in Tony's line of work, but after bringing down two members of the notorious Sinaloa Cartel, he'd have to watch his back more than ever. He stepped into the open. Keeping his gun trained on the men, Tony picked up the weapons. *C'mon, Romero. Get here now.*

As if his boss heard Tony's silent summons, truck engines echoed through the desert. The vehicles drew closer, shining their headlights on the mine, and Tony got his first good look at the men. If he'd seen them walking along the street in downtown Yuma, he would have never guessed they were ruthless criminals.

What followed was anticlimatic. The border patrol agents collected the weapons and handcuffed the men, then called for medical assistance. Tony rushed into the mine and Lucy stumbled into his arms. He removed the gag from her mouth and sobs escaped her as she buried her face against his neck. "Thank God, you're okay," he said, turning her away from him so he could untie her hands. He grasped her arm with the cast. "What happened?"

"I broke my wrist at the rodeo." Her lower lip wobbled. "Don't be mad."

Mad? Hell, he was so damned relieved nothing had happened to her tonight. Not caring that his boss stood in the mine entrance, Tony hugged Lucy again.

A million things could have gone wrong but luckily no one but the bad guys had paid a price. He guided Lucy out of the mine and they watched the agents load the injured men in a border patrol vehicle and drive off to meet the rescue unit at the ranch entrance. Romero and another agent helped the girls from the van and untied their hands, reassuring them that everything would be okay. The girls piled into two of the border patrol vehicles and were driven back to the station for questioning. Tony, Romero and Lucy remained at the crime scene.

"Lucy, this is Deputy Chief Patrol Agent Cesar Romero."

"Are you hurt, Lucy?" Romero asked.

"No, sir."

"How did you get caught up in all this?" he asked.

"Sir, Lucy's been through hell tonight. Can she come into the station tomorrow morning and give her statement?"

Romero stared at Tony as if he'd lost his mind. They'd just arrested two members of the Sinaloa Cartel who'd smuggled kidnapped girls from Mexico into the States and Tony wanted him to wait to learn the details of what had happened tonight. "No, it's not okay, Bravo."

"I'll give a statement, but I'd like to sit down," Lucy said.

Tony walked her over to her truck and she sat on the front bumper. Romero brought her a bottle of water from his truck.

"Thank you." Lucy drank the entire contents then closed her eyes. "Are all the girls okay?" she asked.

"They're fine," Romero said. "What made you come out here tonight?"

Lucy's eyes filled with misery. "It's personal."

Romero frowned at Tony.

"The men must have seen the headlights of my truck coming and hidden, because when I reached the mine, there was no one in sight. I sat in my truck for a minute and looked around, and that's when I noticed the boards had been removed from the mine entrance. I knew something was wrong, so I texted Tony."

"Why didn't you turn around and leave?" Romero asked.

"I tried, but as soon as I put the truck in Reverse, the men came out of nowhere and pointed their weapons at me. I knew if I drove away they'd shoot, so I got out of the truck. I couldn't understand any of their shouting, then one of them tied my hands and gagged me."

"What about the girls?" Tony asked. "Where were they?"

"Already in the mine."

"Did they tell you anything about the men or what had happened to them?" Romero asked.

"No. They were terrified."

"Okay. That's good enough for now."

They all got into Romero's truck and the boss drove them back to Tony's vehicle. After Lucy and Tony climbed out, Romero said, "Assure Lucy's father that I'll be in touch soon."

After his boss drove off, Tony grasped Lucy's hand and stared her in the eye. "Why the heck were you out driving by yourself this late at night?"

"I don't want to talk about it." When she got into Tony's truck she was greeted with a slobbery dog kiss. "You're a sight for sore eyes, girl." Lucy hugged the boxer.

Tony slid behind the wheel. "How did you break your arm?"

"Sloppy dismount. You would have known that if you'd come to watch me." She stared out the windshield.

"I wanted to, but—"

"My father warned you to stop seeing me or he'd make sure you didn't get your transfer to San Diego."

"He told you?"

She scowled. "I didn't think you were afraid of my father."

"The threat of losing my transfer isn't what stopped me from showing up today."

"Then what did?" she whispered.

"My boss banished me to watchtower duty. I was sitting up in a tower in the middle of nowhere when I got your text."

"Oh."

He nodded to the cast on her arm. "Was it a clean break?" He hated that she'd broken a bone, but a part of him was secretly relieved the injury would prevent her from competing in the final rodeo.

"Yes. The doctor said my wrist will be good as new in six weeks."

Tony started the engine and turned the truck toward the highway. "Is Shannon upset that you won't be riding in Cowlic?"

"Who said I'm not riding?"

"You can't be serious." A sense of déjà vu hit Tony, stealing his breath. They'd had this same argument before the rodeo in Cibola.

"I have to ride in all three rodeos or Wrangler won't pay me. I'm going to finish what I started."

Anger burned in Tony's chest. After what had happened tonight he would have thought she'd look at life differently and quit taking unnecessary risks.

Back on the highway Lucy asked, "When are you leaving for San Diego?"

"I don't know. Transfers take time." He refused to allow her to change the subject. "You're in no shape to ride next weekend."

"You're entitled to your opinion, but I'll do as I please."

"Michael wouldn't want you to take this kind of risk."

"My brother's dead. You can't know what he would have wanted."

"Think of your parents, Lucy." *Think of me.* "They lost one child already." *And I don't want to lose you.* After witnessing Lucy in danger tonight, Tony gave up trying to convince himself that he didn't love her.

"I don't want to talk about the rodeo or my parents."

They drove the rest of the way to the ranch house in silence. When Tony parked the truck, he struggled to find the words to change Lucy's mind about competing in Cowlic. "Lucy."

Tell her. For God's sake just tell her you love her. His throat closed and he couldn't speak.

"C'mon, Maddie." The dog jumped out of the truck. "Good luck in San Diego," Lucy said, then shut the door in Tony's face.

Lucy was making a habit of shutting the door in his face and Tony didn't like it—not one damned bit.

CHAPTER FIFTEEN

TONY PARKED IN front of the entrance to the Fiesta Travel Stop. He'd come to tell his mother the good news—he'd been granted a transfer to the San Diego Sector of U.S. Customs and Border Protection. Four days had passed since he and his fellow agents had cracked the human-smuggling ring. The young girls had been reunited with their families and U.S. officials had made arrests in Minnesota and Iowa in connection with a prostitution ring the Mexican gang ran. Tony felt a sense of professional satisfaction that his hunch had paid off and it would be a long time before the Sinaloa Cartel operated along this stretch of Arizona desert again.

The truck stop was crowded for a Thursday. He paused inside the door and searched for his mother among the waitresses. She waved him toward an empty booth by a front window. Five minutes later, she set two cups of coffee on the table and sat across from him.

"I know why you're here." Her smile didn't reach her eyes. "The transfer came through."

Tony nodded. A transfer to San Diego had been his goal for two years, but he hardly felt a sense of relief at leaving Stagecoach and Yuma behind.

"What's the matter, honey? Isn't moving to California what you've wanted for a long time?"

"I thought it was." He gulped the brew, the hot liquid searing his throat.

"Change of heart?" His mother didn't try to disguise the hope in her voice.

"You know I want to leave Arizona because of what happened to Michael."

"Yes."

"But his death wasn't the only reason I thought I needed to leave." Before his mother bombarded him with questions and he lost his nerve, Tony said, "I thought it would be best for Lucy."

His mother's eyes rounded.

"I never told you, but Lucy and I were dating when Michael crashed his truck."

"How? When?"

"We saw each other on weekends. Lucy would leave campus and drive to wherever Michael and I were rodeoing. She didn't watch us ride. She waited for me in my motel room. After the competition, I'd tell Michael I wasn't feeling well or was tired and he'd head to the bars alone while I spent the night with Lucy. The next morning she left before Michael and I hit the road."

"And Michael never guessed what you two were doing behind his back?"

"Nope. We managed to keep the affair a secret from both our families."

"Why?"

"C'mon, Mom. You know Cal Durango would never have approved of me dating his daughter. And neither would you."

Unable to defend herself, his mother remained silent.

"But that's not the only reason we didn't tell anyone.

Michael was winning big-time on the circuit and neither of us wanted to do anything that would create a conflict that might affect his performance."

"That was a very unselfish gesture on your parts."

"Our generosity didn't last long. Lucy and I got tired of meeting on the sly. The last time we were together in Prescott, we decided that we'd tell our families during Lucy's spring break."

"Then Michael died."

"And Lucy and I drifted apart."

"But now you want her back," his mother said.

"I know how you feel about me dating Anglo girls and I don't want to let you down." His heart clenched at the tears that welled in his mother's eyes.

"You could never disappoint me, Tony. You're my son and no matter what, I love you."

"Would you have told me to stop seeing Lucy if you'd known we were dating?"

"Yes." Her chin jutted. "And Cal Durango would have told you to keep away from his daughter, too."

"No man will ever be good enough for Cal Durango's daughter. What I need to understand, Mom, is why you have such strong feelings against interracial dating and marriage."

"I'm not against mixed marriages."

"You're just against them for me?"

"I'm not sure how to explain."

"Try."

"When your father died, I was torn between staying in the United States and returning to my family in Mexico. I chose to stay and become a U.S. citizen because I knew that's what your father would have wanted for you." His mother waved at a coworker who entered the truck stop with her husband. "As you grew older, I worried that your Anglo friends and education would change you, and you'd forget your heritage. I had hoped that by marrying a Hispanic girl, you'd stay true to your roots."

"I know who I am, Mom. I won't ever forget where you and Dad came from."

"I guess I'm selfish. I want to live in America and enjoy the benefits and freedoms I have in this country, but at the same time, I want to honor our family's legacy." The corner of her mouth tilted. "Do you love Lucy?"

"Yes, I love her."

"Then why did you drift apart after Michael died?"

"I blamed myself for Michael's death and I didn't believe Lucy could forgive me for that."

"So you tried to start over with Evita?"

"And I realized I couldn't marry her, because I hadn't stopped loving Lucy."

"Have you told Lucy how you feel?" When he didn't answer she asked, "What are you afraid of?"

"That I don't deserve to be happy after I abandoned my best friend the night he died."

"Honey, you might have left the bar before Michael did that night, but you never abandoned him. In fact, I suspect you were the one to make most of the sacrifices throughout your friendship."

"I don't understand."

"You think I wasn't aware that you wanted to stop rodeoing well before Michael began winning."

"I never told you that."

"You didn't have to. I'm your mother. I know these things. But you didn't quit, did you?"

"Every time I brought it up with Michael he talked me out of it."

"And then you fell in love with Lucy, and you sacrificed spending more time with her so you could stay on the circuit with Michael."

"The night I left the bar, Michael and I argued because I told him I wanted to quit. He trusted me to have his back and he said the only way he'd make it to the NFR was if I was by his side every step of the way."

"Would you have continued to rodeo with Michael if he hadn't died?"

"Yes. I left the bar pissed off at myself because I couldn't say no to Michael, and that meant Lucy and I couldn't make our relationship public until after the NFR—that is, if Lucy didn't break up with me before then."

"You were willing to sacrifice your relationship with Lucy to help your best friend achieve his dream."

"But that doesn't change the fact that I should have stayed with Michael at the bar."

"You and Michael were as close as any blood brothers could be. He'd never want you to punish yourself for his death or allow guilt to tarnish the memory of your friendship."

"I want to believe that, Mom."

"Then allow yourself to believe it, because Michael would be thrilled to know you love his sister. If he were alive, he'd encourage you two to be together."

"If I can convince Lucy to give me a second chance, could you accept a marriage between us?"

"Your happiness means more to me than any of my old-fashioned values. If Lucy makes you happy, then yes,

I will gladly welcome her into our little family and love her like a daughter."

"Good, because I'm planning to ask her to marry me."

His mother squirmed in her seat.

"What's the matter?"

"Nothing…really."

"Mom…?"

"I told Lucy it was a mistake for you two to be together because her father would only make trouble for you."

"When did you talk to her?"

"The morning after you two slept together in the trailer."

No wonder Lucy had acted as if making love had been no big deal. "Do me a favor, Mom."

"Anything."

"From now on, stay out of my love life." Tony slid from the booth then kissed his mother's cheek and high-tailed it out of the truck stop.

THE DAY OF the Cowlic Rodeo dawned bright and hot. Lucy ate her breakfast alone in the kitchen, Maddie lying on the floor beneath the table. Her parents had done an admirable job of avoiding her all week, and she had not exchanged more than a few words with them. Yesterday she'd walked into the kitchen and had caught her mother crying. Their gazes had connected, and Lucy had wanted to hug her mother until the sadness left her eyes, but she'd chickened out and fled the room.

Lucy hadn't felt this alone in a long time. Had she made a mistake in coming clean with her parents? The truth should have set her free. Instead, it had sentenced her and her parents to a private hell. Maybe she should have taken the truth about the night Michael died to her grave.

She finished her oatmeal and banana and walked Maddie around the yard before putting her in the kennel. Gear bag in hand, she headed for the truck she'd leased while her vehicle was in the repair shop. Taking her time, she loaded her things into the backseat, searched her purse for nothing, fussed with the GPS.

In the end, her stalling hadn't brought her parents outside to wish her good luck or offer a warning to be careful.

With a heavy heart, she drove off. Right before the road curved, she glanced in the rearview mirror and her heart leaped in her throat. Her father stood on the porch. With time, would he forgive her? She'd tried hard to make amends for the past and she'd believed for a while that she and her father had been growing closer. Was there still a chance for them?

Then there was Tony. She had to find the courage to tell him about Michael's phone call to her. Once she confessed, Tony would leave Stagecoach and her behind with a clear conscience.

An hour later, Lucy pulled into the parking lot of the outdoor arena in Cowlic. Shannon's truck sat parked by the livestock trailers and Lucy found a spot nearby. She walked through the arena, searching for the Wrangler booth, which was set up next to the stands.

Shannon's eyes widened when she spotted the pink cast peeking out from beneath Lucy's long-sleeved Western shirt.

"Turns out I broke my wrist at the Cibola Rodeo," Lucy said.

"Why didn't you tell me?" Shannon planted her fists on her hips and shook her head. "You can't ride today."

"Why not?" Lucy spread her arms wide. "Cowboys ride with casts, splints and braces all the time."

"You're not a cowboy, Lucy. You're not even a cowgirl."

"Thanks for dissing me." Lucy cracked a smile, hoping to lighten the mood.

"I admire your gumption, but—"

"I have to ride, Shannon. If I don't, Wrangler won't match my earnings and I need that money to keep the Pony Express in business." Lucy hurried away before Shannon registered another protest.

"You're riding Cruise Control!"

Lucy kept walking but lifted her arm to signal that she'd heard. *Cruise Control.* Crazy name for a bull. She stopped at the pen and a livestock helper pointed out a brindle-striped bull with a gray face. Tail twitching at the flies buzzing around his back end, the animal stared at her from across the pen.

"You don't look menacing," she muttered.

"Don't let that bull fool you." The helper spit tobacco juice on the ground. "Once he works himself into high gear he stays there for the rest of the ride."

"So that's how he got his name," she said.

"He's only been ridden ten times in the past eight years."

No worries there. Lucy didn't plan to ride him—she planned to survive him.

"You that Lucy Durango who's raising money for the Pony Express?" the man asked.

"That's me." She offered her hand.

"Name's Aaron." He leaned his head down and whispered, "As soon as you hit the ground, run like hell. Cruise Control's unpredictable."

"Thanks for the warning." Lucy waited for her adrenaline to spike from fear or excitement. Nothing. She didn't break out in a sweat and her muscles didn't turn to jelly. She was going to be in big trouble if she couldn't muster the strength to get on the bull, much less hold on when the gate opened.

The sound of a throat clearing caught Lucy's attention and she glanced over her shoulder. *Tony.* Her heartbeat, which only moments before had been slow and steady, suddenly pounded like a jackhammer.

Tony's dark gaze held hers. "Don't ride, Lucy. Please."

"You don't have to do this, Tony."

"Do what?"

"Try to stop me because you're concerned about your job."

Turmoil darkened his eyes. "You believe I'm here because of my job?" The steely edge in his voice should have warned Lucy that he wasn't backing down, but she was oblivious to anything but her own heartache.

She took her gear bag and returned to the bull chutes, Tony following her. She put on her Kevlar vest then rubbed rosin on her riding glove. "My father won't interfere with your transfer to San Diego."

"I know." Tony stepped closer and tucked a lock of hair behind Lucy's ear, his finger lingering long enough to induce a shiver. "You're the one interfering with my transfer."

The adrenaline rush she'd been waiting for hummed

through her blood, stealing air from her lungs. "I don't understand."

"I declined the job in San Diego."

"Why?"

"Because I'm done running from the past and what I want is right here in Stagecoach." He tilted her chin. "I want you, Lucy. I want what we had before Michael died."

Heart crumbling into pieces, she choked on the words as she forced them from her lips. "Take the transfer. You'll be happier."

The warmth drained from his eyes and Lucy hated that she was hurting him, but he needed to know the truth. "There's something I haven't told you about the night Michael died."

"Lucy, don't—"

"You need to hear this, Tony. After you left Michael at the bar, he called me and asked if I'd pick him up."

Tony sucked in a quick breath.

"I told him to call our father for a ride and then I hung up on him."

"Why didn't you go get him?" Tony's dark eyes reflected disbelief.

"You can't understand what it was like growing up in Michael's shadow." She wiped the tears that escaped her eyes. "Just once, I wanted my father to see that Michael wasn't perfect, but I never wanted my brother to die." Her voice cracked. "And I never meant for my selfish actions to impact your life and leave you feeling guilty. I'm so sorry, Tony."

"Have you told your parents?"

"Yes." And, as she'd feared, she might have lost their

love for good. "I'm sorry for the pain I've caused you, Tony. I don't expect your forgiveness, but I hope you'll be able to move on from Michael's death, because you truly do deserve to be happy." She removed the bull rope from the gear bag and handed it to a cowboy manning the chute.

"You're in no shape to ride," Tony said.

"I have to ride for Michael."

Tony paced five steps away then turned and glared. "That's what you want me and your parents to believe, isn't it?"

"Believe what?" she asked.

"You're not riding for Michael—you're riding for *you*." Tony tapped his finger against her collarbone. "You're punishing yourself for not answering Michael's call for help."

Lucy's eyes widened and Tony hated that he'd upset her, but she had to recognize the danger she was putting herself in.

"You turned your back on your brother, so you're punishing yourself until you end up like him—dead."

Tony knew the moment Lucy accepted that truth. The blood drained from her face and her mouth trembled with the effort to hold back a cry. He gave her shoulders a solid shake. He had to convince her that the forgiveness she desperately sought wouldn't be found in her self-destruction. "Bad things happen to good people, Lucy. We all bear some responsibility for Michael's death, as does Michael himself. Your brother knew better than to try to drive himself home that night, but he chose to get behind the wheel anyway. If we could go back in time, each of us would make different choices."

"But we can't go back, Tony. I've ruined everyone's lives."

"You haven't ruined mine, Lucy." He drew in a steadying breath. "I love you."

Her eyes widened.

"All this time, I've never stopped loving you. I tried, but you're the only woman I want to share my life with. Have a family with. Grow old with."

Tears streamed down Lucy's cheeks. "You can't love me after what I did."

"Yes, he can, young lady."

Tony swiveled and came face-to-face with Cal and Sonja Durango. This wasn't how he envisioned Lucy's parents learning about their relationship.

"Mom… Dad…what are you doing here?"

"Saving our only child from making a huge mistake," her mother said.

"After what I did, how can you—"

"Lucinda." Cal Durango stepped forward and reached for his daughter's hands. "Tony's right. If we could all go back to the night Michael died, each one of us would make different choices." He stared at Tony, his mouth turned down in regret. "Tony would have stayed until Michael had finished his last drink and driven him home." Next he moved his gaze to Lucy. "You would have agreed to pick Michael up at the bar when he called you." His gaze dropped to the ground for several seconds and then he said, "And I would have answered my cell phone when it rang at two in the morning."

"Michael called you?" Tony asked.

Durango nodded. "When I checked my phone the next day, I had a missed call from him."

Sonja Durango sniffed. "I'm the one who told your father to ignore the call and go back to sleep."

"We all have regrets, Lucy. Me, the most." Her father cleared his throat. "I haven't done a very good job showing my love for you. I'm sorry for that. But please believe me when I say that I am very proud to have you for a daughter."

Lucy flung her arms around her father's neck and sobbed. Durango reached out to his wife, and her mother joined in their hug. After a long while Lucy pulled free and faced Tony. "I never stopped loving you, either."

"What do you mean, never stopped? How long have you two been carrying on behind my back?" Durango asked.

"I'll explain later, Dad," Lucy said.

Tony pulled Lucy into his arms and crushed her mouth beneath his. The kiss was slow and sweet and he didn't give a damn if Cal Durango watched. When they broke apart he spoke to Lucy's father. "Sir, may I have your permission to marry your daughter?"

"Not if you're going to move away and raise my grand-children in California."

"We're staying right here in Stagecoach where we both belong," Tony said.

"Then you have my blessing." Durango pulled his wife close. "Michael would approve of his best friend marry-ing his sister, don't you think?"

Sonja Durango nodded. "I bet Michael's smiling down on all of us right now."

The announcer's voice boomed over the loud speakers as he introduced Lucy and spoke about the Pony Express.

"You're not riding, daughter."

For once Tony appreciated Durango's stubbornness.

"Listen to your father, Lucy. I couldn't bear for you to get injured." Sonja hugged her daughter.

Lucy looked at Tony. "You don't want me to ride, either."

"I'd rather you didn't, but I'll support you either way."

"I have to finish what I started," Lucy said.

"Sorry, no can do." Shannon strolled up to the chute, wearing her bull-riding gear. She flashed a brazen smile at Lucy then climbed the rails and straddled Cruise Control as the announcer's voice boomed through the speakers.

"Folks, we've got a change in plans this afternoon. It appears that Lucy Durango broke her wrist in the Cibola Rodeo last weekend. Riding in Lucy's place today is none other than Stagecoach native Shannon Douglas."

The fans cheered and the announcer continued. "You folks know Lucy's been riding bulls to raise money for the Pony Express in honor of her brother, Michael, who died right after he'd moved into the top spot in the rankings two years ago. Wrangler would like to honor Michael's bull-riding career today by matching the pledges Lucy has collected in her prior two rodeos, and if Shannon makes it to eight on Cruise Control, Wrangler will become a permanent sponsor of the Pony Express."

Lucy climbed the chute rails. "Are you sure about this, Shannon?"

"Don't worry, Lucy. I'll make it to eight and your money worries will be over."

Lucy grinned. "Cowboy-up, girl!"

Lucy, Tony and her parents moved closer to get a better view of the action. Shannon went through her pre-ride routine, then nodded to the gate man and Cruise Control leaped into the arena. The bull put Shannon through her paces, but her athletic ability held up against him and fans rose to their feet as the seconds ticked off the clock. When the buzzer sounded, an explosive noise rippled through the arena. Shannon launched herself into the air then scrambled to her feet and ran for the rails.

"Folks, Shannon Douglas made it to eight on Cruise Control!"

Tony swept Lucy into his arms and twirled her. Thanks to Shannon, and Wrangler's generosity, the Pony Express would live to see another day. "From now on, I think you should stick to raising little bull riders instead of competing yourself."

"We'll name our first son Michael, after his uncle," Lucy said.

Cal Durango cleared his throat. "I'll make sure my grandson has the best equipment and coaches around."

"Cal, the baby hasn't even been born yet." Lucy's mother smiled.

"You two better get to work on that." Durango sent Tony a meaningful stare.

"Not before they're married, Cal!"

"Don't be a prude, Sonja. You were two weeks pregnant with Michael when we got married."

Sonja gasped, and Lucy's father led her away. Left alone, Tony pulled Lucy close. "Living with your father won't be easy, but living without you would be impossible. I love you, Lucy."

"I love you, too, Tony."

EPILOGUE

LUCY STOOD AT her open bedroom window on a Thursday morning and watched the sun rise in the east. The swath of pink-and-purple light across the horizon reflected the warmth filling her heart. She closed her eyes and breathed in the fresh, cool desert air. "Are you here, Michael?" she whispered.

The lace curtain fluttered then one panel flew into the air, hitting Lucy's face. She swatted the linen away and laughed. "You always were a big tease."

The bedroom door opened and her mother waltzed in, carrying Lucy's wedding gown. "Honestly, I don't understand why you couldn't get married on a Saturday like normal couples."

"Don't worry, Mom, this is going to be a beautiful wedding and a beautiful day." Lucy hugged her mother then escaped to the bathroom to shower. Her parents, especially her father, had come a long way in accepting a marriage between her and Tony, although they didn't understand Lucy's desire to honor a Mexican tradition.

When Lucy learned about the holiday *El Dia de los Muertos*—The Day of the Dead—she chose the holiday to include Tony's father and Michael in their wedding day. According to Tony's mother, the souls of the dead returned each year to visit their relatives from October thirty-first to November second.

When Lucy broached the subject with her parents, they'd balked at first but relented when she'd told them that the greatest gift they could give her and Tony was Michael's presence at their wedding. The Day of the Dead was a celebration, and that's what she wanted for her special day and for Michael's memory.

Twenty minutes later Lucy emerged from the bathroom in her robe. Her mother was sitting on the end of the bed holding the stuffed teddy bear Michael had given Lucy for Christmas when she was eight years old.

"Lucy," her mother whispered, "I think Michael's here."

"I know. I felt him earlier." She joined her mother on the bed and held her hand.

"I can't believe you're getting married."

"I've loved Tony for a long time. He's the man I'm meant to spend the rest of my life with."

"You know, when you were a little girl I used to imagine planning your wedding."

"You did?"

"Yes, and I can tell you right now that I did not have a cake with a skull and crossbones on it."

Lucy laughed and hugged her mother. "You're a good sport, Mom."

"I believe it's a tradition for the mother of the bride to impart some words of wisdom to her daughter."

"I'm listening."

"One day you'll be a mother." Tears shone in her eyes. "And the best advice I can give you, sweetheart, is to love your children with every breath you take, because you don't know how long they'll be with you."

Lucy's eyes burned, and she squeezed her mother's hand.

"Discipline your children and expect a lot from them but never let a day go by that you don't tell them how much you love them." She caressed Lucy's cheek. "I love you, sweetheart. Know that I'll always be here for you, your husband and your children."

"I love you, too, Mom."

A knock at the door interrupted them.

"Come in," Lucy said.

Her father poked his head around the door. "Where's Tony supposed to put the bucking machine?"

"Behind the barn," Lucy's mother said. "I had Pete set up a table for Michael's things."

According to Maria, the family was supposed to gather and display favorite foods and belongings of the deceased. Tony wanted the bucking machine brought back to the ranch in Michael's honor, and Lucy's father hadn't protested. Her mother had baked a peach cobbler—Michael's favorite dessert—and Lucy had added Michael's lucky boots, his black Stetson, his bull rope, the photograph of him riding Chicken on a Chain and Maddie's princess water bowl to the collection of memorabilia honoring his life.

Her father pointed at his watch. "There's a lot to do between now and two o'clock. You'd better get moving, ladies." The door closed.

"Dad's taking all this Mexican tradition stuff pretty well, don't you think?"

"That's because I threatened him with no sex for a year."

"Mom!" Lucy clapped her hands against her ears and shared a laugh with her mother.

"I suppose we better get moving." Her mother crossed the room to the door. "Maria said her relatives will be over at noon. I'm looking forward to visiting with them before the rest of the guests arrive."

Lucy and Tony's guest list included over two hundred people, and in lieu of wedding gifts they'd asked for donations in Michael's name to the Rider Relief Fund, which provided financial support to injured bull riders and bullfighters.

"I'll be down in a little while." After her mother left, Lucy went across the room to the window facing the barn. Tony and two other men dressed in border patrol uniforms were unloading the mechanical bull from Tony's truck.

Lucy soaked in the sight of Tony in his worn jeans, scruffy boots and T-shirt. He must have sensed he was being watched, because he glanced up at her window. Standing against the backdrop of the Bryon Mountains and a sparkling blue sky, he waved at her. In that moment, Lucy saw the ghostly outline of her brother standing next to Tony. He looked in her direction and smiled and Lucy knew that Michael's gift to her and Tony was the sense of peace that had been missing from their souls since her brother had passed away.

Today would be a celebration of life…death…and rebirth.

And the beginning of the rest of her life with Tony.

* * * * *

A RODEO MAN'S PROMISE

To Kevin—husband and best friend.

This past May we celebrated twenty-five years of wedded bliss! Who would have predicted a few stolen kisses in a dorm stairwell would lead to getting hitched in Vegas and settling into our first home in Phoenix. We didn't stay put long… off we went to the Golden State. Along the way we added two kids and a dog. Then we headed to the Garden State for a couple of years before migrating west again to the Centennial State. From there we planted roots in the Lone Star State, added two more dogs and Taz the hamster to our family before packing up and moving to the Prairie State. This year we finally made it back to the place we began our life together…the Grand Canyon State. What an amazing ride it's been and one I wouldn't trade for the world! But I'm tired. I vote we stay put the next twenty-five years, find us a couple of rocking chairs, kick back and watch our kids navigate life, marriage and children while we grow old together.

I love you, GB!

CHAPTER ONE

FRIDAY AFTERNOON, RILEY FITZGERALD climbed out of a green Chevy cab in front of the Fremont County fairgrounds in Canon City, Colorado. The late-August sun slipped behind a puffy white cloud, casting a shadow over the livestock buildings. He offered the driver a hundred-dollar bill. "Keep the change, Rosalinda."

"A pleasure, Mr. Fitzgerald." The owner of Canon City Cab was old enough to be Riley's grandmother and just as dependable. On his approach to the Fremont County Airport, he'd radioed the control tower to arrange a cab ride for him to the Royal Gorge Rodeo. "Good luck today." Rosalinda waved then drove off.

Riley slung his gear bag over his shoulder and cut across the parking lot.

"Hey, Riley!" A petite blonde sashayed toward him, her perky breasts bouncing beneath a hot pink T-shirt with the words *Cowgirls Ride Better* printed in black lettering across the front.

Sugar waited tables at Dirty Lil's—a roadhouse where cowboys hung out and swapped eight-second stories. Their one and only lusty kiss three years ago had been a bust, but they'd remained good friends. "Did you miss me?" Riley asked.

"Heck yeah, I missed my biggest tipper." She slipped

her arm through his and walked with him to the cow-boy-ready area. "You're comin' to the bar later, right?"

"You bet." Maintaining his championship swagger had become increasingly difficult when he hadn't hit a top-three finish since his July 4th win in South Dakota seven weeks ago.

"Hey, Fitzgerald!" Billy Stover waved his cowboy hat. The bronc rider occupied first place in the standings. "Showin' up kind of late in the day, aren't you?" Stover eyed Sugar while Riley signed in for his event.

"Couldn't catch a tailwind with the Cessna." Riley felt a zap of satisfaction at the smack-down. No matter how great Stover became at bronc-bustin', the cowboy would never earn the amount of money Riley had at his disposal on a day-to-day basis.

No sense trying to downplay his wealth when the media made sure Riley's competitors and rodeo fans knew the Fitzgeralds of Lexington, Kentucky, were rolling in dough. He'd heard the whispers behind the chutes—spoiled rich kid had nothing better to do with his time than play cowboy.

After graduating from college with a marketing de-gree, he'd bypassed the family business—Kentucky Derby horses and a century-old bourbon distillery—and had hit the rodeo circuit, living off his trust fund. Other than sharing a love for the sport, he didn't have a whole lot in common with the average rodeo cowboy. He knew horseflesh—the racing kind—but next to nothing about punching cows, which was what most rodeo contenders did to earn money between rides.

"Forgot you flew your own plane," Stover said.

"You'd forget your brain if it wasn't trapped inside your skull."

Stover spit tobacco juice, the glob landing inches from the toe of Riley's boot. "A win tonight ain't gonna put you back in the running." Listening to the man's crap would be a lot less painful if Riley lasted eight seconds in the saddle. His dismal performance the past month fueled personal attacks and provided fodder for the media.

"Worry about yourself, Stover. Your luck might run out tonight."

"Doubt it." Stover disappeared into the crowd. The sports world was having a field day debating whether or not Riley deserved last year's championship title. Riley's first year on the circuit, he ended the season ranked seventh in the standings. The second year he'd won the title—by default—when Drew Rawlins had scratched his final ride. This year Riley intended to prove the naysayers wrong. He'd had a hell of a run during Cowboy Christmas, but he'd been slipping downhill since then.

"Ignore him." Sugar glared at Stover's retreating back. "Win or lose, you're the hottest cowboy on the circuit."

Too bad Riley's pretty face couldn't keep his butt glued to the saddle.

"Grab a seat, folks, and hang on to your hats." The rodeo announcer's voice boomed over the loudspeakers. "The saddle-bronc competition is about to begin."

"Go get 'em, cowboy." Sugar kissed Riley's cheek then disappeared into the stands.

Rummaging through his gear bag, Riley found his chaps and gloves. He'd put his spurs on during the cab ride to the arena.

"Riley Fitzgerald from Lexington, Kentucky, is up first."

An ear-splitting din echoed through the stands as the crowd stomped their boots on the aluminum bleachers. His confidence might have abandoned Riley but at least his fans hadn't.

"Fitzgerald's about to tangle with one of the orneriest broncs on the circuit."

Riley had ridden Peanut earlier in the season at the Coors Pro Rodeo in Gillette, Wyoming, and the stallion had been hell on hooves. The gelding had practically thrown Riley into the rails. He shoved his Stetson on his head—not that he expected the hat to stay on. Closing his eyes, he inhaled deeply. Large, industrial air vents circulated the smell of horseflesh, urine-soaked hay and sweaty cowboys through the air.

Gotta make it to eight.

He scaled the chute rails and slouched low in the saddle then worked the buck rein around his hand until the rope felt comfortable. As with most notorious broncs Peanut didn't flinch or twitch a muscle—he was every cowboy's best friend until the gate opened.

"You folks may not know that three years ago Fitzgerald won the National Intercollegiate Rodeo Association Championship in saddle-bronc riding his senior year at UNLV. One might recall the story behind that ride…"

The facts surrounding his infamous ride had been embellished through the years until no one believed the truth—sheer luck and not skill had kept Riley in the saddle when Lucky Strike swapped ends—jumped into the air and turned 180 degrees before touching the ground. The ride had vaulted Riley into instant stardom and earned him sponsorship offers from Wrangler, Justin boots and Dodge trucks.

"Hang on, folks. The flagman's signaling a problem with the clock," the announcer said.

A sequence of slow-motion action shots played inside Riley's head as he envisioned his ride. First, he marked out the bronc—touching both heels above the horse's shoulders as the animal exploded from the chute. Peanut bucked, spun and back-jumped. Riley held on, his body moving in sync with the horse while spurring. The image abruptly vanished when loud music blasted through the arena.

"Fitzgerald dropped out of the standings this month. If he's gonna defend his title he's gotta win on the big buckers like Peanut."

Win—exactly what Riley intended to do.

"Clocks have been fixed. Let's see if Fitzgerald can stay in the saddle."

A final squeeze of the rein then Riley signaled the gate man. The chute door swung open and Peanut leapt into the arena. Riley spurred the gelding, goading it to buck harder—the feistier the bronc, the higher the score. But his efforts were in vain. Peanut whirled right, left, then back to the right, but without much vigor.

Son of a bitch. Peanut was acting like a dink—a bucker with no buck.

The buzzer sounded and Riley leapt to the ground, resisting the urge to smack the bronc on the rump as he walked to the chute.

"Don't rightly know what was wrong with Peanut tonight. He sure didn't do Fitzgerald any favors. An eighty isn't good enough for a win. Better luck next time, cowboy."

"Tough draw," Ed Parker said.

Too pissed to speak, Riley opened his gear bag and stowed his rigging. Parker was one of the nicer competitors on the circuit and didn't deserve Riley's cold shoulder; but better to keep his mouth shut than spout statements that would make the morning papers and sully the Fitzgerald name.

Riley's great-great-grandfather Doyle Fitzpatrick had purchased the family's first thoroughbred horse in Ireland and brought the stallion with him when he'd immigrated to America. He sold Duke of Devonshire and used the money to buy Belle Farms—the burned-out shell of a pre-civil war estate on the outskirts of Lexington. Doyle then opened a local bourbon distillery, using the profits to renovate Belle Farms and invest in the world's finest horseflesh.

"You headin' over to Lil's?" Parker asked.

"Yeah." Riley would drink a beer and pretend he didn't give a rat's ass about losing when he did. After socializing he'd phone Rosalinda to fetch him from the bar then he'd fly to his next rodeo in Payson, Arizona.

"I'll give you a lift after my ride," Parker said.

"Appreciate that." Riley headed for the food vendors, where he purchased two hot dogs, fries and a Coke. He sat in the stands and ignored the buckle bunnies with big hair, big boobs and big rhinestone belts, batting their eyelashes at him. Riley's wealth combined with his dark good looks garnered him more than his fair share of female interest. Most of the time, he enjoyed being fussed over but his recent losing streak put him on edge and he didn't appreciate all the female distractions.

He heard the announcer call Parker's name. A few

seconds after the gate opened the cowboy sailed over the bronc's head. Parker was out of the running, too. Riley returned to the cowboy-ready area and followed Parker to his truck.

Dirty Lil's was a hop, skip and a jump from the rodeo grounds. They parked behind the building, near a grassy area where bikers threw horseshoes and played poker at picnic tables.

"You ever think about hanging up your spurs?" Parker asked.

Plenty of times. "Never." That's what champions were supposed to say. "Why do you ask?" Riley didn't know much about Parker's personal life other than his father was the foreman of a corporate-owned cattle ranch north of Albuquerque.

"I've been doing this for eight years and all I've gotten for my time and effort is a handful of broken bones and a divorce."

At age twenty-five, marriage wasn't a topic that came to Riley's mind often. His biggest concern was figuring out what he wanted to do with his life. Until then, he didn't dare quit rodeo or his father would demand he return to Lexington and help run Belle Farms. "You have any kids?" he asked Parker.

"A daughter. Shelly's four. I missed her birthday last week because I was in Texas."

Parker was only a few years older than Riley but already a father. Riley figured he'd have kids one day but he couldn't picture himself as a dad anytime soon.

"I don't know about you, but I could use a cold one," Parker said, hopping out of the truck.

A wooden bust of a woman from an ancient sailing

ship hung above the entrance to Dirty Lil's. A sign dangled from her neck, reminding customers that Friday night was ladies' mud wrestling.

As far as roadhouses went, Lil's was top-of-the-line and plenty big enough for the cowboy ego. A decent-size dance floor occupied the rear of the establishment, where a stage had been constructed for local bands. In the middle of the room sat a twenty-by-twenty-foot inflated kiddie pool filled with mud. A garden hose hooked up to a spigot behind the bar rested on the floor next to the man-made mud bog.

Waitresses dressed as saloon wenches carried drink trays and flirted with the cowboys. "Hey, fellas." Sugar smiled behind the bar. "Don't stand there gawkin'. Sit down and have a drink."

"Two Coors." Riley fished his wallet from his back pocket. "When did you start pouring drinks?"

"Melanie's on break." Sugar leaned over the bar and whispered in Riley's ear. "Heard about your ride. You'll win next time."

Or the next time. Or the time after that.

As soon as Sugar walked off, Riley chugged his beer, then spent the following hour dancing with a handful of women. He bought a round for the house then caught up with Parker and challenged him to a game of darts—and lost a hundred-buck wager.

"You did that on purpose," Parker accused.

"Did what?"

"Gave the game away."

"You're nuts." Riley swallowed a sip of warm beer. He'd been nursing his second longneck for over an hour. "What?" he asked when Parker stared at him.

"You strut around…a big shot with the women." Parker pointed at Riley's waist. "Flashing your world-champion belt buckle and pilot's license. Buying rounds of beer with hundred-dollar bills."

No sense refuting Parker's charges. Riley was set for life. He was aware most rodeo cowboys shared motel rooms, slept in their trucks and skipped meals to scrape together enough cash to pay their entry fees and fill their gas tanks. A few guys even set their own broken bones because they didn't have the money to pay for an E.R. visit.

Riley had never experienced sacrifice—that set him apart from the other cowboys on the circuit. In return, his rivals had no idea how it felt to live with the pressure and responsibility attached to the Fitzgerald name.

When Riley refused to debate his privileged life with Parker, the cowboy muttered, "Thanks for the gas money."

"You beat me fair and square." Riley had believed Parker was one of the few cowboys who'd ignored Riley's wealth. If he'd known otherwise, he wouldn't have played darts with one eye closed—his good eye. He couldn't have hit the bull's-eye if he'd been standing five feet in front of the board. He set his beer bottle on the bar.

"You're not stayin' for the mud wrestling?" Parker motioned to the pit behind Riley. Two women wearing string bikinis—pink-and-white polka dot and cherry-red—taunted each other while drooling cowpokes placed bets.

Both blondes were pretty and not shy about flaunting their centerfold figures. Maybe it wouldn't hurt to watch the first match. Riley found a table with an unobstructed view of the pit and far enough away to avoid the spray of mud.

The antique train whistle attached to the wall behind the bar bellowed. Sugar introduced the wrestlers. "Get ready, boys, 'cause Denise and Krista are gonna give you a fight to remember. Both gals made the finals in last year's Royal Gorge mud wrestling competition."

Wolf whistles filled the air.

The women retreated to opposite corners of the kiddie pool and made a big production out of straightening their swimsuits. When the train whistle blew again, the contestants dove into the pit, spewing mud over the edges of the pool. They tussled, slipped and slid until only the whites of their eyes and their teeth were visible. Riley chuckled at the effort the women put into the act. They knew if they gave the cowboys a good show, they'd earn enough money in tips to cover their rent for a month.

"I thought you were leaving?" Sugar sidled up to Riley's table.

"You know me—can't resist a dirty girl."

"You need a real woman." She snorted at the mud-slinging duo. "Not immature, self-centered brats who only want to get their hands on the Fitzgerald fortune."

"And where is a twenty-five-year-old guy to find a mature, worldly woman his own age?"

"Not at Dirty Lil's, that's for sure."

"If I stop coming here, you'll miss me." Riley kissed Sugar's cheek. "I've got to hit the road."

"Fly safe, you hear?"

"Will do." Riley returned to Parker's F-150, where he'd left his gear bag, then phoned the cab company. By the time Rosalinda arrived, thunder echoed in the distance. She stepped on the gas and issued a weather report. Ominous black clouds threatened the skies to the west. At the airport he tipped Rosalinda another hundred before entering the hangar that housed his plane. The *Dark Stranger*—literal translation of his great-great-grandfather's name, Doyle—was a gift to himself after he'd graduated from college.

Ben Walker, the airport operations manager, stood next to the Cessna 350 Corvalis. "High winds and possible hail are headed this way. You're being routed through Albuquerque, then over to Arizona. You've got to be airborne in the next ten minutes. After that they're shutting us down until the storm passes."

"What about fuel?"

"Took care of that earlier." Walker shrugged. "Heard you lost today so I doubted you'd stick around long."

"Thanks."

"Have a safe flight." Walker returned to his office.

Riley got in the plane and hurried through the preflight checklist, then taxied onto the runway. The control tower instructed him to fly twenty miles east then turn south toward Albuquerque.

Once the *Dark Stranger* leveled off at sixteen thousand feet, Riley relaxed behind the controls and turned on the stereo. Time passed quickly and the plane soon entered Albuquerque airspace. He decreased his altitude and veered west toward Arizona. He'd just straightened the aircraft, when out of nowhere an object slammed into the propeller.

"Shit!"

Flecks of blood spattered the windshield and the plane

vibrated violently. Riley quickly feathered the propeller and shut down the engine to prevent further damage.

He muttered a prayer and searched for a place to land.

OH, MY GOD.

Maria Alvarez stared in horror out the window of her station wagon. The small plane wobbled in the sky, its right wing dipping dramatically before leveling off. The aircraft was losing altitude fast. Maria pressed on the gas pedal as she whizzed along I-40 heading west out of Albuquerque toward Mesita.

Suddenly the plane switched direction and crossed the highway right over her car. He was gliding toward the salvage yard—Maria's destination. Flipping on the blinker, she entered the exit lane. Keeping the plane in sight, she drove along a deserted road for a quarter mile. The road dead-ended and Maria turned onto a dirt path that led to Estefan's Recycling and Auto Salvage. The business had closed to the public years ago but the property had never been cleared of ancient car parts, tires and appliances. The past few months the lot had become the home turf of the Los Locos gang.

Aside from normal gang activities—robbery, drugs and shootings—the Los Locos members were famous for their artistic talent. A recent display of their artwork across the front of an office complex on the south side of Albuquerque depicted an alien invasion of earth. The mural had received praise from the art professors at the University of New Mexico but not the police or the public. Regardless of the gang's creativity, none of its members would escape the 'hood without an education.

Maria was one of five teachers in the city whose students had dropped out or had been expelled from high school. Except for a few instructors, society had written off the troublemakers. Education, not gang affiliation, was the path to a better life. Once the teens joined a gang, leaving alive wasn't an option. Maria's job was to help at-risk teens earn a GED then enroll in a community college or a trade program. Most days she loved her work, but there were times—like now—that her students tested the limits of her patience.

Yesterday, three of her charges had skipped class. When she'd stopped by their homes this afternoon to check on them, their families had no idea of their whereabouts. As she left one of the homes, a younger sibling confessed that his brother, Alonso, had gone to meet the Los Locos at Estefan's Salvage.

As Maria raced toward the junkyard, the plane dropped from the sky and touched down, bouncing twice before racing across the bumpy desert toward the chainlink fence enclosing the property.

He's not going to stop in time.

The aircraft rammed into the fence, ripping several panels from the ground before the nose of the plane crashed into a stockpile of rubber tires, spewing them fifty feet into the air. Amazingly the aircraft came to a halt in one piece.

After parking near the downed fence, Maria clutched the lead pipe she stowed beneath the front seat. This wasn't the first time—nor would it be the last—that she rescued one or more of her students from a dangerous situation. Her father insisted she carry a gun, but after her brother had been shot dead by a gangbanger ten years ago, Maria wanted nothing to do with guns.

Sidestepping scattered debris, she hurried toward the plane. Her steps slowed when the cockpit door opened and the sexiest man she'd ever laid eyes on stepped into view.

He tipped his cowboy hat. "Howdy, ma'am. Sorry about the mess I made of your place. I'll cover the damages."

This past March Maria had celebrated her thirty-fifth birthday. Entering her mid-thirties was tough enough without being "ma'am'd" by a sexy young cowboy. He grinned and she swore her heart flipped upside down in her chest. Embarrassed by her juvenile reaction to the stranger she stopped several yards from the plane.

"You wouldn't happen to have the name of a good aviation mechanic, would you?"

CHAPTER TWO

STOMACH TIED IN KNOTS, Riley walked around the plane, assessing the damage—flat tire. Minor dents. *Oh, man, that couldn't be good*—two mangled propeller blades. Only a bird the size of a hawk could have done that much damage.

Despite a breeze, sweat dripped down his temples as the harrowing descent replayed in his mind. At least his radio hadn't shut off and he'd been able to communicate his safe landing to the control tower at a nearby airport.

"Are you all right?"

The sultry voice startled Riley. He'd forgotten about the woman. He gave her a once-over. Out of habit he catalogued her features, placing them in the plus or minus column. Her voice made the plus column—the raspy quality reminded him of a blues singer.

"Yeah, I'm fine." He moved toward her then stopped on a dime when she lifted the metal pipe above her head.

"Don't come any closer."

This was a first for Riley. Usually, he was the one beating off the women. "I'm no threat."

Keeping hold of the weapon, she crossed her arms in front of her bosom—a well-endowed bosom.

Plus column.

She had curvy hips unlike the skinny buckle bun-

244   A RODEO MAN'S PROMISE

nies who squeezed their toothpick legs into size-zero Cruel Girl jeans. This lady filled a pair of denims in a way that made Riley want to grab hold of her fanny and never let go.

Three pluses—home run.

"Engine trouble?" she asked.

"Bird strike. I'd hoped to make it to Blue Skies Regional—" the municipal airport was located seven miles northwest of the central business district in Albuquerque "—but I lost altitude too quickly."

"Who are you?"

The female drill sergeant needed to loosen up a bit. He spread his arms wide. "A cowboy."

"Aren't they all." She rolled her eyes.

Amused, Riley tapped a finger against his belt buckle. "Standing before you, ma'am, is a bona fide world-champion bronc-buster."

"Don't call me that." Almond-shaped brown eyes flashed with warning.

"Call you what?"

"Ma'am."

So the lady was a tad touchy about her age. The tiny lines that fanned from the outer corners of her eyes hinted that she was older than Riley by more than a few years. She was on the short side, but there was nothing delicate about her. The arm wielding the pipe sported a well-defined bicep. His mind flashed back to Dirty Lil's—he'd give anything to watch this woman mud wrestle.

"I've never met a real cowboy who wears snakeskin boots and flies his own plane. My guess is that you're a drug dealer, masquerading as a cowboy."

Whoa. "Sorry to disappoint you, ma'—uh, miss. I left

Canon City, Colorado, earlier today after competing in the Royal Gorge Rodeo." She didn't appear impressed. "Go ahead and check my plane for contraband." He dug his cell phone from his pocket. "Or call my agent. He'll verify that I'm Riley Fitzgerald, current NFR saddle-bronc champion." Soon to be dethroned if he didn't get his rodeo act together.

"Agent?" she scoffed. "Is that what they're calling drug cartels these days?"

The lady appeared immune to his charm. Riley couldn't remember the last time a woman had rejected him. Her feistiness and bravado intrigued him and he found her sass sexy. "Why would a drug runner risk landing his plane in a salvage yard?"

"I've seen bolder displays of arrogance."

Now he was an arrogant drug dealer? "As soon as I locate a good mechanic I intend to fly the heck out of Dodge." He removed a handful of hundred-dollar bills from his wallet. "Put this toward the damages. You can send a final bill—"

One of her delicately shaped eyebrows arched.

"What?"

"Cowboys don't carry around hundred-dollar bills."

"Take the money!"

Riley jumped inside his skin and scanned the piles of household appliances, searching for the location of the mystery voice. "Who's there?"

"Alonso Marquez, get your backside out here right now." The woman marched toward the graffiti-covered cinder-block hut with broken-out windows and a missing door. The word Office had been painted across the front in big red letters. Rusty refrigerators, washing machines and water heaters sat outside the building. "Victor and Cruz, I know you're there, too." The pipe-wielding crusader halted a few yards before the door when three teens waltzed from the building.

They were dressed the same—baggy pants that hung low on their hips. Black T-shirts. Each wore a bicycle chain lock around their necks and another chain hung from the pocket of their pants, down both sides of their legs, ending an inch above the ground. The baseball caps on their heads were turned sideways—all facing to the left—and their athletic shoes had no laces.

"You guys better have a good reason for skipping class yesterday and missing the quiz."

Quiz? He'd crash-landed his plane, been accused of drug trafficking and now the crazy lady discussed schoolwork with three troublemakers from the 'hood.

"We're not comin' to class no more." The tallest kid of the bunch spoke.

"You're quitting, Cruz? The three of you are this—" she pinched her thumb and forefinger together in front of the boy's face "—close to earning your GEDs."

"We got a better gig goin' on."

"Does this *gig* have anything to do with the Los Locos, Victor?" She tapped the end of the pipe against the boy's chest.

"What if it does?" The teen grimaced, the action stretching the scar on his face. A line of puckered flesh began at his temple and cut across the outer corner of his eye, dragging the skin down before continuing along his cheek and ending at the edge of his mouth. "Hanging with the Locos is better than sitting in class learning stupid stuff, Ms. Alvarez."

Ms. Alvarez was a teacher. Riley didn't envy her job—not if her students were as difficult as these punks.

"Victor—"

"Mind if I butt in?" Four heads swiveled in Riley's direction.

"Awesome landing, dude." The kid named Victor made a fist pump in the air.

"Thanks, but I prefer using runways when possible." Keeping one eye on Ms. Alvarez and her lead pipe and the other on the teens, Riley joined the crowd. "You guys didn't get hurt by flying debris, did you?"

Three heads swiveled side-to-side.

"I'm Riley Fitzgerald." He held out his hand and one of the teens stepped forward, offering his fist. Riley bumped knuckles with the kid.

"Alonso Marquez."

Next, Riley nudged knuckles with the tall teen, who said, "Cruz Rivera."

The kid with the scar kept his hands in his pockets and mumbled, "Victor Vicario."

Riley offered his knuckles to the teacher, but she held out her hand instead. "Maria Alvarez."

Pretty name for a pretty lady. He eyed her weapon. "That's for show, right?"

"No." She smiled and Riley's breath hitched in his chest. She had the most beautiful white teeth and dimples.

"When did you figure out I wasn't a drug lord?" he asked.

Her gaze dropped to his waist. "When you pointed to the horse on your belt buckle."

"I'll be happy to cover the damages if you tell me who owns this place."

"My dad owns it." Cruz and his homies snickered.

"Yeah, Cruz's dad's gonna be ticked when he sees the busted fence," Victor said.

Riley was being conned, but played along. "I'll pay you guys to straighten things up before Cruz's father gets word of the damage." He handed each boy a Ben Franklin. Eyes wide, mouths hanging open, the teens gaped at the money. They'd probably never seen a hundred-dollar bill before.

"Absolutely not." Maria snatched the money from their fingertips. "None of their fathers owns this business, Mr. Fitzgerald."

Mr. Fitzgerald? The only person he'd ever heard called Mr. Fitzgerald was his father.

"Alonso, Cruz and Victor are enrolled in a high school program I teach for at-risk teens."

Cruz attempted to mimic his teacher's voice. "Ms. Alvarez is our last chance to change our ways before we land in prison or fall under the influence of gangs." Laughing, the boys decked each other with playful punches.

"That's enough." Maria scowled. "Get in the car. We'll discuss the ramifications of your actions in a minute."

The boys shuffled off. When they were out of earshot, Maria said, "You landed your plane in an abandoned salvage yard that's rumored to have been taken over by the Los Locos. The boys were hanging out here, waiting for the gang."

"You think the thugs will show up tonight?"

The sexy cowboy pilot was worried about the plane being vandalized. "I don't know."

"Mind if I hitch a ride with you? I need to make arrangements to have the plane towed."

The last thing Maria wanted was a handsome cowboy distracting her while she reprimanded her students. She clearly hesitated too long in answering, because he added, "You don't have to go out of your way. Drop me off wherever you're taking those guys."

She couldn't very well leave him alone in the junkyard with night approaching. "Sure. I'll give you a lift. And I can give you the name of a reliable mechanic."

"I'll fetch my gear bag." He jogged to the plane and Maria had to drag her eyes from his muscular backside.

You're old enough to be his mother. That wasn't exactly true—an older sister, maybe. Regardless, it irked her that a man as young as Riley had thrown her for a loop. With all she'd been through and seen in her thirty-five years she should be immune to a handsome face and a sexy swagger.

"Is the cowboy dude coming or what?" Cruz asked when Maria returned to the station wagon.

"Yep." She settled behind the wheel and glanced in the rearview mirror. The three musketeers sat shoulder-to-shoulder. The boys were all bright and funny, and deserved a chance to escape the gang violence of inner-city life. If only they believed in themselves. Maria was doing her best to nurture their self-confidence and encourage them to study. They had to excel in the classroom if they wanted any chance at a life away from gangs and drugs. The boys' actions today proved that her efforts were falling short.

"We're giving Mr. Fitzgerald a ride into town. You three better mind your manners."

"Are we gonna get to make up the quiz?" Alonso asked.

Of course they would. Maria bent and broke the rules to help her students succeed. "We'll see." Wouldn't hurt to let them stew.

"C'mon, Ms. Alvarez," Victor whined. "We know the material."

Victor and Alonso glanced at Cruz, expecting their buddy to chime in but Cruz remained silent. Of the three, Maria worried she'd lose Cruz to a gang. A few months ago his younger brother had gotten caught in the cross-fire between two rival gangs and had been killed. Maria sensed Cruz wanted revenge. She knew the feeling well, but when she'd attempted to share her personal experience with gang violence, Cruz had shut her out.

"Who gave you guys a ride out here?"

"A trucker dropped us off at the exit ramp on the interstate. We hiked the rest of the way," Victor said.

The passenger door opened and the cowboy tossed a duffel onto the front seat. "Sorry," he said.

"What's in the bag, mister?" Alonso asked.

"Change of clothes and my rodeo gear." He removed his hat and rested it atop his knee.

"Mr. Fitzgerald—"

"Call me Riley." His smile set loose a swarm of butterflies in Maria's stomach.

"Riley," she repeated in her best schoolmarm voice. "Please fasten your seat belt." Once he'd completed the task she made a U-turn and drove away from the salvage yard.

"You ride bulls for real?" Victor asked.

"Nah, I'm not that crazy. I bust broncs."

"You famous?" Cruz asked.

"I won a world title last year at the NFR in Vegas. Ever heard of that? The National Finals Rodeo?"

A resounding "no" erupted from Victor's and Alonso's mouths.

"It's the biggest rodeo of the year. The top fifteen money-making cowboys in each event compete for a world title."

"Does the winner get a lot of coin?" Victor asked.

"Depends on your definition of *a lot*."

"A thousand dollars," Victor blurted.

"Idiot." Alonso elbowed Victor in the side. "He flies a plane, so he's gotta make more 'n a thousand dollars."

"How'd you learn to fly?" Victor asked.

"Went to flight school while I was in *college*."

Maria's ears perked at the word college.

"Why'd you go to college?" Victor asked.

"What else was I going to do after high school?" Riley said.

Victor's eyes widened. "You coulda hung out with your homies."

"Yeah, but that would get boring after a while."

The teens exchanged bewildered glances.

"The truth is," Riley said, "my old man insisted I earn a college degree so I'd be prepared to help with the family business."

Intrigued, Maria joined the conversation. "What does your family do?"

"They breed horses."

Her hunch had been correct. "You live on a ranch."

"No, my family lives on a horse farm in Kentucky."

"You don't have a Southern accent," she said.

"Lost the accent when I went to college at UNLV in Las Vegas."

"I'd go to college if the school was next to topless dancers and casinos," Cruz said.

"I was too busy rodeoing to gamble." Riley winked at Maria and darned if her heart didn't pound harder. She strangled the steering wheel and focused on the dirt road leading to the highway.

"What do you guys do with your spare time?" Riley shifted in his seat. "Are you into sports or clubs?"

"Yeah, we're into clubs." Cruz snorted.

Maria caught Alonso watching her in the rearview mirror. The teen held a special place in her heart—he reminded her of her brother, Juan. Desperate to fit in, he was a follower not a leader. Alonso had much to offer others and she hoped to convince him to attend college after he earned his GED.

"What clubs are you involved in?" Riley asked.

"What do you think?" Cruz said. "We're going to join the Los Locos." The teen acted too tough for his own good.

"Gangs are for losers. Most of those guys land in prison or they get shot dead on the street."

"Gangs are cool," Victor said.

"Then how come all they do is break the law, sell drugs, use drugs and shoot people?" Riley countered.

Maria decided to intervene before the boys went ballistic. "A few of the gangs in the area have unusual talents." She took the on-ramp to the highway. "Members of the Los Locos gang are accomplished artists."

"If they're that good, why aren't they in art school? Or a college program where they can put their creativity to good use?" Riley asked.

"The kids come from disadvantaged backgrounds and—"

"Disadvantaged means poor," Victor interrupted.

"The families can't afford to send their son or daughter to a special school let alone an art camp during the summer months." Maria merged with traffic and headed toward civilization. "Do you know where you want to stay for the night?" she asked Riley.

"Take him to the Lamplight Inn down the block from our house," Victor said. "My sister works there. She'll show you a good time for one of those hundred-dollar bills you got in your wallet."

Riley ignored Victor's comment. "Any motel is fine."

Motel? Maria doubted this cowboy had ever slept in a motel. She'd have to go out of her way and drop off Riley downtown at the Hyatt Regency.

The remainder of the trip was made in silence—the gang wannabes brooding in the backseat and Riley staring at the Sandia Mountains off to the east. When they entered the Five Points neighborhood, Riley tensed. Maria was used to the rough-and-tumble areas in the South Valley, but this Kentucky-bluegrass cowboy had probably never seen urban decay the likes of what he viewed now.

Maria's parents lived in Artrisco, not far from the Five Points, and she'd moved in with them a year ago after ending her relationship with her fiancé, Fernando. Living with her folks was to have been temporary but Maria delayed finding her own place because she felt responsible for her mother's continued decline in health. She turned off of Isleta Boulevard and parked in front of Cruz's home.

The yard was strewn with broken furniture and garbage. The plaster on the outer walls of the house had peeled away and several clay roof tiles were broken or missing. Good thing Albuquerque received less than nine inches of rain per year. Maria unsnapped her belt.

"I don't need an escort," Cruz said.

"I want to speak with your mother."

Cruz hopped out of the car. "You know my mom won't be in any shape to talk."

Sadly, the teen's mother was a methamphetamine addict—all the more reason to make sure Cruz stayed away from gangs and earned his GED. "Promise you'll attend class on Monday."

"Yeah, okay."

"Cruz," Maria called after him.

"What?"

"Be a man of your word."

After Cruz entered the house Maria spoke to Victor and Alonso. "I want you guys to keep your distance from the Los Locos. And both of you had better be ready to take that quiz on Monday."

The boys didn't register a protest as Maria drove them home—two blocks from Cruz's house.

"Thanks for the ride," Alonso said when he got out of the car.

"See ya." Victor followed Alonso into his house.

Maria left the Five Points and made her way toward the river. She drove across Bridge Boulevard then turned on Eight Street. "The Hyatt Regency is on the other side of the Rio Grande."

"Do you do this all the time?" Riley asked.

"Do what?"

"Drive through questionable neighborhoods?"

"Yep. Comes with the job." She also lived in one of those *questionable* neighborhoods Riley referred to. She turned on Tijeras Avenue then stopped in front of the hotel.

Riley faced her, his mouth curving. Maria swore she'd have to ingest a dozen bottles of antacid medicine before her stomach recovered from her run-in with the flying cowboy.

"Let me buy you dinner as a thank you for helping me today," he said.

Dinner...as in a date? It had been months since she'd sat across the table from a man, never mind that Riley Fitzpatrick wasn't just any man. He was a sexy *young* cowboy...man.

"How old are you?" She winced when the question slipped out of her mouth.

"Twenty-five. Does age matter if we're only having dinner?"

Oh, God. Maria's face flamed. Had he guessed she'd been thinking about sex? She really needed to get laid. "Dinner would be nice, but I'm not dressed for the Hyatt. How do you feel about Mexican food?"

"Love it."

"I know just the place." Maria drove back to the other side of the Rio Grande and parked in front of a narrow brick-faced storefront with Abuela's Cocina on the sign, sandwiched between a Laundromat and a liquor store. "'Grandmother's Kitchen,'" Maria said. "Consuelo makes great enchiladas."

"Is it safe?" Riley asked, eyeing the car filled with gangbangers at the corner. The guy in the driver's seat glared at them.

"No riskier than the wild horses you ride." Rodeo could be violent at times, but at least the horses and bulls didn't shoot at the cowboys who rode on their backs.

They made it as far as the restaurant door when a gunshot went off. In a move so quick it snatched the air from Maria's lungs Riley opened the café door and shoved her over the threshold, catching her by the waist when she tripped on the welcome mat in the foyer. Before the door had even shut behind them, Riley had Maria pressed against the wall, his body shielding hers.

"Did you get hit?" he whispered.

Shock kept her tongue-tied.

"Don't move." Riley settled his palm against her hip, exerting enough force to keep her pinned in place. The heat from his hand burned through her jeans, warming her skin. She giggled.

"What's so funny?"

"Are you finished playing hero?"

"*Hola,* Maria." A young woman entered the hallway, carrying two laminated menus. She stared at Riley's hand still attached to Maria's hip. *"¿Quién es el vaquero?"*

"This cowboy is Riley Fitzgerald. Riley, Sonja. Her aunt owns the restaurant."

Riley tipped his hat. "Ma'am."

Ma'am? Sonja was nineteen. Maria snorted.

"Sígueme," Sonja said, disappearing through a doorway.

Maria followed the hostess into the dining room, stunned that a twenty-five-year-old man made her feel as if she were a carefree young girl and not a woman who had seen and experienced a lifetime of tragedy and heartbreak in thirty-five short years.

CHAPTER THREE

RILEY LOST HIS train of thought as he drowned in Maria's brown eyes.

"Do I have food stuck to my face?" She reached for her napkin.

He covered her hand with his, pinning the napkin to the table. "No. Your face is fine. As a matter of fact it's perfect."

Maria's cheeks reddened and Riley chuckled.

"What?"

He released her hand. "I make you nervous."

"No, you don't." The denial lacked conviction.

He eyeballed her fingernail tapping the table and Maria fisted her hand. "Why do I make you uneasy?" he asked.

"Besides the fact that you're a complete stranger?"

"Yeah, besides that." He popped a tortilla chip into his mouth and chewed.

"Let's see." Maria held up one finger. "First, you're sexy and attractive."

Wow. He hadn't seen that one coming. "Thank you."

"You're welcome." A second finger rose in the air. "You're wealthy."

"Money makes you anxious?"

"Didn't your mother teach you that money is the root of all evil?"

"Actually, my father taught me that money solves all problems."

Third finger… "You're young."

He'd read the occasional magazine article that testified to the sexual compatibility of older women and younger men. Made sense to him. He waggled his eyebrows. "Youth has its advantages."

The waitress arrived with their meals and the women spoke in Spanish. Riley guessed they discussed him because the young girl glanced his way more than once. "The enchiladas are great," he said, disrupting the conversation.

"I'll tell Aunt Consuelo you approve of her cooking." The waitress disappeared.

"The whole family works in the business?"

"Years ago Consuelo won the lottery and used the money to open a restaurant. Since then, most of her nieces and nephews have worked here at one time or another."

"I hope she kept part of her winnings and bought a new car or treated herself to a vacation."

"No car or vacation, but she did send her only son to college."

"What does he do?" Riley asked.

"He's an investment banker in Los Angeles." Maria sipped her iced tea. "Pablo visits once a year and attempts to coax his mother to move to California, but Consuelo refuses."

"Why?"

"This is where she was born and raised." Maria smiled. "I know what you're thinking."

"What's that?"

"This neighborhood is a far cry from where you were raised."

"True." No sense pretending he felt at home in the 'hood.

"Consuelo can't retire or close the restaurant because she's the only stable influence in her nieces' and nephews' lives. Without her, the kids would be out on the street running with gangbangers. She pays the kids more than minimum wage, but keeps half their paycheck and deposits the money into a savings account for their college education."

Riley had never had to save a dime in his life. Heck, the day he'd been born his father had opened an investment portfolio in his name with five hundred thousand dollars. Today, the account was worth millions. When it came to college, his father had written a check each semester to the university—not one financial-aid form had been filled out the four years Riley attended UNLV. "Consuelo's a generous woman."

They ate in silence for a few minutes, Riley sensing Maria was eager to end the evening. He wasn't. "You like teaching?" She nodded but didn't elaborate. He'd never had to work at engaging a woman in conversation. "How long have you been a teacher?"

"I taught six years of high school English before volunteering the past five years with the district's at-risk kids. The classes are part of the city's antigang program."

"The boys you gave a ride home earlier…were they expelled from school or did they drop out?"

"All three were expelled. If they fail my class, the educational system writes them off for good."

"Do you have the support of the families?"

"Not as much as I wish. We have students who don't even know who their fathers are and a few with dads in prison or running with gangs."

Riley had experienced his share of disagreements with his father, but the old man had always been there for him; and Riley couldn't imagine not having a male role model in his life. "Tell me more about the boys you're working with."

"Alonso lost his father when he was seven—gunned down by police in a drug raid. Alonso's mother cleans offices at night and works at a convenience store during the day."

The kid's mother worked two jobs in order to feed her family and keep a roof over their heads. Riley's mother had never worked a day in her married life.

"Why did Alonso get expelled from school?"

"He skipped too many days, but he was between a rock and a hard place. When one of his siblings became ill, Alonso's mother made him stay home to care for them so she wouldn't miss work."

"How often do his brothers and sisters get sick?"

"His little sister Lea has asthma and is prone to pneumonia."

"That's too bad."

Maria narrowed her eyes and Riley resisted the urge to squirm. "You really do feel compassion for Alonso, don't you?"

Riley was the first to acknowledge he led a privileged life. He bought what he wanted, when he wanted and without considering the cost. And why shouldn't he? He had an abundance of money at his fingertips. It wasn't his fault he hadn't had to work for a dime of it. Even though he had nothing in common with Alonso and his family, Riley wasn't so coldhearted that he couldn't sympathize with their daily struggles. "What kind of student is Alonso?"

"A good one. Alonso loves to learn. He's smart and organized with his studies and grasps new concepts easily. He's ready to take his GED test but I've held him back because I haven't devised a financial strategy to pay for his tuition at a community college."

"Alonso wants to go to college?"

"He plans to enter the medical field."

"Nurses and technicians make decent salaries," Riley said.

"And the jobs come with health insurance and benefits. Alonso realizes that if his mother had health insurance his sister would have access to better care."

"What about the boy with the scar?"

"Victor is bright, too, but he's very self-conscious of his face."

"Did a gangbanger cut his face?"

"His mother did that to him."

His own mother?

"She attacked Victor's sister after the girl announced she was pregnant—" Maria shuddered "—by the mother's boyfriend. Victor tried to protect his sister and got himself hurt."

"I hope the woman went to jail."

"The hospital called in the cops after they'd stitched

Victor's face but Victor changed his story and said he didn't know his attacker."

"What does Victor want to do with his life?"

"He's not sure. All the kids take career assessment tests and Victor displayed decent math skills and an aptitude for electrical work and plumbing but he's not interested in those fields—which is too bad because a local business has offered to employ students while teaching them the trade."

"What's the deal with the smooth-talker?"

"Cruz Rivera." Maria wrinkled her nose. "Like you, he's popular with the ladies."

Riley placed both hands over his heart. "Was that a compliment?"

"You know you're a good-looking man."

"Thanks."

"For what?"

"For calling me a man." Twenty-five was considered young in many minds; but, at every age, Riley's parents had demanded a level of maturity far beyond his years. In truth, he felt a lot older than twenty-five.

"Cruz prefers to use his muscle over his brain. He's stubborn and bullheaded."

"The kid has the makings of a good rodeo cowboy."

"His father rode bulls before he—"

"Cruz's father was T. C. Rivera?"

"Yes."

Riley had heard stories about Rivera. The man had taken the rodeo circuit by storm when Riley had been in high school. But T.C. had thrown away his chance at a world title when he'd gotten into a brawl in South Dakota and killed a man. "Where's T.C. now?"

"South Dakota State Penitentiary in Sioux Falls."

"Was he close to Cruz?"

"Yes. Cruz is his eldest child. T.C. and Juanita have… had four children."

"What do you mean had?"

"Cruz's younger brother by one year was the victim of gang violence."

"Shot to death?"

"A few months ago. He'd been sitting on his front porch with Cruz when a fight broke out between two gangs and shots were fired. A stray bullet caught him in the chest."

Unable to imagine witnessing a sibling's death in such a violent manner, Riley suspected Cruz's tough-act demeanor was a facade hiding a hurt and angry young man. "Does Cruz ever visit his father?"

"No. Juanita doesn't have a car and she can't waste hard-earned money on bus fare to take the kids to South Dakota."

"How long is T.C.'s sentence?"

"He won't be eligible for parole for another twenty years."

Cruz would be close to forty when his father left prison. Steering the conversation back to Maria, Riley asked, "What do you do when you're not chasing after delinquent kids?" He really wanted to ask if there was a man in her life.

"Nothing as exciting as flying airplanes or busting broncs."

"Have you flown before?"

"I've never been on a plane."

"Bet you'd enjoy the experience."

"Why would you think that?"

He shrugged. "You're a thrill seeker."

"Hardly."

"Sure you are. Your job is one big thrill. You have no idea what you're going to face when you roll out of bed each morning." She didn't refute his charge. "Any brothers, sisters, nieces or nephews?" *A significant other?*

"Afraid not."

"I have one sister," Riley said. "Bree's twenty-eight."

"What does she do for a living?"

"Manages the horse stables at the farm."

"Stables?"

"The Fitzpatricks breed racing horses."

"What kind of racing horses?"

"The Kentucky Derby kind."

Maria's fork clanked against the side of her plate. Depending on their personal agenda, this is where women either pushed Riley away or attempted to get closer. "Our family's been involved in horse racing for generations."

"That explains the plane, but not the rodeo."

Before Riley had a chance to speak, the waitress appeared with dessert. "What are they?" he asked.

"Polvorones. Almond cookies," Maria said.

Riley sampled one. "They melt in your mouth." He helped himself to a second cookie. "When I was in eleventh grade I had the chance to attend the Lyle Sankey Rodeo School—he's a famous rodeo cowboy. I got hooked on the sport." He chuckled. "My father has since regretted giving me that birthday gift."

Maria smiled and Riley's eyes were drawn to her full lips and enticing dimples. "You have a beautiful mouth."

"Good grief, stop that."

"Stop what?"

"Flirting."

"How old are you?"

"You're not supposed to ask a woman her age."

"Why not? Is your age a big secret?"

She scrunched her nose. "I'm thirty-five."

"You're only ten years older than me."

"Only?" She glanced at her watch. "Hurry and finish your dessert."

"Why the rush?"

"I need to check on my mother."

Riley stuffed the remaining cookie into his mouth. "You mentioned that you knew a good aviation mechanic. I'd prefer to contact him tonight. Do you have his number?"

At first Maria acted as if she hadn't heard his question then her shoulders slumped. "Why don't I take you to see him."

Hot dog. "I'll pay him to drive out to the salvage yard and inspect the plane." Tomorrow Riley would lease a plane to fly to the Payson rodeo.

Riley grasped Maria's hand and squeezed her fingers. He expected her to pull away, but she didn't and the longer their skin remained in contact the hotter the heat that raced along his forearm and spread through his chest. If touching the schoolteacher's hand created such an intense reaction then kissing her would be a thrill unlike anything he'd ever experienced before.

She cleared her throat. "We'd better get going."

He set a hundred on the table.

"Is that all you carry in your wallet…hundred-dollar bills?"

Riley moved behind her chair and whispered in her ear, "Would it matter if I said yes?"

Maria squirmed, the movement bringing Riley's mouth closer to her cheek. The smell of lilies teased his nose and he resisted pressing a kiss to her warm skin. He pulled her chair back and she bolted from the dining room.

Riley followed, doubting she'd claim ten years was too great an age difference after he gave her a real kiss—the slow, hot, wet kind.

HANDS CLENCHING THE steering wheel in a death grip, Maria turned onto her parents' street. She hoped her father was in a good mood and her mother hadn't finished off a fifth of vodka—a habit she'd begun after her son died.

Maria parked beneath the carport next to her father's Chevy pickup. He'd forgotten to turn on the outside lights. For once she was grateful. The three-bedroom, two-bathroom ranch was in sad shape. Years of neglect had transformed the flower beds and green grass into dirt and weeds.

"This is where the mechanic lives?" Riley asked.

"Yep." Maria led the way up the front walk. She slid her house key into the lock.

Riley grabbed her arm before she opened the door. "Is the mechanic your…?"

"Father." She stepped inside.

A moment later Riley shut the door and flipped the dead bolt. Obviously he'd noticed the neighborhood wasn't the safest. Twenty years ago the area had been crowded with young families and working couples. Once California gangs began infiltrating Albuquerque, the families that could afford to relocated to the suburbs.

"Make yourself comfortable." Maria disappeared down the narrow hallway leading to the bedrooms. She knocked on her parents' door then poked her head inside the room. Her mother's snores greeted Maria and a half-empty bottle of booze sat on the nightstand. Maria returned to the living room. "Mom's asleep." At her age she should be immune to embarrassment, but she was relieved Riley would be spared meeting her drunk mother.

"Dad's outside in the shed." They left through the sliding glass doors off the kitchen and walked along the brick path that ended at the rear of the property. Light shone through the windows of her father's workshop. "Dad," Maria called.

The shed door opened. Her father wore his favorite cowboy hat—one given to him on his birthday by Maria's brother right before he'd been shot. The brim of the Stetson was frayed and the crown covered in sweat stains. She doubted her parents would ever let go of their dead son—the Stetson and vodka constant reminders that Maria had failed her family.

"Dad, this is Riley Fitzgerald." She spoke in English even though her father preferred communicating in Spanish. "Riley, this is my father, Ricardo Alvarez."

"How do you do, Mr. Alvarez." Riley shook hands with her father. "Maria tells me you're an airplane mechanic. My Cessna suffered a bird strike and I had to make an emergency landing. I was hoping you could check the plane and assess the damage."

"Where is the Cessna?"

"Estefan's Salvage," Maria answered.

"Lucky for me your daughter was out there searching for her students at the time or I would have been stranded."

Maria focused on Riley, ignoring her father's heated stare. Her parents resented Maria for working with delinquent teens, believing her actions sullied her brother's memory.

"I'll pay you for your time," Riley said. "I need to rent another plane from the Blue Skies Regional Airport until the Cessna's repaired. I'll be in Arizona for a rodeo tomorrow evening, but, barring bad weather, I'd return to Albuquerque on Sunday."

The sooner Riley and his crippled plane left the state of New Mexico the better. Maria hadn't drawn a deep breath since he'd emerged from the cockpit earlier in the day. "Dad, will you be able to inspect the plane before Sunday?"

"Sí." Her father had once been a gregarious man but his son's death had left him bitter and remote.

"Thank you, Mr. Alvarez." The men shook hands.

Back inside the house, Maria asked, "Would you care for a drink?" Call her fickle. One moment she couldn't wait to dump Riley off at the hotel, the next she didn't want the evening to end.

"Sure." Riley sat on a stool at the countertop then ran his fingers through his hair—gorgeous, black hair.

"Fitzgerald is Irish, right?" Maria placed a can of cola in front of him.

"Wondering why I don't have red hair?"

Maria laughed. "Mind reader."

"I'm Black Irish."

"What's that?"

"My mother traced her lineage back to the Iberian Peninsula, which means my redheaded relatives cohabitated with the Indians and through the centuries each generation has produced an offspring with black hair."

"Are you the only one with dark coloring in your immediate family?"

"My sister's a carrottop. Dad has brownish-red hair and my mother's hair is a blondish-red." He chuckled. "As she ages, she goes blonder to cover the gray."

Maria fingered the ends of her dark hair. She couldn't recall when she'd had her hair professionally colored and she was certain a few gray strands were visible.

"What about your family?" Riley asked. "Are you Mexican, Spanish, or a mixture of both?"

"My great-grandfather was a bricklayer in a small town outside Mexico City. He married my great-grandmother there then they moved to the States and became U.S. citizens. My father and uncles learned to lay brick from their fathers but after high school my dad went into the air force. When Dad retired from the military, he hired on at the regional airport and has worked there ever since."

"I bet your grandfather was proud his son served in the military."

"He was."

"If your father would rather not have to deal with my plane, I'll find a different mechanic."

This is your out. Suggest Riley find another mechanic to fix his airplane, then you'll never see him again. The thought made Maria sad. She was too old for Riley and they lived very different lives. But the cowboy was a flirt, and he made her feel fresh and young inside. She hadn't felt this invigorated since before her brother had passed away. What could it hurt if she saw Riley one more time?

"Dad will be happy to help." She glanced at the wall clock. 10:00 p.m. "You're probably ready to check in at the hotel."

Maria wrote her cell phone number on a piece of paper. "Call me when you know what time you'll arrive on Sunday and I'll arrange for my dad to meet you at the airport."

Riley took the paper, his fingers caressing hers. A zap of electricity spread through her hand and suddenly Sunday couldn't come fast enough.

CHAPTER FOUR

"LADIES AND GENTS, welcome to Payson, Arizona, home of the Gary Hardt Memorial Rodeo—the oldest continuous rodeo in the world!" The announcer's voice boomed across the Payson Event Center outdoor arena late Saturday afternoon. Over three thousand people packed the stands.

"This here rodeo began in 1884 and hasn't missed a year since." Whoops and hollers followed.

"You ol'-timers out there might recall the original rodeo venue was a meadow near the intersection of Main Street and Highway 87. Back then wagons circled 'round to create the arena."

Riley dropped his gear bag in the cowboy-ready area. As was his M.O. a cab had driven him from the local regional airport to the rodeo grounds and he had less than fifteen minutes to prepare for his ride.

"Hey, Fitzgerald, heard you had trouble with that fancy plane of yours."

What the hell was Stover doing here? Riley thought the man had been headed to Texas this weekend. Ignoring the question about his Cessna, Riley straightened his chaps. "You stop riding for the big money?"

"You oughta know by now—" Stover's smirk widened "—I'm not letting you out of my sight."

Stover had entered every rodeo Riley had since the beginning of the year—not unusual. The serious contenders followed the money trail. Riley had chosen to ride in Payson because he needed a win to boost his confidence and he'd wanted to get the hell away from Stover—the braggart annoyed the crap out of him.

"You tagging along when I head back to Albuquerque?" Riley asked.

"There's no rodeo in Albuquerque," Stover said.

"Who said anything about a rodeo? There's a lady waiting for me in the Duke City." Riley doubted Maria pined for him, but that wouldn't stop him from chasing what he wanted—and he wanted her.

"You're so full of wind you could fly to New Mexico without your plane."

"Jealous?" Riley grinned.

"Women and rodeo don't mix," Stover said.

No kidding. Most cowboys learned that lesson the hard way.

"You go see your lady, Fitzgerald. Have a nice long visit with her."

Maria wasn't Riley's lady—yet—but Stover's words reminded him that he'd better watch his step around the sexy señorita lest he forget his goal of winning a second title. "That's the plan, Stover. I'm gonna drown myself in drink and women."

"Rawlins came out of nowhere last year when he should have retired." Stover fisted his hands. "Then you won the title even though you didn't earn it. This year—" Stover poked himself in the chest "—I'm takin' home the buckle."

Riley turned his back on the cowboy and focused on

his ride. He'd drawn a gelding named Blackheart—a veteran bucker.

"We got plenty of ropin', rasslin' and bustin' activity," the rodeo announcer proclaimed, disrupting Riley's concentration. "As a matter of fact last year's world-champion bronc rider, Riley Fitzgerald, is goin' first today!"

World champion…world champion…world champion…

Repeating the mantra in his head, Riley envisioned Maria's pretty face and flashing brown eyes. She had as much guts and determination as a rodeo cowboy. Tangling with delinquent teens was tougher than riding a wild bronc. He worked three or four times a week for eight seconds. Maria faced gangs and kids living on the edge 24/7 and he doubted her record of success was as good as his.

Today, Riley wanted to impress Maria with a win. He didn't understand why her admiration was important to him—he doubted he'd see her after the Cessna was repaired.

"Folks, the action's at gate number five. Let's see if this world-champion bronc rider can tame Blackheart!"

The roar of the crowd faded in Riley's head as he climbed the chute rails. The familiar pungent smell of livestock calmed his nerves. As soon as he attempted to settle into the saddle, Blackheart rebelled, forcing Riley to hop off. Once the gelding calmed, Riley claimed his seat.

After the dink he'd drawn in Colorado, he was ready for a fight and prayed Blackheart wouldn't let him down. Riley squeezed the buck rein, secured his hat on his head and slid deeper into the saddle. *One. Two. Three.* He signaled the gateman and the chute door opened. Riley's body tensed in anticipation then the horse burst from his metal prison.

Riley raked fur—rolled his spurs high on the gelding's shoulders, inciting the animal to buck harder. Blackheart responded to the taunt by thrusting his hind legs into the air. The horse hit the ground then twirled left, right and back to the left again in quick succession.

Eight seconds passed in a blur. The buzzer sounded but the ride wasn't over until his boots hit the dirt. Dismounts were tricky and had to be timed perfectly so the cowboy didn't break his neck or worse—get his head stomped on. Riley vaulted from the saddle. Luck was with him. He landed on both feet, stumbled once then regained his balance.

"Our world-champion cowboy gave us a world-champion ride. Fitzgerald scored an eighty-six!"

"You lucked out, Fitzgerald," Stover said when Riley returned to the cowboy-ready area.

Before he had a chance to refute Stover's charge, another competitor shouted, "Hey, Fitzgerald! Those kinks the press said you needed to work out just got ironed flat!"

Riley chuckled.

"Don't get cocky. Your eighty-six is about to bite the dust." Stover stomped off.

As Riley stowed his gear, his cell phone rang. He checked caller ID. His father. Perfect timing. "Hey, Dad."

"Where are you?"

"Arizona. Tamed a little booger called Blackheart. I'm in the lead with an eighty-six."

"Congratulations. Got a minute to talk?"

"Sure." Riley grabbed his bag and retreated to a quiet corner away from the bucking chutes.

"I've got a potential buyer coming in sometime mid-October. I want you to show him around Belle Farms."

"Who's the buyer interested in?"

"Bonnie-Blond and Sir Duke's offspring. We're expecting the foal early October."

The mare and stallion were a bit older than other champion horses on the farm but they'd produced the most winners. "Can't Bree give the guy a tour?" Shoot, his sister was in charge of the horse barns.

"The buyer's name is Peter Westin. He's a former PRCA champion steer wrestler."

"I thought my rodeo career was a black mark on the family name," Riley teased.

His father wasn't in a humorous mood. "You have more in common with Westin than I do and I need your help closing the deal."

"I'm riding in every rodeo from here to who-knows-where the next two months."

"You can fly in for one night, can't you?"

"I don't know. Maybe."

"I backed off you because your mother asked me to. You've done what you've wanted most of your adult life. You hardly visit anymore."

Guilt trip. Riley hadn't been home in months. He missed Belle Farms but kept his distance because he didn't care to argue with his father. *Family money pays your entry fees.* "I'll be there."

"Good. Your mother's planning a formal dinner."

"Yeah, sure."

"How's the *Dark Stranger* flying?"

"Runs like a dream," Riley lied. No sense troubling the old man when he hadn't learned the extent of the damages.

"Stay safe, son."

"Will do. 'Bye, Dad." Riley disconnected the call and shoved the phone into his back pocket. There were times that he wished he had his act together. His father's request to schmooze a potential horse buyer was an attempt to lure Riley back to Belle Farms and persuade him to give up rodeo.

Having unlimited funds at his disposal had allowed Riley to avoid making decisions about his future. He'd promised his father if he could bust broncs in college he'd earn a degree then return to the farm. Instead, after he'd graduated he'd decided to try his hand at professional rodeo—two years max. Riley was into his third season of the sport and his father was running out of patience.

Although he'd never admit it out loud, Riley didn't love rodeo as much as he pretended to, but the alternative—working with thoroughbred racing horses—was enough to keep him competing. Until he knew what he wanted to do with his life, he refused to quit the circuit. Not many twenty-five-year-olds had mapped out their lives but Riley feared even by Maria's age he wouldn't have a plan for his future.

Gear bag in hand, he moseyed into the stands to watch the rest of the rodeo. Later he'd grab a bite to eat then find a motel and call it a night. While other cowboys headed to the local watering hole, Riley would end the evening alone…dreaming about a woman more than three hundred miles away.

LATE SUNDAY AFTERNOON, Maria pointed to the sky and said, "That's him." Riley Fitzgerald—the hot, young rodeo cowboy whose memory had disrupted her sleep the past two nights. She checked her watch. Four-thirty on the dot. Riley had phoned her before he'd left Payson and asked to meet her father at the airport.

The moment the plane's wheels touched down, Maria's heartbeat accelerated. Seeing Riley again wasn't a good idea, but that hadn't stopped her from accompanying her father this afternoon. The cowboy excited her and it had been longer than she remembered since a man had rattled her cage.

Too bad more than an age difference raised red flags in Maria's head. In the brief time she'd known Riley she'd sensed he lived life in the moment, thinking only of himself. That wasn't necessarily a bad thing—most young adults were self-centered. Those days had passed Maria by and now her mission in life was to put herself last and help others first.

Riley taxied toward the hangar.

"I'm surprised," her father said.

"About what?"

"That a young man his age is an accomplished pilot."

Landing a plane with winds gusting at thirty-five miles per hour wasn't easy but Riley managed the feat without mishap. Maria guessed that behind his cocky cowboy charm was a serious aviator.

"Twenty-five isn't that young," she said, drawing a frown from her father. When Maria had been Riley's age she'd already earned a master's degree and had begun work on her doctorate. She'd watched her brother die and had helped her parents plan the funeral.

"Your brother would have been twenty-five next month."

"I know." She'd never forget the night Juan had been gunned down. Maria had arrived at the E.R. in time to hold her brother's hand and beg his forgiveness as he'd slipped away.

Less than a minute after Riley parked the plane, the cockpit door opened and he stepped into view. He wore aviator sunglasses but she knew the moment he spotted her—he flashed his devil-may-care grin.

"Nice to see you again, Mr. Alvarez." Riley removed his glasses and his eyes pinned her. "Hello, Maria."

Was it her imagination or had her name slid off his tongue in a husky whisper? "How was your flight?" The question squeaked past her lips.

"Good." Riley switched his attention to her father. "Did you have a chance to drive out to the salvage yard and check on the Cessna?"

"Sí." While her father discussed the list of recommended repairs with Riley, Maria wandered over to the soda machine. Maybe a Coke—make that a Diet Coke— would settle her nerves. She hated diet soda, and was disgusted with herself for caring about Riley's opinion of her figure. What did it matter if she needed to lose ten pounds? She and Riley weren't lovers. Shoot, they weren't friends, either. That Maria was even having this conversation with herself annoyed her.

Propping a shoulder against the wall, she studied Riley. He glanced her way and she swore the corner of his mouth curved in an intimate acknowledgment of her interest in him. Her pulse shifted into overdrive. Oh, who was she kidding? Riley was a cowboy. Flirting was in his DNA. If Maria were five years younger, she wouldn't be as self-conscious of her attraction to Riley. She tossed the half-empty soda can into the recycle bin then joined the men.

"How long until the repairs are completed?" Riley asked.

"It will be ten days before the propeller parts come in."

"I'll pay double your hourly wage to work on the *Dark Stranger.*"

Maria flinched. Ricardo Alvarez was a prideful man. "I will fix it for—"

"Mr. Alvarez. You've already taken the time to drive out to the salvage yard to inspect the plane." Riley fished his wallet from his pocket and handed her father a credit card. "Use this to cover moving the plane, parts and supplies." He turned to Maria and asked, "Will you join me for dinner?"

Oh, my God. He'd asked her out on a date in front of her father? "Ah…"

"I didn't have a chance to celebrate my win this weekend and I was hoping you'd share a victory meal with me." Riley's gaze roamed over her and Maria felt her face flame.

Even though her family never ate together anymore she hoped her father would provide an excuse to decline the dinner invitation. "Did you or Mom have anything planned for supper?"

"No."

Thanks, Dad.

She made a feeble attempt to back out of the date. "Aren't you flying to another rodeo?"

"I'm free until next weekend." He glanced at her father. "I'll hang around Albuquerque this week in case you need an extra pair of hands to work on the plane."

Doubting her father would appreciate Riley's help, Maria said, "We'd better get going." She headed for her station wagon in the parking lot. *She* and not some young, wealthy, full-of-himself, sexy, hot rodeo cowboy would call the shots tonight.

Before she'd put the car in Reverse, Maria's cell phone rang.

"Bad news?" Riley asked after she ended the call.

"It's Cruz."

"What happened?" The note of concern in Riley's voice startled Maria.

"He was arrested."

"What'd he do?" Riley braced a hand against the dashboard as Maria sped from the airport.

"Defacing private property."

"Cruz joined the Los Locos?"

Riley remembered.

Maria ignored the pleasant feeling that rushed through her at the knowledge that Riley had listened to her ramblings about the Los Locos gang. Used to having her lectures go in one ear of her students' and out the other she'd assumed the same for Riley since he was closer in age to Cruz than her.

"I don't know if he was alone or with the gang." Maria's thoughts turned inward. Cruz's mother wouldn't be able to post bail and the school district's strict policy prohibiting teachers from posting bond for students prevented Maria from interceding on Cruz's behalf. What a mess. She pulled into the police station and parked in a visitor's stall. "Wait here."

"Are you kidding?" Riley trailed after her.

As soon as she stepped inside the precinct building an officer intercepted her. "Maria, we can't release him into your custody." Carlos Bradshaw had attended high school with Maria and did his best to help her students when they landed in jail.

Carlos glanced at Riley. "Who are you?"

"Riley Fitzgerald." He held out a hand.

Carlos's eyes narrowed as he examined Riley's attire.

"Riley's a rodeo cowboy," Maria said.

Carlos wasn't impressed. "Cruz has to post bail to get out. And if he doesn't appear at his hearing he'll do time in juvie."

"Cruz's mother doesn't have the money and you know I'll lose my job if I post his bail." Maria shuddered at the thought of Cruz spending the night in lock-up with drug addicts, pedophiles and gangbangers.

"How much is his bond?" Riley asked.

"Ten thousand," Carlos said.

"I'll cover it."

"You must be pretty good at rodeoing if you have that much money to spare," Carlos said.

"Last year's world champion in the saddle-bronc competition." Riley removed his checkbook from his shirt pocket.

"I'll tell them Cruz will make bail." Carlos stopped at the information desk and spoke to the clerk.

"Why are you doing this?" Maria asked.

"The kid needs help."

"You don't even know Cruz."

"I know you," Riley said. "And you care about what happens to Cruz."

Maria's heart melted. Maybe she'd misjudged Riley and there was more to the man than a pretty face, a sexy grin and a fat wallet.

CHAPTER FIVE

RILEY STOOD IN the police station foyer, a shoulder propped against the wall, waiting for Officer Bradshaw to retrieve Cruz from the holding cell. Maria had left to sign paperwork for the teenage delinquent.

"What are you doing here?" Cruz said when he spotted Riley.

"Bailing you out." Riley noted the teen's pale complexion. "First time in the joint?"

Cruz ignored the question and glared at Bradshaw, who had hold of his arm.

"Better be the last time." The officer released the teen. "Maria asked that you wait here for her." Bradshaw shoved Cruz toward the bench in the middle of the hall then lowered his voice. "What's your angle in all this?"

"How do mean?" Riley asked.

"Why'd you post bail for the kid? Trying to get on Maria's good side?"

"Maybe." To tell the truth, Riley wasn't sure if his attraction to Maria had prompted him to intervene or if there was more going on inside him than impressing the teacher.

"I don't know what your game is, but you aren't her type."

Because he was a few years younger or because he was wealthy? "Who is her type?"

Rather than answer, Bradshaw did an about-face and walked off. Riley moseyed over to the bench and sat next to Cruz. "Why'd you spray paint the building?"

The kid gaped at Riley as if he was nuts. "Ahh…cuz I wanted to?"

Riley didn't know the first thing about communicating with teenagers.

"You got any goals in life besides defacing property and causing general mayhem?"

"Why do you care what I do?"

"I don't. I'm curious."

"Doesn't matter what I do 'cause one day I'm gonna get clipped."

"Maria told me about your brother. I'm sorry, Cruz."

The kid shrugged off the condolence. Riley shuddered at the thought of waking each morning worried he'd be dead by suppertime.

"You ever visit your father in prison?" Riley asked.

"No."

"Your father was a heck of a bull rider. I didn't know him personally but his name comes up on the circuit every now and then."

The tidbit of information piqued Cruz's curiosity. "What do they say about him?"

"They claim T. C. Rivera was part bull himself." Riley grinned. "Your father could predict a bull's next move before the bull."

"I never saw him ride."

"You ever think about rodeoing?"

"Where am I gonna get a bull to practice on?"

"You're too lanky to ride bulls. You're built to bust broncs."

"Don't matter. There's no broncs in the 'hood."

An idea percolated in Riley's head. "If I could scare up a practice bronc would you want to try your hand at busting one?"

"Rodeo's stupid. That's why my dad's in the slammer."

Riley baited Cruz. "What's the matter? Afraid you might get hurt?"

"No." The kid glared. "Fallin' off a horse is easy compared to taking a bullet from a passing car."

"You've been shot?"

"Once." Cruz bunched his shirtsleeve, exposing a scar above his elbow. A quarter inch of flesh was missing.

"Bet that hurt."

"No shit."

"How old were you?"

"Nine."

Nine years old? No wonder kids in the 'hood held out little hope for a better life. They were marking time until their end came.

"You must make a lot of money at rodeo if you fly your own plane and wear those sissy boots." Cruz smirked.

"The better cowboys make decent money." If he confessed the cash in his wallet came from his trust fund and not rodeo wins or sponsorships, Cruz wouldn't bother with the sport. "If bullets don't scare you, then why not try—"

"Try what?" Maria appeared out of nowhere.

"Rodeo," Riley said. "Better hobby than drawing pictures on buildings."

"Cruz doesn't have time for hobbies. The judge has

generously decided to give you a community-service sentence rather than make you stand trial for vandalism."

Maria must have done some fast-talking to change the judge's mind.

"What kind of community service?" Cruz asked.

"Garbage detail."

"No way." Cruz popped off the bench. "I ain't bagging no stinkin' trash."

"Then you sit in the waiting cell until your trial."

Riley admired Maria for playing hardball and not backing down to the kid.

"How long do I have to collect trash for?"

"A hundred hours," Maria said.

Cruz's mouth sagged open.

"The earliest the judge would hear your case is in seven weeks. You're welcome to wait in jail until then."

"What about my GED? Did you tell the judge about all the tests I have to take?"

"Yes, but the judge said if you'd cared about your education you would have been at home studying instead of tagging property with the Los Locos."

"She's a juvie judge. Doesn't she give a shit about kids?"

Maria shoved a hand through her hair. "Cruz, you've been offered a lot of second chances and you've done nothing with them. Nobody cares about you or your GED." She set her hand on his shoulder. "Except me."

He shrugged off her touch. "Man, this sucks!"

"Before you two decide anything, give me five minutes." Riley stepped outside the building and phoned Ed Parker. After a quick chat, he asked Ed for his father's cell number. Gil Parker answered on the first ring.

Riley asked the man if he'd allow a teenage juvenile offender to serve his community-service sentence at the Gateway Ranch. Without going into detail Riley explained Cruz's situation and how Maria was helping the teen and two of his buddies earn their GEDs. Gil agreed to take all three boys in for the rest of the summer as long as they worked for their room and board.

"New game plan," Riley said when he entered the building.

"Cruz's situation doesn't involve you," Maria said.

Riley raised his hand. "Hold up a second."

"Yeah, Ms. Alvarez," Cruz said. "Maybe Riley can get me off the hook."

"No can do, kid, but I've got a better idea for you than garbage detail."

"And what would that plan be?" Maria asked.

"First, I need to see the judge." Riley approached the station desk. "Is there any way I can have a word with the judge handling Cruz Rivera's case?" When the clerk eyed him suspiciously, he said, "Officer Bradshaw will vouch for me."

"One minute." The clerk disappeared through a door at the back of the room. A moment later she returned with Maria's cop friend.

"What's going on?" Bradshaw asked.

"Take me to the judge who ruled on Cruz's case," Riley said.

"Why?"

"There's a better way to teach Cruz to stay away from gangs than picking up trash."

"If you're wasting the judge's time, I'll toss you in a holding cell," Bradshaw warned.

After a series of twists and turns through several hallways they arrived at the judge's chamber. Bradshaw knocked twice.

"Enter," a feminine voice called.

"Judge Hamel." Bradshaw poked his head around the door. "Do you have a minute for a friend of Maria Alvarez?"

"Make it fast."

Riley followed Bradshaw into the room, which wasn't much bigger than his mother's master bedroom closet. What happened to judges having plush offices with designer furniture? This woman's desk was a gray metal monstrosity covered with dents and scratches. Instead of original paintings on the walls, a poster of the Eiffel Tower hung behind the desk and a cheap put-it-together-yourself bookcase leaned against the wall with sickly plants resting on the top shelf. The windowless cubicle smelled of coffee and peppermints.

"Sit down." The judge pointed her pen at the folding chair in front of the desk, then removed her reading glasses and tossed them onto the open file in front of her.

"Ma'am, my name is Riley Fitzgerald." He tipped his hat. The judge, who had to be in her sixties, eyeballed him from head-to-toe. He hoped his rodeo-cowboy charisma worked on the judge. "I have a suggestion for Cruz Rivera's sen—"

"Are you telling me how to do my job—" her eyes narrowed "—cowboy?"

"No, ma'am. But I'm hoping you'll be open to the idea of Cruz working off his service hours at a ranch."

Bradshaw chuckled, but Riley ignored the officer.

"What's a city boy going to do on a ranch, Mr. Fitzgerald?"

"Muck out horse stalls for a start, ma'am."

"Hmm…" The judge tapped her pen on the desk then asked, "Where's this ranch?"

"The Gateway Ranch north of Albuquerque. Gil Parker is the—"

"I know Gil. He serves on the city's environmental community board."

Even better.

The judge leaned back in her chair and assessed Riley. "You're a real cowboy, Mr. Fitzgerald?"

Riley poured on the charm. "I'm a rodeo cowboy, ma'am."

"It's 'Your Honor.'"

"Yes, ma'am, Your Honor. I'm the reigning PRCA world saddle-bronc champion."

"I have no idea what that means." She waved a hand in the air. "Nor do I care. Now tell me why you're interested in helping Cruz Rivera?"

Mostly Riley wanted to intervene for Maria's sake. "Maria's working hard to help Cruz earn his GED and she really cares about the kid succeeding." Cruz staying at the Gateway Ranch would give Riley an excuse to keep in touch with Maria. "If Cruz lives and works at the ranch, Maria can focus her energy on tutoring him and not trying to keep him out of trouble."

The judge remained silent.

"Cruz's father was a bull rider—"

"I'm aware of the young man's family history."

"Ranch chores are tough—more difficult than trash detail. Living at the ranch would keep Cruz off the streets and away from gangs. Plus, he'd have to learn to take orders from the other cowboys."

After a long silence the judge lifted her gavel and slammed it against the wood block resting on the corner of the desk. Riley's ears rang. "I'll change his sentence to the Gateway Ranch." She glanced at Bradshaw. "Send Maria back in here." She narrowed her eyes. "Your plan had better work, Mr. Fitzgerald. If I receive one complaint about Cruz from Gil Parker or anyone else at the Gateway Ranch, I'll ship Cruz off to juvie."

"Thank you, ma'—I mean, Your Honor. You won't regret this."

"See that I don't, cowboy."

Bradshaw escorted Riley to the main corridor of the police station.

"Where did you go?" Maria asked.

"To see the judge," Riley said.

"Judge Hamel wants you in her chambers, Maria," Bradshaw said.

"What's going on, Riley?" Maria asked.

"The judge agreed to allow Cruz to work off his community-service hours doing ranch work."

"What ranch?" Maria asked.

"Gateway Ranch—north of the city."

"What do I gotta do?" Cruz frowned.

"Muck out horse stalls," Riley said.

"Huh?" Cruz turned to Maria for clarification.

"Scoop horse poop."

"After Cruz finishes his chores," Riley said, "I'll show him the rodeo ropes."

"You're staying at the Gateway Ranch?" Maria asked.

Riley shrugged. "The foreman of the ranch is the father of a rodeo buddy of mine."

"I won't be able to drive Cruz out to the ranch every day."

"There's a bunkhouse on the property. Cruz can stay there."

Maria folded her arms across her chest, the action raising her breasts higher. Riley did his best to ignore the twinge in his groin. "What about his schoolwork?" she asked.

"What about my homies?" Cruz added.

"Gil invited Victor and Alonso to tag along with Cruz as long as all three work for their room and board."

"I don't get paid?" Cruz protested.

"Nope," Riley said.

"Once I do my hundred hours, I ain't sticking around no ranch."

"With all three guys at the ranch—" Riley spoke to Maria "—you'd only have to make a few trips a week out there to tutor them."

"I can manage that, but I'll have to clear the arrangement with their families."

"So that's it?" Cruz glared. "You guys make all the decisions and I get no say?"

"You lost your *say* when you landed in jail," Maria said.

"Man, this blows."

Maria dug through her purse and handed a set of keys to the teen. "Wait in my car." Once he left the building, Maria said, "I don't know how to thank you, Riley. We could use more mentors in our program."

Riley had never thought of himself as a mentor but the idea of helping Cruz and the other boys made him feel useful and for the first time unselfish. For once he was thinking of someone other than himself.

Maria stood on tiptoe and kissed his cheek. Caught off guard, he had no time to absorb the sensation of her lips brushing his skin, her sigh caressing his chin. "Thank you for caring."

Stunned, he watched Maria head to the judge's chambers. He hoped his plan to help the three delinquent amigos didn't backfire, because Riley intended to earn another kiss from Maria—next time on the mouth.

"YOU SUCK, CRUZ," Victor said in the backseat of Maria's station wagon. "Because of you I gotta go to a stupid ranch and shovel horse turds."

Maria clenched the steering wheel as she felt a wave of heartburn coming on. Victor and Alonso weren't thrilled about keeping Cruz company while he worked off his community-service hours. Their attitude didn't surprise her. The three seventeen-year-olds had never held down real jobs. Local businesses were reluctant to hire them because of their juvenile records and suspensions from school. She didn't envy the cowboy put in charge of supervising the boys.

Gaining approval from the teens' parents had been easier than Maria had anticipated. Once she'd assured them that their sons would continue working toward their GEDs the parents had conceded it was in their sons' best interest to be removed from the influence of the Los Locos gang.

"I didn't force you to come," Cruz said. "Blame it on Ms. Alvarez's boyfriend."

Boyfriend? "Mr. Fitzgerald is not my boyfriend. He's trying to help you, Cruz."

"He wants to get in your—" The rest of Cruz's remark came out in a grunt after Alonso elbowed him in the chest.

Maria slowed the car, then turned off the road and drove beneath a huge arch with the name Gateway Ranch burned into the wood. Three days had passed since Riley had returned from the rodeo in Arizona. Maria had dropped him off at the hotel Sunday night after they'd posted Cruz's bail. She waited until late Monday afternoon to call him to see if he'd wanted to eat dinner with her. The hotel clerk informed her that he'd already checked out of his room. That Riley hadn't told her his plans shouldn't have mattered—they weren't a couple. But he'd offered to help her students and…

And what? That gives you a right to know his every move?

Finally, on Tuesday, Riley had phoned her and said he'd rented a pickup and was staying at the Gateway Ranch getting things ready for the boys. He'd told her to bring the teens out Wednesday and he'd help supervise them until Friday morning when he flew to a rodeo in Nevada.

"There's a lot of stinkin' cows on this place," Victor said as they drove along the gravel road.

Maria glanced at the grazing herd. She'd done a little research on the ranch and decided to share her findings with the boys. "The Gateway Ranch runs over ten thousand head of cattle. Robert Masterson purchased the property back in 1812."

"Guess he's dead now." Cruz snickered.

"Masterson never married. When he died, he left the ranch to a widowed schoolteacher in town."

"What'd she do with the place?" Alonso asked.

"Sold it to the bank. The bank split the property into three parcels then sold off two and kept the third."

"So the Gateway is one of those parcels?" Victor asked.

"Yes." Maria was glad the boys appeared interested in the area's history. "Francis Wellington bought one parcel and a man named Buck Honorable bought the other. As the story goes, Buck and Francis did not get along and fought over water rights and property lines. They even accused each other of cattle rustling."

"What's that?" Victor asked.

"Stealing cows," Alonso answered.

"The fighting got so bad," Maria continued, "that Buck challenged Francis to a duel."

"Who won?" Cruz asked.

Maria didn't answer right away as she maneuvered the car around an outcropping of rock. Once she negotiated the tight turn, she stopped the vehicle and shifted into Park. "Wow."

Thousands of milling cows dotted the green valley below. A collection of barns, corrals, holding pens and various ranch buildings were scattered about.

"This place is huge." Victor pressed his face against the window.

"To answer your question, Cruz, Francis won the duel, because Buck's rifle accidentally discharged and he shot himself in the chest."

"What an idiot," Cruz said.

"Hey, Ms. Alvarez." Victor tapped her shoulder. "You think we're gonna get our own horse to ride while we're here?"

"I don't know. I'm sure one of the ranch hands would teach you to ride."

Victor nudged Alonso. "You wanna learn how to ride a horse?"

"Yeah, sure."

Maria put the car into Drive. "First we need to introduce ourselves to Mr. Parker. He's in charge of the day-to-day operation of the ranch. In other words, all of you had better do as he says."

"Nobody bosses me around," Cruz said.

Maria had had enough of the teen's obstinate attitude. "Say the word, Cruz, and I'll take you back to the police station, where you can wait until your trial."

Seconds passed.

"Whatever. I don't give a crap," Cruz said.

Tense silence filled the car as Maria pulled into the ranch yard. "There's Riley!" Victor pointed out the windshield.

Alonso leaned over the front seat to see out the window. "Where?"

"In the corral."

Riley sat astride a bucking gelding—every inch the quintessential cowboy. He gripped a rope in his right hand, his left arm raised high above his head as he spurred the horse along its neck.

Ranch hands gathered near the pen, straddling the top rail or poking their heads through the slats for a better view. Maria lowered her window and excited shouts filtered into the car.

"Check it out, Cruz. The dude's a real pro." Alonso spared his friend a glance, but Cruz acted unimpressed, arms folded over his chest as if bored by the action in the corral.

Maria forgot about the boys as she watched Riley. His

young, athletic body swayed and jerked in rhythm to the
horse's bucking. Horse and rider melded into one, performing a ballet of wild gyrations and explosive movements. Seconds passed and the bucking grew weaker.
Weaker. Finally the horse conceded defeat and came to
a standstill, its sides heaving.

"That was totally cool!" Victor said.

"Anyone can do that if you hold on long enough,"
Cruz grumbled.

"Let's congratulate Riley." Maria stepped from the
car and slammed the door. The noise spooked the gelding. The horse kicked his back legs out and Riley sailed
over the animal's head.

Oh, dear. Twenty sets of eyes glared at Maria.

Riley got to his feet and dusted himself off. He retrieved his hat from across the pen then turned to see
what had startled the bronc. An older man broke away
from the pack and headed toward Maria. Lines etched
his face and he walked with a pronounced limp.

"Gil Parker." He tipped his hat. "You must be the
teacher Riley mentioned." The foreman didn't smile as
he sized up the boys. Alonso and Victor dropped their
gazes but Cruz stared defiantly at the older man. "You're
the troublemaker." Mr. Parker spoke to Cruz.

Cruz's chin jutted but he remained tightlipped. A
short, gray-haired man with a scruffy beard joined the
group. He turned his head to the side and spit tobacco
juice twenty feet through the air.

"Aw, dude, that was insane," Victor said.

"What'd ya call me, son?" The old man squinted, his
eyes disappearing in the wrinkled folds of skin.

"Sir. I meant, sir," Victor stammered. "Can you teach me how to spit?"

"Depends."

"On what?" Victor asked.

"On how well ya follow orders."

"Hey," Riley called out. He stopped at Maria's side. "Let me introduce everyone." Riley put a hand on each boy's shoulder as he said their name. "Cruz, Alonso and Victor." He moved his hand to Maria's shoulder and her skin warmed beneath his touch. "Maria Alvarez. She's helping the boys earn their GEDs."

Riley motioned to the cowboys. "This is Gil Parker, he runs the place. His son and I compete at many of the same rodeos throughout the year." Riley pointed to the old man. "This here is Shorty. He's worked at the Gateway Ranch for over twenty years."

"How old are you?" Alonso asked.

"Old 'nough to give Jesus a run fer his money."

"Shorty works with the ranch horses," Mr. Parker said. "You boys will report to Shorty and take your orders from him."

"Ya youngins gotta be outfitted proper if yer gonna do cowboy work," Shorty said.

"What's the matter with my clothes?" Cruz tugged on his baggy pants.

"Nothin' less'n ya wanna make a spectacle a yerself." He eyed the teen's outfit. "Looks like ya done dropped a load in yer undershorts."

Cruz's face reddened.

"We'll take good care of your students, Ms. Alvarez." Gil Parker tipped his hat and left the group.

"I'll show ya where yer gonna bunk down." Shorty walked off and the boys followed.

"They'll be fine," Riley said.

"I hope so." Maria wanted this arrangement to work out for the boys; but Shorty was so...short and old that she worried the teens would overwhelm the coot.

"Shorty's been a wrangler all his life and he used to ride bulls in his younger days. Handling three delinquent teens will be a breeze. You wait and see. The boys won't get away with anything under his watch."

Riley grasped Maria's hand. "How about a tour of the ranch?" Riley tugged her after him, his fingers tightening around hers.

He talked about the chores the boys would be doing but Maria didn't hear a word. She was too busy enjoying the warmth of Riley's callused fingers clasping hers.

CHAPTER SIX

"Ya missed a turd."

Riley poked his head inside the barn and caught Shorty pointing the end of a pitchfork into a horse stall. Cruz towered over the old man by several inches.

"One turd isn't gonna make a difference." Despite his protest, Cruz snatched the rake from Shorty and flung the clump of soiled hay into a nearby wheelbarrow. "Satisfied?"

Wincing at the teen's rudeness, Riley hid in the shadows and eavesdropped. Shorty's head wasn't visible but Riley had a clear view of Cruz above the stall door.

"Ain't gonna be satisfied 'til ya do the job right, 'n' that means gittin' rid a the dirty straw."

"Why? The horse is gonna pee and crap all over the new hay."

"That's what horses do best, son. Pee 'n' drop turds."

"Being a cowboy sucks."

"I disagree, son. I'm partial to the cowboy way."

"Quit calling me 'son.'"

"Where'd ya git that chip on yer shoulder?"

"If you lived in my neighborhood, you'd act tough to survive, too."

Shorty moved into view and leaned against the grooming post in the center aisle. He dug out a tobacco pouch from his shirt pocket and stuffed a pinch of chew between his cheek and gum. "If ya don't care fer livin' there, git out."

"It's not that easy to leave." Cruz stepped from the stall.

"All ya gotta do is pack yer bags 'n' vamoose."

"And go where? What would I do?"

Cruz's questions reminded Riley of the privileged life he led. He'd never had to worry about clothes, food, or shelter—all taken for granted. Gangs provided kids in the 'hood with the same securities. The rabble-rousers made easy money dealing drugs, robbing stores, pickpocketing people and selling stolen property. The money they amassed offered its members a lifestyle they'd only dreamed of—cars, expensive clothes, shoes, guns, liquor and all the food they could eat. Aside from escaping poverty, being a gangbanger fed their self-esteem—the kids became big shots.

"Git a job fer starters." Shorty spit tobacco at the drain in the barn floor.

"Nice shot." Cruz set the pitchfork aside and wiped his brow—probably the first time the kid had perspired from honest hard work. "Even if I get my GED who's gonna hire me? I got a juvie record."

"Sellin' drugs?"

"No, but that's where the big money is." Cruz pitched another forkful of soiled hay into the wheelbarrow. "I had a joint in my pocket when the cops nailed me for shoplifting. I was keeping it for a friend."

Shorty snickered at the kid's outright lie.

"Whatever, man."

"The boss said yer doin' community service at the ranch. What'd they catch ya for?"

"Tagged an office building with my homies. The judge gave me trash detail but my teacher's boyfriend convinced her I'd learn my lesson better shoveling horse-shit, so I got sent here."

"Ya any good at drawin'?"

"Do you ask this many questions all the time?"

"Ain't got nothin' better to do while I watch ya work." Shorty ignored the cuss word that slipped from Cruz's mouth. "Ya ever see yer father?"

"You know my old man?"

"T. C. Rivera was a dang good bull rider 'fore he landed in jail."

"He killed a man in self-defense, but the stupid lawyers—"

"Lawyers ain't ignorant, son."

"Then the jury hated Latinos, because my dad got the maximum sentence. If he would have been white he'd have been charged with manslaughter and been out of prison by now."

"Yer dad got what he deserved. I was there. I saw everythin'."

Riley hadn't known Shorty had witnessed the infamous brawl at Deadwood Dick's Gaming Hall in Deadwood, South Dakota, three weeks prior to the finals in Las Vegas.

"Wanna hear the truth or keep believin' the rumors?"

"The truth." Cruz rested the pitchfork against the stall door and sat on a bale.

"I rode bulls in my heyday, kid. Rode 'til I broke most every bone in my body. When I couldn't ride no more, I started clownin' in rodeos. I was at the bar the night T.C. pulled a knife on Clarence Hinkley."

"My father defended himself."

"He tell ya that?"

Cruz shook his head.

"T.C. was drunk. He couldn't hold his liquor—lotta cowboys can't. By the time Clarence walked into the gamin' hall T.C. was a swayin' and stumblin'."

"The other guy should have known better than to harass my dad."

"Cowboys talk a good game, son. Part a bein' a cowboy. Clarence taunted T.C. 'bout his ride that day."

"What'd he say?"

"Said yer father's luck had run out 'n' he ought to use his pretty face fer ridin' women not bulls." Shorty paused to spit.

"If that's all the guy said, why'd my father kill him?"

"Don't believe T.C. meant to. Think he wanted to scare Clarence when he pulled a knife."

"How come no one stopped my dad?"

"I tried."

"You?"

Shorty yanked the snaps apart on the front of his western shirt. Even from his hiding place at the end of the barn, Riley saw the jagged scar that dissected the ranch hand's chest.

"T.C. slashed me when I stepped in front a him."

Cruz's mouth dropped open. "My father did that to you?"

"Other cowboys got nicked, too, 'cause they tried to stop T.C. The barkeep stuck his boot out 'n' tripped yer father. T.C. fell forward and Clarence didn't have time to git outta the way. The knife went straight through his heart. Died right there on the floor."

"It was an accident, then."

"Partly. But at the end a the night a man was dead and yer father was holdin' the knife."

"He was drunk. He didn't know what he was doing."

"There comes a time when a man has to own up to his actions. T.C. might not a meant to kill Clarence, but he did."

"Where do you want me to dump this crap anyway?" Cruz kicked the wheelbarrow.

"Compost pile's out back o' the barn."

Cruz pushed the barrow past Riley and out the barn doors.

"Ya can quit hidin' 'n' come out now."

"Hey, Shorty. How's Cruz doing?"

"His mouth works good—full of wind as a hoss with colic."

"I didn't know you hung around the circuit after you retired."

Shorty waved off Riley's comment. "'Nough talk 'bout me. Hear yer havin' trouble stickin' to the saddle this season."

The very reason Riley had returned to the Gateway Ranch this morning. He'd ushered in the beginning of September with a loss during the first go-round in the Nevada rodeo. "Can't seem to win the big ones."

"Ya got a buckle already. Ain't one enough?"

Riley scoffed. "I didn't *earn* that buckle."

"Well, then, shouldn't ya be practicin' 'stead a hangin' 'round here babysittin' delinquents?"

"I promised Maria I'd make sure the boys settled in

at the ranch." He checked his watch. "She should arrive within the hour."

"Ain't surprised a woman's the reason ya—"

"What are you doing here?" Cruz stepped inside the barn, his glare directed at Riley.

"Got a stubborn horse that needs the wild ridden out of him. You interested?" When Cruz didn't respond, Riley said, "Once I work the kinks out of him, you can take a stab at staying in the saddle."

"Am I done with chores?" Cruz asked Shorty.

"After ya fill the grain buckets yer done."

"Meet me at the corral," Riley said.

"Yeah, whatever." Cruz disappeared into the storage room.

"What happens if ya don't win this year?" Shorty asked.

"Not sure." That was the God's honest truth. Riley left the barn, his purposeful strides eating the ground as he headed to the round pen.

WHAT IN THE WORLD?

Maria parked the station wagon in front of the main house at the Gateway Ranch and watched the crowd gathered near the livestock pen. Unable to see over the heads of the cowboys, she left the car and zigzagged between the trucks parked helter-skelter in the ranch yard.

"Excuse me. Pardon me." Maria pushed her way through the throng of smelly cowboys until she had a clear view of the commotion inside the pen—Cruz sitting atop a bucking horse. She hardly recognized the teen in slim-fitting Wranglers, work boots and a navy blue

T-shirt. Used to seeing him in baggy clothes, Cruz was skinnier than she'd realized.

Right then the horse kicked its back legs out and Cruz pitched forward in the saddle. Maria crossed her fingers, praying he wouldn't land on his face in the dirt.

"Hey, Ms. Alvarez!" Eyes bright with excitement, Victor squeezed past a ranch hand. "Cruz is bustin' a bronc."

"He sure is." She assessed Victor's outfit. The fitted clothes showed he could stand to lose a few pounds. "Nice duds."

"They suck, but I don't care as long as my homies in the 'hood don't see me."

Maria watched Cruz. The horse appeared to be tiring. "How many times has he done this?" She worried Cruz would get injured and be unable to complete his community-service sentence.

"Riley rides the buck out of the bronc first then Cruz finishes him off," Victor said.

Riley was here? She thought he'd left yesterday for a rodeo. Keeping track of everyone's schedules was a losing battle.

"You shoulda seen Riley when he rode the horse the first time. He got thrown twice."

Ouch. "Where's Alonso?"

"In the barn with the vet checking on a sick cow."

The horse in the corral finally settled down and the cowboys whistled and clapped. Cruz jumped off, a huge smile wreathing his face.

Maria hadn't seen the teen smile—a genuine smile— since she'd begun working with him. It was too early to tell if Riley's suggestion to leave the boys at the Gateway

Ranch had been a good idea or not, but Cruz's improved demeanor gave her hope.

"Did you guys finish your school lessons?" she asked.

"We don't have time to study 'cause of all the work they make us do," Victor said.

"Shorty asks you to do chores late at night?"

"No—" Victor's face brightened "—but you should hear the stories the cowboys tell. Big Jim's great-great-grandfather was captured by the Sioux and they cut off one of his ears."

"This is a surprise." Riley's deep voice interrupted.

Amused by Victor's excited chatter, Maria hadn't realized the ranch hands had dispersed, leaving Riley and Cruz standing a few feet away inside the corral.

"Did you see me ride, Ms. Alvarez?"

"I sure did. That was a great performance. I'm impressed."

"Cruz has the raw talent to compete in this sport." Riley patted the teen's shoulder then spoke to Victor. "You want a turn on the horse?"

"Maybe next time. Big Jim wants me to help him fix the baler."

Victor spun but Maria grabbed his arm. "Wait. It's Saturday."

"So?"

"I drove out here to go over your school lessons. I don't want you falling behind." Two loud groans followed her announcement.

"I've got an idea," Riley said. "I'll take Ms. Alvarez on a horseback ride while you guys finish your chores."

Horseback ride? Maria had never ridden a horse on a merry-go-round, never mind a real one.

"When we return," Riley continued, "you have to crack open the books." He faced Maria. "How does that sound?"

"Wonderful." A horseback ride on a beautiful day with a sexy, young cowboy—every thirtysomething woman's dream.

The teens high-fived and walked off toward the barn.

"What happened to the rodeo in Nevada?" Maria decided the beard stubble covering Riley's cheeks made him appear edgier...sexier—if that was possible.

"I lost the first go-round last night, so I returned early this morning."

Maria fought a smile. "I thought you were good at bustin' broncs."

"Full of sass today, eh?" Riley's eyes roamed over her body. "Glad you wore jeans."

"I should warn you that I've never ridden a horse."

"No problem. We'll ride double. Wait here."

Double. The word made her break out in a sweat. By the time Riley led a beautiful white mare from the barn, Maria was a nervous wreck. "This is Zelda. She's a trail horse—sturdy and sure-footed." Riley held out a straw cowboy hat. "To protect your face from the sun."

"Thanks." She plopped the hat on her head.

After lengthening the stirrups, Riley mounted then backed the horse against the corral rails. "Climb on behind me."

Maria eyed Riley's muscular buttocks and thighs. "There's not enough room for two in the saddle."

"Yes, there is. You'll see."

She climbed the rails then swung a leg over the back of Zelda. Riley scooted forward—less than an inch—and

Maria wedged herself into the remaining space. Pelvis snugged against Riley's backside, her hormones sky-rocketed off the charts.

"Wrap your arms around my waist and hang on." Riley clicked his tongue and urged Zelda into a trot. Maria clung to Riley, not caring that her breasts were smashed against his back—the ground was a long way down.

"A quarter mile from here there's a trail that leads to a retention pond with a great view of the mountains," Riley said.

A quarter mile of sensual torture as her breasts absorbed the heat radiating off Riley's back. Forcing her lusty thoughts aside, Maria focused on the scenery, though her concentration was sorely tested by Riley's scent—faded cologne and earthy cowboy.

They rode in silence then turned south and followed a path behind an outcropping of rock. Maria noticed the retaining pond in the distance. Large piñon trees dotted the area, providing mottled shade. Riley reined in Zelda at the edge of the pond and helped Maria to the ground, then tied the horse's reins to a low hanging tree branch. Maria wasn't much of an outdoorsy person but the beauty before her was stunning.

Riley returned to her side and offered her a water bottle. He must have packed the drinks in the saddle pouch before he'd left the barn. "Let's rest in the shade," he said.

Maria checked for creepy-crawlies on the ground before sitting. Riley stretched out next to her—closer than was proper for *friends*. Maria was awed by Riley's masculinity. His muscular frame made her feel feminine and petite. He smiled as if he didn't have a care in the world.

"I envy you," she said.

"Why?"

"I might be wrong but I bet you view the bright side of things first." She shrugged. "I see the bad side. You wake in the morning eager to discover what the day holds in store for you. I roll out of bed and brace myself for what's to come."

"Life is too short to be miserable all the time," he said.

"You're only twenty-five." Maria laughed. "You haven't lived long enough for that saying to mean anything to you."

"Were you always this serious or did something happen to sober your outlook on life?"

The question caught Maria by surprise. Did she dare dredge up the past? The past was one of the reasons she needed to keep her defenses in place around Riley.

"You don't have to talk about it." Riley grasped her hand. "We can enjoy the quiet."

She liked that Riley didn't push her. His demeanor coaxed her to open up to him. "My brother was killed in a gang shooting ten years ago. He died at the age of fifteen."

The fingers around her hand tightened and Maria appreciated Riley's sympathy. "My brother came as a surprise to my parents. They thought they couldn't have any more children after me. I was ten years old when Juan was born and excited at playing the role of a big sister. We all doted on Juan. He could do no wrong in my parents' eyes."

Memories threatened to suffocate Maria. No matter how many years passed since her brother's death, the incident was never easy to talk about. "Juan began running with a wild bunch in his early teens. I was working on my doctorate degree and beginning my teaching career. I wasn't around enough to notice that his friends were members of a gang."

Maria paused, but Riley remained silent—add good listener to his list of admirable traits. "When Juan didn't come home for three days straight my parents phoned me. I tracked my brother down. He'd been hanging out in an abandoned building with gangbangers. Drinking. Smoking pot."

The stench of sewage and rotting garbage. Urine-stained mattresses had been thrown on the floor. Fast-food bags littered the stairwells. Rats scurried through the hallways. The hellhole remained vivid in Maria's mind.

"Juan begged me to give him a chance to leave the gang on his own before I told our parents." She swallowed hard. "I caved in and kept my mouth shut. Three days later Juan was gunned down two blocks from our home."

After all these years, the memory of that day was powerful enough to bring tears to her eyes. "No one came to his aid. Juan laid on the sidewalk for a half hour before the paramedics arrived. There were no witnesses—at least none that were brave enough to step forward. My brother remains another unsolved murder statistic."

"I'm sorry." Riley slipped his arm around Maria's shoulders and hugged her to his side.

"My parents were devastated. They couldn't understand why I didn't tell them as soon as I'd learned Juan had joined a gang. They never said as much but I saw it in their eyes—they blamed me for my brother's death." And rightly so. Maria had been twenty-five—an adult.

She should have known better than to trust a fifteen-year-old to keep his word.

"Mom began drinking after the funeral. Dad shut down emotionally and immersed himself in his job, working overtime at the airport. Their hatred for delinquent teens has grown stronger through the years."

"Is that why you became involved in helping at-risk kids?"

"I believed if my parents could see that not all delinquent teens were bad seeds, they'd move on after my brother's death." And Maria had secretly hoped if her parents were able to put Juan's death behind them, that they'd forgive her for not giving them a chance to save their son.

"I bet your folks are proud of you," Riley said.

"They say I'm wasting my time on the kids."

"For what it's worth, I think what you do is incredible." He looked her in the eye. "I envy you having a purpose in life and being able to go after it in a meaningful way. You're making a difference in these kids' lives."

That was the nicest thing anyone had ever said to her. "Rodeo isn't your passion?"

"Bustin' broncs is a temporary gig. Down the road I want to—" He shrugged. "I don't know what I want to do."

"You have a college degree. Why not put that to use?"

"Maybe one day I will. Right now I can't picture myself sitting in an office eight-to-five. I enjoy the outdoors and I like having space around me."

Riley was a handsome, caring man, who'd offered to help a troubled teen when most people would have turned their backs. "Ever considered a career in social work?"

"Can't say I have."

"You'd be good at it."

"I think I'd be good at this." He leaned forward and brushed his lips over hers. The first touch of his mouth sent a jolt through Maria. When he slid his fingers across her cheek and deepened the kiss, she closed her eyes and gave herself over to the moment.

Riley wooed her with his tongue then gradually ended the kiss with little nibbles on her lip and soft pecks on her cheek. "Mmm. You taste good," he whispered. "Let's do that again."

"Keep your guns holstered, cowboy." A second kiss was a very bad idea.

"Why?"

Because you make me want you and I don't trust myself to stop us from going where we have no business going.

His eyes narrowed. "You think I'm too young for you, don't you?"

"As much as I enjoy your company and appreciate what you're doing for the boys, we're…well, we're wrong for each other on a lot of levels."

He stood and held out his hand. Once he helped her off the ground, he said, "I might be ten years younger, but in time I'll prove that I'm plenty man enough for you."

Riley got in the last word, because Maria was speechless.

CHAPTER SEVEN

RILEY SLOWED ZELDA to a walk as the mare drew near the ranch yard. He squelched the surge of frustration rising inside him. He'd have sold his best bucking saddle for another hour in the shade with Maria. But duty called and Maria was nothing if not dedicated to her charges. He closed his eyes and savored the heat of her lush breasts pressing against his back.

Kissing Maria had surpassed his wildest dreams. He'd expected her mouth to be memorable, but he hadn't been ready for the electrical charge that had hummed between them.

Aside from sexual compatibility, Riley and the teacher had one important trait in common—neither of them backed down from a challenge. Riley was determined to win a second world title and Maria intended for her three students to earn their GEDs. Riley's goal was physical, each step toward it lasting only eight seconds. Bustin' broncs carried risks, but so did Maria's job. Her goal consumed her entire day and most weekends, leaving no room in her schedule for relaxation and fun. Riley couldn't recall ever hearing her laugh—a deep, belly laugh that brought tears to her eyes.

Maria's life doesn't offer much to laugh about, idiot.
Riley admired her resolve to help delinquent teens and

he sympathized with her struggle to come to terms with the role she'd played in her brother's death. He wished with all his heart he could tell her it hadn't been her fault, but the truth… If he'd been in her shoes and Bree had fallen in with the wrong crowd, he'd have felt the same sorrow and pain if he'd ignored the situation and as a result his sister had died.

Plenty of good people in the world suffered—life wasn't fair. Riley couldn't erase the past from Maria's memory, but maybe he could give her new memories to focus on. He guided Zelda to the horse trough then hopped off.

Maria made a move to get down, but Riley set his hand on her leg. "Wait until Zelda finishes drinking." Maria's brow glistened with perspiration and the front of her shirt sported two large damp spots. "You're hot."

"Riley…"

"Sweaty hot." He slid his hand along her thigh and she swallowed a moan.

"Zelda's done," Maria whispered.

He lifted his arms, offering to assist her to the ground.

"I can manage." Ignoring his help Maria shifted in the saddle, presenting him with a bird's-eye view of her fanny.

"A cowboy never allows a lady to dismount by herself." He clamped his hands on either side of her waist and set her on the ground. Taking Maria by the hand, Riley led the horse to the barn, where a ranch hand took the reins from him and escorted Zelda inside.

As they passed an eighteen-by-twenty-foot water-storage tank that stood four feet high, Maria said, "That's one huge horse trough."

"The ranch has a solar-powered well system," Riley explained. "Underground water is pumped to the surface and stored in this tank, then a network of pipes transports water to the horse troughs, the barn and the bunkhouse."

"The water's crystal clear."

Without thinking of the consequences Riley swung Maria into his arms, walked over to the tank and tossed her in. Her blood-curdling scream abruptly ended when she hit the water. The splash from her body soaked the front of Riley's shirt.

When Maria's head popped above the water's surface, she sputtered and gasped for air. "You…you…" She peeled her wet hair away from her eyes and glared.

Chuckling, he said, "You're mighty cute when you're angry."

She cupped her hands and hit the surface of the water, spewing a tidal wave at Riley. Drenched, he chuckled and joined the water fight, leaning over the edge of the tank. His hand accidently bumped her breast and the feel of the soft mound distracted him enough to drop his guard.

Maria wrapped an arm around his neck and tugged. Riley leaned closer ready to claim his reward. Right before their lips touched, Maria's fingers snaked through his belt loops. He lost his balance and tumbled over the side of the trough headfirst, boots pointed toward Heaven.

When he bobbed to the surface Maria stood on the opposite side of the tank laughing. Soaked to the bone she was the most beautiful woman he'd ever laid eyes on. He waded toward her, stopping only when his chest bumped hers.

"Riley, don't you dare—"

His mouth closed over hers and she melted into him. Man, she was good for his ego.

"What are you guys doing?"

Riley broke off their kiss and glanced over his shoulder. Victor, Cruz and Alonso stood outside the tank gaping at them.

"Follow my lead," Riley whispered in Maria's ear. They waded toward the boys then stopped. "On the count of three," Riley said. "One…two…three!"

In a synchronized movement, he and Maria swung their hands below the water surface and sent a huge wave over the edge. The boys yelped and stumbled backward, brushing at their soaked clothes.

"They peed their pants," Riley teased.

"Ah, man!" Cruz yelled.

"I'm coming in!" Victor charged the tank then vaulted into the air. Riley caught the teen around the waist, held him suspended over his head for a moment then released him. Victor hit the water with a smack but bobbed to the surface laughing.

"My turn!" Alonso retreated several feet before making a run for the tank. Maria scrambled out of the way and Riley braced himself when the teen launched into the air. Riley managed to hang on to Alonso long enough to twirl him around once before letting him go.

"Get in, Cruz!" Victor yelled.

Indecision showed on the teen's face. Right then Maria snuck behind Alonso and dunked him below the water.

"C'mon, Cruz. Join the fun!" Maria splashed him.

Riley held Maria prisoner around the waist. "Yeah, Cruz, come dunk your teacher." He kissed Maria right before he pushed her head below the water. When Maria surfaced, Victor and Alonso pounced on her but this time she dragged the boys under with her.

"Watch out, I'm coming in!" Cruz dove over the edge.

"Get Riley!" Alonso led the charge. The boys closed in on Riley and Alonso jumped on his back. Victor grabbed him around the waist and Cruz dove under the water and went for his legs.

"Help, Maria!" Riley pleaded.

"No way. You started this." Maria scrambled toward the edge of the tank but her short legs and constant laughter made climbing to freedom impossible. "Somebody rescue me!"

Shorty appeared with a stepping stool and offered a helping hand. Instead of getting out of the tank Maria tugged Shorty in. The cowboy's hat went flying as he crashed into the water. When his bald head bobbed above the surface, the boys ganged up on him. Together, they managed to lift Shorty above their heads and spin him in a circle.

By now, a crowd had gathered. Maria managed to climb out of the tank and Riley followed.

"Who would have thought a water fight in a holding tank would be so much fun," Maria said.

When Riley noticed a ranch hand gawking at her wet clothes, he offered his soggy shirt as additional cover. She pressed the material to her breasts and giggled.

"What's so funny?" he asked.

"Your nipples are puckering, too," she said.

He leaned in and whispered, "My nipples aren't the only thing that's hard."

The quiet hitch in Maria's breath aroused Riley almost as much as the memory of kissing her.

Gil Parker stopped next to Riley and watched the commotion. "'Bout time someone cut Shorty down to size."

"I'll make sure the boys finish their chores before Maria tutors them," Riley said.

"We're throwing steaks and ribs on the barbecue." Gil glanced at Maria. "Be honored if you joined us for supper."

"Thank you, Mr. Parker. I'm afraid I didn't bring a change of clothes." She scowled at Riley. "I wasn't expecting to go for a swim."

"You're welcome to shower and change at the main house. Harriet will toss your clothes into the washer." Gil tipped his hat then walked off.

"Stay." Riley didn't want the day to end.

"I'll hang around for the cookout on one condition," Maria said.

"What's that?"

"You keep your hands to yourself…in and out of water tanks."

Riley raised his arms in the air. "Promise to keep my hands to myself."

But not my mouth.

MARIA SHOWERED IN the guest bedroom bath while Gil Parker's housekeeper washed her clothes. As warm water cascaded over her shoulders her thoughts shifted to Riley.

The bronc rider had done what no other man had in a very long time—he'd made her laugh. She hadn't had this much fun in weeks…months…since before her split with Fernando. Being with Riley made her feel carefree, desirable and young at heart when most days she felt battered and battle-weary.

Have a fling with him. He's a cowboy. Cowboys do flings. They're not into long-term relationships.

Eyes closed, Maria envisioned Riley's naked, muscular chest. Her pulse pounded when she imagined his callused hands caressing her breasts, thighs… She hadn't had many lovers in her lifetime and she fantasized that Riley was as wild in bed as the broncs he rode.

Her body desired a man—not any man. She wanted Riley. Why couldn't she enjoy the here and now and live in the moment with him? Let whatever happens happen—until he moved on and out of her life for good? A fling sounded sensible but Riley had stolen a little piece of her heart when he'd gone out on a limb for the boys and secured a place for them at the Gateway Ranch.

The boys griped and complained about chores, but she sensed they were learning the value of hard work and that there was more to life than guns, gangs and violence. Even Cruz showed less of his tough-guy attitude.

Maria shut off the water and stepped from the shower. She donned the guest robe hanging on the back of the bathroom door, then rubbed moisturizer on her face and almond-scented lotion on her body. After confiscating a blow dryer from the vanity drawer, she styled her hair. When she entered the bedroom she found her cleaned clothes neatly folded on the bed. Maria dressed then ventured downstairs to the kitchen.

"Thank you for doing my laundry, Harriet." Maria smiled at the older woman who sat at the kitchen table sewing a button on a man's shirt.

"My pleasure." Harriet gestured to the coffeepot on the counter. "Help yourself."

"The Gateway is a beautiful ranch."

"Gil does a fine job taking care of it."

"Have you worked for Mr. Parker long?" Maria joined Harriet at the table.

"Most of my adult life. I was best friends with Gil's wife, Clare. When she died of breast cancer shortly after their son Eddy turned eight, I moved out here to help care for the house and my godson."

"You never married?"

"Never found a man who stole my heart." She knotted the thread.

Maria sipped her coffee and studied Harriet's features. She guessed the woman to be in her early sixties. Her skin was smooth with a few wrinkles around her eyes. Her salt-and-pepper bob flattered her heart-shaped face.

"What about you?" Harriet glanced at Maria's bare ring finger.

"I was engaged once."

"What happened?"

Divulging that her former fiancé had cheated on her was too painful so she settled for telling a half-truth. "Fernando changed his mind and decided he wanted children."

"You don't want to be a mother?"

"I work with delinquent teenagers and practically raise the kids myself. The last thing I want is to go home at the end of the day and have to take care of more kids."

"You'd feel differently toward your own flesh and blood."

Would she? Before Maria had become a teacher she'd desired a family. Then her brother's death had shown Maria that parents' love for their child had the power to destroy them. "I wouldn't want to raise a child in the inner city where I live and work."

"You could move to the suburbs."

Harriet's suggestion made sense but the reason Maria was able to bond with her students was because she understood the challenges they faced—the 'hood was her home, too.

Needing to change the subject, Maria asked, "Can I help with the supper preparations?"

"I don't cook for the ranch hands. Pete does. He uses the kitchen attached to the bunkhouse."

"Are you joining everyone for supper?"

"No." Harriet packed away the sewing kit. "I prefer eating at the house, where I can control my portion size." She smiled.

"So I'm about to put on weight?" Maria took her mug to the sink.

"Pete makes the best cherry cobbler this side of the Mississippi. You'll be lucky if you get away with an extra pound or two."

"Thanks again for washing my clothes, Harriet. I enjoyed our chat."

"Stop in anytime."

When Maria left the house, she spotted Riley and the boys in the round pen with the bucking horse. She crept closer, then propped a boot on the lower rung and listened as Riley discussed the finer points of bustin' broncs.

"I don't get it," Alonso said. "How come you can't use both hands to hang on to the buck rein?"

"'Cause it would be too easy to stay on the bronc," Cruz said.

"Not only that," Riley said, "the cowboy can't touch

the horse with his free hand. If he does, he's disqualified. And—" Riley patted the animal's shoulder "—you've got to mark the horse as he comes out of the chute."

"What does that mean?" Victor asked.

"When the chute opens, the cowboy has to keep his boot heels above the point of the horse's shoulder until the animal's front legs hit the ground."

"There's a lot to remember," Alonso said.

"You ride broncs long enough, it becomes second nature."

"What's a good score?" Cruz's interest in an activity other than tagging buildings and hanging out with gangs pleased Maria.

"Both the rider and the horse earn their own score—as much as twenty-five points each. The meaner the bronc and the nastier he bucks, the more points the horse and cowboy earn. A good score is in the high eighties."

Cruz strolled around the horse, stopping in front of the animal. "How old do you have to be to rodeo?"

"You're old enough right now to compete in junior rodeos. Once you're eighteen you can join the PRCA and buck against the best in the sport." When Cruz remained silent, Riley asked, "Want me to register you for a junior rodeo?"

"Maybe."

"Maybe you should see what your teacher thinks about you bustin' broncs."

"Hey, Ms. Alvarez." Alonso walked over to Maria. "Cruz might join the rodeo."

"I heard."

"Tell you what, Cruz," Riley said. "You and the guys watch me compete next weekend in Las Vegas. Afterward, if you're interested in bustin' broncs—"

"Wait a minute." Maria waved a hand. "This isn't what Judge Hamel had in mind when she handed down Cruz's sentence."

"I wanna try rodeo, Ms. Alvarez." Cruz removed the straw cowboy hat given to him as part of his ranch uniform. "My father was good at it. Maybe I will be, too."

"What if Cruz makes a bargain with you?" Riley spoke to Maria.

"What kind of bargain?"

"If he continues with his studies and does his chores without complaining, I'll teach him how to bust broncs in his spare time. And…" Riley held Cruz's gaze. "I'll sponsor your first rodeo."

"What do you mean sponsor?" Cruz asked.

"I'll pay your entry fee and buy your rodeo gear."

"You'd do that for me?"

"On one condition," Riley said. "You earn your GED."

Out of the three boys, Cruz was furthest behind in his studies. He'd have to work long and hard to catch up to Alonso and Victor.

"Okay. I'll try," Cruz said.

"Trying isn't good enough. If you want to rodeo you'll pass your exams." Riley lowered his voice. "Do you want to bust broncs, kid?"

"Yeah, I want to rodeo." He spoke to Maria. "What if I can't learn the stuff?"

"I'll try to come out to the ranch more often to tutor you. In the meantime you keep up with the homework."

"Can we go with Riley to his next rodeo?" Victor asked.

Riley didn't allow Maria a chance to answer. "Your father called. The *Dark Stranger*'s ready to fly. We'd have to leave early in the morning next Friday and wouldn't return until Sunday night."

The boys begged for permission to accompany Riley to Vegas.

"What's the matter?" Riley asked Maria. "Are you afraid of flying?"

"Maybe."

"Flying's a breeze." Riley turned to the boys. "Have you guys flown before?"

All three shook their heads no.

"Then it will be an adventure for everyone. You'll love it, trust me."

Trust Riley? Easier said than done after watching him land his plane in the salvage yard. "I'll need to gain permission from the boys' parents and Judge Hamel." Maria prayed their answers would be no.

"How far is Las Vegas from Sioux Falls?" Cruz asked.

"It's about a thousand miles northeast of Vegas. Why? You want to go visit your father?" Riley said.

The teen shrugged. "Could you fly me there?"

"That's up to Ms. Alvarez." Riley glanced at Maria.

Maybe a visit with his father would convince Cruz to stay away from gangs and work harder to succeed in school. "I'll check into it," she said.

Right then a loud bell clanged. "Chow's ready. Go on. I'll meet you there," Riley said.

Why did Riley have to be one of the good guys, Maria wondered as she followed the boys to the mess hall.

"Riley's a cool dude," Cruz said.

"Yep, he's a—" *sexy, hot* "—cool dude," Maria concurred.

And very much off-limits.

CHAPTER EIGHT

EARLY FRIDAY MORNING Maria and her father waited for Riley and the boys inside a hangar at the Blue Skies Regional Airport. Gaining her students' parents' permission, and in Cruz's case, Judge Hamel's, had been easy as pie. The parents were appreciative of their sons having an opportunity to travel outside New Mexico and Judge Hamel applauded Riley's involvement with the teens.

The judge had rambled on about how nice Riley was and how she wished there were more young men in the community willing to work with delinquent teens. Good grief, by the time Maria had left the judge's chambers Riley had sprouted wings and was well on his way to sainthood.

Maria wholeheartedly agreed with the judge's assessment of Riley, except for a tiny part of her that questioned his unselfish involvement in the boys' lives. Yes, Riley was a great guy—a well-mannered, mature, genuinely likable *young* man. But aside from "doing the right thing" what motivated Riley to help her students? Maria worried that *reason* was her.

Nonsense. She and Riley were attracted to one another but surely he understood they had no future together.

"Are you prepared for this, Maria?"

Her father's question referred to flying but Maria was

thinking about what might happen between her and Riley in Vegas. "As long as you're certain the *Dark Stranger* won't drop out of the sky, I'll give flying a try."

"I tested the plane myself. You will have no trouble." Her father had kept his pilot's license current after he'd retired from the military, and often took planes on test flights to verify the repairs had been done correctly. "The *Dark Stranger* is a very expensive plane." Translation: Where does Riley get all his money?

"Riley's family raises Kentucky Derby horses."

When her father's eyes filled with suspicion, Maria wanted to shout, "I don't know why he's helping the boys" and "I don't know why he's interested in *me*— an older Hispanic woman from the 'hood," but she held her tongue.

"He's your brother's age."

"Juan is dead, Dad." Her father's mouth grimaced in pain and Maria regretted her words. Why couldn't her parents allow their son to rest in peace?

"You and this…cowboy…it's not proper."

Proper encompassed age, ethnicity, income and social standing.

"Dad, there's nothing going on between me and Riley. He's doing my students a favor, that's all."

"He's wasting his time on those boys. So are you. They're all the same—losers who don't respect human life."

"You're saying Juan was a loser, too, because he joined a gang?"

Her father's face turned ashen. There was plenty of blame to spread around for failing to notice signs that her brother had joined a gang. Maria had desperately wanted to make amends for failing Juan by helping young Hispanic teens. Each boy or girl she saved from a gang would not bring her brother back to life but they reaffirmed in Maria's mind and heart that Juan hadn't died in vain.

"Victor, Alonso and Cruz need a man to inspire them to succeed," she said.

"And a cowboy who throws his money around, flies an expensive jet, and buys anything he wants without working for it is the best person to show those boys how to make their way in life?"

Score a point for her father. Maria had contemplated the same thing after Riley had made arrangements for the teens to stay at the Gateway Ranch, but her doubts about his influence on her students had taken a backseat when she'd gotten sidetracked by her attraction to Riley.

The only way to break the cycle of poverty, drugs, gang violence and unemployment in the 'hood was through education. Would Riley throwing his money around encourage the boys to take a shortcut to fame and fortune? Unable to defend Riley against her father's criticism, she muttered, "He means well."

"You're too old to chase after—"

"I'm not chasing him." Maria curled her fingers into a fist. She'd been devastated when Fernando had ended their relationship. Riley's interest in her—although temporary—was a desperately needed boost to her feminine ego. "We're friends. That's it."

Maria kept her eyes on the airport entrance across the runway, longing for Riley to arrive and put an end to the sparring between her and her father. A moment later, she got her wish. "They're here."

Riley parked in the visitor lot then he and the boys entered the hangar. He removed his sunglasses and grinned. Lord, Maria would miss his smile when he moved on and out of her life.

Each of the boys carried a black leather duffel bag with the Gateway Ranch logo stamped on the side. Riley held out his hand to Maria's father. "How are you, Mr. Alvarez?" He didn't wait for a response before motioning to the plane. "The *Dark Stranger* looks as good as new." Riley walked over to the plane, the boys trailing behind, listening to her father's explanation of the repairs that had been made to the plane.

"Has anyone taken it on a test flight?" Riley asked.

"I flew the plane myself," Maria's father said.

"Great. I'll settle the bill for repairs, file a flight plan, then we'll be on our way." Riley turned to the boys. "You guys board the plane, but stay out of the cockpit." He opened the door and pulled down the stairs. "Ms. Alvarez—" he smiled at Maria "—gets to be my copilot."

"I think I should sit in the back with the boys." *And cross my fingers until we land.*

"First-time fliers fair better in the cockpit." Riley directed his next words to her father. "Isn't that right, Mr. Alvarez?"

Murmuring that he needed to get the paperwork ready, Maria's father walked off and Riley followed. He hadn't imagined the tension between father and daughter when he'd entered the hangar. What had the two talked about before he'd arrived? As much as he respected Ricardo Alvarez and his mechanical talents, Riley sensed the man didn't trust him around Maria. He stepped into the office and shut the door.

"Mr. Alvarez, I want to thank you again for working on my plane." Ricardo handed Riley the work order. He scanned the list of parts ordered, the cost of towing the plane to the airport and Ricardo's fee for labor. "This can't be correct."

"I charged you the going rate."

"You worked on my plane after-hours and on the weekend. That's overtime. This bill should be double the amount."

Ricardo scowled.

Stalemate. Riley waited, hoping the older man would back down. When he remained silent, Riley said, "I won't sign off on this until you change the amount."

Ricardo snatched the paperwork out of Riley's hand, crossed out the total and added two hundred dollars, not nearly enough but Riley suspected this was as far as Ricardo would budge. Riley removed his checkbook from his shirt pocket and made out a draft for the repairs. "Thank you again for taking good care of my plane."

"Don't hurt my daughter."

The statement shocked Riley. "Excuse me?"

"I see the way you stare at her. You're not her kind and—"

"Kind? You mean because I'm a rodeo cowboy or because I'm white?"

"Both."

Experiencing prejudice was a first for Riley.

"And you are too young for Maria." Ricardo's lip curled. "The wealthy believe they can buy anything and everyone they want. My daughter isn't for sale."

Not wanting to argue, Riley spoke in an even tone.

"I'm helping Maria with her students. There's no reason we can't be friends and enjoy each other's company."

"So you want an affair with her and then you disappear?"

Temper flaring, Riley picked his words carefully. "My relationship with your daughter is none of your business. Maria's old enough to know who she wants or doesn't want. She's a beautiful, giving, generous, kind woman. Any man, no matter what his age or race, would consider himself lucky to have her in his life."

"You're too young to know your own mind."

Tired of having his age held against him, Riley said, "Mr. Alvarez, I care a lot for your daughter but frankly it doesn't matter if you approve of me or not." He left the office, closing the door quietly behind him. Shoot. This wasn't how he'd planned to begin the trip to Nevada. Riley hoped Maria's father hadn't convinced her to keep her distance from him in Vegas, because he wanted the trip to be the beginning of a long-term relationship between them. As soon as the *Dark Stranger* was airborne, Riley would focus all his efforts on showing Maria and the boys a good time.

Don't forget about the rodeo.

Riley had become so involved with Maria and her students that he was losing track of his rodeo goals. He needed a win this weekend. Once he boarded the plane, he secured the cabin door. "What do you think?" he asked the teens.

"Sweet!" Alonso said, examining the compartments around his seat.

"Fasten your belts and stay seated until I say it's okay

to move around." He sent the boys a stern look. "I'm serious."

"Yeah, okay," Cruz said.

"Ready?" Riley asked when he entered the cockpit.

"As ready as I'll ever be." Maria smiled but her eyes remained sober.

Riley slipped into the pilot's chair. "You're going to love flying."

"If I don't?"

"I'll put you on a bus back to Albuquerque as soon as the rodeo's over and the boys and I will be waiting for you when you arrive at the terminal downtown."

"Gee, thanks."

With quick, efficient movements Riley ran through his preflight checklist. Five minutes later he flipped on the intercom. "Okay, guys, we're set to leave as soon as the tower gives us permission." A chorus of "okays" echoed from the back of the plane.

Once Riley received the go-ahead to taxi onto the runway he watched the propeller blades rotate smoothly and evenly. "Your father does good work."

"He's the best around."

The tower cleared him for takeoff and the plane's ascent into the sky was smooth and quick. Hoping to avoid another bird strike, Riley climbed to ten thousand feet, then leveled off and informed the boys they were free to unfasten their seat belts.

"You can let go now," he said.

Maria relaxed her tightly entwined fingers. "It's peaceful at this altitude. I bet this is what Heaven feels like."

Was she thinking about her brother? Riley didn't care for the fact that he and Juan—had the teenager lived—

would have been the same age. Riley hoped once they arrived in Vegas, Maria would become too distracted to ponder anything but having a good time with him and the boys.

Riley had two goals in Vegas—to win first place in the bronc-bustin' competition and to show Maria that his feelings for her were serious. If he'd learned anything the past two weeks at the Gateway Ranch it was that he wanted to be more than friends with the inner-city schoolteacher.

"WHOA, WE'RE STAYING HERE?" Alonso said, his face pressed against the window in the backseat of the cab.

The driver stopped outside the entrance of the New York-New York Hotel and Casino on the Las Vegas strip. The exterior of the hotel reflected the New York City skyline...on a much smaller scale. The hotel towers had been configured to resemble the Empire State Building and the Chrysler Building, and the lake in front of the property represented New York Harbor. The hotel also included mock replicas of the Statue of Liberty, Ellis Island and Grand Central Station.

The cab ride from the municipal airport had started out boisterous but the closer they'd driven to the strip the quieter the teens had become. None of them, including Maria, had ever been to Vegas and their wide-eyed gapes seemed to amuse Riley.

"Do they keep the lights on all the time?" Victor asked as Riley paid the cab fare.

"Unless there's a power outage, the lights never dim in Vegas."

The boys piled out of the cab and retrieved their duffel bags from the trunk. A bellman appeared with a luggage cart. "Welcome back to the New York–New York, Mr. Fitzgerald." The young man tipped his cap. "Good luck today at the rodeo."

"Thanks, Mike. You coming to watch the events?"

"Yes, sir. Only a fool would miss a chance to mingle with all those pretty buckle bunnies."

Buckle bunnies set off a warning buzzer inside Maria's head. Until now she'd managed to avoid contemplating that part of rodeo.

"Same suite, Mr. Fitzgerald?"

"Yep." Riley placed a folded bill in the young man's palm.

"Thank you, sir. Enjoy your stay." The bellman bowed, then steered the cart inside the hotel.

"How much does that guy make in tips?" Victor asked.

"I'd guess on a good day two to three hundred dollars."

Victor whistled between his teeth.

"Before you get any ideas about running off to Vegas and becoming a bellman, you should know that Mike graduated from high school and is studying hotel management at the university."

"How come you know so much about the guy?" Cruz asked.

"I stay at the New York–New York when I'm in Vegas. Mike and I talk about sports at my alma mater."

Maria considered it odd that Riley gave the time of day to a recently graduated high school student, until she realized that Riley was fairly close in age to Mike.

"Ready to ride a roller coaster?" Riley asked.

"Where?" Alonso asked.

"Right here in the hotel." Riley pointed to the sky. A red coaster snaked through the mock Manhattan skyline.

"I'm in," Victor said.

"Me, too," Cruz and Alonso echoed.

"What about you, Maria?" Riley asked.

"I don't like roller coasters." The bends and turns made her stomach queasy.

"You'll like this one." Riley grabbed her hand. "The loading station is inside the building at the rear of the casino."

As they made their way through the maze of gaming tables and slot machines, the boys asked Riley how many times he'd ridden the coaster and what he thought of the experience. Maria was grateful Riley hadn't released her hand as he described the terrifying ride.

I can do this. Maria refused to put a damper on the boys' excitement because she was afraid of heights. The boarding area for the ride resembled a mini New York subway station. She released Riley's hand to retrieve her wallet.

"I'm paying." Riley got in line at the ticket booth.

"This is crazy, Ms. Alvarez." Alonso could barely contain his excitement. The ride attendant secured passengers in taxicab cars. Any ride that needed over-the-shoulder harnesses and side-to-side head restraints promised a bruising experience.

"Here." Victor shoved a brochure into Maria's hand.

"Thanks," she mumbled, daring herself to read the literature.

Let the good times roll. The Roller Coaster will lift you up 203 feet, drop you down 144 feet at speeds

*up to 67 mph. Simulating a jet fighter's barrel roll,
you'll turn 180 degrees, hang 86 feet in the air, take
the famous "heartline" twist and dive and get your
negative G's on! Enjoy the rush!*

Rush? How about heart attack?

"We've got an odd number of riders," Riley said
when he returned. Before Maria volunteered to sit out,
he asked, "Who wants to ride alone?"

"Me." Cruz raised his hand in the air.

As the line snaked through the turnstiles, Maria said,
"Are you sure this is a good idea right before you compete?"

Riley smiled. "You're scared."

Of course she was frightened! Any sane person would
be leery of riding a roller coaster that zigzagged through
a miniature New York City.

"You won't fall out." Riley slipped his arm around
her and Maria resisted hugging him back. "I'll keep you
safe."

When their turn came to board the coaster, Maria
chose the inside seat and checked twice to make sure
the harness and lap belt were secured then she closed
her eyes and focused on the seductive scent of Riley's
cologne.

"You're not going to keep your eyes shut the entire
ride, are you?" he asked.

"Yes, I am."

"If you're this scared, why did you agree to ride the
coaster?"

"I didn't want to disappoint the boys." *And I didn't
want you to think I was a boring person.*

The taxicab lurched forward and another group boarded. A few seconds later the attendant's voice bellowed over the intercom. "Ladies and gentlemen, prepare for the ride of your life. Please remain seated until your taxicab returns to the station." A whistle blew. "See you back here in two minutes and forty-five seconds!"

The cars climbed the track, and Maria clutched the shoulder harness until her fingers hurt. The boys raised their hands in the air, shouting dares at each other. As the taxicab neared the summit Maria took in the aerial view of the south end of the strip, where Las Vegas Boulevard met Tropicana Avenue.

The sight lasted only a few seconds before the car plummeted one hundred and forty-four feet, sending her stomach slamming into her throat. Maria became a human pinball as the coaster hung her upside down then flung her through loops and corkscrew turns. She prayed the operator would cut the ride short but the blasted whirlwind experience lasted a lifetime before the train's brakes jerked the ride to a stop inside Grand Central Station.

"Man, that was awesome!" Victor said.

"You hung on when we were upside down," Cruz accused Alonso.

"No way, dude, I let go...for a second." The boys laughed.

Despite the little aches and twinges—souvenirs from the ride—Maria basked in the moment, enjoying the boys' excitement. For the first time since she'd met the teens they acted like typical seventeen-year-olds—friends bantering good-naturedly. A nice change from their usual threatening scowls and I-dare-you glares.

"Did you like the ride, Ms. Alvarez?" Victor asked.

"Awesome." Maria ignored Riley's chuckle in her ear.

"Can we go again?" Cruz asked.

"I've got to head over to the arena, but we'll ride the coaster tonight after the rodeo." Riley led the way to the hotel lobby and secured key cards for their rooms. The elevator stopped on the tenth floor. "You guys are sharing the Skyline Room. The bellhop will deliver a roll-away bed while we're at the rodeo." Riley slid the key card into the lock and opened the door. The boys rushed in to check out the room.

Victor went straight for one of the queen-size beds and flung himself onto the mattress. "I call this bed!"

Alonso took a step toward the other bed but Cruz cut him off at the pass. "No, way, dude. This bed's mine."

"Doesn't matter," Alonso said. "The roll-away will be better than the hard bunks we sleep in at the ranch."

Maria tugged Riley's shirtsleeve. "Where are you sleeping?"

"I've got a single room." Riley pointed to the connecting door on his left.

"Where am I sleeping?"

He motioned to another connecting door on Maria's right. "You're on the other side of the boys' room in the Spa Suite."

Spa suite sounded heavenly. She didn't care to guess how much the rooms had cost Riley.

"We're leaving in twenty minutes," Riley told the teens, then walked Maria to her door and handed her the key card. "The guys and I will meet you in the lobby."

Maria snagged his arm as he turned away. "I can't thank you enough for what you're doing for the boys." *And me.*

"I'm glad you're here, Maria. It's nice not having to travel alone for a change."

She slipped into her room, freshened up then took the elevator to the lobby, where they all piled into a cab and drove along Vegas Boulevard to Mesquite Avenue.

"Hey!" Victor exclaimed. "A carnival. Can we go on the rides?"

"Maybe later," Riley said. "Let's grab supper before the parade kicks off. My event isn't until nine o'clock tonight."

"Everyone hungry?" Maria asked.

"We're always hungry, Ms. Alvarez," Alonso said.

The cab dropped them off at the rodeo grounds, where Riley paid their admission and they got their hands stamped.

"The ink disappeared," Victor complained to the gate attendant who'd stamped the back of his hand.

"It glows in the dark, kid." The man pointed a special light, which revealed the green ink splotch.

They zigzagged through the growing throng of people and made their way to the food vendors. Riley told the boys to eat as much as they wanted. Maria was grateful the teens kept their orders reasonable—chili-cheese dogs, fries and drinks. *When in Rome...* She ordered the same, hoping she'd walk off the extra calories by the end of the day.

"What happens next?" Alonso asked Riley after they found a picnic table in the eating area. Maria noticed Cruz studying the rodeo cowboys milling about.

"I'll give you guys a tour of the livestock pens then we'll head over to Fourth Street for the parade."

"Won't you be tired after all that walking?" Maria asked.

"I'll be fine." Spoken like a true twenty-five-year-old. "Once the parade ends, I return to the cowboy-ready area and—"

"What's a cowboy-ready area?" Cruz asked.

"Where cowboys put on their gear," Riley said. "While I'm doing that, you can find seats in the stands."

"You gonna win tonight?" Victor asked.

"I'd better since you came all this way to watch me." Riley spoke to the boys—the double meaning behind his words not lost on Maria.

Not only did Riley intend to win his rodeo event tonight... But he also intended to win *her*.

CHAPTER NINE

As FAR AS parades went the Helldorado Days event sponsored by the Elks Club was a big hit with the Las Vegas locals, but drew few tourists, who preferred to remain in the casinos and give their money to the great state of Nevada.

Riley, Maria and the boys stood on Fourth Street at the corner of Ogden Avenue near the rodeo grounds. The parade consisted of relic cars displaying ads for local businesses and walking teams wearing themed clothing—Civil War uniforms, Southern-belle dresses, old-West gunslingers and lawmen outfits. The rodeo clowns had dressed early for the event and entertained the kids lined along the sidewalks.

Cruz, Alonso and Victor acted as if the festivities bored them but Riley caught the teens pointing at people in the parade, cracking jokes and laughing. Maria's mood was difficult to judge. She'd been polite but distant toward him since they'd left the hotel. Riley couldn't figure out what he'd done to cause the sudden shift in her demeanor. Her behavior made him feel less than her equal—not in age but maturity—and he didn't appreciate it.

This wasn't the first time Maria acted older than her thirty-five years. Riley blamed her matronly attitude on having lived in the trenches of Albuquerque. Kids in the 'hood matured fast, and the death of Maria's brother to gang violence had left her with deep scars. Riley's upbringing was worlds apart from Maria's, which made their perspectives different. But the very experiences Maria had lived through had molded her into the woman she was today—the woman Riley desired.

He understood her need to help delinquent teens and he admired and envied her noble calling; but a part of Riley wished he could erase her past so that nothing but ten years stood between them. He'd proven they could have fun together. Laugh together. Enjoy each other's company. Add sexual attraction to the mix and Riley believed they were the perfect pair.

"What are you staring at?"

"You have chili-dog sauce on your cheek." He leaned in close. "Want me to lick it off?"

"Stop that," she whispered, the sparkle in her eyes taking the sting out of her threat.

A sudden blast of music ended the intimate moment. One after the other, local high-school bands marched down the street followed by their school float. Centennial High's float consisted of their football team in full uniform with the school mascot—a bulldog—sitting on a cardboard throne, wearing a crown. The sign pinned to the side of the flatbed trailer listed numerous state championships.

The Coronado High float sported a large cougar head, which rotated in a slow circle while red, white and blue streamers decorated the sides of the trailer. Students wore fifties clothing and danced to Elvis's "Jailhouse Rock."

Eldorado High decorated their float in maroon and

gold. One student wearing a Sun Devil costume held a pitchfork above his head. The other students dressed in T-shirts with a picture of their mascot on the front.

The cowboy was Chaparral High School's talisman. The students wore ten-gallon hats, Wranglers and orange-and-black bandanas around their necks.

A red Dodge Ram pulled the final float in the parade—a flatbed covered in sawdust, crowded with buckle bunnies vying for a turn on the mechanical bull that slowly gyrated in the center of the trailer. Cat calls and wolf whistles greeted the float.

As the pickup passed, the blonde swaying atop the bull made eye contact with Riley. He mumbled a curse. Victoria was a casino waitress by day and a rodeo groupie by night. He stepped behind Cruz, hoping the kid would hide him from view. He hadn't been quick enough.

Victoria's whiney voice rang through the air. "Wanna party, Riley?"

Damn. Right when he'd coaxed a smile out of Maria, the buckle bunny had to come along and ruin his progress.

"Hey, Riley," Cruz said. "If you don't wanna party with that chick, I will." The boys chuckled.

Face heating, Riley ignored Victoria. Maria's hot stare was more difficult to discount. "Well?" She nudged him with her elbow.

Play dumb. "Well what?"

"Are you going to party with that bimbo later?"

This was the first time Maria had revealed a jealous streak. "Victoria and I…" Riley clamped his mouth closed when he caught the boys eavesdropping.

"Hey," Cruz said. "I'm serious about the girl. If you don't want her—"

Maria tapped the back of Cruz's head with her open palm. "No hooking up with girls while we're in Vegas. Got that?"

A chorus of "Yes, ma'am" answered.

"That's it for the parade." Hoping to avoid a run-in with Victoria, Riley rushed everyone over to the rodeo grounds. When they arrived at the bucking chutes, he asked, "You guys want to see the horses and the bulls?"

"Yeah, sure," Victor said.

"You're welcome to come, but there's a lot of cussing and spitting behind the chutes," Riley teased Maria.

"Thanks, I'll wait in the stands." Maria pointed to the bleachers on the right side of the arena. "I'll sit near the top."

"Here." Riley removed his watch and handed it to her. "Will you keep this for me?"

"Sure." Maria studied the timepiece, noting the expensive platinum coating and crystal glass under which a cowboy on a bucking horse pointed to the hour and minutes. The watch appeared custom-made. Her jeans were too tight to stow the jewelry in her pocket so she wore it.

As soon as the guys walked off, Maria made her way into the stands. By the time she reached the top bleachers she was gasping for air. She watched a TV broadcaster interview a cowboy near the VIP seating section, then switched her attention to the flag girls practicing their routine while a rodeo crew assembled a platform in the center of the arena.

The stands filled quickly. A beautiful redhead, wearing a tight T-shirt, leather-fringed vest, painted-on jeans with a flashy rhinestone belt and shiny black boots, sat a few feet down from Maria.

She'd never been self-conscious of her physical appearance but one trip to a rodeo and suddenly she was surrounded by hordes of beautiful, flamboyant, young women. She felt drab by comparison.

They may have beauty but you have brains.

The thought did little to lift her spirits.

The redhead's smile froze when she glanced at Maria's wrist. "May I ask where you got that?"

For a moment Maria had forgotten about Riley's watch. "Oh, it's not mine. I'm keeping it for—"

"Riley Fitzgerald?"

The blood drained from Maria's face and she struggled to keep her smile in place. "Yes. As a matter of fact it belongs to Riley."

"I used to keep it for him when he rode."

Oh, Lord. She should have expected she'd run into one of Riley's ex's. "How long ago was that?"

"College. We split before graduation." The soft sigh following the statement hinted that Riley had broken the redhead's heart.

"Please don't take offense," the young woman said, flashing a sweet smile, "but you're not Riley's usual type."

Her comment burned Maria like a nasty wasp sting. "We're friends."

The redhead's expression lightened. "Is he dating anyone special?"

Me, Maria wanted to shout. She knew Riley flew his own plane and came from Kentucky. He'd been born into a wealthy family and attended college at UNLV. He'd won a world title in saddle-bronc riding. But as far as his personal life... Maria knew next to nothing. Maybe Riley had left a string of broken hearts across the country. The moment the thought entered her mind, she regretted it.

She considered herself a good judge of character and Riley was a kind, decent, caring man. No matter that Maria fabricated excuses for their attraction to one another, she believed Riley's intentions toward her—whatever they were—were honest and sincere. If only the odds of a lasting relationship between them were better than slim-to-none.

"Riley's not involved with anyone that I know of at the moment." Maria didn't count herself because she and Riley weren't having sex.

"I'm Amy, by the way."

"Maria."

"Do you live here in Vegas?"

"Albuquerque. I'm a teacher. I help juvenile offenders earn their GEDs."

"Your career sounds challenging," Amy said. "I'm a pediatric nurse. My father wanted me to go to law school then work for him in his firm, but I was interested in the medical field."

"Law doesn't appeal to you?"

"Dad's a pretty famous divorce attorney in Vegas and I've watched him take his clients' spouses to the cleaners. I'm afraid I'm not that cutthroat. I'd rather help people heal, not inflict more wounds."

"I understand the wanting to make a difference in someone's life." Maria regretted that she'd misjudged Amy and had lumped her in with all the other airheads at the rodeo. She yearned to know why Amy and Riley had ended their relationship, but lost her chance to ask when the boys appeared.

"Hey, Ms. Alvarez! We got you nachos!" Alonso led the charge up the bleachers. The boys stopped at the end of the aisle and gaped at Amy.

"Guys—" Maria grabbed the nacho container before it slipped from Alonso's hand "—this is a friend of Riley's. Amy…?"

"Amy Reynolds."

Cruz introduced himself first. Alonso and Victor followed then sat in the row in front of Amy. The boys talked excitedly about the bucking stock they'd seen and the cowboys Riley had introduced them to.

"Ms. Alvarez, we got to meet Mr. Parker's son, Ed," Alonso said.

"Ed told us when he was a kid he used to feed his dad's horse broccoli because it made the horse fart when his dad rode him." Victor jabbed Cruz in the side. "Hey. We should feed Shorty's horse—"

"There will be no feeding broccoli to any horses at the ranch," Maria said.

The teens bobbed their heads.

"How many students do you have?" Amy asked.

"I'm helping sixteen at the moment. Much of the work is self-paced." She waggled a finger at the boys. "Riley arranged for them to work at the Gateway Ranch north of Albuquerque while they earn their GEDs." Maria lowered her voice. "The boys were associating with a local gang and at risk of dropping out of the program."

"Typical Riley," Amy said.

"He has a big heart." And Maria envied the lucky woman who would one day lay claim to it.

"You don't have to convince me. When I was doing my nursing clinicals, Riley helped me throw a birthday party for one of my terminally ill patients—a little boy who wanted to be a rodeo cowboy when he grew up. Riley brought in a clown to entertain the kids and he gave bull-riding lessons on a mechanical bull." Amy's smile vanished. "Santiago died two weeks later. Riley and I went to his funeral."

Maria's eyes stung. The more she learned about Riley the more her heart craved to pull him close. Amy Reynolds appeared to be the perfect match for Riley. They were both attractive, educated and came from well-to-do-families. Why wasn't Riley with Amy?

Maybe he's commitment-shy.

Right then the rodeo kicked off. The mayor gave a welcome speech and two girls—one carrying the American flag, the other the Nevada state flag—raced into the arena on horseback. They stopped their mounts in front of the stands. The spectators stood and a young man with a baritone voice belted out the national anthem.

Once the applause died down, the announcer introduced the rodeo sponsors. The people waved from their leather chairs in the VIP section near the bucking chutes. The bullfighters and pickup men were named next, then the clowns and finally the rodeo queen and her court.

"Ladies and gents, welcome to the Helldorado Day's Rodeo! Tonight you're gonna see the finest bucking stock in Nevada and the best-known cowboys on the circuit competing for thousands of dollars in prize money."

The rodeo clowns strutted in front of the crowd, staggering under the weight of a giant-size cardboard check. The announcer droned on about the evening's events but Maria's thoughts were elsewhere until she heard Riley's name.

"We got last year's world champion in saddle-bronc riding here tonight! Riley Fitzgerald from Lexington, Kentucky."

Amy popped off the bench, stuck her fingers between her lips and let out a shrill whistle. Thunderous applause boomed through the stands and the boys glanced around in shock. Maria had no idea Riley was so popular with fans.

"You may have heard Fitzgerald won the title by default when Drew Rawlins scratched the final ride of his career here in Las Vegas last December. I spoke with Fitzgerald earlier and that young man's on a mission to claim a second title. Keep your eye on him tonight."

Amy sat down. "When Riley competed with the rodeo team in college he drew big crowds and lots of pretty girls."

"Did that ever bother you?" Maria asked.

"Sure it did. That's why we split."

Don't ask. Another voice in her head said...*ask.* Curiosity got the best of her. "Did he cheat on you?"

"Yes."

The bottom fell out of Maria's stomach.

"Groupies drooled all over his boots everywhere he went. I couldn't compete with so many girls."

Any fantasy Maria had entertained about her and Riley becoming more than friends died a quick death. Her ex, Fernando, had been seeing a woman on the side for six months before he'd ended his relationship with Maria—and only because he'd gotten the woman pregnant. Infidelity hurt no matter what the person's age.

This newest tidbit of gossip about Riley confirmed Maria's earlier suspicion that when it came to helping others, Riley was a swell guy. But as far as a personal relationship with him, Maria was convinced it would end in heartache—hers.

"Riley's event is next." Amy clasped her hands together. "I hope he wins."

How was it that Riley had broken Amy's heart, yet she cared enough about him to want him to do well? *Good grief.* What kind of magic spell did the cowboy cast over females? Maria wished she'd never run in to Amy today. Ignorance was bliss. Now that she understood it was all about the chase for Riley, Maria refused to get caught.

Feeling confident in her decision to keep her relationship with Riley on the lighter side Maria joined forces with Amy, praying Riley would win his event.

"MY OLD MAN never said a word about letting delinquent teens work at the Gateway Ranch." Ed Parker stood next to Riley in the cowboy-ready area.

"How long since you last spoke to your dad?" Riley asked.

"A month maybe."

"The boys have been at the ranch a few weeks now." Riley rummaged through his gear bag. "Your dad's got a big heart. Cruz, Alonso and Victor might turn their life around because he's giving them a place to learn what hard work is all about."

Parker stubbed his boot tip against the ground, but didn't speak.

"Your dad misses you," Riley said.

The comment startled Parker. "He said that?"

"Didn't have to. I saw it in his eyes."

"He misses his granddaughter." Parker's shoulders slumped. "My ex took Shelly out to California with her to live with her parents."

"I'm sorry." Riley had heard the same story from more than one cowboy on the circuit. They got a buckle bunny pregnant, married her and then divorced within a year. No way was Riley heading down that path. If and when he decided to marry, his rodeo career would be over.

"Heard you drew Houdini. He won big in Oklahoma last month," Parker said.

He needed a win the first go-round. Riley counted on Houdini's brand of magic bringing him success tonight.

"You listening to the gossip behind the chutes?" Ed asked.

Riley's competitors were jealous. If the boot was on the other foot he'd feel the same. Riley fastened his chaps. "What's everybody saying this time?"

"Nick Bass thinks because you're rich you're a pansy." The twenty-nine-year-old bronc rider stood by himself next to his chute.

Bass was a loner who'd joined the circuit late in the season. He had talent, but if he didn't learn to control his anger, he'd never succeed at the sport. Riley knew for a fact that Bass had grown up dirt-poor and held a grudge against wealthy people. The man was as raw on the inside as he was on the outside.

"Never mind Bass," Riley said. "He can't focus worth a damn."

Speaking of concentrating, Riley waged his own battle as his thoughts drifted to Maria. He ached to sneak off alone with her tonight. He wanted Maria as badly as he wanted to make it to eight on Houdini. Riley glanced toward the stands, searching for her and the boys. As he scanned the rows his eyes landed on a redheaded vixen. *Amy?* He groaned.

"What's the matter?" Parker asked.

"Nothing." Riley hadn't thought of Amy in forever. Even so he was ashamed of how his relationship with his college flame had ended. That she sat next to Maria didn't bode well for him. The last thing he needed was a confrontation with Amy when he was trying to set a spark to his and Maria's relationship. He feared his plan to light Maria's fire tonight was dying a slow death in the stands.

"Good luck." Parker straightened his hat then walked off to prepare for his own ride.

Riley closed his eyes, willing his mind to empty of women. Once his skull rang hollow, he harnessed his energy, turning it inward. Then he gave himself a pep talk.

Don't loosen your grip on the buck rein when Houdini busts out of the chute.

Don't try to outthink Houdini. Follow his lead.

Keep your spurs above the shoulder points and roll 'em slow and steady.

Remember Houdini turns to his right. Be ready but stay loose.

Maria's watching.

Win.

"Good luck, hoss."

A second after the words were spoken, Riley felt a hard slap against his shoulder and, unprepared for the blow, he stumbled forward. He glared at his nemesis, Stover. "I'm feelin' lucky tonight. How about you?"

"This is Vegas. We're all feelin' lucky." Stover sauntered off.

Riley engaged Houdini in a stare down. "You're not throwin' me, you sorry excuse for a bronc."

Houdini neighed.

"Folks, turn your eyes to chute number eight. Riley Fitzgerald from Lexington, Kentucky, is gonna open tonight's bronc-bustin' competition by performing a magic trick on Houdini!" The announcer snickered at his joke.

Riley climbed the chute rails and swung a leg over the gelding, then settled low in the saddle. He tugged at his riding glove before grabbing the buck rein. He worked the leather between his fingers, familiarizing himself with the rope.

Houdini didn't twitch a muscle.

Retreating deep inside himself Riley followed the same routine he'd developed in college—even, quiet breaths. Squeezing the rope then loosening his grip—five times in a row. He attempted to picture his mother, father and sister, but instead saw Maria's pretty brown eyes.

A surge of adrenaline pumped through his veins. This was his chance to show Maria he wasn't playing at being a rodeo cowboy. He was a man on a mission. A man with a goal. A man with skill, maturity and a talent for rodeo.

One. Two. Three. Riley nodded to the gateman. The chute door opened and Houdini vaulted from the gates. Riley set his spurs high against the horse's shoulders until the bronc landed on all four hooves after his first buck. He clenched the rein tighter.

Houdini was unpredictable and threw trick after trick at his riders. The bronc spun to the right in tight circles, blurring the stands before Riley's eyes. He nudged

Houdini's right flank with his spur and the bronc made Riley pay. Houdini back-jumped, slamming his hooves into the dirt. Excruciating pain radiated up Riley's spine and into his brain. He'd have a hell of a backache tomorrow.

The pain intensified when Houdini's head swung right while his body curled left, forcing Riley's hips to twist awkwardly. The muscles in his thighs burned. Sweat stung his eyes.

Riley had never gotten into the habit of counting to eight during his ride—mainly because it interfered with his concentration. Right now he wished to hell he knew how many seconds had passed since the gate had opened, because it felt as if he and the horse had been dancing in the dirt for hours.

Houdini saved his best for last—a vertical jump that would have unseated most veteran cowboys. No way was Riley being thrown tonight—not with Maria and the boys as witnesses.

The buzzer blew and he wasted no time unraveling the buck rein from around his hand. Riley was known for his acrobatic dismounts—he and his college buddies had worked hard to perfect the stunts. He continued to ride Houdini, waiting for the right buck. Riley released the rope and swung his left leg over Houdini's head before leaping to the ground. He landed on both feet, then sprang forward into a front flip. His hat popped off his head, but Riley landed upright and extended his arm, snatching the Stetson before it landed in the dirt.

The crowd went wild.

Riley waved his hat to where Maria and the boys sat

then bowed, which caused the fans to erupt in a second round of boot-stomping and cheers.

"There you have it, folks. Riley Fitzgerald's eighty-seven is the score to beat tonight. That young man sure knows how to entertain!"

"You're nothing but a showoff, kid," Stover said when Riley returned to the cowboy-ready area.

"You beat my score and I'll lick your boots."

Stover didn't have a chance of winning tonight. The man had drawn Black Velvet—a dink. Even if Stover performed well, his horse wouldn't, which put the cowboy out of the running for the championship round on Sunday.

"Careful what you say, Fitzgerald. You might be ridin' Black Velvet one of these days." Disgusted, Stover stomped away.

Riley had had enough of rodeo for one day. His back screamed for a soak in a hot tub—specifically the one in Maria's room. He stuffed his riding gear into the bag and headed for the stands. As far as he was concerned, his best ride was yet to come.

CHAPTER TEN

RILEY WAITED FOR the roller coaster to return Victor, Cruz and Alonso to the mock train station in the New York-New York Hotel. After the rodeo he'd met up with the boys and Maria—thank God Amy hadn't stuck around to speak to him. But the damage had been done. Maria hadn't shown any enthusiasm when she'd congratulated Riley on his win. He guessed she'd discovered he and Amy had dated in the past, but he held out hope that his former girlfriend had spared Maria the details of his infidelity.

Instead of tagging along with him and the boys to the roller coaster, Maria had returned to her room, citing exhaustion. Needing time to devise a game plan to finagle an invitation into her suite, he'd offered to take the boys to the roller coaster before the ride shut down for the night. After three consecutive runs, the teens relinquished their seats in the taxicab cars.

"You sure you don't wanna ride?" Victor asked Riley when they stepped onto the platform.

"Nah, I'm wiped from the rodeo." Houdini had done a number on Riley's back. What he wouldn't give right now to feel Maria's deft fingers massaging his tight, achy muscles. "C'mon. I'll buy you guys a snack at the pizzeria."

"Can we watch a pay-per-view movie?" Victor asked.

"As long as you keep it R-rated. No porn." Riley hated to see Maria get into trouble if word reached Judge Hamel that the boys had watched X-rated movies in the hotel room.

"We've seen titty shows before," Cruz said.

The patrons at a gaming table stared as the boys passed. "Keep your voices down," Riley said.

"We're not virgins," Cruz grumbled.

Riley figured the teens had already experimented with sex, but *this* road trip would be nothing but clean fun— for the boys, that is. "No porn."

They stopped at the New York Pizzeria restaurant and Riley ordered an extra-large sausage-and-cheese pie, pretzel knots and quart-sized sodas, hoping the food would fill the teens until the following morning. Once they returned to the room and dug into the pizza, Riley checked on Maria.

What do I say? Riley hovered in front of Maria's door, struggling with opening lines.

I made a mistake.

I didn't mean to cheat.

I'd planned to break up with Amy anyway. His insides recoiled at the pathetic excuse even though it had been the honest-to-God truth.

Feeling as if he'd lost the round before the opening bell, Riley rapped his knuckles against the door.

"Who's there?"

"It's me, Riley."

The door widened a crack and Maria peeked at him. "Are you and the boys in for the night?"

"Yeah. They're eating pizza and watching a movie."

"What time should I be ready tomorrow?"

Ignoring the question, he asked, "Mind if I come in for a few minutes?"

The door closed and she released the security chain before waving him inside. The air in the suite was humid and heavy with the scent of perfumed soap. He stopped in the middle of the room and faced Maria.

She wore the white hotel robe found in all the bathrooms. He glanced at the hot tub, which sat outside the bathroom, facing the windows that overlooked the strip. The curtains remained open and he guessed she'd dimmed the lights and enjoyed the glittery Vegas skyline while sitting in the tub. "How was your bath?"

"Relaxing." Her mouth curved in a soft smile. "Wish I had one of these at home."

"I rent this room when I compete in Vegas. The hot tub comes in handy after each ride." He rubbed his palm against his lower back.

"Did you get hurt today?" Her eyes wandered over his body, and Riley felt a pang of arousal tug low in his gut.

"Spine's a little stiff. Mind if I take a soak?" As long as they were dancing around the subject, Riley might as well ease his sore muscles.

"Sure. I'll wait in the casino until you're finished." She grabbed her clothes from the back of a chair and rushed toward the bathroom.

Riley stopped her with a hand on her waist. "Don't leave."

Tiny pulses of electricity spread through Maria's abdomen when Riley tightened his fingers against her hipbone. She wanted to stay. She wanted to leave.

She didn't know what she wanted.

He leaned in, his lips brushing her cheek. "We haven't had a chance to talk alone since the rodeo."

What could it hurt if Riley relaxed in the hot tub and she sat in the chair? "Fine."

Flashing his trademark sexy grin he sauntered into the bathroom area. She wished the tub wasn't in the middle of the room but this was Vegas and everything sat out in the open. "Do you want me to close the curtains?"

"Leave them alone." He ran the water.

After she lowered the lights, Maria retreated to the window. Keeping her back to the tub, she watched tourists and gamblers stroll along the strip, ducking in and out of the casinos.

She kept her eyes on the activity outside the hotel but her sensitive ears caught the sound of rustling clothes as Riley stripped. The clank of his belt buckle against the tile floor startled her and she jumped inside her skin.

An image of a naked man appeared in the window glass. Maria blinked hard but couldn't make herself turn away. Riley was magnificent—tall, with lean muscles and six-pack abs. Her gaze skirted his loins, focusing on his legs. His thighs bunched with muscle when he raised his leg and stepped into the tub.

A guttural groan rumbled in his chest. Maria checked over her shoulder and witnessed the grimace on Riley's face as he sank into the water. Had he injured his back more seriously than he'd admitted? Maria retrieved the complimentary bath salts from the counter and dumped them into the hot water, careful to keep her eyes off his naked torso.

"You'll smell like a flower, but the Epsom salts will ease the soreness in your back," she said. Next, she grabbed a hand towel and folded it into a pillow. "Lift your head." He complied and she wedged the cotton between his neck and the tub.

Eyes closed, he muttered, "That feels great, thanks."

Maria gave into temptation and peered below the water level. Her breath caught at the sight of Riley's erection. It had been a long time since a man had made her perspire. Made her heart race. Her pulse pound. And the tiny little sparks that tickled her privates... She couldn't remember the last time she'd experienced those.

"I can explain." Riley grasped her hand, his wet fingers entwining with hers.

With her defenses weakening by the second, she decided to play dumb until she recovered her wits. "Explain what?"

"Whatever Amy told you earlier."

Maria had all evening to come to terms with the information she'd learned about Riley and Amy's relationship. She'd decided she was relieved Riley wasn't perfect—his infidelity made it easier to protect her heart from him.

"I don't want to waste time guessing what you ladies talked about, so you tell me," Riley said.

Most men would have evaded discussing a meeting between their ex and current...whatever she was to Riley. It didn't surprise her that he'd rather face the music than tiptoe around the three-thousand-pound elephant in the room. She, however, preferred to leave well enough alone.

"There's nothing to explain." At his startled expression, she added, "What happened between you and Amy stays between you and Amy."

Learning that Riley had cheated on his former girlfriend had turned out to be a good thing. Until today,

Maria had believed Riley a saint—the only mark against him had been his age. Riley was a nice man with a good heart but now that she'd discovered he wasn't perfect she could lay to rest all her fairy-tale fantasies about a future with him.

No longer did it matter that she was ten years his senior. She didn't have to fret that Riley might want children one day and she didn't. What difference did it make that he came from a wealthy, privileged family and she resided in the inner city? None of it mattered, because she'd never marry a man who'd cheated. *Once a cheater always a cheater.*

After her experience with Fernando, Maria swore she'd never allow another man to hurt her that way again. There would be no guilty feelings for caving in to the desire that had built steadily between her and Riley these past weeks. She was free to be with him for however long their affair—if that's what he wanted with her—lasted. Afterward, she'd walk away with no regrets. No broken heart.

"Are you sure you don't have any questions about my relationship with Amy?"

Maria ignored the suspicious note in his voice and focused her energy on changing the mood. She sat on the edge of the tub and poured a dollop of body wash onto the loofah sponge. Unlike a lot of men the same age as Maria, Riley's body was in prime condition. She slid the sponge across his shoulder, then down his arm, rubbing the large bicep, before moving to his chest, specifically the small tuft of black hair between his pectoral muscles. When her fingernails grazed his skin, he closed his eyes and moaned. Feeling bolder, Maria washed Riley's belly, the action triggering a movement below the water surface. She dragged the sponge along his thigh, then reversed direction and caressed the inside of the leg, making sure she narrowly missed his erection.

Leaning over the tub she soaped his foot. Her bathrobe parted, exposing her breast, and Riley caressed her tight nipple with his wet fingers. An achy knot formed in Maria's stomach as she dropped the sponge into the water and drove Riley wild with her hand. He threaded his fingers through her hair, tugging her head closer until their lips touched. Slow and easy, he kissed her.

"Make love to me, Riley," Maria whispered.

"Are you sure?"

The only thing Maria was certain of was that she couldn't live with herself if she allowed this moment to slip away. "Very sure."

Riley sprang to a standing position, water sluicing down his body, leaving Maria eye-level with a part of his anatomy she very much wanted inside her. Slowly she stood, giving him room to step from the tub. "Leave the jets running," he said, then scooped her into his arms.

"Your back," she protested.

"Sweetheart, the only pain I feel right now is below the waist." He carried her to the bed then covered her body with his.

The flashing neon lights outside the window cast a magical glow over the room. Riley was the sexiest man Maria had ever laid eyes on and he was all hers. *For tonight.*

"Be sure about this." His gaze pinned her. "I don't want any regrets."

She pressed her finger to his lips. "You talk too much."

Hypnotized by his blue eyes, she lifted her head, closing the distance between their mouths. Her bathrobe landed on the floor and Maria resisted the urge to cover herself with the edge of the comforter. Good grief, she was a mature woman whose body reflected her age. She took solace in believing that if Riley wanted young and firm he'd be with a buckle bunny right now.

He kissed a path down the center of her chest and her back arched, begging for more. "Where did you get this scar?" Riley caressed the quarter-size circle of puckered flesh on the outside of her right thigh.

"You'll ruin the mood with questions," she said.

Concern darkened his eyes and a piece of Maria's heart tore off. "Tell me what happened," he demanded.

"A bullet grazed me."

"Who shot you?" He kissed her scar.

Evidently their lovemaking would go no further until Riley had the answers he sought. "It was an accident. A boy entered my class carrying a gun, saying he'd forgotten to leave it at home. I told him to put it on my desk and he did. Then I called school security to collect the weapon. They arrived and when I went to hand it to the officer, the gun discharged, hitting me in the leg."

"You were lucky you weren't injured worse."

"No, I'm lucky the bullet didn't hit the officer or one of my students." She tugged a strand of his hair. "Now can we get back to…"

Riley nibbled a path down her leg, ending at her foot, where he nuzzled the arch.

"Stop!" She giggled. "That tickles."

His mouth moved to her ankle, then along the inside of her leg, his hot breath heating her flesh. "Tell me if this tickles." The air whooshed from Maria's lungs at the intimate caress. No man had ever taken this much care to arouse her. Heat spread through her body, leaving her flushed and gasping for air…a few seconds later her soul shattered into a million bright pieces.

Riley rested on his elbows and stared.

"What?" she whispered.

He tugged a strand of damp hair stuck to her cheek and grinned. "You've been ridden hard and put up wet."

"That's because I'm in bed with a rodeo cowboy."

Capturing Maria's mouth, Riley kissed the sass out of her. Her body shuddered, reminding him of his own unfulfilled need. He fumbled with his wallet on the nightstand. "Fasten your seat belt, darlin'," he said, then took Maria on a ride with more hills and drops than the hotel roller coaster.

IN THE AFTERMATH of their lovemaking Riley tightened his arms around Maria and snuggled her to his side. The soft rumble of the hot-tub jets echoed through the room. Since he'd met Maria, Riley had fantasized about having sex with her. Maria's enthusiastic response had wowed him. Riley groaned when she slid her leg between his, rubbing her lush breasts against his side. All she had to do was inhale and his body was ready for her again.

"Have I told you how much I enjoy being with you?" he whispered in her ear. "You're a special woman. I admire what you're doing for the boys. How you try to protect others."

Her fingers inched their way down his chest and Riley grasped her wrist before she dipped beneath the bedsheet. "Wait." He shifted onto his side and faced her. That Maria appeared reluctant to discuss his past relationship with Amy troubled Riley. He wanted the truth out in the open so they could deal with it. "I'm not making excuses for myself, but—"

"What you did in the past doesn't matter."

If Maria cared the least bit for him, then his cheating on Amy should damn well matter.

"We're having fun together, Riley. Let's live in the moment. No worries about the past. Or the future."

Feeling as if he'd been blindsided, Riley's stomach clenched and he closed his eyes against the pain. He'd finally realized his dream of coaxing Maria into his bed only to discover she was with him for all the wrong reasons.

Maria threaded her fingers through his hair and nudged his mouth toward hers. "Kiss me."

Frustration fueled the urgency behind Riley's kiss. He tried to convey without words that what they'd shared hadn't been a *good time* for him. Maria was the first woman he'd ever envisioned standing at his side a year from now. Ten years from now. Forever from now.

A fist banged against the connecting door between the boys' and Maria's room, abruptly ending their kiss.

"Yeah?" Riley called out.

"Can we watch another pay-per-view movie?" Alonso's voice filtered through the wall.

"Go ahead."

"When you comin' back?" Victor joined the conversation.

"After I discuss tomorrow's schedule with Ms. Alvarez."

"Yeah, sure." Snickers followed Victor's comment.

The mood broken, Riley left the bed.

After Riley retreated to the bathroom, Maria decided she was one fortunate lady. Stretching her arms above her head, she arched her back, relishing the twinges and tiny aches in her muscles. When she opened her eyes, Riley stood at the end of the bed.

"You're a beautiful woman, Maria."

No. She wasn't beautiful. Attractive maybe. But for now…tonight…she wouldn't deny his charge. "You'd better leave before they suspect…"

"They suspect." He winked. "But I'm not one of those guys who brags about his conquests." He shut off the hot-tub jets, then walked to the other side of the bed and re-trieved Maria's robe from the floor.

"What about your back? Will you be able to ride to-morrow?" She slipped on the robe.

"I'll soak in the hot tub beforehand." He stuffed his shirt into his jeans and zipped his pants. "How about letting the boys sleep in and you and I eat breakfast to-gether in the morning?"

"I'd love that."

He kissed her cheek, then her mouth—slow, hot and deep. "Be ready by seven," he whispered.

The quiet click of the door echoed through the room. Grateful for time alone, Maria studied her reflection in the mirror against the wall. She touched her fingertips to her swollen lips. Surely the boys didn't believe she and Riley had…had…

Made love.

There. She'd said it. What she and Riley had shared was more than sex. When Riley had held her in his arms, Maria had forgotten how wrong they were for each other. It would be so easy to lose her heart to Riley. He made her feel young and desirable and he restored her faith in the goodness of people. Riley made each day something to cherish—not just to survive. Though she was tempted to throw caution to the wind and allow herself to be in a committed relationship with Riley, she couldn't trust him not to stray once the newness of their lovemaking wore off. Better for both of them if they kept things light. Easy. Uncomplicated.

What happens in Vegas stays in Vegas.

As long as Maria remembered that, she couldn't get hurt.

RILEY ENTERED THE room the boys shared and three sets of smirking eyes greeted him.

"We heard you guys," Victor said, cracking a smile.

No, they didn't—not with the hot-tub jets running while he and Maria had made love.

"Be careful not to malign your teacher." Riley scowled at the boys.

"What's malign?" Victor asked.

"It means you shouldn't criticize Ms. Alvarez in a mean or hurtful way," Alonso said.

"I meant—"

"Nothing," Riley interrupted Victor. The teens backed off and he asked, "What movie are you watching?"

"A thriller about a man-eating python," Cruz said.

Too agitated to retreat to his room, Riley stretched out on one of the beds and groaned when a sharp twinge zapped his lower back.

"Did you get hurt today?" Cruz sat on the end of the bed.

"Pulled a few muscles."

"Do you get hurt a lot?"

"Not as much as other cowboys."

"How come you keep ridin' then?"

"I entered a junior rodeo on a dare when I was in tenth grade," Riley said. His father had been nagging Riley to take on more responsibility in the horse barns—the last place he'd wanted to spend time. Instead, he'd snuck off with his friends to a local rodeo.

"What happened?" Cruz asked.

"I won."

"So that's why you kept rodeoing?"

"No. I discovered that I craved the adrenaline rush I got from trying to tame a wild bronc." And rodeo had angered his father. What teen didn't find satisfaction in pissing off a parent?

"I get the same high when I break the law," Cruz said.

The more Riley learned about Cruz the more he believed rodeo might be the ticket to prevent the teen from following in his father's footsteps. Cruz lived in a world of gangs, violence and crime—it was all he knew. Riley bet the kid wouldn't be able to turn his back on that way of life without suffering withdrawal symptoms. "You'd be good at rodeo. But there's a price to pay if you get hurt."

"Do you know if my dad got hurt a lot?"

"I don't. You'll have to ask him when you see him on Sunday."

"What are you talking about?"

"Didn't Ms. Alvarez tell you?"

"Tell me what?"

Shoot. Riley should have confirmed the visit with Maria before they'd left Albuquerque, but he'd expected she'd have told him if the prison had denied Cruz a visit with his father. "After the rodeo on Sunday, we're flying to Sioux Falls. Ms. Alvarez arranged for you to see your dad."

"You're not joking, are you?"

"Nope. Barring any bad weather, we should arrive at the prison around six o'clock in the evening."

"Thanks," Cruz said.

"Don't thank me. Thank Ms. Alvarez." With the muted sounds of screaming python victims ringing in his ear, Riley closed his eyes and willed his mind to empty of all thoughts but making love to Maria.

Wow. Double wow. He'd fantasized about having sex with her since the day he'd landed his plane in the salvage yard. His fantasies hadn't compared to the real thing.

He could feel the softness of her skin rubbing against his. Her fingers tickling his thigh. Her nails biting into his flesh. He'd won his first go-round today but he hadn't won Maria. Riley worried over her easy acceptance of their lovemaking. She'd made it clear she was in it for the sex—a wild weekend in Vegas.

This trip was supposed to have been his chance to prove to Maria that there was more between them than sexual attraction. Instead, she'd given him the impression that she wasn't interested in a deeper, more meaningful relationship. Tomorrow was another chance to prove to Maria that what they'd shared tonight was more than just a wild ride.

CHAPTER ELEVEN

"LADIES AND GENTS, this is the final day of the Helldorado Rodeo competition here in lucky Las Vegas!"

Maria scanned the crowd but saw no sign of Amy in the stands. Thank goodness. Even though she'd told Riley his relationship with his ex-girlfriend wasn't a big deal…it was. Maria had difficulty reconciling the cheating Riley with the Riley who'd offered to introduce the boys to his competitors hanging out in the cowboy-ready area. Part of her wished she'd never run into Amy, but then she'd have never learned that Riley wasn't as perfect as she'd made him out to be. In a weird way the knowledge of Riley's past infidelities had both protected and wounded Maria's heart.

The brief time she'd spent in Riley's arms proved how vulnerable she was to the cowboy. The knowledge of why Amy had ended her relationship with Riley had done little to subdue Maria's craving to make love with him. No man had ever made her feel so special and desirable. As long as she kept her feelings for Riley in check and understood that their relationship could go no farther than the bedroom, she wouldn't get hurt.

For a mature woman who'd witnessed events in real life that most people only watched in TV dramas, Maria was embarrassingly gullible. Older didn't mean wiser.

Even though Riley acted mature for his age he was young and entitled to his share of mistakes as he matured. She'd certainly made a few blunders in her twenties.

"Folks, today's pot is worth ten thousand dollars to the cowboy or cowgirl who walks away with first place in their event." The young woman crowned Miss Hell-dorado paraded a trophy in front of the cheering fans.

Ten thousand was a fortune to Maria—pocket change to a man who flew his own plane. This morning Riley had told her over breakfast that a win today would put him in the running for a trip back to Vegas in December. He'd also said he planned to compete in as many rodeos as possible to prepare for the finals.

December was three months away. A lot could happen between now and then. Even so, Maria fantasized about spending Christmas with Riley. The holiday hadn't been the same since her brother had passed away. Maria had stopped stringing lights up and decorating the artificial tree when her mother had complained that the traditions made her more heartbroken over the death of her son.

The shrill blast of trumpets cleared the gloomy memories from Maria's head. A horse-drawn buckboard, carrying the rodeo sponsors to the VIP seating area, entered the arena. While the announcer introduced the men and women, Maria watched Riley and the boys.

Cruz had been especially thrilled when Riley suggested the teens witness today's competitions from behind the chutes. Maria noted a change in Cruz's demeanor this weekend. An aura of new energy surrounded him. Two weeks from now Cruz turned eighteen and Maria hoped he'd continue to pursue his GED and not drop out of her class. With any luck, a visit with his father in jail would convince Cruz to stick to his goals.

"Folks, it's time to kick off the saddle-bronc competition!" Once the cheers died down, the announcer continued. "Gate two's where all the action is. Ed Parker from Albuquerque, New Mexico, is comin' out on Stingray. Parker hasn't had a top-five finish in two years. He's currently in sixth place. Let's see if the next eight seconds changes his luck!"

Stingray bolted from the chute, bucked twice then reared. Maria prayed Gil Parker's son would keep his seat. Stingray established a pattern of bucking twice, then spinning to the right. A half second before the buzzer sounded, Ed sailed over the bronc's head. The pickup men moved in and guided the horse out of the arena.

"Maybe next time, cowboy!"

Five more riders came and went—two managing to remain in the saddle until the buzzer. "Eighty-three is the score to beat and we got two cowboys left who are gonna give it a try!" The announcer spoke over the crowd's applause. "Nick Bass, from Sierra Vista, Arizona, is new to the circuit. You might remember his earlier performance. He came in one point shy of Riley Fitzgerald. He needs a good ride if he intends to upset the reigning world champion."

Once the noise level dropped a notch the announcer said, "The action's at gate five! Bass is gonna strut his stuff on Holly Jolly."

Holly Jolly was an appropriate name for the bronc that jumped out of the chute. All four legs left the ground when the horse performed an equestrian happy dance. After a few seconds, the bronc ran out of jollies and its bucking dwindled to a few kicks. Bass kept his seat until the buzzer then dismounted. Holly Jolly trotted out of the arena on his own.

"Bass made it to eight, folks. Let's see what the judges think of Holly Jolly's performance."

The Jumbotron above the VIP seats displayed an 84.

"Fitzgerald could be our winner today if he keeps his seat on Tranquility!" More applause. "Don't let the horse's name fool you none. Tranquility is notorious for brewin' up a storm!"

The crowd stomped their feet on the metal bleachers. "Let's see if Fitzgerald and Tranquility can get the job done. Gate seven!"

Riley climbed the chute rails. Cruz, Victor and Alonso perched on the top rung to watch the action. Riley didn't waste any time preparing for his ride. A few seconds after he settled into the saddle and wrapped the rein around his hand, the gate opened and Tranquility burst into the arena.

The bronc twisted to the left then reared before slamming back to the ground and spinning right. In a succession of spins and bucks, Tranquility edged closer to the rails. A collective gasp echoed through the stands when the bronc hit the gate. From that moment on, the action in the arena played out in slow motion before Maria's eyes. The boys jumping off the rails… Riley's leg slamming into the chute door… The grimace on Riley's face…

The buzzer sounded but Riley held on through a second round of bucking as the pickup men attempted to corner Tranquility. Riley released the rein and jumped to the ground. He stumbled once, twice, then unable to maintain his balance, he slid face-first into the dirt. The pickup men guided the bronc out of the arena and Riley slowly got to his knees.

"Well, folks, what'd I say about Tranquility? That horse is a cyclone on four hooves!"

Maria pressed her fingers to her mouth as she watched Riley struggle to his feet then limp from the arena.

"Fitzgerald's gonna be okay, folks!" The crowd applauded.

The Jumbotron flashed a score of 85. "Fitzgerald takes first place, which puts him back in the race for a national title!"

"Excuse me. Pardon me." Maria made her way out of the stands then hurried to find Riley and the boys. When she arrived behind the chutes, Riley was surrounded by cowboys. She squeezed into the circle and clutched his shirtsleeve. "Are you okay?"

"I'm good as gold, darlin'."

The crowd snickered, but Maria failed to find humor in his remark. Riley had scared ten years off her life in a little over eight seconds. Reporters were eager for a word with him so she stepped aside. Cruz remained next to Riley listening to the reporter's questions and Riley's responses. Victor and Alonso had lost interest in the commotion and walked off to watch rodeo workers load a bull into a chute. After ten minutes of nonstop questions and autograph signing, Riley glanced her way. His gentle smile tugged at her heartstrings. He thanked reporters, then excused himself and limped to her side.

"I won."

Despite her concern she laughed at his arrogance. "I know. Congratulations. That was an impressive ride. Did you hurt your leg?"

"A bruise. Ready to head to the airport? Cruz is eager to see his dad."

"I'm not so sure about that." Maria pointed to the teen, who was conversing with a blond buckle bunny. As much as Maria had enjoyed the weekend in Vegas, it was time to leave Sin City behind. She signaled to Victor and Alonso and the boys caught Cruz's attention. After Riley collected his winning check, they piled into a cab and swung by the hotel, where a bellman loaded their luggage into the trunk and wished them a safe flight.

When they arrived at the airstrip, Maria pulled Riley aside. "Are you certain you're able to fly with a sore leg?"

"You worry too much." He brushed a strand of hair from her cheek, then limped off to file a flight plan.

Maria wished she possessed his positive view of life. Even if she was able to forget his cheating on Amy, Maria's pessimistic view of the world would drag Riley down and eventually he'd realize that she was a dark cloud hanging over his head and not the ray of sunshine he'd first believed.

THE SOUTH DAKOTA State Penitentiary in Sioux Falls was nothing to write home and brag about. Cruz fidgeted as they stood outside the facility, waiting for Maria to confirm the teen's visit with his father. The kid was nervous. Who wouldn't be, seeing their father behind bars? Victor and Alonso sensed their friend's unease and hovered by his side, offering silent support.

After five minutes, Maria signaled them to follow her. Except for the female prison guard behind the registration window the visitor's welcome room was empty.

"Cruz, it will be about thirty minutes before they bring

your father down." Maria squeezed the teen's arm reassuringly and smiled. "The officer needs you to go with her."

"Why?" Cruz's gaze darted between Maria and Riley.

"They need to screen you for weapons or contraband," Riley said.

"Can we go with him?" Victor asked.

"Cruz is the only one approved for a visit," Maria said. She coaxed the teen to the window, where he answered questions then followed the guard out of the room.

"Look, Alonso. The prisoners are outside." Victor stood before a large tinted window facing the grounds. A sign on the wall assured visitors that prisoners could not see through the glass into the waiting room.

Riley joined the boys at the window. The inmates broke into teams—a few played basketball while others lifted weights or talked and smoked in small groups.

"Look at that tattoo." Victor pointed to a man hovering near the window. "That's the symbol of the Aryan Brotherhood." Right then the convict faced the window and sneered, revealing several missing teeth. Alonso and Victor jumped back and the man laughed as if he knew he was being watched.

"I feel sorry for Cruz's dad," Alonso whispered.

"More incentive to work hard for Ms. Alvarez and earn a GED," Riley said.

Victor grimaced. "What good's a GED if I don't know what I wanna do with my life?" Right then the teen's cell phone bleeped and Victor stepped outside to talk.

Riley lost himself in thought. Shoot, he didn't know what he wanted to do with his life, either; but after making love to Maria he believed it was imperative that he get his act together and make a decision about his future. He couldn't continue to rodeo and rely on his trust fund to pay his way through life.

He believed Maria didn't begrudge him for his privileged upbringing—she wasn't that kind of woman. But the man she gave her heart to and wanted to spend the rest of her years with would be a man who blazed his own trail. If he wanted to be with Maria he needed a game plan for his future—one that included her.

"Everything okay?" Maria stopped by his side.

Riley slung an arm around her shoulders but she moved away, breaking contact. Was she worried the boys would guess they were more than friends or was her lukewarm response a signal that what they'd shared in Vegas had ended when they'd left the city? This wasn't the place or time to discuss their relationship, but before the day was through Riley intended to have a heart-to-heart with Maria.

"Where did Victor go?" Maria glanced around the room.

"He's out front talking on his phone."

Once outside Maria froze when she heard the words Los Locos come out of Victor's mouth.

"Yeah, man, tell the homies I'm in. No, man, I'm for real." Victor kept his back to Maria and continued talking. "I gotta stay a few more weeks at that stupid ranch then I'm comin' back to the 'hood."

Maria's heart sank. Since when had Victor changed his mind about liking it at Gateway Ranch?

"Yeah, I could be a lookout for the gang. Just give me a chance." Victor glanced over his shoulder, his face paling when he saw Maria. "Later, homie." He ended the call.

"Are you running with the Los Locos, Victor?" She engaged the boy in a stare-down.

"What if I am?" The teen jutted his chin.

From the bits and pieces of conversation she'd overheard, Maria guessed that Victor hadn't yet been accepted into the gang but it was only a matter of time before he ran with the hoodlums.

"What about your GED? Are you going to throw all that studying away?"

"No. I'm gonna take the tests, but—"

"But what, Victor?"

"But I'm not Cruz. I don't wanna bust broncs. And I'm not Alonso. I don't wanna go to college." He scuffed the toe of his shoe against the cement. "I can make a lot of money in the gang."

"Why all of a sudden are you worried about making money?"

"I wanna be like Riley. The dude walks around with hundred-dollar bills in his wallet. He stays in fancy hotel suites in Vegas and flies his own plane."

"Then go to college and earn a degree, get a good job and save your money."

"Riley didn't get his money from no college degree. He said his grandpa left him a bank account." Victor's eyes narrowed. "I don't have a grandpa who's gonna leave me millions of dollars. But I can buy stuff and get me a bunch of those Benjamins if I hang with the Los Locos."

"You believe becoming a member of a gang is the fast track to fame and fortune?"

"It's the only track in the 'hood, Ms. Alvarez. As soon as I save enough money I'll quit the gang and move away from the 'hood and get a real job."

They both knew once Victor joined the Los Locos he'd never leave the gang or the 'hood alive. Maria's father had been right—Riley wasn't a good role model for the teens. Cruz, Alonso and Victor weren't mature enough to understand that not everyone in life received a free ride. That the majority of the people on earth had to *work* for the things they desired.

"Promise me one thing, Victor."

"What?"

"You won't have any more contact with the Los Locos until you earn your GED and leave the ranch."

"But—"

"No calls. No texts. Nothing." If Maria believed it would prevent Victor from contacting the gang she'd confiscate his phone. But if the teen was determined to stay in touch with the Los Locos there was little she could do to stop him. "If you can't keep that promise then you pack your bags and leave the ranch when we return tonight." She was relying on Victor's friendship with Cruz and Alonso to keep him at the ranch until she found a way to deter him from joining the gang.

"Everything okay out here?" Riley poked his head outside the building.

"We're fine," Maria said.

Victor shoved his phone into his pocket. "Is Cruz back?" he asked.

"Yep. We're ready to leave." Cruz and Alonso pushed past Riley out of the building. The stony expression on Cruz's face gave no indication how the visit with his father had gone. A moment later the same cab and driver that had dropped them off at the prison arrived and they headed to the airstrip in silence.

After Riley filed another flight plan, Cruz asked Maria if he could switch places with her and keep Riley company in the cockpit. Thirty minutes later the *Dark Stranger* was airborne. Once the plane reached cruising altitude, Riley leveled off.

"My dad's heard of you."

"Yeah?" Riley didn't know how unless the man had caught a televised rodeo on TV.

"He wanted to know why I was hanging around with a rich cowboy."

"What'd you tell him?"

"I told him about Ms. Alvarez and how I got kicked out of school and she was helping me get a GED and you got us a place to stay at the ranch where you were teaching me about rodeo."

"What'd he say?"

"That I should find a better teacher."

"Did he mean me or Ms. Alvarez?"

"You."

Go figure. "Did your dad recommend anyone in particular?"

"Yeah, a dude named Drew Rawlins."

Riley's ghostly nemesis.

"My dad said Rawlins is really tough."

"Rawlins was good but he struggled with injuries and had to retire."

Riley doubted he'd ever earn the respect he deserved unless he won the NFR outright this December. One thing for sure, he wouldn't win if he didn't focus on rodeo. He needed to keep his priorities straight or he'd lose his chance to prove he was the best in the world at bustin' broncs.

"My dad said rich people don't know how to fight for what they want 'cause they never had to go without."

Riley's father had warned him others would believe as much and that he'd have to work twice as hard to earn respect. Case in point—Maria. He had to find a way to prove to her he was more than a good time or temporary amusement. "A bronc can't tell a rich cowboy from a poor one nor does he care." Irritated, he changed the subject. "Did you and your dad talk about anything else?"

"He asked about my mom. I told him the truth. That she gets high all the time."

Riley remained quiet and waited for Cruz to volunteer more information.

"No one told him my brother was dead," Cruz whispered.

"Your father must have been pretty upset."

"He told me no matter how long it takes, I should stay in Ms. Alvarez's class and get my GED."

"Good advice."

After a short silence, Cruz added, "My dad didn't mean to kill that man."

"I'm sure he didn't." But T.C. *had* killed a man and now he had to pay a hefty price.

"He doesn't want me to end up in the slammer like him."

"Most fathers want their kids to turn out better."

"Yeah, I guess."

"Did your dad say what he does to keep busy?"

"He's got a job in the prison factory making commercial draperies." Cruz glanced at Riley. "Does that mean he sews stuff?"

"Probably."

"That sucks."

It sure does.

"He said to thank you for bringing me to visit."

"Ms. Alvarez should get his thanks. She's the one who arranged the meeting."

Riley spent the next few minutes communicating with Blue Skies Regional Airport. After he'd been cleared for landing, he said, "There's a junior rodeo in El Paso at the end of October."

"That's two months away."

Not quite. "Seven weeks. Think you can pass your GED exams by then?"

"Yeah. But I'd need a saddle."

"I'll buy you one before I leave."

"I thought I had to earn—"

"Consider the equipment a loan." The kid couldn't very well learn how to rodeo without gear. "If you don't earn your GED, the gear's mine."

"You gonna be around to help me?"

"I've got a string of rodeos to get in before the finals in December, but I'll squeeze in a few lessons before the El Paso rodeo." Riley turned the plane eastward. "And I'll make sure the other cowboys at the ranch help you."

"What about you and Ms. Alvarez?"

"What about us?"

"Aren't you guys…you know, doin' it?"

"Ms. Alvarez and I are good friends."

Cruz frowned. "I thought you and her…you know?"

"You leave Ms. Alvarez and me to our own business. Okay?"

"Just sayin', man." The teen listened to his iPod the

remainder of the flight. When Riley landed the plane at the airport, Maria's father waited inside the hangar.

"You did a fantastic job on the repairs," Riley praised Ricardo.

"Are we going back to the ranch?" As soon as Alonso asked the question, Maria's father excused himself and retreated to his office—obviously the older man was uncomfortable around the teens. "Load your bags into the truck. I'll be right there."

Once the teens left the hangar, Maria spoke. "Thank you for making this weekend special for the boys."

What about you? Had Maria's time in Vegas been special? "I wish you could come on the road with me but you'd be a major distraction." He leaned in to kiss her cheek but she dodged the caress. He was batting oh for two so far today. "Cruz wants to compete in the junior rodeo at the end of October. I told him to keep studying and that I'd try to return to the ranch between now and then to give him a few lessons."

"That's not a good idea."

"What do you mean?" Riley's gut clenched when Maria refused to make eye contact.

"It's best if you keep your distance from the boys."

He opened his mouth but shock barred the words from escaping.

"I appreciate everything you've done, but—"

"Stop." Riley shoved his fingers through his hair. "Did the guys tease you about us sleeping together in Vegas?"

Maria glanced over her shoulder to check on her father but he'd disappeared inside the office. "This has nothing to do with us. I caught Victor on his cell phone talking to a member of the Los Locos gang."

"What does that have to do with me?"

"Victor believes joining a gang is a shortcut to making a lot of money."

"He should know better than that. You have to work hard if you expect to own the finer things in life."

"I agree, Riley, but Victor sees you throwing your money around, paying for fancy hotels in Vegas, flying your own airplane…don't you understand? He wants to live your life, only he doesn't have a wealthy grandfather. The only way he believes he can make a lot of money is by joining a gang."

"I'll have a talk with Victor and—"

"It would be best if you stayed away from the boys."

Frustrated, Riley clenched his hands into fists. "And do you believe I should keep my distance from you, too?"

"Yes."

The whispered word sliced Riley's heart in two. "Then it's a good thing I'm on the road until the middle of October." Maybe it was wishful thinking or a trick of the lighting, but he swore Maria's eyes shone with tears. He wanted to ask if she regretted making love with him but didn't have the guts. He prayed Maria's heart would grow fonder of him over the next several weeks. "Walk me to my truck?" He didn't want to leave without kissing her.

"Sure." They stepped into the shadows outside the hangar and Riley slowed his steps. "This weekend meant a lot to me." When Maria remained silent, he pulled her close. "I care about you, Maria. More than I've cared about any woman. Don't quit me."

"We'd be dragging out a relationship that has nowhere to go and—"

"If this is about Amy, I—"

"What happened between you and Amy doesn't matter, because we can't be together." Maria's smile wobbled. "Fly safe, Riley."

Damn, this was not the memory he wanted to take with him after a great weekend in Vegas. Maria might believe she'd gotten the final word in, but, as far as Riley was concerned, they were far from finished. He kissed her, pouring his emotions into the embrace, showing her how much he wanted her...heart, soul and body.

Then he left her gasping for breath and walked away.

CHAPTER TWELVE

SIX WEEKS.

Six long weeks had passed since Riley left Albuquerque and hit the rodeo circuit.

Late Friday afternoon Maria stood outside the corral at the Gateway Ranch, watching Cruz practice his rodeo skills on a horse named Skippy. She shivered as the brisk October breeze whipped her hair about her head. She'd arrived late to tutor the boys, because Judge Hamel had requested a meeting with her to discuss Cruz's progress. Cruz had fulfilled his hundred hours of community service, but both she and the judge agreed that it was in the teen's best interest to remain at the ranch until he completed the requirements to earn his GED. One test remained—math. Not Cruz's strong subject.

Since the rodeo in Vegas, time had crawled to a standstill for Maria. No matter how busy she kept herself, every other thought centered on Riley. Her feelings for the cowboy were a tangled mess, and she missed him. Missed his smile. His grin. The way he goofed off and made the boys laugh.

"Cruz looks as if he'll be ready for his first junior rodeo at the end of the month," Gil Parker said when he stopped at Maria's side.

"He's getting better, isn't he?" Maria was impressed

with the way Cruz listened to the ranch hand giving him pointers.

"Riley phoned an hour ago. He should be here by supper time."

Maria's heartbeat jumped out of sync for several seconds before returning to a normal rhythm. "Has he been winning?"

Gil frowned. "I thought you two were—" He cleared his throat. "I'd presumed he'd been calling you with updates."

"I've been busy with my students." She'd listened to Riley's first voice mail message weeks ago. He'd pleaded for a chance to make things right with Victor and with her. Tears had filled her eyes and from that day forward she'd deleted his messages without listening to them. One of them had to be the adult. Since she was older...

"Spoke to my son Ed last night. He said Riley moved into the top ten. He's taken first or second place in every rodeo since his big win in Las Vegas. Billy Stover beat him out in Phoenix two weeks ago, but Ed claims Riley drew a lazy bronc in that go-round."

"I'm glad he's doing well." That Riley was winning again proved he hadn't lied to Maria when he'd insisted she was a distraction. She hadn't wanted to believe she interfered with his concentration, because then she couldn't dismiss Riley's feelings for her as those of a young man with his first crush on an older woman.

Gil tipped his hat toward Cruz. "How's he doing with his schoolwork?"

"He'll be ready to take his final test next week."

"Think he'll pass?"

"I hope so." Victor and Alonso had completed their

exams and earned their GEDs two weeks ago. Gil had offered to pay the two teens for their work if they decided to remain at the ranch while Cruz studied. Alonso jumped at the opportunity but convincing Victor to remain hadn't been easy when he was eager to join the Los Locos gang. In the end Cruz and Alonso had been the ones to talk him into staying.

"What you're doing for the boys..." Maria blinked back tears. "Thank you for opening your heart and this ranch to them."

Gil smiled. "Everyone deserves a second chance."

As much as they might want to, the boys couldn't live at the ranch forever; and Maria worried that if she didn't persuade Victor to walk away from the Los Locos he'd be lost to her forever.

"Here he goes." Gil pointed to Cruz.

Shouts of encouragement erupted from the cowhands when Cruz settled onto the back of the bronc. Pride filled her as she watched her student cling to the saddle. The horse didn't buck as violently as the animals in the Vegas rodeo, but the bronc had plenty of spunk for a beginner. Cruz slid sideways but managed to remain in the saddle. Eight seconds passed and Alonso clanged a cow bell. Several cowboys leapt into the pen ready to intervene should Cruz need help.

The teen swung his leg over the saddle and launched himself into the air. He landed on both feet, but the impact sent him sprawling forward and he slid on his belly.

"Dismount needs a little work, Cruz!"

Maria whirled at the familiar voice. Riley strolled toward the corral, his sexy swagger and engaging smile sending a tiny thrill through her. She waited for him to notice her but he focused on the action inside the pen.

"I made it to eight, Riley!" Cruz spit dirt from his mouth.

"I saw. Good job!" Riley stopped near Gil and the men shook hands.

"Didn't expect you for another hour or two," Gil said.

"Caught a tailwind." Riley spared Maria a quick glance. "Hello, Maria."

Hurt by the tepid greeting, she responded in kind. "Riley." What had she expected after she'd ignored his phone calls and text messages?

"Heard you set fire to the rodeo circuit these past few weeks," Gil said.

"I had a good run."

"Look forward to hearing about your rides. See you folks at supper." Gil walked off.

Aside from the nick on his chin and a bruise on his right cheekbone Riley appeared in good shape. Maria never got the chance to ask how Riley's leg was healing before Cruz demanded his attention.

"Hey, Riley!" Cruz ducked between the slats of the pen. "Did you win a lot of rodeos?"

Alonso and Victor joined Cruz, peppering Riley with questions. Forgotten for the moment, Maria waited for a pause in conversation, then said, "Don't forget to tell Riley your good news."

"We passed our tests and got our GEDs," Alonso said.

"Alonso scored higher than me, but I still passed." Victor fist-pumped the air.

"That's great, guys. I'm proud of you," Riley said. "What about you, Cruz?"

"I have to take the math test."

"Math is tough, but I'm sure you're working hard with Ms. Alvarez on mastering the subject."

"Victor and Alonso have been quizzing Cruz to help prepare him for the test next week," Maria said.

"You'd better pass, Cruz. I paid your entry fee into the El Paso junior rodeo at the end of the month."

Maria squelched her anger at Riley's announcement. Was he purposefully going against her wishes that he keep his distance from the boys?

"Oh, man, really?" Cruz's eyes lit with excitement.

"Can me and Victor go, too?" Alonso asked.

"As long as Cruz passes his math exam, I'll fly all of you, including Ms. Alvarez, to El Paso."

"You gotta pass, Cruz," Alonso said.

Victor didn't appear as eager to watch Cruz compete as Alonso. Maria suspected he'd rather return to the 'hood. As much as she believed Riley's jet-setting lifestyle and big spending was responsible for Victor's desire to join the Los Locos, attending the rodeo in El Paso would keep the teen away from the gangbangers a while longer.

A ranch hand shouted for help stowing the rodeo gear and the boys took off at a sprint.

"That's an improvement." Riley watched the teens haul the equipment into the barn.

"Gil Parker is a saint in my book," Maria said. "Such a shame there aren't more people willing to offer at-risk teens a safe place to live, work and study their way to a better life."

Riley's expression sobered. "You didn't return my calls."

"I didn't see the point."

"We were friends before we slept together, weren't we?"

Maria glanced around, making sure no one eavesdropped on their conversation. "I did a lot of thinking while you were away." A little bit of crying, too. "Riley—"

"I want you to meet my parents, Maria."

What?

"My father's trying to close a deal with a former PRCA steer-wrestling champion and he needs me to schmooze the guy. My mother invited Peter Westin for dinner tomorrow night and I agreed to fly home for it."

"Riley, I don't see the purpose of meeting your parents when we're—"

"Friends?"

"Right."

"I can't think of a better reason than being friends to introduce you to my family."

Although Maria had decided that allowing her relationship with Riley to progress further was out of the question, a part of her wanted to see the place where he'd been raised—the environment and people who had molded him into the man he was today. A visit to Riley's childhood home would strengthen her memories of him—and memories were all she'd have once they parted ways. Even so, common sense insisted she offer a token protest. "I'm sure your mother wouldn't approve of you bringing home an older—"

"Please, Maria."

After all he'd done for the boys, Maria couldn't refuse him. "All right. I'll go."

"Good. Meet me at the airport tomorrow morning at ten."

"I have to work on Monday."

"We'll return Sunday."

"Casual or formal?"

"Formal."

Maria hoped the one and only cocktail dress she owned fit her. The last time she'd worn it she'd attended a co-worker's retirement party two years ago. She studied Riley's retreating backside as he headed for the barn. All these weeks she'd agonized over how she'd set Riley straight about their relationship only to learn he'd already decided they were better off being friends not lovers.

Maria didn't know if she was relieved or hurt that Riley had accepted defeat without a fight.

RILEY WATCHED MARIA out of the corner of his eye as he drove twenty miles south of Lexington along the road bordering Belle Farms. Maria stared out the passenger window of the Lincoln Town Car, which had been dropped off for them at the estate's private airstrip. Maria's silence worried Riley. Hell, he'd been a mental mess since the rodeo in Las Vegas.

Maria was the first woman Riley had ever been serious about—really serious. When she hadn't returned his phone messages he'd deduced that she was intent on ending their relationship. The thought scared and angered him and he'd channeled that raw emotion into rodeo. The broncs hadn't stood a chance against Riley's bottled-up orneriness.

His goal had been to return to Albuquerque and pretend Maria hadn't ignored his calls, but he'd lost his courage and confronted her. As he'd predicted, Maria appeared intent on keeping that distance between them.

In a panic he'd invited her to Belle Farms, hoping to prove his feelings for her were honest and sincere. "The entrance is right here," he said, breaking the silence. He drove the Lincoln beneath the arching stone pillars and down the tree-lined drive. Maria's eyes widened—a common reaction by first-time visitors.

Albuquerque was unique in its own way, but the desert's brown-and-red clay colors paled in comparison to Kentucky's rich verdant pastureland, freshly whitewashed fencing and hunter-green horse barns. The road circled around a profusion of blooming rosebushes in front of a life-sized sculpture of a racing horse. He parked the Lincoln in front of the main house.

"It's beautiful," Maria whispered. Six massive pillars supported the overhang protecting the porch. A set of rocking chairs sat on both sides of the front door and large hanging baskets of red and yellow flowers added a splash of color to the home.

"My great-great-grandfather completed most of the renovations during his lifetime."

"It's remarkable and I haven't even seen the inside," Maria said.

He got out of the car, rounded the hood and held the door open for her.

"What about our bags?" she asked.

"I'll fetch them later." Halfway up the steps, the front door opened.

"Hey, Eunice." Riley greeted the housekeeper with a big hug. "I've brought a friend home to visit. Maria Alvarez, this is Belle Farms' housekeeper, Eunice Mays. She's been with the Fitzgerald family since before I was born."

The older woman with striking white hair hugged Maria, squeezing the air from her lungs. "Welcome to Belle Farms, Miss Maria."

"Thank you, Eunice. It's a pleasure to meet you."

The housekeeper waved them into the foyer. "There's fresh-squeezed lemonade in the fridge."

Maria's feet remained rooted to the marble floor as she took inventory of the opulence surrounding her. Matching red velvet drapes with gold fringe adorned the floor-to-ceiling windows in the living room to her right and the dining room to her left. Mahogany bookcases lined the walls at the far end of the living room, where an antique desk sat. Maria guessed the piece of furniture was a family heirloom that had made the trip across the Atlantic. Persian rugs adorned dark wood floors, which gleamed in the sunlight pouring through the windows. Portraits of Fitzgerald ancestors hung on the foyer walls and along the staircase leading to a second-floor landing.

"Quit gawking at all the old stuff and come along, Miss Maria," the housekeeper said.

"Eunice hates antiques," Riley whispered. "She thinks the house is a museum."

"I heard that, young man."

The kitchen was a bit more modern—all the usual appliances. The double-wide refrigerator was built into the wall and a huge marble island sat in the middle of the room.

"You know what I think, Eunice? You hate being older than half the furnishings in this house," Riley teased.

The housekeeper smacked Riley across the shoulder. "Sit down before I send you to the corner."

Maria joined Riley at the island. "The corner? What's that?" she asked.

After setting a plate of cookies on the counter, Eunice retrieved a pitcher of lemonade from the refrigerator. "When Riley was naughty his mama would make him sit on a stool over there." Eunice pointed next to the back door.

"I hated that corner," Riley said. "Every time the door opened I got smacked."

Eunice laughed and the tension that had built in Maria since leaving Albuquerque eased. She hoped Riley's parents were as friendly and welcoming as the family housekeeper.

"Most of the time Eunice came to my rescue and convinced my mother to shorten the punishment time."

What an amazing childhood Riley must have experienced in the lap of luxury surrounded by love. No wonder he only saw the good in people.

"Is Bree out in the barn?" Riley asked.

"Where else would that girl be?" Eunice scoffed. "Your mama's in town talking to the caterers for tonight's dinner."

"Mom's not cooking?" Riley said.

"She took a tumble off her horse last week and sprained her wrist."

"She's okay otherwise?" Riley asked.

"Your mama's fine. But until she can cook again we've been eating take-out from the restaurants in town." The housekeeper leaned across the island and whispered,

"Don't tell your mama, but I'm glad she's taking a break from the kitchen."

"I thought you loved my mother's cooking."

"I do. But lately she's been on a health kick. Worried about our hearts and cholesterol." Eunice grimaced. "We eat so many vegetables now my skin's turning green."

Maria and Riley laughed.

"I snuck into town last week and had me a Big Mac." Eunice smacked her lips. "Thought I'd died and gone to heaven."

"What time is dinner tonight?" Riley asked.

"Seven. Don't be late." Eunice turned to Maria. "Have Riley put your things in the yellow bedroom at the top of the stairs. We keep that room clean in case we have an unexpected guest." Eunice glanced at the wall clock above the sink. "Time for my nap. Holler if you two need anything."

"Thank you, Eunice."

The housekeeper patted Maria's hand. "No trouble at all, Miss Maria."

"She's a lovely woman," Maria said as soon as Eunice left the kitchen.

"I have a lot of happy memories at Belle Farms."

"I'm surprised you'd want to leave this place."

"I don't have the same passion for horse racing that my father and sister have." Riley stood. "Speaking of fathers and sisters…ready to meet mine?"

"Sure." Maria followed Riley out the back door, then along a stone path. She took in the bustling activity around her—trainers walking horses in and out of barns. Hay bales being unloaded from a truck. A horse being hosed down. Another groomed and yet another examined by a veterinarian.

Riley left the path and approached an enclosed pen where a young woman guided a horse through a series of jumps in an obstacle course.

"I thought your family was into racing," Maria said.

"My sister competes in show jumping in her spare time. She's training Princess Leia." Bree sat tall and straight in the saddle, a long red braid swishing across her back. She coaxed the beautiful brown-and-white mare over three gates, then turned a corner and leapt across a water hazard, before slowing the animal to a trot.

"Riley!" Bree reined in Princess Leia in front of the fence, then hopped off and swatted the mare's rump. The horse trotted away.

Bree slipped through the rails and brother and sister bear-hugged. Maria felt a twinge of envy, their closeness reminding her of how much she missed her brother. Pasting a polite smile on her face she waited for an introduction.

"I want you to meet a very special friend of mine— Maria Alvarez."

"Hello." Bree scowled at Riley. "Mom never mentioned that you were bringing a guest tonight."

Maria's stomach plummeted. Why hadn't Riley sought his parents' permission before inviting her on the trip?

"I wanted to surprise Mom and Dad." Riley slid his arm around Maria's waist and pulled her next to him. "Maria and I met in Albuquerque when my plane went down."

"Went down?" Bree's eyes widened. "Dad never mentioned you'd had trouble with the plane."

"He doesn't know, so keep my secret, okay?"

"What happened?"

"Bird strike. I landed the plane in an abandoned salvage yard."

Bree's expression grew more horrified by the second and Maria wished Riley would spare his sister the particulars.

"Maria happened to be checking on her students who were waiting in the salvage yard for a gang called the—"

"I'm sure Bree doesn't care to hear all the boring details," Maria interrupted. "My father's an airplane mechanic and he worked on Riley's plane."

"Oh." A curious expression remained on Bree's face, but she refrained from prying. No doubt she'd corner her brother later and badger him with questions.

"Good thing you didn't cancel at the last minute. Dad's worried the deal with Mr. Westin will fall through. He expects you to charm the pants off him and Serena."

"Serena?" Riley asked.

Maria was all ears.

"Mom didn't tell you?" Bree glanced between her brother and Maria. "Serena's Mr. Westin's daughter. She's a concert pianist."

"Why was she invited to the dinner?" Riley asked.

"Why do you think?" Bree batted her eyelashes. "Mom's matchmaking again." She flashed Maria an apologetic smile. "If Mom had known Riley was bringing you, she wouldn't have invited Serena."

"No worries. Riley and I are just friends." Maybe if she said it aloud enough times, Maria's heart would believe it.

"Good. Then there won't be any awkwardness." Bree

hugged her brother a second time. "It was nice to meet you, Maria. I'll see you at dinner."

As soon as Bree was out of earshot, Maria hissed, "How could you, Riley?"

"How could I what?"

"First, you didn't tell your parents I was coming and now they've invited a woman to the dinner who expects you—"

"Expects me to what?" Riley inched closer to Maria.

Flustered, Maria glared. "To be unattached." She couldn't be with Riley, but, darn it, she didn't want any other woman to be with him, either.

You can't have your cake and eat it, too.

"I had no idea that my mother invited Mr. Westin's daughter. When I spoke to my father several weeks ago he never mentioned Serena."

"I'll keep Eunice company in the kitchen while you entertain the *pianist*." Maria swallowed a groan at the waspish tone in her voice.

"Jealous?"

"Absolutely not."

"My mother's been playing matchmaker since she introduced Amy to me," Riley said.

Good grief. Why did Riley have to bring up his old flame?

"Mom and Amy's dad were friends in college. You know—" Riley waved his hand in the air "—the whole sorority-fraternity thing."

No, Maria did not know the whole sorority-fraternity thing.

"They remained good friends through the years even

after they'd married other people. Mom was pretty angry at me for ruining things with Amy."

Maria sympathized with Riley's mother. She must have been embarrassed by her son's infidelity.

"Mom believes she knows what's best for me—but when it comes to women, only I know the kind of woman I want." Riley's confession sent Maria's heart tumbling. "Will you let me tell you what happened between me and Amy?"

If she didn't, he'd never drop the subject. In truth, Maria was curious about Riley's affair with Amy. "Give me the shortened version."

"I cheated on Amy."

"I know. Amy told me." Maria expected Riley to fire off one excuse after another for his actions. He surprised her.

"My feelings for Amy began to weaken the second semester of my senior year of college. I was focused on rodeo and making plans to ride the circuit after graduation. I spent less and less time with her and—" he shrugged "—I expected her to realize our relationship had run its course."

"Why didn't you tell Amy you wanted to break up?" Maria had questioned why Fernando hadn't told her he'd fallen out of love with her. It would have hurt Maria but at least she'd have been spared the humiliation of having been cheated on.

"I realize I should have made it clear to Amy that I didn't want to be with her anymore, but I took the easy path, hoping she'd figure it out on her own."

"But she didn't until you cheated on her."

"I'm not proud of hurting Amy with a one-night stand."

Maria didn't know if a one-night stand was better or worse than an affair.

Riley stared down at the grass. "I know what I did was wrong. I'm not going to make excuses for myself or say that I was immature. But I've learned from my mistakes and I'd never intentionally hurt you, Maria."

Intentionally being the key word.

"Maria." He clasped her hand. "I invited you to Belle Farms because I want my parents to meet the woman who makes me happy. The woman I want to be with. The woman I intend to be faithful to."

Heart crawling up into her throat, Maria struggled to speak. Before a word came out of her mouth, Riley said, "There's my dad."

CHAPTER THIRTEEN

"DID YOU BREAK the news to Mom, yet?" Riley had asked his father to warn his mother about Maria before their dinner guests arrived.

"I did." The lines bracketing his father's mouth deepened.

The two men stood outside on the patio waiting for Westin and his daughter. Lantern lights swung from the trees and four umbrella heaters placed strategically around the space warded off the chill in the evening air. "What did Mom say?"

"She's not happy, so do me a favor and be nice to Westin's daughter."

"And ignore Maria?" *Not a chance.*

"Maria's older than you, isn't she?"

"Ten years."

His father's scowl deepened.

"The age difference doesn't bother me, Dad. Maria's an intriguing woman."

"She mentioned being a teacher."

"Maria tutors at-risk teens."

"Challenging work."

And not safe.

"Why isn't she in a traditional school classroom?" his father asked.

Without going into detail, Riley said, "She wants inner-city kids to have a better life. She's a crusader."

"Crusaders don't make much money."

Increasing the family coffers was his father's passion in life—the reason he and Riley didn't see eye-to-eye.

"Have you decided what you'll do after the finals in Vegas?"

"Yes." Riley had done a lot of soul-searching while flying from rodeo to rodeo the past few weeks. The one thing he knew for certain was that he wouldn't be returning to Belle Farms. "Horse racing has been part of our family for generations and I want Belle Farms to flourish, but I'm not the right man to carry on for you."

"Belle Farms provided you with a privileged life."

"And I appreciate all it's given me, but instead of making more money I'd rather spend what I have helping others."

"You're talking philanthropy work?"

"Something along those lines."

"I'm listening."

Riley had a plan in mind even though he hadn't worked out all the details. "I'm thinking of purchasing a working ranch where at-risk teens can get a second chance to turn their lives around while earning their high-school diplomas." He braced himself for his father's objection. One never came. "If Belle Farms helped sponsor the ranch, the publicity would go a long way with the racing public," Riley added.

"I'm guessing this ranch would be near Albuquerque."

"Yes." Maria was an integral part of Riley's plan and he refused to consider that she might not want to be involved with his project.

"I'll consider your idea. In the meantime where are you spending Thanksgiving?"

Riley was holding out for an invitation to join Maria and her family. "I'm not sure yet."

"Your mother and I have decided to visit her cousin in San Diego for the holiday. Bree's staying here to watch over the farm. Keep Eunice posted about your plans. She'll be around to cook if you want to spend the holiday at home."

Home. Since Riley had met Maria, Belle Farms didn't feel like home anymore. "I'll know what I'm doing shortly."

"If you're—"

Riley turned to see what had interrupted his father. Through the windows along the back of the house Riley spotted Maria chatting with his mother in the kitchen. Maria wore a knee-length red cocktail dress with spaghetti straps. The satiny bodice hugged her breasts and the pleated skirt swirled around her hips. Red high heels added a few inches to her height and tonight she'd styled her hair in curls that bounced against her bare shoulders.

"Well," his father murmured. "I can see why you find her attractive."

"She thinks I'm too young for her."

"Smart woman."

"Dad, I'm a competitor. It's only a matter of time before I persuade her that we belong together."

"You're that serious about her?"

"I'm surer of Maria than I am of winning the title in December." Riley set his beer down and went to meet her as she stepped onto the patio.

The first words out of her mouth were "I met your mother."

The first words out of his mouth were "You're beautiful."

"Did you hear what I said?"

He threaded his fingers through hers. "What happened?"

"Your mother was very polite to me but I can tell she isn't pleased about my presence tonight. Riley, I think it would be best if I waited in my bedroom until dinner is over and the guests leave."

"No. You're staying by my side." Right then the back door opened and Riley's mother escorted Pete Westin and his daughter outside. Riley eyed Serena from head-to-toe and in less than three seconds decided his mother had missed the mark again. The blonde wasn't his type.

"Pete, good to see you again," Riley's father said to the former rodeo cowboy. "This is my son, Riley, and his friend Maria Alvarez."

"Heard you're chasing a second title this year," Westin said.

"Not many cowboys can match your success, Mr. Westin."

The former rodeo star preened at the compliment. "This here's my daughter, Serena. She graduated from Yale and recently returned from touring overseas."

"My mother said you're a gifted pianist," Riley said.

"I'm afraid I was destined for a career in music." Serena smiled. "My mother tied me to the piano bench because she was afraid I'd follow in my father's footsteps and become a cowgirl."

"You ladies won't mind if we men discuss business before dinner?" Riley's father said.

"Of course not." Riley's mother slipped her arm through Serena's. "I want to hear all about your concerts in Europe."

Riley waggled his eyebrows at Maria then followed his father and Mr. Westin.

"Oh, dear," Riley's mother said. "That was the doorbell. If you'll excuse me a minute, I believe the caterers have arrived."

Left alone with Serena, Maria asked, "Would you care for a drink?"

They walked over to the built-in grill and bar. Maria picked out a bottle of red wine and Serena said, "That's fine." She glanced around. "Belle Farms is very impressive. Do you visit often?"

"This is my first time here." Maria handed Serena a wineglass.

"Do you know much about horse racing?"

"Not a thing."

"I don't particularly care one way or another about the sport." Serena nodded to the men. "Your cowboy is very hot."

"Riley's a great guy, but he's not my cowboy."

"I do love their swaggers, but I wish my father would stop trying to marry me off to a cowboy." Serena sipped her wine. "I prefer city life over country living."

After all her visits to the Gateway Ranch, Maria had grown fond of fresh air and wide-open spaces.

"Riley hasn't stopped staring at you since we walked over here," Serena whispered.

Maria resisted the urge to glance over her shoulder. "We're friends."

"Friends with sleeping privileges?"

"We're too different to make a long-term relationship work." Maria was saved from having to explain when Riley's sister arrived outside. Following introductions Bree launched into a conversation about the farm's past Kentucky Derby winners.

Dinner was less stressful than Maria anticipated mainly because talk centered on rodeo and horse racing. Riley's mother attempted to change the subject to Serena's concert tours but Serena didn't cooperate, which amused Maria. The men declined dessert and disappeared into the library to conclude their business deal while the women remained at the table and devoured slices of cheesecake drizzled with raspberry sauce. Following dessert Bree excused herself to check on the horses and Serena offered to play the piano.

A half hour later the men emerged from the library flashing smug grins. Shortly afterward, Serena and her father departed and Riley's mother pleaded a headache then retreated to her bedroom. Time for Maria to retire to her room. She held out her hand to Riley's father. "It was very nice to meet you, Mr. Fitzgerald. Belle Farms is a beautiful piece of paradise and I enjoyed seeing Riley's childhood home."

"You're not turning in already, are you?" Riley asked.

"You and your father should have time to talk." Maria retreated to the guest bedroom, relieved to avoid further scrutiny. She had her dress unzipped halfway when the door flew open.

"Riley!"

He closed the door then leaned against it. "What's the matter?"

"Nothing. I thought you'd want time alone with your father since we're leaving early in the morning."

"I want time alone with you." He crossed the carpet and stood before her.

"Kissing isn't a good idea," Maria warned as his mouth drew near.

Riley stared at her. Seconds passed, their mouths inches apart, then he abruptly pulled back. "Let's get this over with."

"Get what over with?"

"You refusing to accept that you're in love with me," he said.

Where did Riley get off...

Dear God. It was true, wasn't it? She was in love with Riley.

"I'll go first." The blue of his eyes deepened. "I'm in love with you, Maria."

Rattled, she struggled to collect her thoughts, an impossible task after Riley's confession. "We can't."

"Can't what? Love each other?"

Why did he insist on making this so difficult? "We're too different. A long-term relationship would never last."

"Different how?"

Was he kidding? "I'm ten years older than you, Riley."

"Ten years isn't much these days. Besides, older women-younger men marriages are more common than they used to be."

Marriages? "I'm not ready for this." Maria pressed her hand to her thumping heart, angry she'd opened the door to questions about her past—humiliating questions she didn't care to answer.

"What did he do to you, Maria?"

Tell him. Then he'll finally understand.

"Fernando said he didn't want children—"

"Who's Fernando?"

Maria moved across the room, putting the bed between her and Riley. "My ex-fiancé."

"I'm listening."

"Since Fernando and I worked all day with at-risk teens we decided we wouldn't have enough emotional energy left at the end of the day to raise our own children."

"And…"

"Fernando changed his mind and wanted kids. We argued a lot about it."

"But you refused to reconsider having a family."

Damn you, Riley, you're going to make me say it, aren't you? "Yes. What happened to my brother left me with a deep scar. I don't want children because I won't risk losing them."

Riley's expression gentled as if he'd known her fears all along.

"Fernando dropped the subject of having kids and I assumed we'd settled the matter. Then he met a woman. They had an affair and she got pregnant."

"Do you think he got her pregnant on purpose so he could have a child?"

That's exactly what she'd accused Fernando of doing, although he'd denied the charge. "I don't know."

"I'm sorry he hurt you, Maria." Riley skirted the end of the bed and put his arms around her. "I can understand why you'd be afraid to have children but don't you believe you'll feel differently once you hold your own baby in your arms?"

"Of course I would feel differently. That's why I can't allow myself to fall in love." She brushed a lock of hair from Riley's forehead, knowing that if she gave her heart to him he'd have the power to make her change her mind about having a baby—his baby. "You need a haircut."

"Don't change the subject," he said.

"At twenty-five, most men your age aren't thinking about marriage, let alone fatherhood." She pressed a finger to his mouth when he attempted to protest. "One day, maybe in your thirties, you'll be ready to start a family. And I would be in my forties."

"Lots of women get pregnant in their forties. Look at all the movie stars who—"

"It's not simply age, Riley. There are cultural differences we've ignored until now."

"You're prejudiced?"

"I'm referring to our parents. Neither of them would have picked us for each other. And if family approval means nothing to you then the fact that our lives are going in different directions should be a cause for concern."

"I'm not going to rodeo forever."

"I realize that, but I *am* going to help inner-city teens forever. I've found my calling and it's right in my own backyard. I'll never leave Albuquerque."

Riley released Maria and walked to the door. He paused with his hand on the knob. "Your arguments are sound, but you forgot one thing."

"What's that?"

"You didn't take into account that you've already

fallen in love with me and you don't want to live without me." The quiet click of the door followed his statement.

Maria battled tears. Riley had guessed the truth— she did love him. What she'd felt for Fernando paled in comparison to her feelings for Riley. She worshipped the ground the cowboy walked on for all he'd done to help Cruz, Victor and Alonso. If she took a chance on Riley and their relationship didn't last or if tragedy struck and she lost him... Maria wasn't strong enough to survive losing another man she'd come to love.

"THANKS FOR COMING home with me," Riley said, breaking the strained silence that accompanied their flight back to Albuquerque.

"I enjoyed meeting your family." Their goodbyes to Riley's parents had been stilted but polite. Both had invited her to return for another visit when she and Riley had more time, but Maria sensed their reservations about their son's involvement with her.

Riley guided the *Dark Stranger* into a hangar at Blue Skies Regional Airport then cut the engine. He grabbed Maria's hand when she attempted to unhook the seat harness. "We need to talk."

Fearing she'd break down and cry if Riley pleaded his case again, she shook her head.

"You're not even willing to give us a chance?"

It wouldn't work, Riley.

"I need you, Maria. You're a strong, generous champion for the kids that society has cast aside." He shoved a hand through his hair. "Don't you see? You inspire me to be a better man."

Her eyes watered.

"People view me as a rich, spoiled guy who doesn't have to work for anything. No one gives me credit for my rodeo talent. They insist that it's easy for me to succeed because wealth gives me advantages most cowboys can't match. I fly to rodeos instead of driving long hours. I sleep in the best hotels instead of my truck. I don't have to hire on at ranches between rodeos to earn entry-fee money. Instead, I can rest and allow my injuries to heal."

Heart aching, Maria hated seeing Riley upset.

"You're the first person who sees beyond my wealth to who I am in here." He thumped his fist against his chest. "I don't want to lose you, Maria. Give me a chance to make you happy."

Maria was too torn inside to speak.

"I know Albuquerque is your home. I'm willing to make it my home, too."

She had to escape from the plane before she gave in to Riley's impassioned plea. "I'm sorry." Her voice cracked. She scrambled from her seat, leaving Riley no choice but to unlock the door and lower the steps. As soon as he joined her on the tarmac he pulled her into his arms.

Her defenses decimated, Maria melted against him.

"I love you," he whispered. "I honest-to-God, seriously, with-all-my-heart love you."

Maria loved Riley more than she'd ever loved Fernando and she'd be devastated if one day Riley woke and decided she was too old for him. Or that she didn't excite him anymore. Or that he was tired of her devoting all her time and energy to at-risk kids and not him. And if her parents eventually accepted Riley, Maria feared they'd view him as a replacement for the son they'd lost. Then one day when Riley decided he'd had enough of being tied down to Maria and left, her parents would lose a second son.

Riley's mouth crushed Maria's, awakening her desire. She tasted desperation on his tongue and her heart wept at the hurt she was inflicting on him. A throat clearing startled them and Riley ended the kiss. Maria's father stood ten feet away, glaring.

"Mr. Alvarez."

"I was saying goodbye to Riley, Dad. He's heading out to the ranch, so I'll have to hitch a ride home with you."

Maria spun but Riley grabbed her elbow. "Remember, Cruz is competing in the El Paso junior rodeo at the end of the month. Victor and Alonso are welcome to tag along if it's okay with their parents."

"I'll check into it."

"Nice seeing you again, sir," Riley said. He shifted toward Maria and she swore his blue eyes glistened with moisture. "'Bye, Maria."

Once Riley left the hangar, her father spoke. "Have you no shame?"

"I'm not in the mood, Dad."

"If your mother knew you were involved with a man your brother's age—"

"Riley's a great guy. Yes, he's the same age as Juan would have been had he lived, but why should that matter? Riley is decent, caring and he's genuinely concerned about the boys I'm trying to help."

"Those boys are a waste of time. They'll end up dead. The same as your brother."

"I never thought you'd remain bitter the rest of your life."

"You don't know the pain of losing your only son."

"Is that why you and Mom don't want me to be happy? You want me to be as miserable as you two the rest of my life?" She waited for her father to deny the accusation. He didn't. They headed for his truck in the parking lot, Maria's feet dragging—guilt, anger and sadness weighing them down.

CHAPTER FOURTEEN

"THANKS FOR ALL the bucking lessons." Cruz spoke to Riley inside the barn where the two males organized and stowed the teen's rodeo equipment. "I didn't think you were gonna be here this week. Ms. Alvarez said you were too busy competing to help me get ready for El Paso."

"I had to withdraw from a rodeo." Riley had hated walking away from another win but he'd hated even more the idea of giving up on him and Maria. Thoughts of Maria had begun to interfere with his concentration and he'd decided to return to Albuquerque and remind Maria why they were meant to be together. The only problem with his plan was that Maria was nowhere to be found. She wasn't returning his calls and she hadn't stopped at the ranch since he'd arrived six days ago. She couldn't avoid him forever—the junior rodeo was tomorrow.

"Why'd you withdraw?" Cruz asked.

"Sore shoulder." He rubbed his arm.

Cruz narrowed his eyes. "You said the best of the best ride with injuries."

"They do." Riley shrugged. "I can afford to sit out a rodeo with a small purse."

"How much was first place worth?"

"A grand."

"That's a lot of money." The comment came from the

other end of the barn, where Victor held a pitchfork in his hand. Shorty must have assigned the teen to muck stalls.

"Mind if I have a word alone with Victor?" Riley spoke to Cruz.

"Yeah, sure." Cruz left the barn.

"You and I need to talk, Victor."

The kid tossed a pitchfork-full of soiled hay into the wheelbarrow, narrowly missing Riley. "Talk about what?"

"Ms. Alvarez believes I'm a bad influence on you." Riley wondered if Maria was using her concern over Riley spending time with the teens as an excuse to keep him from getting too close to her.

"What do you mean a bad influence?" Victor asked.

"Heard you were trying to get into the Los Locos gang."

"So."

"You think that's a smart idea?"

"I earned my GED. You and Ms. Alvarez can't tell me what to do anymore." Another clump of dirty hay flew past Riley's head.

"You're better than a thug, Victor."

"The Los Locos aren't thugs. Besides, I can make a lot of cash being a lookout for the gang and—" Victor spread his arms wide "—I can be somebody important. I don't have to be a nobody my whole life."

"There are other ways to make a name for yourself aside from joining a gang and breaking laws."

"Who says I'm gonna break the law?" Victor's chin lifted defiantly. "Don't matter none 'cause nobody cares what I do anyway."

"Ms. Alvarez and I care."

A rude bark of laughter erupted from the kid's mouth.

"The only reason you're even here is because of Ms. Alvarez. You're helping us 'cause *you* like her."

"What's wrong with that?"

Silence.

"Ever thought about using your GED to enroll in a community college or study to be a plumber? You can make good money in the trades."

"Why should I work my butt off for a few bucks when I can rake in the dough being a lookout for the Los Locos?" Victor straightened his shoulders and grinned. "I wanna wallet full of hundred-dollar bills like yours."

Score a point for Maria. Victor had noticed the way Riley spread money around. He didn't have the right to tell the kid he had to work hard for his money when Riley hadn't earned a dime of the funds he had access to.

"What if you had the opportunity to make a lot of money doing honest work?"

"How much money?"

"What will the Los Locos pay you?"

"I don't know. A Benjamin or two."

"A hundred dollars an hour? A day? A week? Or a month?"

"I don't know."

Riley doubted Victor would earn any substantial amount of money in the gang. He'd be lucky if the group repaid his service by buying him a fast-food meal. "What will you do with that much money?"

"Shoot, man, I'm gonna buy me a jacked-up car with a kick-ass stereo." Victor wiggled his fingers. "Maybe get me some bling."

Fancy gold necklaces and rings would only make Victor a target for rival gang members. "Will you miss working at the ranch after you leave?"

"Nah." Victor shrugged. "Maybe a little."

"What will you miss the most?"

"Not shoveling horseshit, that's for sure."

"I'm serious."

"I'd miss Shorty."

"I thought Shorty made you work too hard."

"He does. But he gives a crap about me—I mean people. He's not prejudiced against Latinos and he says I do a good job."

"You think the Los Locos will treat you with the same respect?" Riley asked. "What if you screw up? Will the gang give you a second or third chance like Shorty does?"

Victor didn't have an answer to that question.

"Life isn't easy—"

"What would you know about easy? You fly a plane and have a ton of money. I bet you've never had to go a whole day without eating 'cause you had no money and your mom hadn't been to the grocery store in over a month."

"You're right. I've never gone hungry. But think about this, Victor. We have no control over what family we're born into. No control over our ethnicity or how our parents earn a living or where they live."

"You got lucky, man."

"I agree. I'm fortunate and blessed. My ancestors struggled and went hungry so that I didn't have to. They didn't break the law—they broke a sweat and shed their own tears and blood to leave a legacy for future generations. You can do the same."

"What are you talking about?"

"Put your GED to good use. Carve out your own path in life. Show your siblings that working hard at an honest job is the way to get what you want. Be a role model for your friends and family."

"Me, a role model? Get real, man."

"Think about it, Victor. You've got the brains to succeed at whatever you choose to do. Leave your mark on the world not on the side of a building. Dream about being more than you ever believed you could be."

"Dreams don't matter none if you don't have a way to make 'em come true."

"Nothing worth having comes easy." Riley shuffled his feet. "Think about what I've said. Once you join the Los Locos there's no turning back. The life you could have had will be lost to you forever."

"My life ain't gonna last long anyway, so why should I care about how I make my money? I'm never gonna get out of the 'hood. Might as well take the easy money and party before a bullet takes me down." Victor tossed the pitchfork into the stall and pushed the wheelbarrow out a side door that led to the compost bin behind the barn. If Victor didn't place any value on his own life, the teen would never believe he deserved better than a day-to-day existence in the 'hood.

Riley believed each time Maria lost a student to a gang she was forced to relive her brother's death. The thought of her experiencing that kind of pain over and over again twisted Riley's gut. Right then Riley decided that if he couldn't be a ray of hope in Maria's life, he wouldn't be in her life at all.

MARIA SMILED AT the excitement on the teens' faces as they entered Fifer's Arena in El Paso, Texas. True to his word, Riley had returned to Albuquerque at the end of October for Cruz's first junior rodeo competition.

She wasn't happy that Riley ignored her request to keep his distance from the boys, but at the same time she admired him for keeping his promise to Cruz and helping him prepare for the rodeo. Because she'd missed Riley more than she'd ever believed possible, Maria hadn't trust herself to be around him so she'd avoided the Gateway Ranch.

When Riley arrived at the Blue Skies Regional Airport earlier in the morning, she'd waited for him to turn his smile on her, but he ignored her and greeted everyone else. If he'd been surprised that her father and Judge Hamel were tagging along, he hadn't said a word.

Maria had persuaded her father to attend the rodeo, hoping he'd witness a different side of the teens and acknowledge the importance of her work.

"Good luck, Cruz," Maria said. "We'll be cheering for you in the stands."

Cruz caught Maria by surprise and hugged her. "Thanks for not giving up on me, Ms. Alvarez."

He turned to Judge Hamel and offered his hand. Cruz's court hearing had been two weeks earlier and had lasted all of five minutes. Judge Hamel had given Cruz a stern warning to stay away from gangs and that if he appeared in her courtroom again she'd send him to jail. "Thank you for giving me a second chance."

"You're welcome, young man." The judge pumped his hand. "Make us proud."

Cruz bumped knuckles with Victor and Alonso. "This one's for all the homies in the 'hood."

Riley motioned for Cruz to follow him to the bucking chutes and Maria led the way to their seats.

"Maria, I'm impressed with the changes in Cruz. What you're doing with these kids is terrific," Judge Hamel said.

"Thank you." Although Maria's father pretended interest in the rodeo clowns entertaining the fans, she sensed that he had eavesdropped on her conversation with the judge.

"I'm amazed by parents of teens who pass through my chambers, insisting they had no idea their kid had been involved in a gang. Parents are notorious for blaming others rather than acknowledging they should have paid closer attention to their child's activities."

"The allure of gangs is difficult to resist when gang-bangers make big bucks, drive fancy cars and wear diamond rings and expensive clothes," Maria said. "And they get a kick out of people fearing them."

"Well, at least you're making progress with a few of the kids." Judge Hamel stood. "I'm going to the restroom before the action starts."

Once the judge was out of earshot, Maria turned to her father. "What's the matter, Dad? You're awfully quiet. Aren't you feeling well?"

"I'm sorry, *cariño*."

Surprised by his statement, Maria asked, "Sorry for what?"

"For blaming you when your mother and I should have realized Juan had fallen in with the wrong crowd."

"Dad, Judge Hamel made a generalization—"

"Don't make excuses for me, daughter. I was Juan's father. I should have known his friends." The folds around his mouth sagged with sadness. "Your brother stared me in the eye and lied about where he was going. I knew he lied but I didn't want to believe it."

"If we could turn back the clock, we'd all make different decisions. I tried to help Juan but in all the wrong ways."

Her father clutched her hand. "You were a good sister."

Stunned by her father's turnaround, Maria said, "It's too late for Juan, but there's time for them." She pointed to Victor and Alonso, sitting two rows away. "I see Juan in the eyes of every boy I help. There are so many good kids who make bad choices."

"The hurt never goes away." Her father sniffed.

"I know."

"Your mother will never stop drinking."

Maria ached for her parents' marriage. Her father had not only lost a son but he'd also lost the woman he'd married over thirty years ago. "You could help me make a difference, Dad. You could be a mentor for at-risk teens."

His eyes narrowed. "How?"

"You could teach boys and girls about airplane mechanics and discuss your career in the military."

"*Sí.* I will think about it."

She hugged her father. For ten long years, he'd buried his anger and guilt over his son's death. Today marked a new beginning for their relationship.

And you have Riley to thank for this moment.

Maybe it was time Maria admitted that Riley's presence did more good than harm to those he touched. Yes, Victor intended to take a shortcut to living the high life, but Maria doubted the boys would have earned their GEDs if they'd remained in the 'hood. Riley had provided the teens with a safe environment to study and work away from the influence of gangs. Shorty and the Gateway Ranch had brought about positive changes in all three boys.

Judge Hamel returned to her seat and a moment later the announcer's voice bellowed over the loudspeakers. "Ladies and gents, it's time to begin our pro-am junior rodeo!"

Hoping to catch a glimpse of Riley and Cruz, Maria scanned the chute area.

"We've got twelve young men here today who're waiting to strut their stuff on a few ill-mannered bucking horses."

"Got any questions?" Riley asked Cruz as they stood next to Dark Magic's chute.

The corner of Cruz's mouth curved. "Yeah, how do I keep from falling off again?"

Even though Cruz joked, he couldn't conceal the fear in his eyes. Riley had experienced the same jitters the first time he'd competed. "Stick like glue to the saddle and you won't take a tumble."

"If I don't do well, I can't blame it on my equipment," Cruz said.

Riley had heard kids gossiping with envy over Cruz's saddle. They'd probably had to scrape and save for a year to buy second-hand gear in order to compete today and in walks the new kid with expensive equipment and a world-champion sponsor.

"Shut them up," Riley said.

"If Judge Hamel catches me fighting, she's gonna throw me in jail."

"I'm not suggesting a brawl." Riley chuckled. "Ride

well and win." Winning was the only way to silence the critics.

Cruz scaled the chute rails and straddled the bronc. "I think I'm ready."

"You're more than ready. Remember, when Dark Magic makes his move out of the chute, keep your spurs above his shoulders until he completes his first jump. Don't forget to lift the buck rein and keep spurring the horse front-to-back finishing behind the saddle."

"Got it," Cruz said.

"One more thing," Riley said.

"What?"

"Have fun."

Cruz fiddled with the black Stetson Shorty had given him for good luck then signaled the gateman. Dark Magic bolted from the chute and Riley watched the kid mark out.

Six seconds...

Dark Magic wasn't anywhere near the size and strength of the broncs Riley rode but the young horse was riled. The animal spun twice then bucked his back legs high off the ground, forcing Cruz to use every ounce of his strength to remain in the saddle.

Three seconds...

Another series of spins and bucks.

Two seconds...

The bronc rocked forward and Riley guessed what was to come.

One second...

Dark Magic used the momentum he'd built for his final buck, which brought all four hooves off the ground.

The front of the bronc rolled right, testing Cruz's physical agility. The kid slid but managed to cling to his seat.

The buzzer sounded and Cruz jumped off Dark Magic, landing on his feet. The crowd cheered his performance and Riley never felt prouder as he watched the teen's face glow with pride.

"That was such a rush!" Cruz pumped his fist in the air.

"You've got what it takes to be one of the best, kid. You have to decide how bad you want it."

"I know."

"Here come a few people who want to congratulate you." Riley couldn't take his eyes off Maria. Today she wore her hair down, the dark strands brushing her shoulders. Her jeans and long-sleeved blouse weren't fancy but they hugged her shape, showing off her curves. She was a beautiful woman. A woman he wanted for himself.

Her eyes shimmered with emotion and he hoped she'd missed him as much as he'd missed her. While the others congratulated Cruz, Riley inched closer to Maria. He yearned to take her in his arms. Hold her. Kiss her. Instead, he clenched his hands into fists to keep from grabbing her.

"Thanks to you, Cruz might have a career in rodeo," she said.

Riley didn't want to discuss Cruz or rodeo. He wanted to talk about them—their future. "I've decided this is going to be my final run at another title. Whether I win or not in December I'm leaving the circuit."

"Why?"

"I've got other interests—" *people* "—I want to pursue." And he'd devised a plan on how to convince Maria that *he* was integral to her mission to prove to at-risk teens that education not gangs was the path to a better life. But until he worked out the details and gained his father's approval, he didn't want to raise Maria's hopes. "I'll be on the road until the finals in Vegas the first week of December." He wished she'd give him a sign that she'd miss him, but her schooled expression hid her thoughts.

"I'll be cheering for you in Vegas," Maria said.

If all went as planned, Maria would be cheering for him in person in Vegas.

CHAPTER FIFTEEN

"THANKS FOR THE LIFT, Ms. Alvarez." Victor hopped into Maria's station wagon and buckled his seat belt.

"You're welcome. I'm glad you decided to come along." A week ago Gil Parker had invited her and Victor to Thanksgiving dinner at the Gateway Ranch. "Cruz and Alonso will be glad to see you."

"Yeah, I guess."

After the junior rodeo in El Paso, Cruz and Alonso had asked Gil Parker if they could continue to work at the ranch. Cruz wanted to hone his rodeo skills and Alonso wanted to prepare for the SAT and ACT college entrance exams he intended to take in the spring. Gil had extended an invite to remain at the ranch to Victor, but the teen declined, citing that he couldn't wait to return to the 'hood.

"How are things going?" she asked.

"You mean with the Los Locos?"

Maria clenched the wheel tighter. "Yes."

"I didn't join the gang," Victor said matter-of-factly.

Startled, Maria glanced at the teen. "How come?"

"I thought a lot about what Riley said."

Riley hadn't phoned her since El Paso...since *forever*. "When did you speak with him?"

"Before Cruz's rodeo."

"What did Riley tell you?"

"He said I should dream big—bigger than the Los Locos. And I told him that it didn't matter what my dreams were 'cause I didn't have a way to make 'em come true."

"Nothing worth having comes easy," Maria said.

"That's what Riley said, Ms. Alvarez. He told me that once I joined a gang I couldn't change my mind and my life wouldn't belong to me anymore. It would belong to the Los Locos."

Bless you, Riley. He'd been able to reach Victor when she'd failed.

"He told me I was better than a thug."

"He's right."

"And Riley said we can't help what family we're born into or who our parents are. It's up to me to show my brothers and sisters that we can change how we live if we want to bad enough."

"So what are your plans?" Maria asked.

"I'm gonna ask Mr. Parker if he'll let me come back to the ranch. I wanna work with the horses and maybe if I do a good job for Shorty, Mr. Parker will let me be a real ranch hand for him one day."

Oh, Riley, why did I ever doubt you? Maria blinked back tears. "I'm proud of you, Victor."

"Thanks, Ms. Alvarez. Is Riley gonna be at the ranch for Thanksgiving dinner?"

"I don't know." She hadn't asked Gil because she'd been afraid to learn the truth—that Riley had washed his hands of her.

A half hour later, Maria and Victor learned that Riley would not be present. He was in Florida riding in one last rodeo before the finals the first week in December. Maria hid her disappointment behind a brave smile.

Supper in the bunkhouse was a lively affair. Harriet sat on Gil's right. The couple bent their head in conversation throughout the meal and Maria sensed there was more to their relationship than boss and employee and the knowledge made Maria miss Riley even more.

Not a day went by since El Paso that Maria hadn't been tempted to contact Riley. She'd stayed busy working with a new group of students, but at the end of the day she returned to her parents' home feeling empty inside. Before she'd met Riley she'd been content to devote her life to troubled teens, but now she believed there was more to life than helping others. She was entitled to her own happiness.

Maria had finally accepted that the key to her happiness was Riley. All of a sudden their ten-year age difference no longer mattered. Life was short—very short in the 'hood. She wanted to live each day to the fullest and she couldn't do that without Riley by her side.

"Hey, Ms. Alvarez, what do you think of Victor's new snake tattoo?" Alonso said.

Maria stared at Victor's forearm. "It's ugly."

The cowboys around the table chuckled and Shorty teased Victor about his baggy jeans. Victor took it all in stride and Maria was pleased to see that the boys had truly become part of the ranch family. Following supper, Pete served coffee and dessert—a variety of cobblers, pies and cookies.

"I'll be right back," Gil announced. He returned to the bunkhouse a few minutes later carrying a large box wrapped in shiny red Christmas paper with a fancy white ribbon. He set the box in front of Maria. "This came for you a few days ago."

Maria's eyes widened. "From who?"

"Riley."

Maria's heart thumped wildly in her chest.

"Riley got you a Christmas present, Ms. Alvarez!" Alonso said.

"Hurry and open it. Maybe it's a new bucking saddle," Cruz said.

"I doubt he bought me rodeo gear." Maria laughed.

"Want me to help?" Victor asked.

"Sure." Maria clutched her hands in her lap and watched as the boys tore off the ribbon and paper.

Cruz lifted the lid. "There's another box inside."

Alonso removed a medium-size box wrapped with the same paper and identical white ribbon.

"You'll have to open that one." Maria's heart beat faster.

"Uh-oh. Another box," Alonso said.

The ranch hands placed bets on how many more boxes the boys would uncover.

When Victor opened the next one, which was the size of a candy box, he discovered six plane tickets to Las Vegas dated December ninth—the day before Riley's final ride. Each of the boys' names was on a ticket as was Maria's and her parents'.

"Does this mean we all get to go to Vegas to watch Riley at the NFR?" Cruz asked.

"I believe it does." If Maria's heart pounded any harder, the organ would explode inside her chest.

"There's one more box hiding in here." Cruz handed Maria a small red-wrapped box with a tiny white ribbon around it.

Maria unraveled the ribbon and carefully tore the paper away to reveal a black velvet jeweler's case. Silence filled the bunkhouse and all eyes remained riveted on the object in Maria's hands. With shaking fingers, she popped open the lid. The breath in her lungs escaped in a loud whoosh. The most beautiful diamond solitaire she'd ever seen glittered and sparkled beneath the room lights.

Wedged inside the box was a tiny note. Maria unfolded the paper and read out loud. "If you trust me with your heart, wear this ring and meet me in Vegas."

Victor tugged Maria's sweater sleeve. "Does Riley want to marry you?"

"No kidding, dumb-ass. That's an engagement ring," Cruz said.

"Are you gonna marry Riley, Ms. Alvarez?" Alonso asked.

Tears burning her eyes, Maria smiled. "As a matter of fact, I am." She slid the ring over her finger and the room erupted in applause.

"HEY, FITZGERALD, DON'T blow it tonight!"

Riley scanned the cowboy-ready area at the Thomas and Mac Center on the campus of the University of Nevada-Las Vegas. Out of the crowd walked Billy Stover.

"*You* better not blow it tonight, Stover," Riley said. This evening seven world champions would be crowned and Riley, not Stover, would win the saddle-bronc championship—that is if Riley could keep his mind on business and not Maria.

Gil Parker had phoned him the evening of Thanksgiving to tell him Maria had opened her gift and had left the ranch, wearing the diamond engagement ring. Riley anticipated a call from Maria but one never came and he worried that she'd worn the ring home only to have changed her mind later. Fear and anxiety had eaten away at his gut all week but miraculously he'd come out on top each go-round.

He'd receive a great deal of satisfaction if he silenced the naysayers that had followed him around the circuit this year, but more than anything he was ready to put rodeo behind him and move on to bigger and better things—the most important, beginning a new life with Maria.

If Maria refused to marry him she'd find out soon enough that he wasn't a quitter. He'd already begun making plans toward their future together by purchasing an abandoned ranch southwest of Albuquerque. Riley believed he and Maria would make a great team and with a little TLC the ranch would become a safe haven for the at-risk teens in Maria's program. She'd be a fool to walk away from a chance to help more of her students because she was afraid of her feelings for him.

"Stover, quit hassling Fitzgerald," Ed Parker said as he entered the cowboy-ready area.

"You can boss me around when you become a winner, Parker, but not before." Stover stomped off.

"You ready to take home the championship?" Ed asked.

"If I don't win, it won't be because of my horse."

"Heard you drew White Lightning."

The bronc had thrown all but two riders during the finals—Stover and, after tonight, Riley.

"If you don't have the best ride of your life, Stover's going to edge you out," Ed said.

"Not a chance."

"I do admire your cockiness." Ed grinned. "Dad said you proposed to that schoolteacher over Thanksgiving."

"How come you weren't at the Gateway Ranch for the holiday?" Riley asked, changing the subject.

"I was in California visiting my little girl." Ed stuck a pinch of chew between his lip and gum. "Win or lose, you gonna retire after tonight, settle down and play house?"

"Yep. What about you?"

"What else am I gonna do if I quit? I sure don't want to punch cows for my old man."

"Would you work for me?" Riley asked.

"Doing what?"

"I'm going to start up a rodeo program for teenage boys who've dropped out of high school. I'll need a few rodeo cowboys on hand to teach the kids." The idea was ambitious, but Riley's trust fund would cover the initial investments and he had a few fundraising ideas to keep the ranch open year-after-year. Riley's father had expressed interest in investing in the program and using the publicity to draw attention to Belle Farms.

Riley's parents and sister had arrived earlier in the week and when he'd explained his intention to marry Maria after his final ride tonight his mother had almost fainted. But after spending several days with Riley and listening to his plans for the future and the role Maria played in those plans his parents had accepted the fact that their son was in love with an older woman.

"When you get the ranch up and running give me a shout. I'll drop by for a look-see," Parker said. "Sure would be nice to settle in one place for a spell. Maybe I'd get to see my daughter more often." Ed tipped his hat. "Good luck tonight."

Riley inched closer to White Lightning's stall. The rodeo workers had loaded the gelding into the chute a few minutes ago and the animal acted jittery. Riley hoped by the time the chute door opened the bronc would be pissed as hell and ready to rock 'n' roll. He rummaged through his gear bag and put on his chaps, spurs and riding glove.

Focus, damn it. Riley blocked out the noise around him, willing his mind to empty of all thoughts but White Lightning—fat chance.

"Riley!"

Cruz, Alonso and Victor rushed toward him. Frantically he searched for Maria. She stood off to the side, her hands stuffed into the pockets of her jeans. Was she wearing his ring or not?

"Glad you guys made it," Riley said, his attention riveted on Maria.

"A dude in the stands says you drew the best horse," Alonso said.

"I sure did. He's right here." Riley pointed to White Lightning.

"Good luck, Riley. I hope you win." Cruz bumped knuckles with Riley, then he and the other boys walked off. Maria edged closer.

God, he'd missed her.

"You came." *Dumb-ass. Tell her you love her.*

"I'm sorry," she whispered.

"For what?"

"For being a coward."

Her confession surprised him. "You're one of the bravest women I know." *Except when it comes to love.*

"I let my fears dictate my actions when I should have listened to my heart."

Speaking of hearts, Riley's was racing. "What's your heart saying now?"

She pulled her left hand from her pocket and raised it high in the air, where the arena lights bounced off the diamond solitaire. "It's telling me to take a chance on you, Riley."

"You don't have to take a chance on me, honey. I'm the real deal." Riley tugged her closer.

"You're the first man who's come into my life and challenged me to seek my own happiness. To forgive myself for the role I played in my brother's death. To not be afraid of the future. To live in the moment."

"Is that what you're doing now—living in the moment? 'Cause if it is that's not good enough for me." He pressed his palm to her lower back, exerting enough pressure to close the gap between their bodies. Her breasts bumped his chest and Riley swore her heart thumped as hard as his. "I don't want to live moment-by-moment with you. I want forever with you. Maria, I love you with all my heart."

"I'm not going to change my mind about children."

"We don't need to make a decision about having a family anytime soon."

"If I still say no?"

"I can live with that. It's you I can't live without."

"What about your parents? I'm not the woman they would have chosen for you."

"They're coming around. They understand that you're the inspiration for all I want to be in life."

"I don't know if I can ever leave Albuquerque."

"You won't have to."

"You're okay with living in New Mexico?"

"It's where we both belong. Where we can do the most good."

Maria smiled. "You're very wise for a young man, Riley."

"'Bout time you noticed."

"Are you sure?" she asked.

"Only when it comes to you, me and our love."

Her eyes glittered with tears. "I do love you, Riley. I'm glad you made me see the light."

"I'd have fought for your love forever if that's what it took to make you admit that we belong together."

"Really?"

"Yeah, really." Riley kissed her—a teasing, fleeting brush of his lips that left her moaning for more when he pulled away.

"Ladies and gentlemen, it's time to begin the last night of the National Finals Rodeo here at the Thomas and Mac Center in Las Vegas, Nevada!"

Riley ducked his head and spoke in Maria's ear. "I've got our future all mapped out, honey. You hang on to my saddle and I promise you it'll be a hell of a ride."

Ignoring the cowboys who'd gathered around Riley's chute, Maria planted a big wet kiss on his mouth. Wolf whistles echoed through the cowboy-ready area. "Win this one for all the boys out there who dream of being you." Maria kissed him one more time then sashayed away.

"Before we kick off the bronc-bustin' competition, let's give a round of applause to our judges...."

The announcer's voice faded in Riley's head as he struggled to tamp down his excitement at Maria finally accepting his love for her. Turning his thoughts to White Lightning took more strength than Riley anticipated.

"Do-or-die time, big fella." He glanced out of the corner of his eye and watched Stover pace nervously in front of his bronc's chute. He'd drawn Bull's-eye—a horse known for throwing its riders into the rails.

Right then Stover glanced his way and Riley sent him a silent message. *This is my moment, Stover, not yours.*

"Well, folks, it's down to the final two rides of the season here in Vegas." The crowd applauded. "Billy Stover from Waco, Texas, is going to try and tame Bull's-eye. He needs a good score to build a lead over Fitzgerald, the reigning saddle-bronc champion."

Riley retreated to the shadows to watch Stover's ride. The damned cowboy took forever to find his seat in the saddle but once the chute door opened and Bull's-eye bolted for freedom, Stover was in the battle of his life. Bull's-eye was more of a spinner than a bucker, making it difficult for the cowboy to spur. If Stover didn't force the bronc out of his spin he was going to lose valuable points.

The buzzer rang and it was no surprise that Stover had kept his seat—the man rarely got thrown. "Let's see what the judges think of Stover's ride…eighty-two!" The applause was lukewarm at best.

Riley needed an eighty-four to win. "Okay, White Lightning. It's me and you and a date with destiny." Riley climbed the chute rails and slid low in the saddle, then worked his gloved hand around the rope.

"Folks, Riley Fitzgerald's had a rocky run at the title this season. He's been in and out of the standings more times than I can count, but he made it back to Vegas this year and he's vying for a repeat title." Music blared over the loudspeakers and snippets of Riley riding in last year's finals flashed across the Jumbotron.

Win it for the boys. Maria's voice blocked out the noise around Riley.

A world title would lend respect to the rodeo program Riley wanted to establish for troubled teens. A title might also bring in lucrative sponsorship offers. More than a gold buckle rested on this one ride. Riley couldn't afford to fail.

"Chute number seven is where tonight's final action takes place. Riley Fitzgerald from Lexington, Kentucky, is gonna tame White Lightning."

A few more words from the announcer and Riley's date with destiny arrived. The chute door opened and White Lightning leapt for freedom.

Riley's body was pumped full with adrenaline and he had no trouble keeping his spurs above the points of the horse's shoulders. The gelding performed beautifully, throwing its body into buck after buck. The stands blurred before Riley's eyes. As if he and White Lightning were one body, Riley rode out the bucks, keeping his hand high above his head.

When the buzzer sounded, Riley continued to ride, knowing once he got off the horse that would be the end of his career. White Lightning must have sensed Riley's emotions because the horse kept bucking, challenging Riley.

Satisfied he'd done his best on White Lightning, Riley flung his leg over the saddle and leapt for the ground, stumbling twice before regaining his balance.

The crowd stood on its feet, stomping and cheering. The Jumbotron replayed Riley's ride as the announcer said, "Folks, I do believe Riley Fitzgerald settled the debate—he is the reigning saddle-bronc champion of the world! We'll have to wait for next year to see if Fitzgerald can capture a third title."

Not a chance. Riley slipped into the cowboy-ready area and came face-to-face with Maria, the boys, her parents and Riley's family. His throat swelled with emotion. Everyone that mattered most to him was present to help close one chapter of his life and open the next.

He gathered Maria in a hug. "I love you, Maria. Will you marry me tonight?"

Maria's eyes shone with tears. "I love you, too, Riley. And, yes, I'll marry you tonight."

The coliseum crowd roared with approval after witnessing Riley's proposal on the Jumbotron. He kissed Maria, fueling the fans response.

"Fitzgerald got lucky twice tonight, folks—he's not only a world-champion cowboy, he's caught himself a world-champion bride!" the announcer chuckled.

"Good thing you said yes because Elvis is waiting to marry us." Riley ignored his mother's shocked expression. "C'mon, everybody. We've got less than an hour to get to the chapel I booked for our wedding."

Riley's mother gasped. "We haven't sent out announcements! Or decided on colors and flowers and what about the rehearsal dinner?"

"I don't know about you—" Riley gazed into Maria's eyes "—but I sure don't need to rehearse. I'm ready for the real thing."

"Me, too."

"Everyone who means the most to Maria and I are here right now." Riley addressed Maria's parents. "Mr.

and Mrs. Alvarez, I know I'm not the man you would have picked for your daughter. But I am the man who will love her and honor her and treat her with all the respect and dignity she deserves."

Ricardo cleared his throat. "That's all a father can ask for. Be happy together."

"Ready?" Riley asked Maria.

Maria giggled. "Viva Las Vegas!"

"I CAN'T BELIEVE you bought this place, Riley," Maria said Christmas morning when Riley stepped onto the porch of the run-down ranch house outside Albuquerque. They'd spent Christmas Eve at her parents' home, where they'd opened gifts. Riley's present to her had been the key that had unlocked the front door of this ranch house.

He slipped a jacket over her shoulders to ward off the chilly morning air. "Five hundred acres of second chances." Riley wrapped his arms around Maria and pointed to the east where a crumbling barn sat. "We'll replace the barn with a new one and fill it with horses. Then add corrals and a bunkhouse." His finger moved west. "We'll string a fence for bucking stock out there."

Maria leaned into Riley, content to listen to his ramblings about improving the property. With the sun rising in the east, casting a pink glow across the morning sky, Maria had found her paradise. She envisioned the hustle and bustle of teenagers doing ranch chores, studying for GEDs and learning that a brighter future was within their grasp if they stayed out of trouble and worked hard.

"Over there, we'll build your classroom and install the latest technology and computers to help with homework."

"I vote we put a new roof on our house first," Maria

said. They'd slept in their clothes on the living room floor Christmas Eve and stared at the stars visible through the holes. She faced Riley, wrapping her arms around his neck. "I've decided on a name for the ranch." Riley had given Maria the honor of choosing the name.

"What is it?"

"Riley Fitzgerald Ranch for Boys."

"No way. That's a dumb name, Maria."

"It is not!" She snuggled her head against his chest. "You're the best thing that's ever happened to me. Let me be reminded of how lucky I am each time I answer the phone 'Riley Fitzgerald Ranch for Boys.'"

"I thought you'd name the place after your brother," Riley said.

Caught off guard by the suggestion, Maria blinked back tears.

"Juan Alvarez Ranch for Boys," Riley said.

Maria pressed a soft kiss to Riley's mouth. Long. Slow. Sweet.

He broke off their kiss and said, "Looks like the cavalry has arrived." A caravan of trucks and construction equipment wound their way along the ranch road.

"What's going on?" Maria asked.

"This is our first Christmas at the Juan Alvarez Ranch for Boys and I wanted it to be memorable. We're having a barn-raising today."

"But it's Christmas. Who works on Christmas day?"

Riley grinned. "Money talks."

"You shouldn't have. This must be costing you a fortune, Riley."

"*Us* a fortune. When it comes to making you happy, Maria, money is no obstacle. Now stop worrying. The cowboys are from the Gateway Ranch. Pete's bringing the chuck wagon and he's cooking Christmas barbecue for everyone. My parents are flying in later today and your folks are picking them up at the airport and driving them out here. Cruz, Victor and Alonso and their families are coming, too."

Tears burned Maria's eyes. "This is really happening, isn't it?"

Riley placed her palm against his heart. "Merry Christmas, darlin'."

"I love you, Riley."

"I know. Now let's go welcome everyone to our new home and you can help Pete set up the chuck wagon."

"Sounds like a plan. And, Riley…?"

"What?"

She'd been thinking a lot these past weeks about having a baby with Riley. She was still scared, but not as scared now that she knew they'd raise their child on a ranch and not in the 'hood.

"Never mind." She smiled, tucking her secret away. Once life settled down a bit and the ranch opened its doors to at-risk teens, Maria would discuss starting a family. Or better yet, maybe she'd wait and surprise Riley a few months later with the good news. Right now Maria intended to enjoy every single second with the man who showed her that real-life heroes really do exist.

* * * * *

#1557 TEXAS REBELS: FALCON
Texas Rebels • by Linda Warren

Falcon Rebel's wife, Leah, did the unthinkable: she left him and their three-month-old baby. Now she's back, wanting to see her daughter. Will Falcon allow her into their lives again or refuse to give her a second chance?

#1558 FALLING FOR THE SHERIFF
Cupid's Bow, Texas • by Tanya Michaels

Kate Sullivan is busy raising her teenage son, and she has no interest in dating again. But single dad Cole Trent, the sheriff of Cupid's Bow, Texas, may make her change her mind!

#1559 THE TEXAS RANGER'S WIFE
Lone Star Lawmen • by Rebecca Winters

To protect herself from a dangerous stalker, champion barrel racer Kellie Parrish pretends to be married to Cy Vance, the hunky Texas Ranger assigned to her case. But it's impossible to keep their feelings about each other completely professional...

#1560 THE CONVENIENT COWBOY
by Heidi Hormel

Cowgirl Olympia James only agreed to marry her onetime fling Spence MacCormack to help him keep custody of his son. But when she discovers she's pregnant—with Spence's baby—this convenient marriage might turn into something more.

We hope you enjoyed reading this
special collection from Harlequin®.

If you liked reading these stories,
then you will love
Harlequin® American Romance® books!

You love small towns and cowboys!
Harlequin American Romance stories are
heartwarming contemporary tales of everyday
women finding love, becoming part of a
family or community—or maybe starting a
family of their own.

Enjoy four new stories from
Harlequin American Romance
every month!

Available wherever books and
ebooks are sold.

A truck pulled up to the curb and her thoughts came to an abrupt stop. It was Falcon.

There was no mistaking him—tall, with broad shoulders and an intimidating glare. She swallowed hard as his long strides brought him closer. In jeans, boots and a Stetson he reminded her of the first time she'd met him in high school. Being new to the school system, she was shy and didn't know a lot of the kids. It took her two years before she'd actually made friends and felt like part of a group. Falcon Rebel was way out of her group. The girls swooned over him and the boys wanted to be like him: tough and confident.

One day she was sitting on a bench waiting for her aunt to pick her up. Falcon strolled from the gym just as he was now, with broad sure strides. She never knew what made her get up from the bench, but as she did she'd dropped her books and purse and items went everywhere. He'd stopped to help her and her hands shook from the intensity of his dark eyes. From that moment on there was no one for her but Falcon.

Now he stood about twelve feet from her, and once again she felt like that shy young girl trying to make conversation. But this was so much more intense.

Be calm. Be calm. Be calm.

"I'm…I'm glad you came," she said, trying to maintain her composure because she knew the next few minutes were going to be the roughest of her life.

His eyes narrowed. "What do you want?" His words were like hard rocks hitting her skin, each one intended to import a message. His eyes were dark and angry, and she wondered if she'd made the right decision in coming here.

She gathered every ounce of courage she managed to build over the years and replied, "I want to see my daughter."

He took a step closer to her. "Does the phrase 'Over my dead body' mean anything to you?"

Don't miss TEXAS REBELS: FALCON
by Linda Warren, available August 2015
wherever Harlequin® American Romance®
books and ebooks are sold.

www.Harlequin.com

HAREXP0715